The Decoy Bride

LIZZIE SHANE

Copyright © 2018 Lizzie Shane

All rights reserved.

This is a work of fiction. Names, characters, places, brands, media and incidents are either the product of the author's imagination or are used fictitiously. Any resemblance to actual events or persons, living or dead, is entirely coincidental.

ISBN: 1719178046
ISBN-13: 978-1719178044

Some books write themselves. Others…don't. This was definitely one of the latter, and I have to dedicate it to my Isle of Palms ladies, who got me through the sticky parts.

Thank you. You know what you did.

CHAPTER ONE

"May I be honest with you?"

Bree kept her face carefully blank as she swallowed down the dread roiling in her stomach. Somehow she didn't think the owner of the premiere gallery in Santa Monica was going to follow up that question with *I think you're brilliant and would love nothing more than to launch you into the art world*—but in her eleven years in LA, she'd never once puked on a gallery owner and she was *not* going to start with Olivia Hwang.

Bree folded her hands as if they were discussing any old piece of art and not the magnum opus she'd spent the last six months slaving over. "Please."

Olivia cocked her elegant head, studying the fifteen-foot collage that took up the entire showroom wall. "It's beautiful," she said, like someone else might say *it's blue*, as if it was a fact, and not a particularly interesting one.

Bree was tempted to leave it at that—just say thank you, gather up her things and go, holding onto the illusion of the compliment. Olivia Hwang had called her work beautiful. She could dine out on that for months.

But she would know it was an illusion. And she'd never been good at leaving society's pretty illusions intact. She'd always had to push, slave to a compulsion to find the truth beneath. "And?" she prompted.

"And boring."

She couldn't contain her flinch, though Olivia was too engaged in studying the collage to notice. *Stupid compulsion.* "Boring," she echoed, voice empty, ears ringing.

"It's the sort of piece you would expect to see in an airport. Universal in a sort of bland, inoffensive way. Like something a computer could produce."

Another surge of nausea sloshed in her stomach, but Bree forced her voice to remain steady as she pointed out, "I did it all by hand."

Two thousand photos. Each painstakingly developed and carefully crafted into a larger piece until the pictures taken all over Los Angeles came together to form a giant wave crashing on the shore.

"I can see that," Olivia said, still speaking in that matter-of-fact, almost clinical way. She reached out as if she would touch the piece, but stopped short, her hand hovering in the air over the lines. "The technique is lovely. Composition, form—you have a good eye. It just lacks perspective. *Soul.* Obviously it's beautiful, but what's it saying?"

"Does beauty have to say something?"

"If it wants to be art it does." Her tone was dry, this tall, thin woman in a skirt suit designed by a man who outfitted First Ladies. *She* was beautiful, but it wasn't the first thing anyone noticed about her. Her composure, her exquisite poise, outshone everything else.

Bree knew who she was, of course, but she'd still Googled Olivia Hwang as soon as Alan told her he'd managed to get her a meeting with *the* Hwang Gallery. The billionaire philanthropist's wife had started the gallery over a decade ago and quickly become one of the most influential voices in the California art community, launching careers with a single sentence. She didn't look like a woman on the far side of fifty—but even without the help of a skilled plastic surgeon, money could work miracles on the fountain-of-youth front. The lowlights in Olivia Hwang's elegant updo probably cost more than a month's rent for Bree's apartment.

"Art is only as meaningful as the emotion it inspires," Olivia went on, taking a step back to take in the scope of the piece. "This? It's pleasant. It doesn't hit you in the gut. Do you want to be pleasant?"

Well, I was raised in Minnesota. Bree bit her tongue on the urge to snark at the preeminent gallery owner in southern California. She smoothed sweaty hands down her Walmart skirt, and angled her body toward the photos resting at the foot of the adjacent wall. "What about the prints?"

They weren't on the same scale as the wave collage, but if Olivia Hwang saw something in them it would still change her life.

"Pedestrian."

Bree flinched at the casual indictment.

"Lovely," Olivia qualified, "but generic. The sort of art you could buy at a farmer's market."

I do sell them at farmer's markets. Bree swallowed back another tide of nausea.

"That isn't really what we do at the Hwang Gallery." The gallery's owner waved a long-fingered hand at the prints lined up along the wall, somehow both praising them and dismissing them with the gesture. "You're a talented photographer—obviously. I wouldn't have agreed to look at your work if I hadn't seen potential in the piece Alan showed me—but I don't see *you* in any of this. Where's your voice? Your point of view? What makes this a Bree Davies photograph?"

Besides the fact that I took it? Bree stared at the print.

She'd been proud of it twenty minutes ago. It had been one of her favorites when she was picking which pieces to load into the car to bring to the meeting with the great Olivia Hwang. Back when she'd been dreaming of words like *big break* and *turning point*. Now all she could see was Olivia's words in neon letters across the vivid bridge scene.

Pedestrian. Generic.

At her continued silence, Olivia added, her voice gentle, "There are thousands of truly excellent photographers who don't have anything to say. And the world needs them as well. There's no shame in commercial photography. We can't all be artists."

The words echoed against another voice from another time, that one harsh and deep. *You can't just decide to be an artist. That isn't how it works, Bree.*

Her stomach gurgled and Bree pressed a hand to it, determined not to lose her breakfast burrito all over Olivia Hwang's three thousand dollar shoes. "Thank you so much for your time," she said hurriedly, hunched over like Quasimodo as she collected her prints, sliding them back into the plastic crate.

Olivia stepped back, the corners of her mouth tugging down with sympathy. "I'd be happy to see your work again," she offered. "If you find your voice."

Bree nodded her thanks, pressing her lips together to contain the emotion that was suddenly pushing against her from the inside out. She'd been so worried about throwing up on one of the most powerful gallery owners in southern California, she'd completely missed the very real threat that she might burst into tears in front of her.

She blinked rapidly, trying to focus her suddenly blurry vision on the prints beneath her hands. Olivia must have sensed what an edge she was on, because she murmured, "Justin will help you if you require any assistance. Best of luck, Miss Davies," and retreated with a soft click of expensive heels, leaving Bree alone with her disappointment.

It wasn't like she hadn't had disappointments before. Rejections were easy to come by in this business and she'd learned early on that she would need a thick skin to survive. But this time had felt different. She'd let herself get her hopes up.

Two weeks ago, her friend Alan had thrown the art equivalent of an open mic night in his tiny little gallery in Venice. It was a monthly ritual and one that Bree participated in more out of habit than any real sense that it might lead to her big break. But that night a miracle had occurred. Olivia Hwang herself had dropped by, perusing the art with pursed lips and the occasional encouraging twitch of an eyebrow. And she'd stopped in front of Bree's piece—a double exposed photo that had given the eerie impression of a hidden self. She'd been experimenting—the effect more accident than art.

We can't all be artists.

Bree sniffed hard and climbed the step stool to release the clips holding her magnum opus in place. The collage sagged, one end sinking toward the floor as the other stayed clipped up—would Olivia have been impressed by her vision if she'd seen it like this? The city of LA as a wave, half crumpled in on itself. Would she have been *saying something* then?

The other side released, slithering to the floor, and Bree looked up to see Olivia's assistant guiding it gently down. "It's a beautiful piece," he said—and she forced herself to smile even though the last thing she wanted was his pity.

"Thank you." She bent and began to briskly roll it—

taking much less care than she had an hour ago in her studio when she'd oh-so-gently packed her *pièce de resistance* for transport to the illustrious Hwang Gallery. But the world had looked different then. Olivia Hwang had singled her out, asking to see more of *her* work. Everything was hope and technicolor fireworks in that moment.

But now...back to beige.

We can't all be artists.

Justin helped her carry the collage out to her car and brought out the crate of prints while she was maneuvering it into the hatchback. She'd bought the used Honda Fit off a surfer three years ago. He'd bragged that he could fit three surfboards into the tiny car and she'd discovered it fit easels and tripods just as well. Not to mention massive—*bland*—collages.

Her phone buzzed as she was jockeying the rolled collage to make room for the crate. She balanced the crate on the edge of her bumper as she fished in her pocket for the phone, the face lit with a text alert.

MT: I need you! 911!

Bree snorted. Since nothing in Maggie Tate's life was ever a 911 emergency—at least nothing that she would be texting Bree about—she pocketed her phone to finish shimmying the crate into place before acknowledging the text.

But since she also needed the job with Maggie more than ever, she texted back *On my way* before slamming the hatch closed and climbing into the driver's seat. Driving away from the Hwang Gallery and leaving all her stupid, overly optimistic hopes behind.

Maggie's Hidden Valley estate wasn't far, by LA standards—the ten miles inland would probably only take a half hour if the traffic stayed bearable. Bree pointed her car toward the familiar destination and let instinct take over, not bothering with GPS.

There was something oddly soothing about the stop-and-go Thursday morning traffic. It let her shut off her brain and try to forget the words that kept echoing inside her mind.

Banal. Generic. Pedestrian.

Her phone rang through the car's Bluetooth and Bree reached to connect the call, grateful for the distraction. "Hello?"

She'd expected Maggie—the star wasn't known for her patience—but instead an all-too-familiar voice came through the speakers. "Bree?"

She barely managed to keep her groan internal. "Hi, Mom." Her mother was psychic. It was the only possible explanation for how she always knew exactly when to call when Bree's doubts were loudest in her ears.

"Are you all right? Your voice sounds strange."

"I'm driving," she offered as an excuse, silently hoping her mother would take the hint and let her go lest she become another distracted driving statistic.

"I won't keep you," her mother said—then proved the words a lie in the next breath. "I just had a job opportunity fall into my lap for you and I wanted to let you know before someone else snapped it up."

Bree sighed wearily. "I have a job, Mom." Too many jobs. Nothing but freaking jobs and no *career*.

Was it time to face facts and admit the dream was never going to come true? That she was never going to make it as an artist?

We can't all be artists.

"Not like this," her mother went on, plowing over her objections as always. "Graphic design! You'd be doing something artistic. Wouldn't that be better than scooping ice cream?"

"It's soft serve. We don't actually scoop it."

She'd never told her mother about the job with Maggie Tate. There was probably a parental loophole in the non-disclosure agreements she'd signed, but she'd never wanted to tell her parents about her side gig—or admit that it had been the only thing keeping a roof over her head for the last three years.

The job had been fun at first—and perfect in that it gave her some extra cash but never took her focus away from her real goals.

"You know what I mean," her mother said with a familiar flicker of impatience. "You'd be making a good living and doing something with your artistic talents at the same time. Most artists have to have a day job to keep the lights on."

"I take it this graphic design job is in Clement?" Her mother was a small business and financial advisor in the town where Bree had grown up—and where she'd never fit.

"You can still take photos in Minnesota. Cameras do work here."

Bree tightened her grip on the steering wheel, only resisting the weary urge to close her eyes because she was driving. "I wouldn't grow as an artist in Clement, Mom."

"Why not? Lots of artists never got out into the world. Look at Monet. He spent years at that Giverny place your father and I visited when we were in France last year."

"Monet grew up in Paris. I somehow doubt he was lacking cultural stimulation."

A minute pause. "Aaron Cooper just moved back to town."

"Are you trying to say Aaron Cooper counts as cultural stimulation in Clement?"

"He's single."

Bree groaned. "He's, like, seven years younger than me. You really want me to move home and date Andi's baby brother?"

"I know you remember him when he was a kid, but the age difference doesn't matter so much when you're older. He's a very attractive young man."

"Mom."

"I'm just saying. When was the last time you had a date?"

"I have other priorities, Mom." A car horn blasted in the lane next to hers and Bree jumped at the excuse to get off the phone. "Look, I've gotta go. Traffic. I'll call you later."

"No, you won't." Her mother sighed heavily into the phone. "You don't have to ignore us, Breanne. We just want you to be happy."

"I am. I'm happy right where I am," Bree insisted—though right this moment, as she pulled off the main road and up to the gatehouse guarding Maggie Tate's exclusive neighborhood, the words felt a lot like a lie. "I'll call you later."

She disconnected the call and pulled out her ID to be scanned into the neighborhood. Five minutes later she was driving past the house Jennifer Lawrence had bought from Jessica Simpson a few years back. Or rather the gate for the house. Known as one of the few neighborhoods in LA that was completely paparazzi proof, Hidden Valley was its own world. Each of the mansions in the posh guarded community was tucked behind a long, gated drive of its own—for those who were rich enough to buy their privacy in twenty acre plots in Beverly Hills.

Bree pulled up to the gate at Maggie's place and scanned her ID again, waiting as the massive metal gates swung ponderously open before continuing up the curving drive. Lush landscaping encroached on either side and she drove down the middle of the cobblestone driveway to avoid brushing the sides of her car on her way to the six-thousand square foot "cottage" that Maggie Tate called home.

The stone façade and vines tumbling from the eaves gave the home a vaguely European feel, an effect which Bree knew carried on inside where the designer had gushed, "I see French Country" in every room. It was a far cry from the stucco-and-sand design aesthetic of Bree's Mar Vista apartment—which only emphasized the feeling of entering a different world. And Maggie's world was definitely different.

In the wide, cobbled parking area in front of the garages, a silver Lexus crouched like a panther.

A new toy? Maggie wasn't one of those celebrities who collected sports cars, preferring to be chauffeured in luxury SUVs, but if she was going to start a sports car collection, the Lexus looked like a good place to start.

Bree wasn't usually a fancy car person—they always seemed excessive when she could literally live for three years on what something like that cost. But for a car like that—all muscle, chrome and sex—a girl could almost make an exception.

Maybe she'd get to drive it.

She parked her slightly dented Honda Fit alongside the unfamiliar car, eyeing its liquid lines. There were worse things in the world than being Maggie Tate.

Tearing her eyes off the sexy beast, Bree climbed the steps to the front door, which opened before she reached it, revealing Maggie's business manager Mel.

Six-four in flats, Mel—*never* to be called Melanie by anyone except Maggie—could have been a dead ringer for Jane Lynch if not for the vivid red color of the spiky haircut that gave her an extra two inches of height. She lived in tailored pant suits—in a variety of colors, today's was a deep navy blue—and always seemed to be suppressing a sort of superior amusement at the world around her.

"Hello, darling," she said as Bree reached the top of the steps, and as always the simple greeting held something else, an echo of droll amusement at the ridiculous wonderland where they found themselves.

"I hear there's an emergency," Bree said, going up on her toes to air-kiss beside Mel's cheek in greeting. It was an affectation of Maggie's, but one that had become second nature to Bree.

"There's something," Mel replied, dry as dust. "Come on. Maggie will want to tell you herself."

They wended through the French countryside of Maggie's foyer, living room and den—a familiar path that Bree knew would lead through the kitchen, breakfast nook and out onto the side patio with its outdoor seating area and cascading ponds. It was one of Maggie's favorite spots on the property—and Bree's as well. There was something almost magical about the little oasis, where the only sound was that of water trickling between the ponds—

And the yapping of the most obnoxious dog on the planet.

Cecil B. DeMille, Maggie's Cavalier King Charles spaniel, was in rare form this morning. She could hear him yelping before she even got to the kitchen—but then, even on his calm days, Cecil had a bark that could pierce soundproof glass. And Cecil was not known for his calm days. Especially not around Bree.

She'd never had a problem with dogs before, but that animal hated her.

There was some kind of echo effect going on, making Cecil's cries reverberate even more. His standard bark sounded half pained yelp and half panicked yip—like he was being stepped on by an elephant—but this morning it sounded like more than one dog was being tortured by pachyderms.

Mel glanced at her as she opened the patio door, a terrifyingly knowing smile quirking her lips, and then they stepped outside—and *two* Cecil B. DeMilles suddenly stopped yelping and tore across the pavers to yap and nip at Bree's ankles.

"Bree!" Maggie Tate, darling of the silver screen, leapt up from her lounge chair and threw open her arms like Bree was her BFF and not her employee. "I'm getting married! And I got you a dog!"

To her left, Mel snickered softly as Bree's jaw fell. "Oh."

CHAPTER TWO

Maggie Tate was eccentric. It had always been one of Bree's favorite things about her.

Bree couldn't be sure whether Maggie had always been a little odd or if it was a side effect of the fame and outrageous wealth since Maggie had already been terrifyingly famous and disgustingly rich when she'd first hired Bree. The sheer all-consuming scope of her celebrity was what had made Bree's job necessary.

She was the decoy. The lookalike. The one who played Maggie for the paparazzi when the real deal wanted them off her back.

There were differences in their appearances—Maggie was an inch taller and her breasts were two cup sizes bigger, but heels and padded bras could work wonders. One of Hollywood's leading blonde bombshells, Maggie was actually a natural brunette—which had always amused Bree since she *was* a natural blonde, whose hair had been dyed hot pink when they met. Now Maggie paid to have her ridiculously overpriced stylist give Bree darker roots so they would match.

Their mouths were a little different, Bree's upper lip not quite so full, but make-up helped there. Bree's unremarkable hazel eyes had nothing on Maggie's naturally turquoise ones, but colored contact lenses made up the difference.

The things they could change to make them more similar, they did—but the things that were harder to change? Those nature had already taken care of. The long thin nose. The slant of her jaw. The high cheekbones.

They were both photogenic, but learning to *be* Maggie—how to work the angles of her face, how to smile and frown just the way she did, how to be aware of the shape of her body at all times—had been surprisingly challenging. The phrase *beauty is as beauty does* had taken on whole new layers of meaning when she realized exactly how much Maggie *did* every day to be "naturally" beautiful in every photo taken of her.

And now the effervescent beauty was bounding over to her, beaming like the sun.

"Isn't he the cutest? You would not *believe* how hard it was to find Cecil B. DeMille's twin. Harder than finding you!" Maggie giggled, scooping up one of the dogs—though Bree couldn't have said whether it was Cecil B. DeMille or his doppelgänger.

The one left on the ground continued to yap shrilly at her ankles, darting forward as if to bite her before stopping just short and retreating to begin another attack run—which was a very Cecil thing to do, but maybe his twin was like him in that way as well.

"Here. This is Cecil Two."

Maggie dumped the dog she was holding against Bree's chest and Bree's arms closed automatically around him. The animal, which had been lying docile against Maggie's chest and gazing adoringly up at her, began to whimper and squirm as soon as he landed in Bree's arms, his sharp little nails scraping the skin on her arms as he tried to wiggle away from her. *Oh joy, he really is just like Cecil.*

Also like Cecil he was heavy for a pocket pooch and his continuous wriggling had her grappling to support his butt so she wouldn't drop Maggie Tate's precious dog. Or—dear God—*her* dog. "Why are you giving me...?"

"The paparazzi would never believe that I would go away for three weeks without Cecil—and I couldn't bear the idea of being parted from my baby for three whole weeks. Could I, baby? No, I couldn't." Maggie bent gracefully, scooping Cecil up easily and tucking him against her side as she baby-talked into his worshipful furry face. "It was just unthinkable, wasn't it, baby, yes it was—so we found Cecil Two! Isn't he perfect?"

Maggie reached to scratch him behind the ear and as soon as she extended her hand, the dog in Bree's arms stopped struggling and went limp with adoration, black eyes liquid as he gazed at his goddess. "Aren't you just the sweetest?" Maggie cooed at him. "Yes, you are. I just want to keep you myself. Yes, I do."

By all means, keep him. Bree somehow resisted the urge to shove the dog back at Maggie, adjusting his weight in her arms—which started up the whimpering struggles again. "Three weeks?"

"I'm getting married!" Maggie squealed again, waving a blinding diamond while Cecil B. DeMille punctuated the announcement with a series of high-pitched snarling barks in Bree's direction, as if the marriage were her fault.

"Cecil, shush," Maggie scolded. "We like Bree, remember?"

Do we? Do we really? Somehow she doubted Cecil shared Maggie's affection. "Who are you marrying?"

Maggie's name was linked to so many men in the tabloids it was impossible to keep up with the carousel of famous hunks, but last Bree had known Maggie had been claiming repeatedly in interviews that she was focusing on her career and taking time for herself.

"Demarco Whitten!"

Bree frowned, trying to place the name—and keep from dropping the dog in her arms as he made a break for freedom over her shoulder, his tiny claws scrabbling up her chest. "The basketball player?"

"I know it's fast," Maggie gushed, as if Bree already knew all the details. "But he just gets me. You have no idea how refreshing that is. He really *knows*, you know?"

"That's great," she said, feeling like she was still three steps behind—and somewhat distracted by being mauled by a freaking mini-Spaniel. "So when are you...?"

"Next week! His team just got knocked out of the playoffs—which is awful and all, but it means we don't have to wait until the finals are over to tie the knot *and* we'll still have two weeks for a honeymoon before I have to be in Hungary to shoot the next Alien Adventuress movie. I know it's like *no* notice, but you can do it, can't you?"

"Do it?" Was Maggie Tate inviting her to her wedding? They didn't really have what could actually be termed a friendship since their entire relationship hinged on the two of them never being seen together in public, but Maggie wouldn't need someone to pretend to be her at her own wedding, would she?

At the look on her face, Maggie laughed the bright, sunny sound that made audiences the world over fall at her feet. "Listen to me! I'm getting it all backwards. I'm hiring you!"

Maggie danced over to the seating area, still carrying Cecil, and Bree followed, trying to keep a firm grip on

Cecil Two. As soon as she sat down on the chaise, she released the kraken and the furball escaped her lap in an explosion of yips, darting over to fling himself worshipfully at Maggie's feet, making high pitched noises of distress until his personal deity reached for him.

"My wedding is going to be a media feeding frenzy as soon as word gets out—especially my wedding to *Demarco Whitten.*" Maggie bent to boost the fretful Cecil Two onto her chair and he instantly settled against her. She smiled with a Cecil cuddled against each hip, the patron goddess of annoying yappy dogs. "We both want something really intimate and romantic—which is why I need you to throw the press off the scent. We're going to leak my plans to get married on a private island in the Caribbean. You'll fly down there with Melanie and plan every little detail of the wedding—and while the press are watching you, Demarco and I will be at an undisclosed location, getting married and spending two blissful weeks as husband and wife without the world looking for us. It's brilliant, isn't it?"

Bree frowned, trying to catch up. "Does Demarco have a double?"

"No—but you won't be faking the wedding, just the wedding planning, and what groom wants to be part of that, right? Melanie will be there with you, along with security. You remember Cross?" She turned to Mel. "Is he still here?"

Bree looked up to see that Mel had been joined by her assistant, a petite dark-haired woman Bree had never heard speak. The girl shook her head now and Mel verbalized for her, "He had to see to preparations."

"Oh well." Maggie shrugged. "You'll see him tomorrow. You know Cross, don't you? I've had him accompany you on some of my appearances. Since he's sort of semi-famous in his own right, he's recognizable and the media love the idea of him as my favorite bodyguard so his presence will help sell that you're really me."

Maggie said it all as if it was already a done deal—and maybe it was.

If she sounded like no one ever said no to her that was because no one ever did. Maggie Tate was a force of nature even when she wasn't giddy and in love—and if she barely knew her groom-to-be who was Bree to question the foibles of true love? She couldn't exactly argue against impulse decisions. She'd once dropped out of school and moved halfway across the country for a guy. Of course, that hadn't really worked out the way she might have wished and she'd more or less sworn off men in the last decade, but that didn't mean she had any right to judge Maggie's turbo-engagement. Sometimes life came at you fast.

"We'll pay you, of course," Maggie went on when she didn't speak right away—Bree had a tendency to zone out in conversations, falling into her own thoughts—but Maggie rarely noticed since she loved to fill silences. "And Mel will take care of everything for you at the resort. You just have to be me. Is sixty thousand all right? I know three weeks is a long time."

Bree nearly choked on her tongue. *Sixty thousand.* It was more than she made in a year. Hell, it was more than she made in *two* years.

Sixty thousand for going to a fancy resort and pretending to be Maggie Tate for three weeks.

Admittedly, it was longer than she'd ever tried to be Maggie before. Most of her "appearances" were only a few hours long—highly public shopping trips on Rodeo

Drive when Maggie was having a little "procedure" done with her nip-tuck specialist or a night dancing at a premiere night club when Maggie didn't want anyone to know she was at home with Ben & Jerry's sulking after Alien Adventuress 2 got seventeen percent on Rotten Tomatoes.

Usually the appearances involved as little speaking as possible, since Bree hadn't quite managed to master Maggie's verbal mannerisms as well as she had her physical ones. But in three weeks she'd have to talk. Though the wedding planner was unlikely to know Maggie well enough to know what she sounded like.

Sixty thousand dollars.

"You'll do it, won't you?" Maggie said, as if the question was a formality. "You'd leave tomorrow. We'd need you here bright and early to get on your Maggie face. Cecil One and I will sneak out tonight, so I'll be gone when you arrive. Cross will collect you and Melanie from here and take you to my plane. You didn't have plans, did you?"

Nothing beyond burning all my photographs because it turns out I'm a talentless hack with nothing to say.

She needed to get away. Needed to run. Three weeks on a private island avoiding the disheartening truth of her real life? It sounded too good to be true.

Bree met Maggie's stunning turquoise eyes, filled with hope and bright with love. "No plans. Of course I'll do it."

"Perfect! Oh, thank you!" Maggie squealed, clapping her hands like a child and sending both of the dogs into a yapping frenzy. "And just think! The next time you see me, I'll be a married woman!"

* * * * *

"Well? How did it go? I'm dying here! Are you about to be wildly famous?"

Bree's thoughts were so filled with Maggie's news that it took her a moment to realize that wasn't what Andi was asking about. Her former roommate had called her as she was walking back out to her car. The Lexus was gone, leaving the Honda and its cargo of rejected art as a lonely reminder of her morning.

She opened her mouth to tell Andi that there would be no catapult to famous artist status, that her work was apparently pedestrian and had nothing to say, but the words caught in her throat.

She'd known Andi since Clement. They'd grown up together—or close to it, only a year apart in school. Andi had gone back to Clement after college and married her high school sweetheart while Bree moved to Venice Beach and tried to figure out how to make a living as an artist. The two of them hadn't really kept in touch, but a few years back when Andi's perfect husband had handed her divorce papers, Bree had perfectly understood the need to run away from all the expectant eyes of Clement, Minnesota. Her last roommate had recently moved out and Bree had been happy to have her friend—and someone to split the rent with.

She'd helped get Andi a job as a production assistant—which had led to a gig as personal assistant to TV heartthrob Ty Walker. Andi had barely tolerated the man with a reputation as one of the most shameless playboys in Hollywood until last Christmas when his daughter had arrived on the scene and everything had changed. Andi had fallen head over heels for her boss— and his little girl—and now the three of them were living a life of domestic bliss.

Which left Bree without a roommate.

It wasn't easy to find someone who didn't mind darkroom chemicals in the bathroom.

Of course, if she made a cool sixty grand in the next three weeks, she wouldn't need to worry about a roommate for a while. She wouldn't have to consider moving back to Clement and selling her pictures on stock photo websites for pennies a piece. She wouldn't have to graphic design headers for websites and pretend it was fulfilling her artistic hunger. She could keep the dream going for a little while longer, buy herself a little more time to be herself and try to make something happen before she was forced to admit that not everyone could be an artist.

"It went great," she heard her tongue lying without any direction from her brain.

"I knew it!" Andi whooped in the phone. "I knew she would love you. How could she not? What happens next? Is she going to give you a show?"

"Uh, no, that's, uh, still a long way off. She wants me to…refine my concept for the show. Figure out what the overall message will be." Which wasn't a total lie. Olivia had told her to come back if she found her voice. Now all she had to do was find it.

"Bree, that's awesome," Andi enthused. She knew next to nothing about the art world, but she'd been Bree's roommate long enough to have picked up some information around the edges. "I'm so happy for you."

Bree climbed into her car and tried to avoid looking at the massive rolled collage poking between the front two seats. Why was she lying? Andi had held her hand through dozens of rejections. She would understand.

"I knew this would be it," Andi gushed. "It feels like everything we've worked for, everything we've dreamed of is happening all at once."

And there it was. The reason she'd lied.

Andi's life hadn't been perfect or easy, but she was *so happy* right now and something about that happiness made it impossible for Bree to admit that she'd failed again. That she wasn't finally getting her own happily-ever-after.

"Are you excited?" Andi asked, accustomed to Bree's long silences.

"It doesn't feel real," she admitted. Because it wasn't real. Because she was lying to her best friend. But the happier Andi was for her, the harder it was to admit the truth.

"I can't wait to say I knew you when. I expect a Bree Davies original for my birthday."

Her birthday. Bree cringed. "Crud, I forgot. I'm sorry, Andi. I just took a job for Maggie. I'm going to miss your birthday." Andi was the only person in her life who knew about her gig with Maggie, who'd been with her when Mel first approached her about the job.

"You're still working for Maggie? I thought you'd be focused on your show."

"The show's still a long way off—" *Second Tuesday after never.* "—and I've still gotta pay rent. This way I can afford to use your bedroom as a studio instead of taking another roommate."

"Well then I'm glad you're going," Andi said firmly, endlessly supportive, "even if you are going to miss the ridiculous party Ty is insisting on throwing me. What does she have you doing this time?"

"Top secret. But I promise I'll tell you all about it after."

"Ooh, a mystery. I love it. Just be careful. There are a lot of crazy fans in the world," Andi cautioned, the voice of experience after meeting some of Ty's most zealous fans.

"I'll be fine," Bree assured her. "She's sending her security guy with me."

"The one you said was hot?"

She could practically hear Andi perking up on the other end of the phone. "I never said he was hot."

Though he definitely was. In that Midwestern All-American way that reminded her entirely too much of her childhood.

"Yes, you did. His name's Cross, right? We were having margaritas and I distinctly remember something about Hot Cross's Buns."

Bree felt her face flaming—damn fair complexion—and was grateful no one was there to see her turning scarlet. "I'm an artist. I'm trained to evaluate the male form. Like the David."

"Uh-huh. You just keep telling yourself that, sister. So you're going off alone with Hot Cross and his buns?"

Bree rolled her eyes. "One—Maggie Tate is never alone. There will be entourages and paparazzi and nothing remotely romantic about the entire experience. Two—Hot Cross and his buns have never said more than two sentences to me, and even if he did he'd be talking to *Maggie*, not to me. And three—when did you get so obsessed with my love life? You were never like this when we lived together."

"I'm in the love bubble. I feel the need to sow the seeds of romance wherever I go and inflict joy and happiness on others. Get used to it."

"Well, you're going to have to sow your seeds elsewhere. I couldn't be less interested in Hot Cross and his buns," she insisted—though she really needed to stop lying to her best friend.

CHAPTER THREE

Aaron Cross Jr., a man once called the bane of wide receivers across the Pac-12 and AFC West, known for his lightning feet and hard hits, slammed onto the mat on his back and groaned.

Candy, the five-foot-nothing bane of his existence, frowned down at him. "What are you moaning about? Did you hurt something?"

He snorted. "Only my dignity." He sprawled on his back as Candy wandered over to the edge of the mat to check her phone.

"Dignity's overrated." She grabbed a towel off the bench beside the sparring mats and flung it at his chest. He caught it one handed, curling to sit up. "Though if it's any comfort you're a lot better than you were."

Better isn't good enough. Only the best is good enough. Cross ignored the voice in his head—the one that always somehow sounded like his father even though he wasn't sure he accurately remembered the sound of the man's voice—and swiped at the sweat on the back of his neck. "I still can't land a hit."

Which was frankly embarrassing. Cross had always been fast, but Candy had been dancing circles around him—literally—ever since the pocket ninja had agreed to help him with his hand-to-hand training when he started at Elite Protection. That was over three years ago and he still couldn't score a freaking touch.

"Yeah," Candy agreed, "but that's not because you're slow and I can tell by the way you move that you know how I'm going to countermove." She briskly wiped the sweat from their session off her arms and flicked her towel into her gym bag. "I have a theory about why you've plateaued."

"Oh yeah?" He looped his towel around the back of his neck, holding the ends. "Care to share?"

"You're too nice."

Cross snorted and levered himself to his feet. "That's one I haven't heard before." Nice didn't get you to the NFL.

"Or too much of a gentleman," Candy went on, speaking over him. "Deep down, I think you can't stand the idea of hitting a girl."

"I promise I am genuinely trying to knock you on your ass every time you hand me mine."

She shook her head. "You probably think you are, but it's so ingrained in you. Nice Midwestern boy, always the biggest and the strongest growing up—your whole life you've been conditioned to be careful of your strength so you wouldn't hurt anyone, right?"

"Except on the field," he admitted. The football field was the one place where he could run as fast as he could and hit as hard as he could, never holding anything back. He'd loved that about the game—even if other parts had sucked, it had always felt amazing to push himself to the max.

"Yeah, but we aren't on the field," Candy argued. "You're on a sparring mat with someone your gentlemanly instincts are telling you is a dainty little female and you don't want to actually land a hit because you know your big ole fists could do some serious damage if you did. Am I right?"

He picked up his gym bag, looping the strap over his shoulder. "You're saying I could kick your ass if you looked like Tank?"

"I don't know about that—I'd be pretty badass if I had Tank's reach—but you could definitely kick Tank's ass any day of the week. You train a helluva lot harder than he does."

You have to train the hardest to be the best. Cross ignored the ghost voice. "You saying we don't need to train anymore?"

"Do you *need* to? Nah. You're a beast, Cross. You've got this. You can probably take down anyone in the company except me and maybe Pretty Boy. But I still like sparring with you if you want to keep it up." She grinned at him. "You're a challenge now."

"Thanks." Being called a challenge by Candy was probably one of the best compliments he'd ever received, but all Cross could hear was that he still couldn't take down her or Pretty Boy. Even if Candy and her former-model fiancé had both been studying martial arts their entire lives and he'd only started when he joined EP, he wanted to be on that level. To be the best. "You heading out?"

Candy slung her bag over her shoulder, shaking her head. "Max wants me to go over the background checks for the new applicants before I go. Though he'd probably appreciate it if I showered first. Smell me. On a scale of one to ten, how rank am I?"

She raised her arm to wave her armpit at him and he backed away, hands raised defensively. "I'm not going to smell you. Where's Pretty Boy? Isn't that his job?"

"He's packing the gear for our early honeymoon."

Cross snorted at Candy's description of the trip. She

and her fiancé Ren, whom she'd dubbed Pretty Boy when the former male model joined EP, would be handling the security detail on the real Maggie while Cross was putting on a show with the decoy. A natural chameleon, Candy excelled at the kind of protection duties that involved blending in. Most of the Elite Protection personal security work was for celebrities who wanted a bodyguard who was visibly intimidating—and eye-catching in their own right. That was part of the Elite Protection luxury brand—the sexiest personal protection money could buy. But this time Maggie didn't want her bodyguard to draw attention, so Candy had been called up, with Pretty Boy backing her up.

"You two thinking of making it a double wedding?"

"Nah. I keep trying to convince Pretty Boy to elope, but he seems to think my parents will never speak to us again if we do. Not that that's a deterrent, necessarily. And at this rate if we don't elope we'll never get married. Who has time to plan a wedding with everything that's going on here? We haven't even had a chance to take a day off in over a year. Remind me to send you a thank you note for the vacation, by the way. Three weeks in Fiji? Maybe I'll go nuts and send you a fruit basket in a fit of gratitude."

Candy might call it a vacation, but Cross knew no one took their job more seriously than she did. "No fruit baskets necessary. I already owe you for all the training."

"My guidance is a priceless gift," Candy agreed with exaggerated humility. "But you would have been fine even without my wisdom. Your overachiever syndrome would allow nothing less."

He frowned. "You make it sound like a disease."

"Do I?" she asked innocently, then her gaze turned speculative. "I admit I am curious why I didn't see your name on the list of candidates for the new position."

Elite Protection had been expanding rapidly in the last year to keep up with increased demand for their services. Max Dewitt, the founder and head badass of EP, had hired four more bodyguards, an in-house accountant, an admin assistant, and a full-time IT person to assist Candy in the last six months alone, but now with his wife seven months pregnant, their boss wanted to have a right-hand man in an executive position to take over some of his own duties. Hence the job hunt for a partner.

"I'm surprised you didn't put your own hat in the ring," Cross countered. "You'll be giving up your second-in-command status."

"Nah, I like what I do. If I had to do all the businessy crap, I wouldn't get nearly as much time to play with my toys." Candy was their resident tech expert, keeping EP current on all the latest security gadgets. "But you forget I did your background check. I know you have an MBA."

Another voice woke up in his head, but this one was definitely his ex-wife's dulcet tones. *No one wants a dumb jock giving them business advice, Aaron.*

"I think Max would probably prefer someone who got their degree from Yale, rather than Online MBA dot com."

Lauren had hated those online classes, bitching about them constantly. But then, Lauren had hated any mention of a life after football. In retrospect, he shouldn't have been surprised that his marriage had only lasted a few months longer than his career in the NFL. He could have put "torn ACL" instead of "irreconcilable differences" on the divorce paperwork.

"I think Max would prefer someone he can trust who knows this business inside and out," Candy argued, "but shouldn't that be his call? Why won't you tell him you're interested?"

Because Cross didn't do failure.

He could hear his father's voice again, whispering in the back of his thoughts, *you never get anything if you don't go after it*—and the old man wasn't wrong. But you also had to know what you could go after and what was out of your reach.

Elite Protection wasn't the first successful company Max Dewitt had started. His father was Titus freaking Dewitt, for fuck's sake, and everyone said Max had inherited his father's Midas touch. He didn't need business help from some meathead who'd gotten his degrees from an online college after dropping out of UCLA for the NFL draft.

It went against the grain for Cross to walk away from a challenge. When something intimidated him, he ran right at it, pushing harder, bellowing over the fear until it was the other guy who was shitting himself. But this was different. He couldn't power through this. He couldn't train harder and longer, do more crunches, run more laps, until exhaustion silenced that damn voice in his head telling him *only the best is good enough.*

"Is there a candidate from Yale?" he asked instead of answering Candy's question.

"Two," she admitted. "Plus Wharton and Kellogg and all the other fancy-ass business schools. Doesn't mean they're any better for the job than you."

He glanced pointedly at the clock on the wall. "Shouldn't you be going? You still have to talk to Max and you don't want to be late picking up Maggie tonight." The world waited for movie stars. Not the other way around.

Candy grimaced at the reminder. "Any tips on handling the great Maggie Tate?"

"No tips. Usually Mel does most of the handling—" At Candy's puzzled look, he clarified. "Her manager. Melanie." Though the one time he'd called her that she'd given him a look like she would remove his spleen with a carving knife if he ever did it again.

"The tall one? Looks kind of like Brienne of Tarth?"

"Who?"

"*Game of Thrones?*" Candy shot him an incredulous look. "Seriously? Who doesn't watch *Game of Thrones?*"

He shrugged. "I've been busy."

"For six years?" At his look, she rolled her eyes. "Fine, so Mel is my point person."

"She would be, but she'll be with me and the decoy. You're getting the assistant. Tera. She doesn't talk much, but if you have a problem with Maggie, probably best to go through her."

Candy arched a brow. "You think we're likely to have a problem with Maggie?"

He shrugged. "She wants what she wants when she wants it and she wants you to be able to work miracles to make it safe to do whatever the hell she wants rather than listening to your advice about what would be safer."

"So pretty much every client we've ever had. Got it." She cocked her head, studying him. "What's the decoy like?"

He shrugged. "Exactly like Maggie. I can't even tell them apart. Unless they tell me which one I'm getting, I never know the difference."

"Really?" Candy's voice lifted, intrigued. "Is she an

actress?"

"Didn't you do her background check?"

Candy made a face. "That doesn't tell me what she's like. Her hopes and dreams."

"She's a job."

Candy had a tendency to change her appearance to get reactions out of people, so he shouldn't be surprised that she was so fascinated by the idea of the lookalike, but he'd never really thought much about who the decoy was when she wasn't Maggie. She was impressive, he knew that much. Her impersonation was note perfect, but that was as far as it went.

Candy sighed dramatically. "Your lack of curiosity appalls me. Do you even know her real name?"

"I'd still have to call her Maggie, regardless. If I called her the wrong thing in front of the wrong person I could put our real client at risk."

Candy lifted one brow, her lips quirking. "You have a history of calling women by other women's names?"

"Not that I know of," he said calmly, unoffended by her delight in giving him shit.

"It would be understandable. I know you ball players get around. It must be hard to keep the ladies straight."

"I was married when I played ball. Which I believe you know."

She shrugged. "Doesn't mean you didn't play around."

"Yes. It does."

Candy cocked her head, studying him for so long he frowned at her. "What?"

"You're just such a good guy. I was trying to think if I have any single friends to hook you up with, but I don't really hang out with women. Maybe Parv knows somebody good for you," she said, referring to their boss's very pregnant wife. "Or Elena. She was on that reality show. Some of those girls must still be single."

"I do not need to be hooked up with a woman from a reality dating show," he insisted. "Or anyone else." The last thing he needed was to become the company project. Tank's wife already seemed determined to introduce him to a "nice girl"—he didn't need Dylan and Max's spouses getting in on the action. "I like being single."

Looking back on it, it was hard to remember why he'd thought getting married was a good idea in the first place. He certainly hadn't missed marriage since his divorce. The last five years had been *peaceful*. He'd been able to focus on the things that mattered to him, finally the master of his own life.

"I *really* like being single," he repeated. He liked not feeling like he was disappointing someone all the time. He liked not having anyone else rely on his emotions.

Candy wrinkled her nose at him—which she would have hated knowing made her look adorable. "I'm siccing Parv on you. She has a huge family. I bet she has a hot cousin."

"Tragically, I'll be on a tropical island for the next three weeks and won't be able to date anyone's hot cousins," he said, moving toward the door to the changing rooms in an attempt to cut off the conversation.

"You have to come back sometime," Candy said.

"That sounds like a threat." Which was about right if she was trying to get him married again.

She still hadn't moved toward Max's office, her head cocked to one side. "Pretty Boy used to date this girl he knew from his modeling days. I wonder if she's still single."

And now she was trying to set him up with her fiancé's exes. "Not everyone has to pair off to be happy."

"Are you happy?"

Define happy. Cross kept walking, inexplicably annoyed by the question. Candy gave him shit, but she usually stayed away from the personal stuff, keeping it light. It was one of the things he liked about their friendship. "Elia's single. Why don't you inflict your matchmaking on him?"

"Elia's doing fine on his own."

And I'm not? He *liked* being single, damn it.

His cell rang and he fished it out of his pocket. "Oh, look, I've got to take this."

"You can run but you can't hide!" Candy shouted at his back.

He shook his head, not turning as he moved steadily toward the outer door.

He was happy Candy and Pretty Boy were finally officially *on* after years of on-again-off-again bullshit, but if she was going to suddenly start matchmaking he could almost wish things would have stayed rocky. Tank had been married to the same woman since he and Cross had been teammates in the NFL, but the last few years had seen an epidemic of marriage proposals at EP. Dylan and Elena. Max and Parv. Candy and Pretty Boy.

Candy seemed to think he was next, but Cross would rather pin that particular target to someone else's back. Maybe someday down the road he would decide he wanted that again—*far down the road*—but right now he had other priorities. Like being the best damn bodyguard EP had ever had.

He glanced at the name on the screen and another priority sprang to the front of his mind. Building his father's legacy.

He connected the call before it could go to voicemail. "Hey, Mike."

"Aaron Junior! I'm glad I caught you. We have a little situation with the equipment deliveries," the man known as Mayor Mike to all of Harris, Iowa began—and Cross could feel his wallet lightening by the second. "It's the six man blocking sled we picked out—turns out it's backordered. Now, we might be able to get it here in time for the beginning of the football season, but I know how important it was to you to have all the equipment in place and ready to go when we have the Aaron Cross Senior Field House dedication next month, so we have a solution. It's the deluxe sled. Now, mind you, it is an extra twelve hundred dollars, which would put us farther over our equipment budget, but we can get that baby here in two weeks and I know—"

"It's fine, Mike. Get the deluxe."

"I knew you'd say that. I told Tammy you'd say that. Spare no expense, that's our Aaron Junior. He knows how important this Field House is to Harris. That's what I said."

Cross winced at the words *spare no expense*, since he'd already sunk over a million dollars into the new athletic center for his old high school, but at this point an extra twelve hundred would hardly make a dent and he did want everything to be perfect for the dedication. The day his father's name was revealed on the building's façade.

They'd been planning and building the field house for nearly three years now and the project was almost over—which meant Mayor Mike had only three and a half weeks left to squeeze him for money in the name of his father's legacy.

Maybe he'd get lucky and there wouldn't be cell service at the Luxe Resort and he could avoid Mayor

Mike's daily *we have a little situation* calls.

"I have to get going, Mike, so if there's nothing else—"

"Actually, there was one more thing," the mayor's frantically cheerful voice babbled. "It's the RSVPs for the dedication events—now, mind you, I know not everyone pays attention to RSVP deadlines, but we did request that replies be returned no later than last Wednesday—"

"I thought I already RSVPed."

"Oh, you did! You absolutely did. It's your mother. We haven't heard from her. Now I'm sure it's just an oversight, so we've included her on all the guest lists even though she didn't follow the protocol and RSVP—" Mayor Mike did love his protocol. "But I just wanted to make sure she hadn't said anything to you about boycotting the events. I didn't want her to feel slighted that she wasn't more involved in the planning of the dedication—"

"I'm sure she doesn't feel slighted."

"I'd just hate for anything negative to touch the dedication—"

Cross repressed a sigh at Mayor Mike's dramatics. "I'll talk to her. I'm sure it just got lost in the mail."

"Oh good. Thank you. I didn't want to worry you, but we can't be too careful. Your father's legacy is at stake, after all."

Believe me. I know. Every day of his life, he knew. It was all about chasing the ghost. Living up to the memory. Being the best. Because only success mattered—and he was his father's legacy.

CHAPTER FOUR

"I can't do this."

Bree had always made decisions impulsively—which had led to a pretty impressive resume of mistakes, but this might be her worst yet. Did she really think anyone would believe she was Maggie Tate? For three whole weeks?

The reality of what she'd agreed to had set in last night when she realized she didn't have to pack, because there wouldn't be a single second when she wasn't being Maggie.

She hadn't slept well. Whenever she'd managed to stop worrying about whether she could actually pull off three weeks of playing Maggie Tate, she'd heard Olivia Hwang's words echoing in her brain, that blithe indictment that she had no voice. When she'd finally managed to fall fitfully asleep, that voice had blended with another, deeper voice, a masculine echo from memory.

Not everyone has what it takes. You can't just decide *to be an artist.*

She'd jerked awake at two in the morning with that voice lodged in her brain, and hadn't been able to get back to sleep. Pacing. Staring at her work, the pieces crammed into her apartment. Wondering if she should just quit. If it was time to move back to Clement. If she'd been fooling herself this entire time.

She almost hadn't gone to Maggie's that morning. But sixty thousand would help—even if she did run home with her tail between her legs—and she didn't renege on promises. She'd told Maggie she would do this and she would.

So she'd arrived at dawn—eyes bloodshot and face drawn from a sleepless night—to be transformed into a goddess.

Then Mel had dropped her bombshell.

The brilliant make-up artist and stylist who made her over into the movie star each time wouldn't be traveling with them—but one of Maggie's small battalion of personal assistants *would*. Kaydee. And she wouldn't be in on the secret.

"I can't..." she repeated.

"Sure you can," Mel said, glancing up from the tablet in her hands from which she managed Maggie's world. "Just add more contouring."

"Not the make-up." After the two hour tutorial, she was actually reasonably comfortable with the make-up, painting shadows and accents on her face. "*This*. The rest of it."

"Of course you can," Mel insisted, as if the alternative wasn't even an option. Mel had sent Kaydee to walk Cecil Two, leaving them alone for the moment in Maggie's vaulted-ceiling bathroom—which meant it was Bree's last chance to panic.

And she was taking advantage of it.

"I might be able to fool the people on the island who've never met her before, but Kaydee *knows* her. You can't seriously expect me to fool a friend."

Her only comfort last night had been the knowledge that the people she was going to be meeting didn't know the real Maggie. They only knew the parts she played on film and the persona she put on for her publicity appearances. If Bree slipped up a little, Mel would be the only one to know. But if she had to perform for Kaydee *all the time* she was going to make a mistake. She knew it.

Mel wrenched her attention off her tablet with a frown. "First of all, people see what they expect to see. And Kaydee isn't a friend. She's a yes man. Yes girl. Whatever. Her job is to agree with everything Maggie says and confirm to Maggie that every choice she's making is the right one—even if Maggie wants to dye her hair purple and streak across the Golden Gate bridge. She won't be looking at you critically."

"But she still knows Maggie—"

"Not like you're thinking. She may know how to bring Maggie her coffee the way she likes it and look after Cecil when Maggie can't, but I picked her in part because she's only been with us for two months—which makes her eager to please. *Desperate* to please. So just remember that you're the boss. Be confident and commanding and she won't suspect a thing."

But it would still be twenty-four seven. She would have to always be Maggie. Always be on. For three solid weeks. Panic began to squeeze her throat.

Mel's tablet released a muted chime and she glanced at it, giving a satisfied nod. "Cross is here and the drivers are en route. We should be ready to roll in ten."

"Should we?" Bree demanded, a little hysterically—because she certainly didn't feel ready to roll. She felt like she was about to asphyxiate from sheer panic.

She'd played Maggie dozens of times before and it had never made her airway feel tight with nerves like this, but she'd never had to keep it up for three weeks either. It had always been a few hours—five or six at the most—and she'd always been able to look ahead to a time when she could let Maggie's persona fall away and be herself again. This time it would be all day every day.

Three solid weeks.

What did she think she was doing? She was an imposter. Not just as Maggie, but as an artist. As *everything*. What the hell was she doing with her life?

At a soft knock on the door, Mel called, "Come in," and the door opened. She was braced for the return of Kaydee and Cecil Two and the weight of the Maggie mask to crash down on her. She wasn't braced for the man who walked through the door.

He really was hot.

Cross looked like something out of a James Bond movie. Tall, blond, and sexy as hell in a dark, tailored suit. Square-jaw, strong profile, cut shoulders—he even *looked* like a bodyguard. She'd noticed his physique before, his aura of authority, but this morning the low hum of awareness that always lived beneath the surface when she was with him had been cranked up to eleven and she felt his presence in her skin, felt his eyes on her amplifying her nerves.

Brown. He had such a generic Midwestern hero look she'd been expecting his eyes to be generic Midwestern blue, but they were brown. Rich and dark, burnt umber with a note of amber, and thickly lashed, but with blond lashes that almost disappeared.

Pretty. The man had seriously pretty eyes.

Bree's heart lurched, something a little desperate inside her latching onto the sight of him because he *knew*. He knew she wasn't Maggie and there was a startling comfort in that. Of course, Mel knew too, but that was different. Mel was the director of this farce, whereas Cross was inside it with her and seeing him there made her feel less alone. They'd done this before, dozens of times, and the familiarity comforted her.

"I believe you know Bree?" Mel said into the suddenly thick air.

He was watching her, bringing to bear on her all the intensity of his focus, and she felt her cheeks warming.

"Bree?" he echoed, studying her face, as if trying to see beneath the Maggie mask.

She fluttered her lashes and flashed him her very best Maggie smile, purring, "Hello, handsome."

His answering smile burst out, fast and lethal, while his voice stayed deep and calmly professional. "Ms. Tate."

"*No.*"

Bree jumped at the sudden outburst from Mel—and the reminder that she and Cross weren't alone in the master bathroom. "What?"

"No flirting."

Bree felt her face heating and very pointedly did not look at Cross, though she caught a glimpse of his lips twitching in the mirror. "Maggie flirts constantly."

Mel gave her a pointed look. "Not like that. Not with intent."

Her face had to be bright red now. She refused to look at Cross, focusing on Mel. "I wasn't—"

Mel held up a hand to cut her off. "Those aren't the kind of rumors we want to start."

"I wasn't aware we *wanted* to start rumors."

"This is fame, darling. We always want to start rumors."

Before Bree could respond, a bright voice sing-songed from the attached master. "Here we are!"

Cecil Two returned in a clatter of tiny puppy toenails against the tile and Kaydee bounced in behind him with an equal degree of youthful enthusiasm. She looked about the same age Bree had been when she first came to LA—so bright-eyed and young it almost hurt to look at that much hope and fresh-faced optimism.

And this little girl could bring the entire house of cards toppling down if Bree wasn't careful.

She had to sell it. So she threw out her arms to the dog and cooed, "Baby!"

* * * * *

Damn, she was good.

Cross watched as Maggie's persona fell seamlessly over the decoy—Bree. He hadn't even realized she'd let the act fall away until it was back, subtly transforming her face. Her adorable blush was gone, the vulnerable uncertainty in her eyes gone, and only Maggie's flashy, flirty confidence remained as she baby-talked at the dog.

Mel was right. Maggie always treated Cross like he was part of the scenery—absently flirty and friendly without ever looking directly at him—but Bree looked him straight in the eyes and it had been almost unnerving, though not unpleasant, that look. Not in Maggie's vague, oh-are-you-here kind of way, but right at him. Into him. Like she saw him and wanted him to see her.

Suddenly she'd been real—not the Movie Star, a real person with Maggie Tate's face—and it was surreal.

He found himself studying her, stealing glances as Mel herded them downstairs to the waiting pair of SUVs that would take them and their luggage to the airport.

Even knowing for a fact she was the decoy, all Cross saw when he looked at her was Maggie Tate. With the giant floppy hat, oversized sunglasses, and designer tote carrying a designer dog, she could have been any wealthy woman on her way to a beach vacation, but the smile was all Maggie.

Her face was exactly the same. Her mannerisms. She didn't say much, but when she did speak it was all Maggie—the cooing baby talk for the dog, the flirtatiousness for the drivers that was delivered in an automatic, almost absent way, like a habit she'd forgotten to turn off.

Cross couldn't resist glancing down to try to spot the differences. Surely there was no duplicating Maggie Tate's legendary ass. But there it was. Perfect. Flawless.

The fact that she was a decoy had never bothered him in the past—but he'd rarely thought of her as anything other than Maggie before. Now...it was disconcerting, *knowing* she wasn't Maggie, but seeing only Maggie when he looked at her.

Once "Maggie" was settled in one SUV with Cecil B. DeMille in a designer dog carrier at her side, Kaydee retreated to the second SUV and Mel grabbed Cross's arm before he could take his own place in the passenger seat. Her manicured nails creased the fabric of his coat as she yanked him to a stop.

"Stop it," she hissed under her breath.

"What?"

"Stop looking at her like you're trying to see through the cracks. You're going to tip Kaydee off." Mel pointed with one perfect nail toward the star in the SUV. "That's Maggie. Treat her like Maggie. We picked you because you've always been good at treating them both like Maggie in the past. Don't make me regret the choice. And stop staring at her ass."

She released him, stalking around the SUV to her own place as Cross mentally kicked himself and his face heated with mortification. He'd been warned that they would be traveling with someone who wasn't in on the deception. Only a few in the inner circle—those who *needed* to know in order to pull off the lie—even knew Maggie had a doppelgänger. Mel had explained that the driver, as well as the pilots and Kaydee, were all part of Maggie's carefully crafted publicity machine.

The most trusted members of the entourage were with the real Maggie and Demarco on a Fijian island right now, while the ones with the decoy's team were those who were loyal to the actress—to a point. They would never say a negative word about her—but they could also be relied upon to be bribed by paparazzi for information about where she went and who she was going to be with.

It was useful to have a few of those in a celebrity's retinue—the people you knew would leak information, and so by controlling what information those people had, you controlled what the public learned—and everyone was more likely to believe the whispers told by make-up artists and chauffeurs than the press releases Maggie put out herself. It was how Mel controlled Maggie's image.

But it also meant Cross couldn't slip up like that again. He couldn't forget himself again. He had a job to do. A story to sell. The client's security and privacy depended on them being able to pull this off.

The decoy—whoever she was beneath that Maggie façade—was just a job. End of story. And Cross *always* did his job. He was the best.

He wouldn't forget again.

CHAPTER FIVE

It really should have been fun.

The fancy car. The private plane. Being whisked off to a private island while wearing designer everything.

Bree *wanted* to gape and squeal and touch everything. She wanted to be excited. She owed it to everyone who'd ever dreamed of spending three weeks living like a movie star to *enjoy* this, but she was too nervous to feel like Cinderella. She was the imposter, impersonating the princess, and if her mask slipped even for a second, if she let herself indulge in the experience as *herself*, then the entire illusion would come crashing down around her.

So instead of gasping as she stepped aboard the luxuriously appointed Gulfstream, she yawned.

There were buttery leather captain's chairs arranged in two separate seating areas, a low couch, a flat-screen TV, a shiny table—and a bedroom. The plane had its own bedroom. And she couldn't even stare.

Catching the yawn, Mel nodded toward the bedroom. "Why don't you go get settled and I'll check on you after I talk to the pilots? Kaydee, can you make sure we have Cecil's puppy pads on board?"

Grateful for the distraction that got Kaydee's enthusiastic chatter away from her, Bree hitched up Cecil's Louis Vuitton carrier and headed toward the bedroom. Ever since the two SUVs had arrived at the airfield, Kaydee hadn't been more than a few feet away from her, orbiting her like a very eager planet. Bree had never realized how exhausting it was to be the sun. She sank down on the edge of the bed—and the lack of sleep and stress pulled at her until she wanted nothing more than to curl up and sleep for ten hours.

Was that a Maggie thing to do? That question dominated all of her thoughts now. W.W.M.D. What would Maggie do?

The paparazzi had followed them to the airport, IDing the SUV's license plate as belonging to one of her regular cars as soon as they pulled out of Hidden Valley. Bree had ducked her head beneath her sunhat to deny them a picture as she was walking toward the plane with Kaydee chattering at her side—but then she'd second guessed herself. Would Maggie duck? Or would she strut? And even if Maggie would *normally* duck, did Bree need to *not* duck so the pictures would encourage the paparazzi to follow them to the Caribbean rather than searching out the real Maggie in Fiji?

She was getting a headache just thinking about it.

Right on cue, Cecil Two began his high, penetrating yelp of a panic-bark and the headache began to throb in earnest behind Bree's eyes. Trying to channel Maggie's way with animals, Bree used her drippiest, gooeyest voice and cooed, "Hush now, baby, you just rest," at the dog—which had no impact whatsoever on the yelping.

Cecil Two definitely seemed to know the difference between her and Maggie. Though maybe he just didn't like traveling. Being hauled around with no control over his life. She couldn't blame him there.

"Who's a sweet baby?" she baby-talked, removing her giant floppy hat and using it to shade the designer pet-carrier from the sun coming through the windows.

"You all right?"

She looked up at the deep voice. Cross stood in the doorway, his brown eyes concerned.

"Yeah, of course," she assured him, unsure whether she was speaking as herself or as Maggie. He'd been distant since Mel scolded them. Professional and reserved. She wanted to tell him that she hadn't been flirting *with intent*—but Mel appeared in the doorway before she could make her tired tongue form the words she needed.

"Everything all right here?" Mel shot Cross a pointed *those-are-not-the-rumors-we-want-to-start* look, shooing him back to his seat, and stepped into the bedroom, sliding the door shut behind her.

Mel had kept everything running smoothly, like a well-oiled machine, and Bree wondered how the real Maggie was doing now that she only had Mel's silent assistant to see to the details of her life.

"Did the other group make it to their destination okay?"

Mel narrowed her eyes. "We aren't going to talk about that. *You* need to focus on the here and now." Her frown intensified. "What's wrong with you?"

"What?" Bree blinked, startled by the sharp question.

"You haven't said two words since we left the house. You know that isn't Maggie. She hates silence."

"I know...I just...what if I say the wrong thing?"

Mel frowned, unimpressed by her nerves. "You're Maggie Tate. Nothing you say is the wrong thing. Everyone you meet wants to please you. *They* are nervous to meet *you*. And they won't be looking for anything other than what they want to see."

"And what's that?"

"A movie star. And movie stars are never nervous."

She laughed shortly. "Wanna bet?"

"You need to own it. If you can't commit then we may as well stay home. Can you do this or not?"

Bree swallowed down a rush of nerves that rose up at Mel's question. Part of her desperately wanted to just say no and retreat back home, but then she remembered Maggie's face. Her effervescent smile. Her sheer joy at the idea of marrying Demarco without the rest of the world looking on. Didn't she deserve that just as much as the next person? And hadn't Bree promised to help her with that?

Not to mention the money.

"I can own it," she promised, stiffening her spine.

"Good." Mel opened her satchel and whipped out her tablet. "I made this for you to study. Don't worry. You've done this before. You're going to be great. I'll tell Kaydee you aren't feeling well and keep her out of your hair until we land." She snorted. "Hell, if we're lucky we might even get a pregnancy rumor out of it."

Pep talk complete, Mel set the tablet on the bed beside Bree and stepped out of the small room, closing the door behind her. The engines fired up and Cecil Two immediately resumed his shrill baying. Her headache throbbed. If Cecil Two made that unholy noise the entire flight, she wouldn't have to worry about having a dog as a prop on the island—she would smother him.

Bree reached into the carrier to lift Cecil Two out, but it was like trying to hold a furry eel, all wriggling and slippery and he shattered her eardrums with a series of pained yelps as if she was torturing him when she finally got her hands on him and lifted him out. His tiny claws scrabbled frantically at her arms, leaving pink grooves in her skin, and she hissed out a curse, dropping him onto the bed. The spaniel was off like a shot, leaping to the floor and darting around the bedroom to sniff everything, his entire little body shimmying with excitement—but at least he was being quiet. He could run to his little heart's content if he stopped making that ungodly noise.

The plane began to move, taxiing toward take off, and her instincts urged her to buckle in or at least locate the nearest emergency exit, but stars apparently played by different rules. Cecil yipped nervously, scrambling back up on the bed and onto her lap. She soothed the wriggling mass of puppy as the plane lifted smoothly into the air, the force barely pressing her down on the bed.

The tablet began to slide and she caught it with one hand, the other bracing Cecil in place. Scooting farther onto the bed, she glanced at what Mel had left her. The tablet was paused on a video of Maggie on a late night television show.

She hit play and listened to the rise and fall of Maggie's voice, her bright, sweet laugh. This was what people were expecting of her. This was what she had to give them. Bree settled in to watch with Cecil tucked against her side.

* * * * *

"How is she?"

Kaydee glanced up, also listening for Mel's answer to Cross's question as the manager sank onto one of the leather captain's chairs. "She's fine. Just a little under the weather."

Kaydee started to get up. "Should I—?"

Mel waved her back to her chair. "She just wants to rest. I'll check on her in a bit."

Cross glanced past Mel's shoulder to the closed door behind her, wondering if Bree was really ill or if the "sickness" was for Kaydee's benefit. He didn't like knowing there was someone in the entourage they didn't entirely trust.

It went against the grain for him to pretend he was securing the client without actually protecting her privacy but that was the name of the game this time. A carefully constructed farce, complete with a decoy dog. Which sounded insane, but he'd seen how far the paparazzi would go for that shot.

He'd had his own little flirtation with fame as a professional athlete, but it hadn't been in the same league. Most people hadn't recognized him, even when he was at the top of his game. He was a ball player, not a personality. His wife had wanted him to be showier, to make a name for himself and stand out beyond his actions on the field, but he'd never wanted that. He couldn't imagine seeking out the lack of privacy that true celebrities had.

Now Bree was at the center of that hurricane of attention. It was only natural that he would feel protective of her. This urge to check on her was normal. Professional. She was the client—sort of. It wasn't personal. It was the job.

And if he was a little more interested than he should be, he blamed Candy. He'd guarded the decoy before and he'd always marveled at how perfectly she pulled off the act, but Candy's words from yesterday had burrowed into his brain and now he couldn't seem to stop wondering about the woman behind the Maggie act.

She'd seemed nervous when she got on the plane. Vulnerable.

His gaze went to the bedroom door, but Mel caught him looking and glared until he returned his attention to familiarizing himself with the security of the villa where they would be staying. Best not to think about Bree. He had a job to do.

* * * * *

Bree jerked awake, one hand flung out in an attempt to brace herself as the bed jolted beneath her. Disorientation swamped her as her gaze darted around the unfamiliar space—until the bed shuddered again and she remembered where she was. Forty thousand feet in the air, shaken awake by turbulence, inside the insane bubble of Maggie Tate's life.

She must have fallen asleep while watching her Maggie tutorial videos. Groggily, she scrubbed the sleep from eyes that itched from the turquoise contacts and swiped at her chin. Did movie stars drool when they slept? Somehow she doubted it.

She sat up, searching the compartment for Cecil Two, her stomach clenching when she realized someone must have opened the door to let him out at some point. Someone who would have seen her sleeping. Had it been Kaydee? Had she already messed things up by not sleeping like Maggie?

The weight of everything she was trying to do pressed on her stomach, the absoluteness of it. She couldn't let her guard down, even to sleep.

There was no clock in the room—not that she would have known what time zone they were in or what time they were supposed to arrive if there had been. She glanced out the window, trying to get her bearings and figure out how deep they were into the seven hour flight, but her gaze caught on the view outside, the sun painting the tops of the clouds.

She hadn't been able to bring her camera.

The luggage was all Maggie's. Maggie's clothes. Maggie's wallet. Maggie's dog. The only thing she had of her own was her cell phone—and she only had that because it looked exactly like Maggie's—and while the cameras on phones may be getting better all the time, they still left something to be desired.

She wanted that shot. The clouds out the window seemed to be speaking to her, somehow perfectly encapsulating the surreal reality of this moment, flying high above the world she normally saw, luxury at forty thousand feet, seeing life through Maggie Tate's eyes. A beauty that was impossible to touch, turning to vapor when you got too close.

But even if she took the shot, it probably wouldn't say what she wanted it to say.

How could she explain to the Olivia Hwangs of the world that it wasn't that she had nothing to say, it wasn't that she lacked a perspective, it was that she never seemed to be able to break through that barrier that stopped her from being able to execute her vision perfectly so that it said what she needed it to say.

Was that why she wasn't an artist? That frustrating disconnect between what she wanted to say and what was actually said? Like struggling to find the right words when she was exhausted and her entire vocabulary seemed to have slipped out of her brain.

She wasn't sure how long she stared out the window, lost in her thoughts, before Mel knocked on the door and poked her head inside. "Oh good, you're awake."

The dog slipped through the opening, scurrying over to the bed and popping up on his hind legs, his little front paws braced on her thigh. She scooped him up as she'd seen Maggie do a thousand times, and crooned to him wordlessly, which he seemed to like this time since he settled down, a soft, furry weight in her lap. He was sort of sweet, Cecil Two. When he wasn't making that hideous dying seal noise.

Mel stepped into the bedroom and shut the door behind her. She produced a comb from her Mary Poppins satchel of All The Things and matter-of-factly strode over to fix Bree's bedhead. "We'll be landing in about twenty minutes," she explained as she gently tucked and tugged at Bree's hair. "A helicopter is meeting the plane which will take us to the resort's private island. Right on schedule."

"Do we know anything about the others?" If she knew this was working, if she knew Maggie was getting her dream wedding, then maybe it wouldn't be quite so hard to focus on doing what she needed to do.

"Don't you worry about the others. Your focus is here." Mel tucked away the comb and considered her work with a satisfied nod. "We'll see you in twenty."

And with that she left Bree alone again with her doubts—for twenty minutes that passed in a blink. Probably because she wanted time to move slowly, dreading their arrival when she had to sell the lie.

How was she going to do this?

After the plane's wheels touched down, she settled Cecil back into his carrier and tucked the tablet with her Maggie primer into the purse that probably cost more than a month of rent for her. When the plane stopped moving, she opened the door into a bustle of activity. Cross was already halfway out the jetway door, seeing to whatever needed seeing to, securitywise. Kaydee relieved her of Cecil's carrier, moving quickly after Cross, and Mel stood with her satchel over one shoulder, sending Bree a questioning glance.

"Ready?"

"Any tips?" she asked under her breath, though they were alone in the cabin.

Mel gave a droll look that was somehow encouraging. "Own it."

Bree took a deep breath, hoping her nerves weren't visible beneath the hat and sunglasses. "Right."

The helicopter waited to whisk them to the tiny island resort that was their final destination, but she couldn't tell anyone it was her first time on one or even act like she enjoyed it without blowing her Maggie cover. Maggie, who had been on so many helicopters they were as boring to her as limousines.

She was going to screw this up somehow.

Then not only would she not get the money, she'd destroy her chance of ever working for Maggie again—and for the last couple years, the jobs with Maggie were the only thing keeping her financially afloat.

When she'd first moved into her Mar Vista apartment, there had been five of them sharing the two bedroom space. A cabal of starving artists, living off Ramen noodles and ambition.

It had been heady. Even being broke had felt like a magical dream back then. But over the years, her roommates had gradually moved on and moved out—getting their own apartments and jobs with benefit packages—while Bree stayed in the same place, both literally and figuratively, clinging to the dream of being an artist and always on the verge of going broke.

Andi had been a good roommate—always paying her rent on time and understanding Bree's tendency to get sucked into her art for days at a time—but it had been almost six months since Andi had moved on and

Bree still hadn't gotten another roommate. Or four. Though the idea of living without personal space was much less appealing now than it had been when she was twenty-two.

Was she too old for this? Was she just another dreamer who'd wanted to be an artist until reality kicked in?

Her mother told her she should be proud of herself, that most people never even tried to chase their dreams—but it was always a preface to "and now you can come home" which lessened the feeling of pride it inspired. As if she was bound to grow up and stop fooling herself at some point and everyone in her life was just waiting to see when it would happen.

But who was she if she wasn't an artist? She couldn't exactly be Maggie Tate for the rest of her life. Even if she did somehow manage to get through the next three weeks without screwing things up. Was she just resisting her inevitable future as a graphic designer and mall Santa photographer?

Andi had suggested that she could move to a cheaper apartment—a one bedroom in a part of town that wasn't so location-pricey—but Bree knew that would be the first domino falling. As soon as she stepped away from Venice Beach and Santa Monica and the creative fuel her soul got in those artistic communities, it would be a tumble downhill away from her dreams until she landed back in Clement again. She would know she'd given up.

But if she could make people believe she was Maggie for the next three weeks, she could buy herself another two years in Venice. Two years to focus on her art and make it happen. And if, at the end of two years, she still couldn't hack it, she would know she'd done all she could.

Provided she could sell the lie.

The pilots were lined up on the tarmac at the base of the stairs, like soldiers awaiting inspection. She half-expected them to salute, but when her foot hit the ground the pilot simply said, "Always a pleasure flying you, Ms. Tate."

"Thank you. Magnificent as ever, gentlemen," she declared with a breezy smile as Cross fell into place beside her, putting a hand on her back to steer her toward the waiting chopper.

She was disproportionately aware of that hand, gently encouraging her to bend forward and duck under the spinning blades, but she didn't look toward him, instead focusing on pinning her giant sun hat to her head with one hand as its brim rippled wildly in the wind. He was the bodyguard. Part of the white noise of Maggie Tate's life. Not a strong, sexy man with his large hand spread on her lower back.

Kaydee and Cecil were already inside when Mel climbed in. Bree took Cross's hand, letting him boost her into the helicopter's cramped interior. The noise was deafening—but she could still hear Cecil Two's high pitched yelping over the thunder of the helicopter.

Their luggage took up half the passenger compartment, but Cross found room for his long legs, wedging himself onto a seat that seemed too small for him between Bree and the door. And her mouth went dry.

Was Maggie this aware of him when he was pressed up against her side? The firm, muscular presence of him? His legs splayed out in front of her? The length of his thigh pressing against hers?

Bree caught Mel studying her and smoothed out her face before she found herself as the recipient of a "Those aren't the rumors we want to start" speech later on.

Abruptly, the helicopter lifted—and Bree's hand shot out, reaching for anything steady to grab onto and landing on Cross's thigh, gripping it tight.

Okay.

She was okay. She wasn't scared of flying. She'd been on planes. Lots of them. This was just like that. But as the helicopter swooped into the air, her stomach fell behind and her hand tightened on Cross's thigh. She closed her eyes behind her sunglasses, but that only made it worse, visions of fiery crashes dancing in her head.

Maybe she should have mentioned that she didn't like heights. Not that she was terrified of them or anything. She could go on balconies and in glass elevators without batting an eye. She'd swung out on the rope swing over Martin Lake more times than she could count as a kid. She'd even entertained the idea of taking flying trapeze lessons at one point, though she'd never actually gone.

But this—as the helicopter angled sharply, banking into a turn and she had to swallow the squeak that wanted to leap out of her throat—this was different. This was climbing the two story ladder to paint a mural on the wall of the gym senior year of high school, her palms sweaty and heartrate galloping faster with every second that passed. This was the eighth grade fall carnival, stuck at the top of the Ferris wheel with Marcus Bradley, whom she'd been told had a crush on her, but who'd laughed when he saw her gripping the safety bar and swung the basket, whooping the entire time.

She *didn't like this*.

A hand closed over hers and, startled by the touch, she looked down. Cross's hand. The grip fear had on her trachea eased, allowing oxygen into her system again.

Her gaze jerked up to his face. She couldn't see his eyes behind his reflective shades, but he wasn't looking at her, his face turned to the view outside the window and the brilliant turquoise seas. He didn't even seem to be aware of her, but his hand was warm and firm over hers, squeezing gently, comfortingly, where she clutched his leg.

She averted her gaze before she earned another "Thou shalt not spread rumors about lusting after thy bodyguard" lecture...but she turned her hand over beneath his.

Their fingers linked together, pressing her palm against his palm, the back of her hand resting against his thigh, and Bree closed her eyes to focus on the feeling of his skin. Breathing in the reminder that she wasn't alone.

Cross was in this with her.

CHAPTER SIX

"She's here!"

Cross had a feeling they weren't supposed to hear the excited gasp from the assembled staff when the golf carts carrying them from the helipad pulled up in front of the massive villa. The exclusive Luxe Resort prided itself on ensuring the privacy of its high profile guests with VIP villas separated from the resort's main compound by a dozen acres and several layers of security—but within the restricted VIP enclave everything was open and airy in true tropical style, so there were no walls to stop the breathless exclamation from carrying easily above the whispersoft engines of their golf cart caravan.

A tall woman with a blue-on-blue skirt and blazer combo setting her apart from the white-and-khaki line-up shushed the speaker and stepped forward as the first golf cart came to a stop. Her black hair was tugged into an elegant poof on the crown of her head and an engraved silver name tag read "*Dominique, Personal Concierge.*" She beamed as she approached, her smile poised and professional, as if she worked with movie stars every day, though the dazed sparkle in her eyes when she clapped eyes on the Great Maggie Tate gave her away.

"Welcome to the Belle Mer at Luxe Villas, Ms. Tate,"

she said, a soft accent touching the words as a small battalion of bellboys swarmed the second cart to collect their bags. "My name is Dominique, and I'll be your personal concierge while you're staying with us. Anything you need, at any time, day or night, simply say the word and it's yours."

"Thank you," the celebrity in the giant hat and sunglasses purred, cuddling her spaniel close to her chest as she climbed out of the golf cart. Cecil B. DeMille hadn't enjoyed the helicopter ride any more than his mistress had and he'd refused to stop yelping hysterically until Bree had removed him from his carrier and tucked him beneath her chin. He now curled passively against her neck, periodically releasing little post-traumatic whimpers.

Looking at Bree now, as she smiled her breezy Maggie smile, he would never have guessed she'd gone white as a sheet in the helicopter and grabbed his leg hard enough he'd probably have a bruise in the shape of her hand.

She'd clung to his hand like a lifeline until the chopper touched down, but now she was back to being Maggie, looking past him like he was part of the scenery.

Not that he minded being part of the scenery. That was his job. And it was pretty damn fantastic scenery.

Lush tropical fronds wafted in the breeze, waters of exquisite turquoise blue surrounded them on three sides, and the villa sat in the midst of it all like a pearl. Cross had familiarized himself with the security set up, but even the pictures he'd studied hadn't prepared him for the effect of the place. Luxury and indulgence seemed to saturate the humid air.

And the villa itself...*damn*.

He should have been expecting it, but he still

couldn't quite seem to wrap his head around the scale of Maggie Tate's life.

"Is this my villa?" Maggie-Bree asked. "It's just *darling*. I love all the little balconies."

Cross almost snorted at the idea of calling anything that size *darling*—it had to be four thousand square feet if it was an inch—but managed to keep his reaction to himself as Dominique launched into a description of the property.

"There are five king suites, in addition to the grand master—each with its own private balcony with an ocean view. As you can see, we're out on our own little peninsula here, so there are full ocean views on three sides. You also have three-hundred meters of private sandy beach cove in addition to the two hot tubs and of course the three swimming pools—the garden grotto pool with a waterfall feature, the salt-water infinity pool overlooking the ocean, and the courtyard lap pool. The property also features a private fitness studio, a screening room, and a gourmet kitchen, though of course we have a private chef on call for you at all times. You also have two private butlers, three housekeepers, and a personal recreation director should you decide you'd like to take advantage of any of the resort's many amenities—from spa treatments to flyboarding."

The swarming bellhops had already surged ahead, their baggage disappearing into the house as Dominique guided them toward another path lined by mosaic tiles.

Mel inserted herself between Bree and Dominique with the deftness of years of practice at keeping the staff from fawning directly over Maggie without being obvious about the buffer she provided. "Mel Walters. We spoke on the phone. I understand you'll also be helping us with the planning of our *special event*." She gave Dominique a meaningful look—and the slim Caribbean woman beamed.

"I will! And may I just say you have chosen the perfect venue for your special event. I can assure you that your time at Luxe will be unforgettable."

If he hadn't been watching, he wouldn't have noticed it, but a flicker of a frown passed across Bree's Maggie Face. It vanished quickly as she adjusted Cecil in her arms, managing to flash her replica engagement ring at the same time. "I can't *wait* to get started, but right now I just want to get my sweet baby settled. He didn't like the trip. Did you, Cecil? No, you didn't, did you, baby?"

"Of course!" Dominique exclaimed. "We have everything prepared for Cecil, just as you specified."

The concierge led the way into the air-conditioned interior where everything was white and bright and open.

"This is the formal living room," Dominique explained, as they stepped into a room with a white sectional that could easily hold twenty, a white baby grand piano, and a chandelier that looked like a pink glass sculpture hanging from the center of the ceiling. "There's also a family living room upstairs and the outdoor living room on the covered beachside patio. You'll notice we've placed a dog bed in every room so Cecil can be comfortable, no matter where you are. To your left is the formal dining room and beyond that the kitchen, screening room and fitness studio, but the suites are just up these stairs to afford them the best ocean views."

Mel stepped in then, collecting the keys from Dominique and ushering the staff out with a series of "Maggie's" instructions as the star attraction stood off to one side and cuddled her dog. Dominique left only after promising profusely to be at their beck and call should they require anything, *anything at all*.

Once the door clicked shut behind the concierge, Mel moved to where Bree was gazing out the floor-to-ceiling windows at the sunset view and scooped Cecil B. DeMille from her arms. "Kaydee, would you take Cecil for a walk and unpack his things? I know Maggie won't rest easy until he's settled."

"Of course!" Kaydee had been trailing behind, taking everything in, but now she rushed forward to take the pooch from Mel.

"Make sure they know about his dietary restrictions!" Bree-Maggie called as her assistant hurried toward the gardens with the dog.

When Kaydee was out of sight, Bree turned to Mel and tugged off her sunglasses, her Maggie persona falling away. She still had Maggie Tate's face and Maggie Tate's body—but suddenly someone else was looking out of Maggie Tate's turquoise eyes. A little uncertain. No longer queen of everything and used to having her every whim indulged. "What now?"

Mel shot a deliberate glance toward the doorway which Dominique had said led to the kitchen. "Now you rest up after your trip. I know how travel always exhausts you. I'll arrange for dinner to be brought in so we won't have the chef underfoot tonight while you're recovering," Mel said pointedly and Bree pursed her lips, chastened by the reminder to stay in character. "Tomorrow is early enough to start thinking about planning your big day." Bree opened her mouth, as if to argue and Mel gave her an unblinking stare. "There's no need for you to worry about anything outside this villa."

Bree grimaced—a definite Bree face. It was amazing how quickly he'd become able to tell them apart—or maybe it was just amazing how easy it was to tell them apart when Bree let the mask fall. She'd have to be careful of that. Once the paparazzi found them, their long-range cameras wouldn't care that she was inside the villa.

"I guess I'll go check out this grand master suite," Bree said without enthusiasm, trudging up the stairs like a toddler being sent to her room.

Mel watched Bree go, then turned to Cross when she was out of earshot. "She'll feel better after she's rested."

Cross had his doubts about the effectiveness of trying to operate Bree using Maggie's manual, but running Maggie was Mel's job. His was to keep her safe—and to that end, he had work to do.

The resort had an excellent reputation, but Cross was responsible for Bree and he wasn't going to assume everyone else had done their job.

He needed to check in with the local security team. Set up the additional motion sensors and cameras that Candy had sent along with him. Touch base with Max at EP and text Candy to make sure there hadn't been any developments on the Fijian end. Sweep the entire villa for recording devices—Luxe may have an excellent reputation for ensuring their guests' privacy, but that didn't mean an enterprising maid hadn't dropped a camera in a palm tree when she found out who was going to be occupying the villa.

Not that he'd be able to remove them if he found them. He had to keep reminding himself that they were trying to be found. Hoping to be caught. Though only in a highly controlled way.

The games of celebrity.

Still, he would search. He wanted to know what they were up against.

And then, once he got through all of that, he had three missed calls from Mayor Mike—probably reminding him that his mother still hadn't RSVPed, or asking for more money. He needed to call his mother, and to go through the package she'd sent him with the latest round of bills for the field house.

He'd told all the vendors to send the bills to his California address, but Harris was a small town and several of the local vendors seemed to think the best way to bill him was to send the invoices to his childhood home. His mother had gotten in the habit of dumping all his mail into a manila envelope once a month and sending the bills to him so he could keep on top of things.

Just one more headache that he wouldn't have to deal with when the field house was done.

He had the latest envelope in his luggage, but he couldn't get to it until Bree was secure.

"Do you need me for anything?" he asked Mel. "I'd like to do a full security run down and touch base with the resort crew."

"We're good. I'll manage things here. You do your thing."

Cross nodded, leaving Mel to quietly rule the world, and went to collect his gear from the luggage the bellmen had left neatly stacked in the foyer.

With all the balconies and patios, the house had clearly been designed for indoor/outdoor living—a luxury for many celebrities who were targets for telephoto lenses as soon as they stepped outside the walls of their homes. The resort was banking on their isolation and the security on the island, which he knew had been designed to be as invisible as possible, blending into the landscaping.

And here they were, banking on the fact that the paparazzi would be determined enough to break through that security to get to Maggie.

For the first time, Cross felt a flicker of remorse—if their plan worked, they would ruin Luxe's perfectly secure reputation. But they would also keep Maggie's real wedding safe and private, which was what they were being paid to do. Luxe would recover. They might even benefit from the publicity of having the fake Maggie camp out there for a few weeks.

The games of celebrity.

* * * * *

Bree had never been much of a napper.

Restless excess energy was more her style—especially when she was nervous, as she was now. Simply walking into the master suite made her feel miles out of her league, reminding her exactly how out of her depth she was.

It had its own sitting room, two walk-in closets, a giant bathroom with the biggest shower she'd ever seen, a soaker tub, a polished marble double vanity and a fluffy bathrobe hanging on a hook with orchids tucked into the lapel. And if that wasn't enough, there were three sets of French doors leading out onto a private wrap-around balcony the size of her apartment, with views of an ocean so blue it could make you cry.

She was in heaven. And it was terrifying.

After sleeping for hours on the plane, the last thing she needed was another nap. Especially when she was afraid to lie down on the bed. Afraid of disturbing the artistically arranged pillows.

Her entire body was humming with too much energy, nervous agitation making her feel caged.

Trapped. She wanted to *do* something—anything, it didn't even matter what—but that wasn't Maggie.

Maggie was a napper. She was self-indulgent and languorous and loved having things done for her. She would never unpack her own suitcase or cook her own dinner—which meant if Bree was going to pass herself off as Maggie for three weeks there was nothing for her to *do*.

She actually felt jealous of Kaydee for having a task— *she* wanted to walk Cecil. *She* wanted to explore the island and sink her toes into the sand. She craved useful activity and watching Kaydee walk off with Cecil she'd felt like an alcoholic watching someone else pour herself a drink.

Bree had never done well with forced inactivity. She needed to *move*, to burn off her agitation, to *use* the energy that felt like it was consuming her from the inside out. But she couldn't without blowing her cover.

Maggie may work out fanatically to maintain her movie star bod, but Bree couldn't even go for a run because Maggie didn't believe in letting people see her looking anything less than flawless and never ever sweated where anyone might see her.

Though she thought someone had said the villa had a fitness studio. Maybe she could run her jitters into exhaustion.

Provided Mel ever let her out of napping time out.

A soft knock sounded at the main door of the suite and Bree barely stopped herself from lunging toward the sound. What would Maggie do? Go to answer it? Lounge in bed and call *enter*? She needed to know these things. She was going to screw up all the details.

Or give herself a nervous breakdown.

She settled for staying on the big, comfy reading

chair in the sitting area where she'd been rewatching her Maggie primer and calling, "Come in."

The door opened and Cross paused on the threshold, a small electronic device in one hand. "Will I disturb you if I sweep in here for recording devices?"

"No, come in," she urged, ready to beg him to disturb if it gave her something to focus on besides her own panic, but when he stepped into the room and let the door fall shut behind him the reality of what he'd asked hit. "Do you think there are really recording devices in here?"

He grimaced. "Better safe than sorry."

Bree's heart sank. She'd wanted him to say *no, of course not, this is just an excess of caution*. But that was only her wishful thinking. In Maggie's world, the walls had ears.

Which only drove home the fact that there was nowhere she could be herself. For three weeks.

She glanced toward the balcony. Everything was glass and blue water—it was gorgeous—but suddenly she felt exposed looking at it. Her gaze went to Cross's shoulder holster, visible now that he'd taken off his sport coat.

"Should I be worried?"

He looked up from his task, his dark eyes serious. "I'm not going to let anything happen to you."

The vow sent a little shiver down to her most primal self. He would protect her—on some instinctive, animalistic level, she'd known that, but that wasn't what she'd meant to ask. She'd wanted to know if there was anywhere she could go where she wouldn't be watched...but she was afraid to ask again. Afraid she wouldn't like the answer.

"Is this going to be a regular occurrence?" she asked

instead, as he ran the device in his hand over the bedside lamp.

He answered without taking his attention from his task. "I'll sweep regularly for recording devices, but even with the resort's security measures a really determined photographer with a telephoto lens or a reporter with a parabolic mic at the window could get something. Not to mention a maid with a cell phone who was willing to risk her job for a big enough check. I'd be surprised if anyone has anything set up yet since so few people knew we were coming and the Luxe has a reputation to protect, but just to be safe it's probably best to always be on guard."

Bree felt herself wilting at the prospect, but forced herself to nod. "Right. Thanks."

Always be Maggie. For three weeks straight. She could do this. For sixty thousand dollars, she could play the pampered movie star. Lots of people in the world had much harder jobs. Nearly everyone. Talk about your first world problems. She just needed to suck it up and be Maggie. Easy.

So what if she didn't know what the hell she was doing? Lots of people were faking their way through life.

"Do you think this is crazy?" she heard herself asking, her mouth, as usual, forming the words before her brain caught up.

Cross paused, meeting her eyes, and she had the sense that he knew exactly what she was trying to ask. *Can I do this? Will it do any good?*

"I think..." He paused, giving her question genuine thought. "I think privacy is a luxury that's worth the effort."

His eyes were dark and steady and something deep

inside her throbbed as her breath went short.

He really was unfairly gorgeous. A square-jawed golden god.

They'd worked together in the past—she'd even flirted with him, but she'd always been playing Maggie and Maggie was blithe and flirty. But when she was herself with him, even if it could only be for a few minutes, it felt different. More real.

He was the one person in this entire situation that felt real.

Cross turned his attention back to the device in his hands, his concentration complete, and she watched him while trying to pretend she wasn't, trying to ignore her hyperawareness of his every move—and blaming Andi for even planting the idea in her head that he might be fling-worthy.

She was Maggie for the next three weeks. She couldn't exactly have a fling with her bodyguard when she was supposed to planning her wedding.

Though they wouldn't *always* be in the public eye, would they?

And her bodyguard was definitely appealing.

Kind of a control freak, but undeniably hot. Serious. The kind of guy who would probably think she was silly. Flighty. She didn't know his first name, but Cross suited him. It was firm. Commanding. He was definitely a take-charge kind of person—and in Bree's experience take-charge men didn't always know what to do with her go-with-the-flow ways. But she was intrigued, in spite of herself.

Though at the moment, the feeling didn't appear to be mutual. He was focused completely on his task, seeming to have lost interest in her. She tried to stifle her disappointment at the thought.

He'd probably thought she was coming on to him. Probably trying to let her down easy. Should she say something? Assure him that she could be professional?

"I didn't mean to flirt earlier, not with intent," she blurted and his gaze snapped toward her—right as the door opened and Mel appeared.

"There you are," the manager said, her gaze moving between Bree and Cross as she let the door close gently behind her.

Bree froze, feeling her face flame like a teenager caught with a boy in her room—even as she reminded herself that she was a grown woman on the far side of thirty and she hadn't done anything to deserve a reprimand.

"Cross was just sweeping for bugs," she said too quickly, defensively, as Cecil Two darted into the room, his long ears flapping as he yelp-barked and raced toward her.

"You about done?" Mel aimed her question at Cross, who frowned at the device in his hands.

"Nearly. Nothing yet, but I'll keep scanning periodically."

The knowledge that no one was listening—and she had no idea how long that would last—had words tumbling out of Bree's mouth. "Do you really think this will work?" she asked Mel as Cross stepped out onto the balcony to work his magic out there. "You think the paparazzi will go to all the expense of flying to a tiny island in the Caribbean just to get pictures of me planning a wedding?"

Mel arched a brow, one side of her mouth lifting sardonically. "Honey, if it meant a payday they'd fly to Antarctica for pictures of Maggie Tate. When the Instagram post of the engagement ring goes live tonight, the media are going to go into a feeding frenzy. They're probably already bribing everyone they can think of to try to get our flight plan. For a sneak peek at the wedding of the century? Trust me. The pictures will be worth much more than the expense. They'll come. Which is exactly what we want them to do."

Bree's stomach churned at the thought. She'd known that celebrities had to deal with that degree of insanity, had known it was Maggie's reality, but it was different when it was happening to her in real time. "Do I need to be posting pictures while I'm here? Of wedding stuff or the beach?"

"You don't need to worry about any of that. Maggie almost never touches her own social media. If you want to pose with a veil and have Kaydee snap a pic and post it, that'll be in character, but otherwise, just leave your online presence to me."

"You're the expert."

Mel's smile was wry. "Even Maggie doesn't know her brand as well as I do." She tilted her head. "Do you need anything else? Those videos good?"

She'd been chafing under Mel's management, but the other woman wanted her to succeed as much as Bree did. She needed to remember that Mel was an ally and a resource, not the principal waiting to send her to detention if she didn't behave properly. "They're great. Thank you."

Cross reentered and gave them both a nod before exiting the suite, which Mel took as her own cue to depart.

"I'll have dinner sent up when it arrives," she said, retreating to the door. "Try to get some rest. Busy day tomorrow."

Bree's stomach knotted nervously at the reminder.

Tomorrow she had to sell the lie.

CHAPTER SEVEN

The house was too quiet.

By the time dinner arrived, Cross had already set up the additional equipment Candy had sent along—motion sensors and cameras tied to his phone so he would get alerts whenever someone approached the villa—which may drive him crazy with all the staff coming and going, but no one would ever accuse him of slacking on the job.

Anything worth doing is worth doing one hundred and ten percent. He'd always hated that phrase—the idea that anyone could give more than their most was a sportsism that had always annoyed him, but the words still echoed in his mind in his father's voice. *Be the best. Push the hardest. Do the most.* Always. The words pushed into the back of his mind and refused to quiet.

He hadn't found a single bug—which wasn't surprising. He'd expected nothing less. The only people who'd known they were coming to this villa were the hotel staff. The real games would begin once the paparazzi hit the island, but tonight all was well.

And it was driving him crazy.

After he'd finished the security preparations, Cross had picked a bedroom close to the master suite so he'd be able to get to Bree quickly in case of emergency and began to unpack. His room was just as lavish as the master, only on a smaller scale. Instead of an entire sitting room, he had an arm chair. There was a built in desk off to one side—as if people came to the Caribbean to work—but it looked out over a smaller version of the master balcony.

Dominique had explained as Mel was ushering her out that a butler would be available at their convenience to unpack for them, but Cross didn't like the idea of anyone else handling his things. He'd unpacked quickly, setting up his surveillance console and throwing the envelope with the Harris bills into one drawer of the desk, before roaming the house under the pretense of a security sweep.

His body was still on Pacific time—which he knew would suck when he had to wake up at dawn the next morning, but right now he was too restless to sleep.

Deciding to burn off some energy in the fitness studio, he first walked a circuit of the house, registering the sound of a television from one of the other upstairs bedrooms before he made his way downstairs. The sound of the treadmill whirring greeted him before he reached the door and he paused with his hand on the knob, eyeing the light seeping beneath the crack.

He told himself his hesitation was because he didn't want to intrude, but if he was honest, there was something else at play. Bree was...distracting. And he couldn't afford to be distracted.

But he still opened the door.

He didn't know why he'd been so sure it would be her. It could easily have been Mel or Kaydee on the treadmill, but somehow he'd known who he would see—a slim figure with a blonde ponytail swinging in time to her steps.

Between the sports bra and the snug workout pants

that ended below her knees, her outfit left little to the imagination—and showed exactly how similar her body was to the one the entire world had seen on the silver screen. Sweat glistened on her shoulders and down the line of her back, proving she'd been keeping up the bruising pace on the treadmill for some time already.

Her focus was locked on the tablet propped on the treadmill console, a pair of noise-cancelling headphones covering her ears.

She hadn't noticed him yet. He could slip out and no one would be the wiser. Wasn't discretion the better part of valor? The last thing he needed was to be noticing her ass or the taut line of her stomach.

Even if she hadn't been off limits for the next three weeks while she was playing Maggie Tate, he wasn't looking for a relationship—and now wasn't the time for a fling. No, it was better if he walked away before he got any closer to Bree...

But then, as if she'd sensed him there, she turned her head, catching sight of him in the mirror, and his opportunity to retreat gracefully vanished.

She reached up, tugging off the headphones with one hand while the other went to the treadmill controls, lowering the speed to a walk. "Hey. Everything okay?"

He came more completely into the room, letting the door fall shut behind him. "I was going to ask you the same thing. You all right?"

"Couldn't sleep." She hit another button and the treadmill slowed to a stop as she hooked the headphones over one of the hand-bars. "Nervous energy," she admitted with a grimace—an expression that was so incredibly Bree it was hard to imagine anyone could mistake her for Maggie.

The fitness center was windowless and the door was

closed. They weren't likely to be more private than this for the next few weeks, so he let himself speak to Bree candidly, rather than through the filter of Maggie. "You'll be fine," he assured her. "I've stood right next to you for years and never known the difference."

"Yeah, but not for three weeks straight. Trying to fool everyone. Trying to *be* her. Doesn't it feel different this time?" She waved at their surroundings, taking in the entire villa. "This isn't exactly a stroll down Rodeo Drive."

Her words called to mind the first time he'd guarded her. Maggie had been trying to attend a family funeral without being hassled by the press. Candy had tucked herself invisibly into Maggie's retinue for the funeral while Cross had taken the decoy out to entertain the press on Rodeo Drive.

He'd felt noble at the time, protecting a grieving family from the paparazzi by taking a lookalike shopping in Beverly Hills, but now he found himself wondering about Bree. If she had been as nervous that day as she was now.

"If it makes you feel any better, I've been wondering all day how many times I was with you when I thought I was with her. You're that good. It's disorienting. Especially when I don't know anything about you."

"It's weird, isn't it? Having spent all this time together without ever being properly introduced." She thrust out her hand. "I'm Bree. Bree Davies."

"Aaron Cross."

Her hand was small in his—and he only realized he was still expecting Maggie's perfectly moisturized hands when he felt the slight roughness and callouses on Bree's. Did she work with her hands?

"I don't think I ever knew your first name," she

commented, her head tilted inquisitively. "Does everyone call you Cross?"

"Aaron was my father's name too," he explained. "Cross felt more like mine."

Why had he told her that? He didn't talk about his father. Big Aaron. A legend larger than life. A shadow he could never get out of.

"Well, it's nice to finally meet you, Cross," she said—and he realized he was still holding her hand. He dropped it, rocking back on his heels.

"How long have you been Maggie's decoy?" he asked, moving past her to inspect the free weights.

"Not quite three years."

He went still. That was the entire time he'd been working for Maggie. He could have been guarding the decoy the entire time. "You're an actress?"

"Artist, actually. Or trying to be." She grimaced—the self-deprecating expression so un-Maggie-like it was almost jarring on the actress's face.

"So why...?" Why pretend to be someone she wasn't? What did she get out of it? Just the chance to play celebrity for a little while?

Bree shrugged one shoulder, avoiding his gaze. "It's a job."

Her body language was totally different. Less sultry. More unsure. She could be so convincing as the movie star and then a heartbeat later she would be someone else entirely. Even her voice was different, not as high pitched, with the slightest Midwestern twinge of an accent. She could have been from his home town. "How did you learn to do it?" he asked. "To be Maggie."

"She taught me. Trained me. It was fascinating, actually. To her it was all about the details. How to hold her head to get the best angles. How to smile. How to laugh. Everything she does is choreographed and it was incredible to see the way she saw herself. How controlled she was, for someone who seems so effortless, you know?" She wrinkled her nose. "Of course it helped that I had teams of stylists to make me look exactly like her. I'll have to do all that myself here. And sound like her. That's the hard part. That and keeping it up twenty-four seven."

"If you ever need a break, the theatre room and this one are good places to hide out. No windows."

"I'm just afraid I'm going to say the wrong thing to the wrong person and ruin everything."

"Relax. You've got this." Movement on the tablet she'd been watching caught his attention and he saw a clip of Maggie being interviewed on the screen. "Studying?"

She made a face. "Psyching myself out is more like it."

He studied her face, the tight lines around her mouth, the nervous tension in her eyes. "Why agree to do it if you're so nervous?"

She grimaced. "The money. And because I genuinely like Maggie. Her life is an insane zoo, but everyone deserves a dose of normal now and then and if I can help her with that, I will."

The answer, instead of enabling him to put her into an easily quantifiable box, only stirred up more questions. Who *was* she? This woman who pretended to be Maggie? She seemed so open, so matter-of-fact, but she had to be an amazing liar to pull off her job. It was a strange sort of contradiction. "How did you start doing this?"

"Chance?" She smiled wryly. "I dressed up as the Alien Adventuress for Halloween one year and a friend posted pictures of the party on his Instagram. Next thing I knew Mel had gotten my number and was asking if I was interested in working for the Great Maggie Tate. At first it seemed like this fantastic game—and the first time I did it...it was crazy. Everyone treats you differently when you're famous."

He frowned, vaguely disappointed in spite of himself to hear her sounding like a Hollywood cliché. "So you wanted to be famous?"

Bree laughed. "God, no. But I got to see people through the lens of fame. I got to walk a mile in someone else's shoes. To *see*, you know? Life is different as Maggie Tate. You wake up in this completely different reality with Gulfstreams and helicopters and crazy villas." Her wave seemed to encompass not just the villa, but the entirety of Maggie's world. "It isn't about the wealth or the fame—it's about... the view. About the chance to see how looking through someone else's eyes could change you. Who wouldn't want that?"

Lots of people.

Most people would have been all too eager to use the movie star to get ahead, but very few would have wanted to understand what her life was really like. He'd seen all too much of that, but Bree...she wasn't what he'd expected. He wasn't sure what he'd expected. He hadn't thought he had expectations, but she'd somehow defied them.

"You're going to be great tomorrow."

"You think?" Her voice was so soft, so vulnerable.

Somehow he'd drifted back to her until they were separated by only a foot. Alone together in the quiet of the fitness studio, he looked down at her. She seemed so small, so fragile. Cross cleared his throat. "We should both get some sleep."

Her gaze shuttered. "Probably a good idea." She reached for the towel hanging off the treadmill to dab at the sweat above her sports bra and he turned away from the sight. "Cross?" she said softly when he reached to open the door—his own plans for a workout forgotten.

He turned back. "Yeah?"

"Thank you." She smiled, a slight, nervous curve of her lips. "I just needed to feel like me for a minute, you know?"

He nodded, unsure why those words should make him feel so off-balance. "Good night, Bree."

She smiled. "Good night."

He exited the fitness studio and climbed the stairs quickly without looking back. Whatever that moment had been, he needed to forget it. He didn't need the distraction from his goals. No matter how intriguing she was.

CHAPTER EIGHT

By six o'clock the following evening, Bree was reasonably certain she was a horrible human being.

On the plus side, she'd forgotten her nerves about being found out. Now she almost wished they would discover her so this churning guilt would go away.

She'd spent all day with the endlessly patient Dominique—a wedding planner who really ought to be sainted—while Mel and Kaydee helped her explain her "vision" for the ceremony. A vision which changed approximately every ten minutes.

She'd gushed about sunset weddings and brunch weddings and weddings where the beach was lit by two hundred candles and moonlight. She waxed poetic about an old Hollywood theme, and a basketball theme, and blending them into an old Hollywood/basketball theme to please *all* their celebrity friends. She'd namedropped shamelessly—Ed Sheeran would be singing, Vera Wang would be designing her dress by hand, and an Oscar-winning director friend was just *dying* to officiate. But it would be an intimate little affair. Private. Just the two of them. And perhaps two or three hundred friends.

She'd requested a red carpet of rose petals and a trellis arch woven out of tropical flowers—then promptly turned around and professed her love for all things minimalist. She'd played Maggie at her most dramatic and indecisive—and every time she'd told another lie, she'd felt like a worse person.

Bree didn't like lies. She didn't like the idea of conning all these people. She didn't like using them. And it didn't make her feel any better that it hadn't been her idea, her plan—it just made her feel weak for going along with it.

Now, back in one of the few rooms where she could be herself, her feet pounded on the treadmill as she tried to outpace her guilt, to run it into exhaustion. And, yes, she was also hoping that Cross would come down here as he had last night because she needed to talk to someone, needed him to tell her that what they were doing was for the greater good. Because right now she just felt slimy.

And she had to do it all over again tomorrow.

No one had ever been hurt by the deception before. When she played Maggie on Rodeo Drive, the shop clerks got commissions they wouldn't have gotten if "Maggie" hadn't appeared that day, but this…

Dominique thought she'd been hired as the wedding coordinator for an A-list actress. Something like that on her resume could completely change her life. She hadn't said as much, but it was there behind the stars in her eyes.

The owners of the resort had flown in to meet with Maggie personally, to assure her that everything would be flawless on her big day. They'd already started recruiting extra staff for the event—each hire carefully vetted by their in-house security team. And every reassurance about every measure that was being taken to ensure her happiness and safety only made her feel worse—because the wedding wasn't happening. Not here, at least.

It had taken her all day—through discussions of flowers and catering options and the logistics of bringing in top recording artists to perform at the reception—before she'd realized that the resort wasn't even getting paid. They were "sponsoring" the wedding for the privilege and publicity associated with being the resort where Maggie Tate got married.

That was when Bree had really started to feel sick.

At four, she'd pleaded jet lag and retreated upstairs while Mel cleared the villa of the cast-of-thousands the wedding plans seemed to require.

She was wasting their time. Using them. And she hated users. Hated liars. Hated seeing one in the mirror while she tried to outrun her guilt.

She'd been on the other side of it, been hurt by deception, and now she was just as bad as Zander had been. Just as manipulative.

"There you are." Mel appeared in the doorway, her focus half on the tablet that was never far from her hand—right on schedule to get Bree back on schedule. "Your dinner has arrived."

Bree sighed and hit the button to stop the treadmill, riding the conveyor belt to the back and hopping off as it slowed. She knew Mel was trying to help, but Bree had never done particularly well with schedules. She always felt restless inside them. Confined.

At home she would pour her excess energy into her work and completely forget about the time. She'd lost more day jobs than she could count because she lost track of the days, let alone the hours. Schedules were not her friend. Time was a flowing, flexible thing. When she was creating something, life would fade away into that perfect, sharp focus of absolute purpose and a feeling would fill her like she was doing the one thing she'd been put on earth to do...

Except no one wanted her art.

How could it be her reason for existence if she was boring and pedestrian? If she'd never had talent and was only fooling herself that she might actually be able to make a meager living as an artist at some point?

Maybe it was time for her to grow up and learn how to live inside a schedule. Past time.

Realizing she'd been silent too long again, she forced a smile. "Thank you," she said as she fell obediently into step with the woman currently managing her life.

"Kaydee's out walking Cecil and the resort staff have left for the night." Mel kept her voice carefully low, even though they were alone in theory, adding softly, "You did well today."

The words brought back that sick feeling. "Do you feel bad at all? About lying to all these people?"

Mel's smile was lightly patronizing, as if her naiveté was *adorable*. "They'll be fine."

Would they? Bree wanted to demand. Would Dominique, who thought they'd just made her entire life? Or the resort's owners who were going to who knew how much expense to make this wedding perfect?

What was the plan for the end of the three weeks? Bree was here, planning an entire wedding, but the real Maggie was off getting married somewhere else. Would the truth come out? Would Maggie admit she had a decoy? It seemed unlikely, because then they'd never be able to use the ruse again, but then what story were they going to sell? How were they going to explain it? Bree should have asked more questions at the beginning, but all she'd been thinking of was how sixty thousand dollars could change her entire life.

Seeming to sense her unease, Mel stopped at the hallway leading to the main part of the house. "You don't need to worry about anything but your part and you're doing that beautifully. Look. We already have some buzz."

She tapped something on her tablet, showing Bree an article from the *Fame Game* website from that morning.

Wedding Bells for Alien Adventuress?

Are Maggie Tate and Demarco Whitten really tying the knot? After the Alien Adventuress star Insta-flashed her stunning nine-karat blush diamond yesterday, the celebrity wedding watchers all salivated at the thought of the spectacular bash these two are bound to throw—and rumor has it we may not have to wait long. A source close to the actress says Maggie can't wait to marry her baller honey and is already scoping out tropical venues for the big day.

Bree frowned. "How do we know they mean *this* tropical island and not the other one?"

"Don't worry about that. Trust me. There will be paparazzi in the bushes any day now. Just keep doing what you're doing." Then Mel paused, adding, "Though maybe be careful of the way you look at Cross."

Bree snapped her mouth shut on the words she'd been about to say. "Cross?"

"I don't need to remind you that we aren't trying to start rumors about Maggie and her bodyguard."

"I didn't—I don't look at him." But she'd been aware of him. All day. Her shadow, his presence a weight against her spine—somehow comforting and agitating her at the same time.

Mel's eyes were entirely too knowing. "He's an attractive man, I can see the appeal, but even if no one notices you sneaking off to the fitness studio together in the middle of the night, the way you act around him could give the wrong impression."

Bree blushed, feeling like she'd been caught necking on the couch by her parents. "Nothing happened."

"Good." Mel patted her arm. "Why don't I have your dinner brought to the master suite and run you a bath? Something nice and soothing."

Bree wasn't sure how much more *soothing* she could take. Mel's attempts to calm her did nothing but rub against her nerves, making her agitated. Making her want to push against the restrictions and do something crazy. Something *real*.

But she wouldn't.

Sixty thousand dollars. A new lease on life. That was what this was. So she would take her freaking bath and stop looking at Cross and keep lying to the people who had been nothing but kind to her. Because apparently that was who she was now.

The girl who lied.

* * * * *

Cross moved rapidly through the darkened villa. It was late and he'd already done his last security sweep, but after the call with Max he'd just ended he needed something to do. The rapid click of doggie toenails against the tile let him know he had a canine shadow and he paused with his hand on the patio door, looking down as Cecil B. DeMille sat at his feet, his tail sweeping the floor eagerly, his little furry face hopeful.

"You wanna come too? Inspect the perimeter and guard your mistress?"

He knew the dog was spoiled rotten, pampered endlessly and walked four times a day, but Cecil B. DeMille held himself perfectly still, as if by turning into a small, furry statue he could impress upon Cross the epic importance of one more walk. His dark eyes were liquid—and it would take a harder man than Cross to resist that pleading gaze.

"Come on," he murmured, making a quick detour to grab Cecil's leash from the table where Kaydee had left it after their last walk and clip it to his collar. "And don't say I never did anything for you." Cross opened the patio doors then and Cecil burst through in a rush, wriggling in excitement.

The warm, humid air hit him as soon as he stepped out of the air conditioning, a weight against his skin even after the sun had set. Exterior lights illuminated the paths and Cross stepped onto the one that circled the house, Cecil cavorting euphorically at the end of the leash.

Happiness was so simple for him. Walks, food, chew toys, new things to sniff, and life was complete. If only they could all take such pleasure in the simple things. If only life weren't so freaking complicated.

Cross had done his best to simplify—but in spite of his best efforts, life seemed to keep throwing him curve balls.

Like this freaking partner position.

Candy had apparently put his name in for it behind his back. And when Max called to talk to him about his application just now—the application that Candy had apparently forged for him—for some reason Cross hadn't explained the mix-up and retracted it. He'd let it ride. Put his name in for something he knew he wasn't going to get. Set himself up for failure. Which was something he never did.

Candy was, predictably, ignoring his texts on the subject—which was annoying in itself, but then there was also the strange voicemail message he'd gotten from his mother saying she wasn't sure she was going to be able to make it to the dedication. After twenty-five years of her cultivating his father's legend in the town of Harris, he couldn't wrap his brain around it.

Then, of course, there was Mayor Mike. Calling repeatedly now because apparently he felt the students of the Harris County High School desperately needed a victory flag to fly after each win like the Chicago cubs.

The idea of pitching his phone into one of the luxurious swimming pools was surprisingly tempting.

At least things were going well on the job. Smooth. Simple. Bree had done a good job today, and Cross had managed not to stare at her like he was trying to see the woman beneath the Maggie act.

He rounded the house to the beach-facing side, greeted by the shushing sound of the waves and a cool breeze off the moonlit water. The setting was gorgeous, everything about it designed to encourage the release of cares from the outside world—but Cross was still wound tight. He'd never been good at relaxing.

A high school guidance counselor had once called him a super achiever, using her two semesters of psychology to diagnose why he had two modes—push and push harder. It had always been hard for him to turn off. Lauren had accused him of being a workaholic more times than he could count. She'd bitched that work-hard-play-hard was one thing, but work-hard-work-harder wasn't nearly as much fun—but she hadn't bitched too hard. That had been when he was still playing football and she hadn't minded his single-minded focus so much when it included the promise of being an NFL wife. She'd only complained to guilt him into giving her what she wanted—and it had usually worked. Easier to say yes than to fight it out. One of the few places in his life where he hadn't cared if he got the win.

He was competitive, not masochistic—and Lauren could be vicious when thwarted.

The end of the leash tugged and Cross paused, turning back to where Cecil had stopped to investigate something in the sand, his tiny muzzle burrowing a hole with single-minded focus. Cross could respect that focus.

Days like this he missed the NFL. Missed having his entire life have one purpose—a win on Sunday. And that win...it was like a fix for a junkie. The thrill he had lived for. Nothing felt like that.

He didn't miss the way some part of his body had always hurt. Or the constant comparisons to his father's legend and always coming up short. He didn't even miss the team so much anymore—not since he'd started working at Elite Protection. But he missed the feel of the win. You didn't get that in everyday life. That fight. That rush. That high.

Maybe that was why he sparred with Candy. Going for that feeling any way he could.

Cecil abandoned whatever he'd found in the sand and bounded over, ears flapping.

There would be no wins here. No clear cut sense of victory. At least not until it was over and Maggie was home from her honeymoon, safely undiscovered.

No sense of purpose or satisfaction.

A light came on inside the second story above him, casting a swath of yellow light over the beach and Cross looked up, identifying the source as a lamp in the master suite—right as the balcony door opened and a figure stepped out into the night, backlit by the golden light.

She wore a silky pearl white bathrobe that stopped

halfway to her knees and seemed to catch and capture all the different colors of the night—the moonlight on the sand, the warm glow of the light behind her. Blonde hair curled over her shoulders, moving gently in the breeze.

If this had been a Maggie Tate movie, the soundtrack would have swelled and every move would have been captured in lush slow motion.

She looked like a mirage. Or a movie star. Some creature composed as much of fantasy as flesh and bone.

He frowned at the thought—and at the lurch of attraction in his gut.

She was a job. Not a fantasy.

And right now she was standing on the balcony like a freaking bulls-eye.

CHAPTER NINE

The bath actually had soothed Bree's nerves—which was almost annoying in itself. She wasn't sure she deserved to be soothed tonight, but Mel and the luxury of the villa were conspiring against her stubbornness. The view from the balcony was breathtaking. It was nearly impossible to be anxious with her muscles warm and loose from the bath and the sound of the waves lapping against the sand.

She'd kept her hair out of the water, piled in a knot on top of her head so she wouldn't have to worry about flat irons and products, and now it fluttered in the breeze off the water. She breathed in the salt-tinged air—and almost didn't feel guilty for all the lies she'd told today.

Almost.

If only she didn't know how much this meant to them. How the appearance of the benevolent goddess Maggie Tate could change lives.

She *liked* Dominique. Related to her entirely too much. They could have been friends. If she hadn't been lying to her all day. Tricking her into believing her big break was coming when this was nothing of the sort.

Just like Zander had done to her, once upon a time. When she was nineteen and too stupid to know any better. Too eager to realize the truth that was staring her in the face. Blinded by the hope that her dreams really were about to come true.

She cringed internally at the parallel—as she'd been cringing all day.

Sixty thousand dollars could change her life—but if she was only in it for the money that made her feel like an even worse human being. She'd seen the people who sucked up to Maggie because of her wealth, eager to use her for what they could get—and here she was, letting money persuade her to use people.

She'd always had the tendency to slip into her own thoughts, losing track of her surroundings and checking out of conversations—but before it had always been an image she saw or the inspiration for a future piece that distracted her. Today it had been guilt. Sinking into the morass of it, until Mel jogged her back into the present.

"You shouldn't be out here."

Bree jumped, sucking in a breath and spinning at the sound of the voice behind her. Cross stood in the doorway that opened onto the balcony, the light behind him in the bedroom casting his face in shadow and making it impossible to read his expression.

She pressed a hand to her racing heart—and told herself it was only galloping because he'd startled her, not because he was here. She tugged her bathrobe tighter around herself, though it was already closed, grateful he couldn't possibly see her blush in the low light.

Mel would have a fit if she caught them together. The beach below was supposed to be private, but that was no guarantee that someone wouldn't wander where they weren't supposed to and see her standing there in nothing but her bathrobe with her bodyguard. It would be a paparazzo's dream.

She glanced out over the water, but she saw no tell tale reflections off telephoto lenses. "I'm here to be seen, aren't I?"

He stepped deeper onto the balcony. "I still don't like you out here."

She arched a brow at him, at the gruff tone of his voice. "You realize you aren't actually here to guard me, right?" He was here to sell the story. Just like she was. An accessory like Cecil Two. Though he probably wouldn't appreciate the comparison. And he was a much more attractive accessory than the dog.

Cross took another step, closing the distance between them until awareness of him pricked over her skin. He lowered his head until his lips almost brushed her hair and she could feel his breath against her neck when he murmured, so low she could barely pick out the words, "As far as the world is concerned, you are Maggie Tate, which means you're just as much at risk as she is. So I *am* actually here to guard you." He stepped back, and she sucked in a breath, realizing belatedly that she'd been holding it. "Now please come inside."

She would have obeyed, but her spine had been liquefied under the heat of his proximity and she needed the support of the balcony railing at her back to stay upright. He was gorgeous—all dark eyes and muscles—and smart. Driven. Capable. She didn't know much about him, but she knew that much. He was the kind of man who could have done anything with his life and the world would have been his oyster. What made a man like that want to step in front of bullets for celebrities?

"Did you always want to be a bodyguard?" she heard herself asking. "Some secret desire to be Kevin Costner when you grew up?"

His lips didn't even twitch at her attempt at a joke.

"If I tell you, will you come inside?"

"Tell me first." She wasn't ready to step into the light of the bedroom. He would leave then, and she didn't want him to go.

Cross's jaw tightened, but he answered. "I grew up in a football family in a football town. It was all I knew how to do. Then I tore my ACL and couldn't play anymore. I needed something to do and one of my old teammates thought I'd be good at this job." He shrugged. "That's all there is to it."

But she knew that wasn't true. There was something in him, some instinctively protective core that drew him to this job and made him good at it.

And also made him sexy as hell.

Bree flushed, looking out over the beach again so she wouldn't start openly drooling over him. Off limits. She needed to remember that or she really would be starting a scandal. Not that he would be interested in starting one with her. He was probably taken... "Your girlfriend doesn't mind you taking off for weeks at a time to get up close and personal with Maggie Tate?"

"No girlfriend," he grunted. "I'm more the married-to-my-work type. Will you come inside now?" He held the balcony door for her and she hesitated, trying to think of some reason, any reason, to keep him here, talking to her.

"Me too." She pushed off the railing, moving slowly, reluctant to let the moment end. "Married to my work, I mean."

Why did she tell him that? Why did she need him to know she was single? *Available...*

"Must be a hard way to make a living," Cross commented as she stepped into the light, the carpet plush beneath her bare feet. He closed the door softly behind them, sealing them in the relative privacy of the master. "Art."

"It is," she acknowledged. Which was why she wasn't really making a living. Just making enough to string her hopes along that something could break for her. That it might still happen.

Cross pulled the drapes to block out the beach—and a shiver rippled down Bree's spine at the thought of being alone with him where no one could see them.

Until his phone rang.

Cross shifted away from her as he reached into his pocket, his body language somehow putting even more distance between them than the two feet that separated them. He glanced at the screen and his expression closed off before he shoved the phone back into his pocket without answering.

"You can take it," Bree urged, moving back to give him more space, suddenly feeling awkward after the delicious tension that had tightened her bones vanished as if it had never existed.

"No, it's fine," he said curtly. "I know what it is. Just another reminder to call my mother."

"I get that. I dodge my mom's calls all the time."

Cross frowned, visibly irritated. "I'm not dodging her. I don't do that."

"Okay." Her easy capitulation seemed to bother him just as much as her implication that he was avoiding his mother, so she tried again. "My mom drives me crazy sometimes too. There are lots of times when I ignore her calls."

"I'm not ignoring her," he snapped. "Just stay off the balcony."

Crap. She'd done it again. She always seemed to say the wrong thing, but before she could apologize, he was halfway to the door, his long strides eating up the yardage.

"Cross…" But he was already gone.

Leaving her feeling stupid in his wake. She always did that. Crossed some line she never saw until she was past it.

She wished she could talk to someone. Someone who would tell her how to smooth things over. Andi. Or her mom. But even if she could have risked using her phone, she'd have to admit where she was if she called. Which would mean admitting she hadn't gotten the Hwang exhibit as she'd originally implied. And she wasn't ready to admit the truth.

At least not until she knew whether she'd be able to afford to stay in LA a while longer.

Two weeks and five days. She just had to be Maggie for two weeks and five days more. But she hadn't realized how lonely it was going to be inside the fishbowl. How isolated she was going to feel. Or how badly she would want advice on how to deal with a certain sexy bodyguard. The man who felt like a lifeline every time she saw him. The only thing that was real.

* * * * *

Cross stalked out of Bree's room, nearly bumping into the Kaydee, who was standing entirely too close to the door. What the hell was she doing there?

"Have you seen Cecil?" she asked before he could figure out how to ask how long she'd been lurking there without making it look like he had something to hide, coming out of the master suite at night.

"He's downstairs. I just walked him."

"Great. Thanks!" she bubbled, moving quickly away—and in no way putting his mind at ease.

Had she heard anything?

He frowned, staring after the girl, but if she had overheard something there was nothing he could do about it now. He didn't think they'd said anything that couldn't have been said by Maggie. Bree had given him a hard time about ignoring his mother. He'd told her to stay off the balcony. Nothing scandalous there.

He walked to his room, replaying the conversation in his head—and getting irritated all over again.

He wasn't dodging his mother's calls. Cross didn't do that. That wasn't him. He didn't run away from things. He ran *at* them. Screaming at the top of his lungs, making the other guy shit himself. That was who he was, damn it.

Except...he should have called her days ago. When Mayor Mike first asked.

His mother had always been the first champion of his father's legacy. The charter member of the Aaron Cross Senior Fan Club. He'd expected her to RSVP for the dedication of the field house on the first possible day. For her to now say she was thinking about not even going...

Something was wrong. And his brain was supplying a thousand versions of what might be wrong. And he didn't want to know which one of them might be right.

But he wasn't avoiding her. Even if Bree's appeasing *okay* did dig underneath his skin and make him want to go ten rounds with the punching bag in the fitness studio.

His phone binged with a voicemail alert, but instead of listening to Mayor Mike's latest rant, he pulled up his mother's number as soon as he reached his room. She answered on the second ring.

"Hello?"

"Are you sick?"

"Aaron? Where did that come from?"

He hadn't meant to ask that. He hadn't meant to blurt out his worst fear. That she was dying. He'd joked at one point that only mortal illness would keep his mother away from an event celebrating his father, but it didn't seem like a joke anymore. "This stuff about not going to the dedication—are you okay? Is something wrong? You'd tell me, wouldn't you? If something happened? If you were sick?"

Linnea Cross—for all her husband's fame and glory—was an intensely private person, sharing little of herself with her friends and even less of her troubles with her son. It was her job to worry about him, she'd tell him whenever he wanted to shoulder some of the burdens.

"Is that what you thought? Oh, Aaron, no. I'm fine. Everything's fine. I just wasn't sure it was a good idea."

"Why wouldn't it be a good idea? You love Harris. You love Dad. You love all things Harris and Dad—I thought this would be right up your alley."

A slow pause seeped through the phone. "Did you get the package I sent you with the latest bills?"

He frowned. Why was she changing the subject? Was this about money? Did she think he'd spent too much on the field house? She'd never said much about the project, pro or con, but he'd always thought she was in favor of it. "I got it, but I haven't gone through it yet. Why?"

"No reason," she said quickly. "I just wanted to make sure it hadn't gotten lost in the mail."

"I got it. Thank you for forwarding that stuff. I know it probably hasn't been fun having all of it come to your house, but it's almost over." He stared out over the black ocean. After he left here, he'd be heading straight back to Harris for the big event. "So you'll go to the dedication? I can tell Mayor Mike you RSVP?"

"Sure. All right," she agreed, still strangely subdued.

They spoke for a few more minutes before saying goodnight and he didn't hear any red flags, but he still disconnected the call with a frown on his face.

He'd thought she'd be excited. Admittedly, the multi-year project had been a marathon and in Harris no one had been able to escape it. If he was ready for it to be over, she had to be doubly so, but he'd never expected her to balk at the idea of attending the dedication. She was a very private person, so maybe it was the idea of being on display that bothered her. She'd never liked that.

Maybe that was all it was. She would tell him if it was something serious. Wouldn't she?

CHAPTER TEN

After a restless night, Cross was up at dawn. Back in go mode. Checking the perimeter with Cecil scurrying around his ankles. Checking his emails and shooting updates on their status to Max in California and Candy in Fiji. Going for a quick run—familiarizing himself once again with all the paths around the compound, swinging by the security office at the main resort to touch base with the men there and ensure there had been no developments he should know about. Pushing himself faster on the return to the villa, pushing his own limits until he was breathing hard, the air thick in his lungs and against his skin until he stepped into the arctic blast of the air conditioning in the villa and the sweat on his skin chilled in an instant.

The villa was still, silent as Cecil scampered over to greet Cross, releasing a single, echoing yelp. He crouched to pat the dog—and decided now was the perfect time to get some squats in. He'd spotted free weights in the fitness studio. He may not be as fit as he'd been when he was sprinting down the field after wide-receivers every Sunday, when his entire life had been about his physical capabilities, but he still needed to stay toned in his current job. To stay sharp.

His phone pinged with an alert and he listened to a weather report tracking the beginnings of a tropical storm that might have the island in its path if it gathered momentum. It was early in the season for a hurricane, but Cross liked to be aware of *every* possible risk and variable, and a hurricane was a pretty freaking big one.

The details of wind speed and likely trajectories filled his ears—so he didn't register the treadmill whirring until he opened the door to the fitness studio.

She had a gorgeous stride. Long and graceful. A runner's stride.

She wasn't watching anything on the tablet this morning, no giant noise-canceling headphones on, and her head turned toward him the second he opened the door. "Hey." She was breathing fast, the color high on her cheeks.

"Hey."

He remembered suddenly, viscerally, the way she'd looked last night, wrapped in silk and moonlight, but forced the unprofessional thought from his mind. "You're up early."

She made a face as she continued to run, her pace remaining steady and strong. "Mel had a lazy morning scheduled. I don't know how Maggie stands it—being told when to eat, when to sleep. It would drive me crazy."

He shrugged. "The price of fame."

"Which keeps us all employed."

"Mel seems to know Maggie's habits pretty well. It's probably less restrictive when it's tailored to your natural routine. And I somehow doubt Maggie lets Mel tell her to do anything she doesn't already want to do."

"Yeah. She owns it. I need to own it." Her feet pounded hard on the treadmill. "I shouldn't be complaining about being told to sleep in, but this whole thing has me on edge and I've never been good at sleeping in unless I was up all night the night before."

He shoved images of what could keep her up all night out of his brain. "Painting?"

Her brows pulled into a sudden frown. "I don't paint." She hit a button and the treadmill instantly slowed. "Not that kind of artist." She climbed off the machine, grabbing for the towel hanging on the bar. "Look, about last night...I shouldn't have said anything about your mom—"

"It's fine," he cut her off before she could get going. "We're fine," he assured her. He didn't mean to say more, but he heard himself explaining, "My hometown is dedicating a building to my father and my mom has been acting strangely. Like she didn't want to go. I was worried something might be wrong, but I talked to her last night. She's fine."

"Oh." Bree blinked. "Good. I mean, I'm glad."

"I got an update from the other team," he offered, moving to the free weights. "So far so good. No paparazzi on their tail."

"None on ours either from what I can tell." She grabbed a water bottle from the treadmill cup holder and drained a third of it. "I keep staring at the bushes, expecting to see some guy with a camera lurking in them, but so far it's almost annoyingly quiet. Are we really doing our jobs as decoys if the paparazzi don't even know we're here?"

He shrugged, stacking weight. "It's Mel's show. She certainly knows what she's doing when it comes to the publicity crap."

"But don't you wish we could *do* something?"

"Of course," he acknowledged, beginning his reps.

"Then why can't we? We were hired to draw attention to ourselves, weren't we?"

"Not my call."

Bree made a sound that was almost a growl. "What good does it do Maggie if we're sitting here on our hands and no one knows we're here?"

"We aren't sitting on our hands. We're planning a wedding. And Mel is confident the news will leak when it needs to."

Bree shook her head, thumping the water bottle against her thigh. "Doesn't that bother you?"

"How so?" His muscles began to ache with the familiar pull of the exercise.

"Lying to everyone. Letting them think they're going to get to host this amazing wedding, but what happens to them when the truth comes out? It doesn't feel right. Aren't you at all uncomfortable with the fact that they don't know?"

"We're protecting Maggie."

"*How*?" she burst out. "If the people at the resort are doing such an amazing job of protecting our privacy that no one knows we're here, *how* are we protecting her? Doesn't it feel wrong to you?"

She had a point. As much as it went against his instincts to expose the client to publicity, that was exactly what they needed to be doing in this case. They were doing too good a job of protecting her.

He set the weights gently back into the cradle. "I'll talk to Mel."

Her smile was blinding—bright and fast and so artless it was a pure Bree expression, without any of Maggie's careful nuances.

"Talk to Mel about what?" Another voice came from the doorway and Bree spun toward the manager as she stepped inside the small room—and Cross kicked himself for not hearing the door open.

"About getting out there and being *seen*," Bree said when Mel shut the door behind her. "We aren't doing anyone any good if no one knows we're here." Mel frowned, but Bree rushed on before she could object. "The paparazzi don't even seem to be on the island. Or if they are, they aren't bothering me. Shouldn't we do something to draw attention away from the real Maggie? Even if I just go sunbathing over on the non-VIP part of the island and get caught on some tourist's cell phone? What's the point of being the decoy if no one knows we're here? We're supposed to be a distraction. So let me distract!"

"It will get leaked organically at some point and be more believable if we aren't fishing for attention—"

"I'm not saying we should go fishing, but the resort is being diligent, taking such good care of us and guarding our privacy so carefully. If we leave things organic no one may ever know we're here, which totally defeats the purpose. And screws the hotel over. If they aren't going to get the publicity of the wedding later, the least we can do is give them some exposure now."

Cross watched the exchange with interest—and saw the exact moment Mel warmed to the idea, her eyes going speculative.

"You aren't entirely wrong," the taller woman acknowledged. "Maybe it wouldn't be such a terrible idea to be more visible. But we have to be careful about how we go about it. It has to be authentic to Maggie."

"Perfect." Bree bounced on her heels. "What would Maggie do?"

Mel eyed her. "How do you feel about jet skis?"

* * * * *

They needed a believable excuse for Maggie to go to

the public side of the island. Luckily, Maggie's affection for jet skis was well documented. And just as luckily, Bree had spent her childhood summers careening around Martin Lake.

She would go out, zip around the island, get close enough to be seen by swimmers or boaters or whoever looked most likely to post on social media about her presence, and then retreat back to the villa to await the inevitable ripples her presence would send out.

Cross would follow her on a second jet ski, to ensure no rogue pirates tried to kidnap her between one side of the island and the other, or whatever it was he was afraid would happen to "Maggie" on this little expedition.

On their private pier, Bree swung her leg over the jet-ski, settling into position. The padded bra she wore beneath the swim-suit cover-up made her life-jacket feel unnaturally tight and she fiddled with the straps, trying to get a little more breathing room as Cross mounted up beside her.

She resisted the urge to look at him while Mel's eagle eyes were on her. The manager had not been pleased to find Bree and Cross alone together in the fitness studio again—though it hadn't been Bree's fault Cross had showed up to use the weights while she was running. Mel hadn't been impressed by the excuse...and Bree couldn't blame her. She was the one who had stayed to watch the gun show, though she'd done her best not to openly drool.

The man was built like a freaking action star and watching all those muscles in action...*whoo, mama.*

But now she kept her eyes virtuously forward, while the jet-ski guy went over the controls with the bodyguard.

Bree may have spent the better part of her childhood zipping around on the lakes of northern Minnesota, but Cross's Iowa upbringing had apparently not included the same training. She snuck a glance at him from behind her sunglasses without turning her head, and found him frowning intently as he listened to the operational instructions.

It was sort of hot—that focus. That concentration. The visible need to master this. To be the best.

Overachiever in action.

"You ready for this?" she called when the jet-ski guy fell back.

"Ready," he shouted back, crisp and precise.

Bree bared her teeth in a grin and shoved away from the private pier with one foot, floating a couple yards away before she cranked the engine and it roared to life, the machine shivering beneath her. "Try not to fall behind!" she shouted over the noise, and shot off over the water.

She didn't hear what Cross shouted after her, her ears filled with wind and the drone of the engine. Salt water sprayed her and she laughed as she revved the jet-ski faster. Finally, after days of being penned in, playing Maggie in a cage, she finally felt free.

She flew, the jet-ski racing across the glassy surface of the lagoon where her villa was located—until she sailed through the opening in the reef that protected the inlet and a wave hit the jet-ski broadside. She swore, yanking the handlebars into a tight turn and standing to drive all her weight down on one side to force the jet-ski to pivot into the wave. The engine nearly guttered at the sudden move, but she managed to stay upright as the wave rolled beneath her.

Cross wasn't so lucky.

She heard his shout and looked back in time to see him try to duplicate her move, only to get dumped off as his jet-ski rolled.

"Oops." She turned carefully, watching the swells, and returned to help him get back on his jet-ski, which was already being carried away from him on the waves. He bobbed in his life-jacket as she approached and she studied his face, unsure how the big, strong alpha male would take to being dumped in the ocean. "Sorry about that," she said when she cut the engine and floated up beside him. "I'm used to lakes. No waves to watch out for."

He hauled himself out of the water, his weight dipping the jet-ski, but he corrected his balance before he tipped them both. "Here I thought you were trying to lose me," he said, though there was no acrimony in his voice as he shook his head, water droplets flinging off his hair and raining over her shoulders.

"You have your uses." She puttered the idling jet-ski over to his.

It took him a couple tries to roll the jet-ski back upright and get seated again, but he never once bitched about the faulty machine or tried to make some excuse for his unexpected trip into the water, like all the jocks she'd known in high school would have done if they'd been dumped. For someone who seemed to put so much focus into perfection, she'd expected a much more dickish response, but Cross was nothing if not surprising.

"You gonna go full throttle again?" he asked, the water revealing a slight curl to his blond hair she hadn't noticed before.

"Too fast for you?" she challenged.

He flashed his teeth. "Never."

She grinned. "Good."

She cranked the jet-ski up to the max, racing across the waves.

CHAPTER ELEVEN

Cross had never been particularly good at having fun. He knew how to laugh as well as the next guy—but usually in the pursuit of some more serious goal. Training. Always working harder than the next guy.

Fun for fun's sake wasn't really part of his MO. It always felt like a waste of time he couldn't justify, but with Bree...She'd been going crazy, cooped up in the villa—even if it was several thousand square feet of luxury. He'd seen the restlessness in her. She needed to do. She needed to move. And she needed *fun*.

She bared her teeth, face into the wind, laughing as the jet-ski shot up the side of a swell and caught air before crashing down the other side in a shower of salt spray. He knew they were on a mission, knew there was a purpose to this—to be visible enough for word to start to spread that Maggie was on the island—but somehow that was secondary as they rounded the curve of the island into calmer water and she began to slalom toward the public pier, her laughter lifting on the wind.

It was intoxicating. *She* was intoxicating. She flicked a glance back at him, over her shoulder, and his blood rushed, his entire focus on chasing her when she was in this wild mood.

Then another engine sounded, deeper than the higher whine of the jet-skis, and he saw the exact moment Bree vanished into Maggie.

The jet-ski slowed, just a fraction. Her posture changed, just a bit. Her chin went up, just an inch. And suddenly he wasn't chasing Bree, totally uninhibited and free, but Maggie, poised and posed and knowing exactly how she would look to the cell phone cameras that would be pointed her way as soon as the tourists on the parasailing boat realized who she was.

They passed the boat—close enough to be identified, but far enough away that they weren't rocked by the larger craft's wake. They were already past the boat when Cross heard a startled, "Was that Maggie *Tate*?"

Mission accomplished.

The tourist likely hadn't gotten a picture, but the rumors would start and that was all they needed. A few regular tourists bragging about their brush with fame. Done deal.

Cross pulled his jet-ski alongside "Maggie's", jerking his chin toward the villa. "We should head back."

Her eyebrows arched high over the top of her sunglasses. "Should we?" she asked sweetly—and he realized the gross error he'd made in giving her her own jet-ski when she smiled. "Gosh, I'm *parched*. I could really use a drink."

She was zipping toward the main resort's dock before he could say a word—and there was nothing he could do but curse and follow her.

She was better on the damn jet-skis than he was. It took him two passes before he managed to get the damn thing close enough to the dock to catch the rope one of the resort employees tossed to him. He reeled himself in and the dock hand secured the jet-ski as he scrambled onto the dock—where Maggie was already stripping off her life jacket, revealing the curves barely hidden by the sheer white cover-up she wore.

"Maggie..."

She turned, running a hand through her hair to make it flow even more perfectly around her shoulders. "It's a resort, Cross. What can possibly happen to me with you here?" she asked, fluttering her lashes at him.

She turned toward the beach and he hurried to shed his own life-jacket and follow her. "I've only done the most basic security review of this side of the island," he said as he fell into step beside her, scanning the area and kicking himself for not doing a more thorough sweep of this side.

Out of the corner of his eye, he caught the droll look she threw at him as they hit the beach and passed a couple lolling in the sun as their kids built a sand castle nearby. "I promise if anyone comes at me with a tiny plastic shovel, I'll let you take the first hit."

He glowered, still scanning the beach. "It would help if you took this seriously."

"I think you're taking it seriously enough for both of us," she said. "And doing an excellent job of drawing attention to the celebrity in their midst."

He swore under his breath. She was right. His overprotective behavior was more noticeable than any famous face could be from a distance—and people were definitely taking a closer look at Bree/Maggie now that he was acting like a hyperactive Secret Service detail.

What the fuck was wrong with him? Admittedly, his training and his previous jobs had always focused on scenarios where the client wanted him to be as visible as possible, but he should be able to pivot better than this. He just hated the thought of her being so exposed.

Bree-as-Maggie traipsed toward the open air restaurant with tables set right in the sand and approached the bar with woven palm fronds shading the seating area. She bellied up to the bar, smiling a trademark Maggie Tate smile, and requested in Maggie's high, sweet voice, "One vitamin water, please."

The young male bartender gaped a little—obviously not as accustomed to seeing VIP guests on this side of the resort—but he moved quickly, opening a chilled vitamin water and passing it to the star with a glass and a straw that she accepted with a fluttery, "Thank you."

She didn't bother with the glass, putting the straw straight into the bottle and lifting it to her lips—the poor bartender watching the action as if hypnotized as she wrapped her lips around the tube and nearly moaned in relief.

"So refreshing," she purred—and the bartender nodded helplessly, completely caught in her spell.

Cross was tempted to growl at her to stop messing with the kid, but he was too busy studying a family that had taken a seat at one of the larger tables nearby. Two men, two women, three children under six. Lots of noise, lots of movement as they got the kids settled—and one of the men twisted, revealing a bulge of a certain shape beneath his loose fitting Hawaiian shirt.

A bulge that exactly matched the shape and size of a man carrying concealed.

Cross frowned, shifting his body to put himself between Bree and the threat and trying to get a better angle to confirm what he'd seen. He kept a hand on the small of her back to stay aware of her position at all times as he studied the man at the table, who turned toward one of the children at the sound of her high, continuous giggles—

And the fabric of his shirt caught on the bulge

beneath. Holster. On the hip.

Cross stiffened. "Time to go."

* * * * *

Bree's gaze jerked toward Cross at the hard tone in his voice. His hand was on her back, but he wasn't looking at her. He'd shed his sunglasses when they stepped into the shade and his attention was locked on a family at one of the tables even though his eyes never stopped moving, taking in every detail of their surroundings.

The family looked like any other—the kids hamming it up for attention and the parents laughing as they indulged them—but Cross's awareness of them stayed sharp. She'd been on Maggie jobs with him before when he'd been on alert, but never like this—his jaw locked even as his body stayed somehow fluid, ready to act.

"I…"

She wasn't sure what she would have said, hadn't even formed a thought, but the words died on her tongue when his head turned and his gaze locked on hers, hard and unwavering. "*Now*, Maggie."

"Okay," she whispered, fighting the urge to shiver. She'd already told Ethan the Awestruck Bartender to charge the vitamin water to the villa and signed for the drink and an exorbitant tip.

Cross's command didn't scare her—it turned her on. Which was the absolutely wrong reaction to this scenario, but *damn* the man was hot when he was in Protector Mode.

It had been impulse to come ashore. What Cross had said about Maggie only letting Mel tell her to do things she already wanted to do had hit home. She'd been letting the manager run her too much. If she wanted to do something a little splashier to make the rumors spread faster, she needed to *do it*. At least that had been her thought as she raced toward the dock.

Now, as Cross steered her toward the beach, his body shielding hers from whatever he'd seen at the restaurant, she wasn't so sure she'd made the best call—though the chance to see Cross in uber-protector mode was pretty damn hot. He hustled her down the beach and she was acutely aware of him, the heat of him at her back, the careful way he touched her like she was precious even as she could feel the tension in his body.

Her breath came quick and her steps came faster, until she was fighting the urge to run down the beach, her bare feet sinking deep into the sand with each step.

When they reached the jet-skis, he untied hers first while she was donning the life-vest and helped her climb on, shoving her away from the dock before moving to his own. She turned on the engine, puttering at the lowest speed until she was a good distance away from the dock and Cross's jet-ski joined hers.

She looked at him questioningly, but he jerked his chin back toward the villa, his eyes hidden once again by his sunglasses and his jaw hard. "Let's go."

She didn't argue, cranking the jet-ski up and taking off toward their side of the island—but it felt different now. She couldn't focus on the rush of the wind and the water. All she could feel was her tight awareness of Cross—as if they'd been tied together by a bungee cord and the more distance was between them the more she felt pulled back. She was intensely aware of exactly where he was—off her left shoulder, between her and the shore—until they rounded the reef at the edge of the island where the surf kicked up and they were no longer in sight of the people on shore.

A parasailing boat droned in the distance, but they were as alone as they were ever going to be as she slowed her jet-ski until it was idling and waited for Cross. The machine rolled up and down on the swells, but she kept her balance and her eyes on him as he came alongside.

"What just happened?" she asked, hyperaware of the man drifting at her side. His body was still tight beneath his life-jacket, the muscles in his bare arms flexed, but something of the battle readiness seemed to have left him. "Did you see a camera?"

Though why he would react that way to a camera when they *wanted* to spread the news that she was here was beyond her. Maybe her Maggie act had been slipping and he was afraid someone would spot it? But she'd been in full Maggie mode, fluttering at Ethan the Eager Bartender.

"Not a camera. A gun."

She blinked, her jaw dropping. "Seriously?"

She watched for a flicker of a smile, some sign that he was putting her on, but he nodded, sober and intent. "One of the men at the table. Looked like he was carrying concealed."

And all she'd seen was a kid laughing with her father.

The sharp difference in their perspectives, in what they saw in the world could not have been more clear than it was in that moment. What must life be like through Cross's eyes? What must it be like to be the man who saw a threat—and immediately put himself between her and the danger?

"Probably not a threat," Cross said. "Off-duty cop, most likely. Someone in the habit of carrying everywhere. But better safe than sorry. Especially where you're concerned."

She felt uneasy at his words, but she couldn't have explained why. She'd felt safe the entire time, oblivious to the possible threat and shielded by Cross, but now something shifted through her—not for herself but for him. "You never shut down, do you?"

"You're not paying me to shut down."

"I'm not paying you at all."

He frowned. "You know what I mean."

She cocked her head, studying him, the hard lines.

She wanted to kiss him. The urge was sudden and a little wild. To climb over onto his jet-ski and straddle his lap, facing him, to frame his face with her hands and kiss him until he forgot to be so serious, so responsible all the time. "What does the great Cross do to unwind?" she murmured.

"I don't," he said, the words blunt. "Let's get you back to the villa."

His words carried an edge that signaled his hair-trigger readiness wasn't going to completely unlock until she was back inside the safety of her gilded cage. She wanted to tempt him to put that fierce adrenaline to good use, to see if he would ignite as fast as she thought he would if she lit the fuse, but he wasn't hers. And she couldn't risk the rumors. So she cranked up the jet-ski without another word, heading back to their lagoon.

CHAPTER TWELVE

The villa was quiet again. Safe.

Kaydee had taken Cecil for a walk. Mel and Bree had been holed up inside the upstairs living room with the wedding planner since they got back, discussing *visions* and *ambience*. The last time he'd seen her, Bree was wearing a little diamond tiara and a wedding veil over her sundress, fluttering her lashes at one and all. Totally fine. Everything was as it should be, but Cross paced in his room, still wound up from their afternoon on the other side of the island.

She shouldn't have gone off script. Anything could have happened to her.

Needing something to occupy his brain—something calming, mechanical—Cross yanked open the drawer on the desk, pulling out the manila envelope his mother had sent him before he left LA. Paying the bills, comparing them against the budgeting spreadsheets—it was busywork. Automatic.

Which was perfect right about now.

He ripped open the envelope and dumped the contents on the desk, quickly sorting them into stacks. Anticipated expenses, Mayor Mike's add-ons, and likely junk mail. The anticipated expenses stack went quickly—all of the bills but one matching up against the expected charges. Mayor Mike's discretionary fund required more concentration and Cross made notes on several of the bills to remind himself to talk to the mayor about exactly how much other fundraising sources had been able to chip in.

By the time he got to the junk mail stack, his thoughts were calm and focused again as he ripped open credit card offers and coupons for window cleaning services and oil changes. Once he'd confirmed they weren't field house expenses, he tossed them into the trash, until only one envelope remained.

It looked different than the others. A plain white business envelope with his name and address handwritten on the front and the return address on the reverse side. *Rachel Leigh Persopoulos*. And a Boulder address in a loopy, feminine script.

Cross had never been to Boulder that he remembered. He hadn't been back to Colorado since his father died when he was five.

Unsure what to expect, he broke open the envelope and pulled out a single piece of stationery with a handwritten letter.

Dear Aaron,

I hope you won't think I'm too familiar, calling you Aaron, but I've thought of you that way my entire life, as my brother Aaron I've never met, and so it feels strange to think of calling you anything else. I'm not sure if you know about me. My mother said you did, and that if you wanted to have any contact with us, you could easily pick up a phone, but some things have changed for me recently and I find I'm no longer comfortable with the idea of family I've never met. I'd like to know my brother. And I'd like to believe he wants to know me too. I'm in Boulder, but I can drive out to see you some weekend or you're welcome here. I hope I'll hear from you and that you will be happy to have heard from me.

Your half-sister,
Rachel

Cross stared at the page, at the phone number written in neat numbers across the bottom, at the loopy, girlish signature.

It had to be fake. Some kind of money grab. Some bullshit claim.

He didn't have a sister, half or otherwise.

His parents had been high school sweethearts. They'd gotten married in college and stayed together until the day his father died. Their love story was a legend in Harris. The idea that his father could have cheated, that he could have fathered a child with someone else, simply made no sense. Not the Aaron Cross Senior who was the pride of Harris. Not the man his mother had told him stories about growing up.

It had to be a scam.

He didn't get targeted for many cons—he hadn't been in the NFL long enough to get a very big target on his back—but he'd seen his fair share and this definitely smelled like that. Though it was pretty amateurish. No fabricated details. No doctored photos. No fake birth certificates with his father's name on them. Really, it was almost insulting how little effort this woman had gone to.

It would be so easy to debunk and brush aside.

Cross called his mother's house, the ridiculous letter held loosely in one hand.

"Hello?" she answered.

"You won't believe the letter I just got."

A long silence greeted the words—so long he glanced at his cell to make sure it hadn't dropped the call. Then, finally, "A letter?"

Her voice was thready. Weak. Cross frowned. "Are

you all right?"

"What kind of letter?"

"It's a paternity claim. For dad. Some woman in Colorado."

"What does she want?"

"She says she just wants to meet me—her 'brother'—but I'm sure if I met her there would be a request for money in it somewhere." Another lingering silence made him frown. "Mom?"

"I wondered why she was contacting you," his mother said slowly. "When I saw the return address on the envelope."

A high ringing began in his ears and his fingers tightened automatically on the paper in his hands as the implications of his mother's words penetrated. She'd recognized the name on the envelope. She *knew* the name on the envelope. *Rachel Leigh Persopoulos*.

Holy shit.

"It's true."

His mother said nothing—she didn't deny it.

"You knew." Shock shuddered through him, hard and fast. "You knew about her."

"We kept it quiet," his mother admitted softly.

"So quiet you never told me I have a sister? How old is she? Why didn't you—" He broke off, too many questions crowding for space.

"I never meant to keep it from you—"

"But you did. That's exactly what you did."

"You have to understand—"

He cut her off with the only question that mattered. "How long have you known?"

Silence stretched and he knew the answer was going to be bad. "Since she was born," she finally admitted—and Cross didn't need to hear anything else.

"I have to go."

"Aaron, you have to understand—"

"Not right now I don't."

He'd never hung up on his mother in his life. Never snapped at her. But he knew if he stayed on the phone another minute he was going to say something he would regret.

She'd lied. For *decades*. His father had been dead for twenty-five years. She'd known. She'd known he had a sister. But it wasn't only that. She'd known all along that the legend of his father was a lie.

The legend Cross had spent his life chasing.

All of it a lie.

He stalked out of the bedroom without any idea where he was going, instinct driving him toward the beach. Sunset splashed across the water, painting everything in vibrant shades of pink and orange. It was gorgeous. Breathtaking. And he couldn't see it. His feet sank into the sand and all he could see were the lies.

Thirty years of chasing a ghost. Thirty years of always feeling like he had to do more, as if nothing he could do could ever live up—and it was bullshit. All of it.

Had his grandparents known? They'd only passed on in the last few years, until then living in Harris, feeding the myth. How many people had known the truth? How many people had hidden this from him?

He'd spent his entire childhood trying to live up to the legend of Big Aaron—not only was his father the best football player who would ever come out of Harris, Iowa, he was the best man. The best father—though Cross barely remembered him. The best friend—though few who claimed so had actually known him. The best husband—though apparently he'd cheated on the love of his life.

Big Aaron. The Saint of Harris.

When Aaron Cross Senior made it to the NFL, the entire town had celebrated as if they'd won the Superbowl. When Aaron Cross Junior got drafted, the reaction was *well, what do you expect from Big Aaron's kid? He's got the genes.* As if it was entirely genetic. As if it was expected.

Coaches had all wanted him to play his father's position, to chase all his father's state records, but he'd been determined not to be a wide receiver, but a defensive back—the one chasing the wide receivers down. Always chasing that fucking ghost.

He'd been to the NFL. Played two years longer than his father had—though whenever the stats were brought up there was always an asterisk on his father's NFL career. What he *would* have accomplished if he'd lived. It wasn't enough to compare Cross to what his father had done, he had to spend his entire life being compared to who his father would have been.

Even if the people doing the comparing had no fucking idea.

The legacy had been a legend. Due in large part to his mother. She'd told the stories. She'd kept the legend alive. She'd played her part as the grieving widow who never dated again because no man could ever compare to Big Aaron.

And all the time she'd been hiding the fact that he had cheated. That he had another child no one ever spoke of.

Rachel.

Who was she? What did she want? Cross hadn't given the letter much thought when he first read it. He'd been so certain it was ridiculous. So sure it was a hoax.

THE DECOY BRIDE

But now...

He had a sister.

He closed his eyes, centering himself, breathing deep. Instinctively, he began going through the motions of the kata Candy had taught him. After a few minutes, he toed off his shoes and began moving faster, fighting invisible foes until his skin began to heat and sweat began to itch along his spine. He paused only long enough to strip off his shirt, tossing it on top of his shoes, and continued to move, his thoughts racing as his body moved.

What did she look like? What was she like? *Why hadn't his mother told him?*

His cell phone pinged a warning, letting him know when the wedding planner left the villa, tripping the security sensors, but Cross didn't stop moving even as he checked the screen, his breathing slow and even as his feet slid through the sand.

The sun had set in spectacular style and now the moonlight blanketed the beach in calm. A calm he couldn't feel, though he made sure his face revealed nothing when, fifteen minutes later, his phone pinged again and Mel started down the beach toward him.

"It worked," she called out when she was still ten feet away. "The first pictures are on the web."

Cross stopped moving, turning to face the manager. She was barefoot, having taken off her heels at the edge of the patio, but thanks to the slope of the beach he was still looking up at her. "Mission accomplished," he said, hoping the conversation would end there.

It didn't.

"A couple outlets have already reached out for comment on the photos."

"Oh?"

"Mm-hmm." She nodded, but she wasn't smiling. "You know the first thing they asked? Not *why is Maggie on the island* or *is this for a movie* or even *is that where the wedding is going to be.* Can you guess?" He figured the question was rhetorical and waited her out. She didn't make him wait long, her voice snapping sharply in the dark. "*Who's the guy?* That's what they all want to know." She took another step closer, until he could see her eyes in the dark, and the irritation in them. "That isn't the narrative we want to sell, Cross. You're supposed to be invisible. I'm spinning it the best I can, but this—"

She held up her tablet, showing him a photo of him and "Maggie." He had his hand on her back, his body curved protectively around hers, and they were looking at one another...

"*This* is entirely too intimate, Mr. Cross."

In the photo, they were standing at the bar. By the look on her face, it must have been taken right before he ushered her back to the jet-ski. Cross frowned at the photo—though not for the reason Mel wanted him to.

Irrational anger rose up at the memory of him rushing Bree down the beach, his hand on her back.

He'd overreacted.

He'd been too on edge. Things had felt...fuck, they'd felt *personal* today. And that had never happened to him on a job before.

Mel wasn't wrong. He hadn't done his job well. He hadn't handled Maggie—or Bree—well. He couldn't even keep straight in his head how he was supposed to be thinking of her.

"Look," Mel said when he didn't answer. "I know, all right? I understand that life with Maggie can be intoxicating. She's a great actress and she has this aura about her that affects everyone around her. But I need to know that you won't be sucked in, Cross."

He frowned, trying to read between the lines of the warning, unsure he understood exactly what she seemed to be trying to tell him with her eyes. She'd said Maggie had an aura. Maggie, not Bree. Life with *Maggie* was intoxicating. "I won't," he promised. "It won't happen again."

"Good." Mel opened her mouth, as if she would say more, but closed it after a moment with a nod. "Good," she repeated. "Good night, Cross."

She turned back up the beach and Cross frowned after her, playing her words over in his mind, trying to figure out what she'd been trying to tell him.

Why say life with Maggie? Was that just because someone could overhear them down on the beach? Or was there more to it? Had she been trying to send him a message? A hint of some kind?

Had they pulled some kind of double switch?

She was Maggie's most trusted handler, the one who knew her best. But he was here with Bree. Wasn't he?

He'd never actually seen them in the same place at the same time. The only reason he knew there was a decoy was because he'd been told.

There were differences though. The way she smiled. And her cup size, for one. The woman who ran on the treadmill was nowhere near as filled out up top as the star of the silver screen. But what if that was just padding and movie magic? Maggie Tate had never done a topless scene that he knew of.

What if Bree was who Maggie was when she didn't have to play the great Maggie Tate? Or even a character Maggie was playing, a persona she was trying out as she got ready for a role? He'd heard of actors doing stranger things.

Was this entire trip a ruse?

But why? Why go to all that trouble?

He'd never seen Maggie with Demarco either, not even in the tabloids. It was only their names that had been linked. Was the wedding a sham too?

Cross shook away the thought. He was seeing lies everywhere now. Making himself crazy. This entire day had him off balance.

He turned back toward the ocean, breathing in and out with the waves, centering himself—

And his phone buzzed in his back pocket, alerting him that someone had left the villa.

The hairs raised on the back of his neck and he knew who he was going to see even before he pulled out his phone and checked the camera that had been activated by the motion sensors.

Bree walked down the beach, like a freaking siren on her way to sing him to his doom. Or Maggie. Fuck, he didn't know anymore.

He bent and grabbed the shirt he'd tossed into the sand earlier, tugging it over his head before he turned to face her.

The great Maggie Tate. Outlined in moonlight.

He needed to stop meeting her in places like this.

Balconies. Beaches. Moonlight and waves on the shore. It was like the setting had been designed to get his brain thinking the wrong damn thing—which was probably exactly what the resort had designed it for, but he was the bodyguard not the lover. As Mel had *just* reminded him.

Even if Bree was Maggie. Either way, she was off limits.

"You should go inside," he called out when she was

within earshot, trying to force conviction into the words—but she kept walking, and for the third time that day, he had the disorienting feeling that he wasn't in control.

CHAPTER THIRTEEN

Bree's feet sank into the sand as she descended the slope of the beach, making her steps feel unsteady even though she'd only had a single glass of champagne in her suite. The resort had sent over a bottle of Maggie's favorite brand with dinner and Mel had grudgingly agreed that it would be an insult to their hosts not to open it, though she'd sternly cautioned Bree against overindulging—lest her Maggie mask slip.

She'd allowed herself one glass, the bubbles fizzing deliciously down her throat as she stood just inside the balcony doors where no one could see her and watched Cross moving like a ghost in the moonlight below.

One glass of champagne was no excuse for the way she felt—drawn to him by instinct more than thought, but she could no more have stayed away from something that beautiful than she could have excised the piece of her soul that made her an artist.

God, she'd missed her camera. It wouldn't have been able to capture the motion, just allude to it, but not having the weight of it in her hands, lifting it to her eye, losing herself through the lens—it felt like she was missing a limb.

She was losing herself inside the box of Maggie's life and if she'd just been able to capture that shot maybe it would have satisfied the restlessness in her—but her camera was in LA. And Cross was here. So she made her way down the beach to see if he could make her feel like herself again. These last few days he'd been the only one who could.

She'd had her lines planned out—composed in champagne courage. *Fancy meeting you here.* She'd pretend she was bumping into him. That she hadn't been watching him from above. *We really need to stop meeting like this.* Like it was fate. And not just two restless people trapped in a small space. Trapped in a small life that seemed to be closing in around her.

But when she got down to the beach, his first words were to shoo her away and she lost all desire to play flirtatious games.

Cecil Two had escaped the house with her and scrambled over the sand as quickly as his short legs would allow, his tail wagging frantically as he rushed Cross with a little yip of excitement. Cross knelt to greet the dog, dusting the sand off Cecil's silky ears where they had dragged along the ground. The spaniel gazed adoringly up at Cross and Bree felt an irrational surge of jealousy—and wasn't even sure which one of them she was jealous of.

"I think he likes you more than me," she said. "Not that his affection for me sets the bar very high."

"He just wants attention," Cross said as he continued to lavish affection on the dog. "Don't you, Cecil?"

As if in response, the dog flung himself onto his back, splaying all four legs and revealing his belly in a wildly undignified display—and Bree's lips twitched helplessly at the sight. He really was an adorable little attention whore.

Cross flicked a look at her that she couldn't read in the darkness. "Mel just finished telling me to keep my distance from you. Apparently the press is getting the wrong idea."

"Me too," she said, then stammered to clarify when she realized it sounded like she was getting the wrong idea too, "I mean, Mel talked to me. About the pictures."

He nodded, straightening—much to Cecil's dismay. "You should go inside." He glanced up the beach, toward the brush that made it feel so secluded, blocking them from the rest of the VIP side of the resort. He met her gaze. "It isn't safe out here."

Did he mean because the paparazzi were coming? Because anyone could see them? Or that it wasn't safe for the two of them to be alone together? Because he was as tempted as she was to break the rules?

Then he looked away and she realized what a reach that was. She had no indication that he felt anything for her other than professional obligation. Yes, he was perfectly nice to her when they bumped into one another in the fitness studio and, yes, he was incredibly diligent in his protection of her person, but that didn't mean he felt any of the same sizzling awareness beneath his skin that she felt beneath hers.

Their relationship was professional. She could do professional.

"I wanted to thank you for this afternoon," she said. "I wasn't scared at all."

"You didn't know there was a gun in play."

She shook her head. "I knew you would protect me." He still wasn't looking at her, scanning the beach—once again in his default bodyguard mode, hyperaware of his surroundings and aware of her only in that she was the center of the sphere he cast. She didn't know why she said it—maybe because in that moment she would have given anything for him to look at *her*, but she blurted,

"You're kind of hot when you're in glorious protector mode. You know that?" Completely ruining her short-lived attempt at professionalism.

He looked at her then—a victory in itself, until he murmured, "You should go inside."

"I know. It isn't safe." She studied his face in the low light. "Has anyone ever told you that you're a little too security conscious?"

"It's my job."

What if I don't want to be your job? "What are you like when you aren't on the job?"

His jaw hardened at the question. "I'm always on the job."

And with those words, the truth that she hadn't been aware of woke in her like a sunrise, the reason behind the instinct that had driven her to seek him out tonight suddenly as clear and bright as the moon above them.

She wanted to see this man when he let loose. She wanted to show him how to unwind. To be his fun. His ease. His haven. She wanted to grab his hand and drag him into the silly parts of life, laughing all the way. He *pulled* at her. But all she could say was a soft, "You could unwind with me…"

He met her eyes again and she felt temptation pull tight between them, that cord she'd felt between them growing more tangible, taut and breathless. *He wanted her*. The knowledge sent shivers down her arms and she caught a ragged breath, feeling like her breasts were swelling and pressing against her bra, like she was becoming more desirable the longer he held her gaze.

Then Cecil yelped to get his attention, shattering the moment, and Cross's jaw shifted as he looked away. "I can't do that here. I have a job to do." He looked back to her, his gaze stern. "We both do."

"I'll do my job," she promised, not wilting under that stern gaze, still feeling the aftereffects of the moment that had strung between them. "But you can still be yourself with me. And I'll be the same with you." *You're the only one who makes me feel like me,* she barely stopped herself from adding.

"I don't think that's a good idea." He shook his head, as if dispelling the last vestiges of temptation. "I think you should go inside."

"Does Maggie let you tell her what to do?" He looked at her sharply, his gaze almost angry, and she realized it was the reference to her "self" in third person. They were in the middle of a beach with no one in sight and only the sound of the ocean for company, but God forbid anyone overhear. She rolled her eyes. "Fine. I'm going."

She started up the beach, hoping he would call after her, not looking back. She felt as much as heard him fall into step a few feet behind her. Was she being too obedient again?

She'd wondered that this afternoon, after they got back from their little jet-ski jaunt. If she should have let him whisk her back to the villa without protest. Would Maggie have done that? Bree had fallen back on her own instincts—biddable. Accommodating. But that wasn't Maggie. Maggie was willful. *Strong*.

Maybe she should be a little more like Maggie. Push back more. Play the diva card.

Have that confidence.

If she were the great Maggie Tate, he would have kissed her. Maggie would have settled for nothing less than exactly what she wanted. And Bree wanted to kiss him. The feeling had been coming on ever since he'd walked into Maggie's dressing room back in LA.

THE DECOY BRIDE

Bree turned when she reached the patio, pausing to dust the sand off her feet so she wouldn't track it all into the house. They had a battalion of invisible maids who somehow kept the villa spotless without ever being underfoot, but no sense making their jobs harder than they had to be.

Cross stopped at the edge of the patio as well, though he didn't bend down to brush the sand off his feet. He simply frowned at her, as if he was trying to figure out some puzzle while Cecil scampered around their ankles.

Bree studied his face in the low light. "Everything okay?"

"Mel said something earlier..." He trailed off, shaking his head. "Never mind."

"What?" Bree asked, suddenly dying of curiosity. What had Mel said? Something about her? About them? Something that might make him want to kiss her? Because now that she'd thought about kissing him, she couldn't seem to stop thinking it.

The shadows from the house kept her from seeing his face clearly, so she stepped closer to him, trying to read his expression. "Cross?"

"It's nothing." He shook his head, bending to knock the sand off his feet. "It doesn't matter."

She thought that was all he would say, that it would be the end of it, but then right when she was about to give up and go inside, he spoke.

"Have you ever had a day where everything you were so sure of turns upside down?"

"I'm never sure of anything," she admitted.

"I'm sure of everything." He frowned. "I'm building a freaking field house. That's how sure I was."

"A what?"

He shook his head as he explained. "Sort of an

athletic center. At my old high school. In the town where I grew up."

Her brow furrowed as she tried to follow, unsure what he was talking about. "That's a nice thing to do for the town."

"I didn't do it for the town. I did it for my father. I'm building a freaking monument to him."

"Is that a bad thing?"

Cross laughed softly without humor. "I don't know anymore. He died when I was five and I only have a few memories of him, but I spent my entire life being told how amazing he was and trying to live up to this icon of manhood. Big Aaron. Pride of Harris. I have been chasing a ghost my entire life and tonight I found out he wasn't perfect. He wasn't the personification of everything good. He was just a football player who cheated on his wife and had a kid with someone else. A sister I never knew about."

"Whoa," she whispered. "That must be hard, learning that about someone you idolized."

"It's not that. It's my mother. It's the lies. For years, she never told me I had a half-sister. For decades, she knew the truth and she let me worship him. Let me build my life around trying to be like him. Let me think he was some saint. And build a *monument* to him. I'm so fucking angry. And when I'm not pissed, I feel like a fool."

"I'm sorry." Bree gazed through the darkness at this man, an overachiever who had spent his life competing with a memory. She didn't know much about that, but she knew about lies. The big ones. The ones that made your entire world feel like it was tilting on its axis. "I moved out to LA because of a lie," she said before her brain caught up with the words. "I needed someone to believe in me and this guy online told me I was good. That I could make it as an artist. He promised me a show at his gallery, told me he wanted to launch me into the art world. A bright new talent. That's what he said. Except he didn't have a gallery. Or a show. Or any of the contacts to launch me anywhere. He'd just lied. And I felt so stupid for believing him. I felt like the foundation I wanted to build my life on had turned out to be made of mist—and that wasn't even my mother. I can't imagine what you must be feeling."

He looked at her, dark eyes seeming even darker in the low light. "Then why is it I feel like you are the only one who can?"

Her heart stuttered—and his gaze dropped to her lips.

He wasn't going to kiss her. She knew he wasn't. He was too freaking good. Too freaking noble. Too freaking *controlled*.

He always did what he was supposed to do and he was supposed to stay far away from her—but Bree had never been good at doing what she was supposed to do. She hated repression. She hated caution and good sense.

She wanted *real*. She wanted *truth*. She wanted the honest, raw, piercing emotion beneath the surface.

She wanted to *erupt* with him.

He was never going to kiss her.

So she kissed him.

* * * * *

He wasn't expecting it. Wasn't expecting the distance between them to vanish from one second to the next and for Bree to go up onto her toes, framing his face with her hands, and press her lips to his on a rush of beautiful impulse.

He wasn't expecting it, but he got on board fast.

He closed his arms around her, bending so the discrepancy in their heights was erased. She made a soft, breathless noise against his lips and her arms curled around his neck, arching into him.

He shouldn't be kissing her. He knew he shouldn't be kissing her. He should have pushed her away as soon as he realized her intention, but they were in the shadows, shielded on nearly all sides by the house and the heavy pillars that supported the massive balcony above. It would take a miracle for someone to spot them here.

At least that's what he told himself. Because he wasn't going to stop.

She'd startled him, but when her lips had settled, soft and warm and firm and a little wild against his, he'd had the sharp, clear thought that he shouldn't have been surprised. He'd always sensed the impulsiveness in her, this restless wildness, caged inside her Maggie persona. She'd done her job, she'd been good, but she could only restrain herself so long before the fire inside her needed to get out. And for that fire to ignite him…

He groaned, gathering her against him. He couldn't straighten all the way, not without lifting her off her feet, but somehow the fact that he was curved over her, his body her shield, felt incredibly natural. Incredibly right. He parted his lips—and she was right there with him, stroking her tongue against his, teasing and tempting, this wild, frantic, butterfly of a woman.

She arched her body into his, going up on her tiptoes, stretching into him, the feel of her intoxicating—

Cecil barked, high and shrill, and Bree startled in his arms, jerking back enough to break the kiss, both of them breathing hard. The dog was at the door to the house, whining to be let in, and Cross stared at Bree's face, so close to his in the darkness, trying to find some coherent thought.

"So that happened..." Bree whispered.

A startled laugh slipped past his lips. It shouldn't have happened—but he framed her face with his hands, ignoring the dog and all his good sense. For the first time all goddamn day, something felt right. Something felt real.

"You are so goddamn beautiful." It was too dark to see her face very well, but he knew the lines of it by heart. Knew her lips would be glistening from his kiss, her eyes—those incredible eyes—looking up at him like she saw right past the face he presented to the world to the truth of him, somehow understanding him without even trying. "Your eyes..." he whispered. "You have the most incredible eyes."

Bree went stiff in his arms, her hands suddenly between them, braced on his chest. "What does that mean?"

"What?" He released her instantly when she pressed against him. His arms suddenly empty, he peered into the heavy shadows of the patio as she put a rocking chair between them.

"Who were you kissing? Me? Or her?"

It took him a moment to realize what she was accusing him of, and then irritation flared. "You think I can't tell the difference?"

Though he had wondered, earlier, when they were down on the beach, if she really was Maggie. If this was some kind of game she was playing. Her way of seducing him.

Something of his thoughts must have shown on his face, because she reacted as if she'd read his thoughts.

"I'm not *her*," she snapped.

"I know that."

But she was already through the door, back inside the house, leaving him wondering what the hell had just happened.

CHAPTER FOURTEEN

He'd been kissing Maggie.

Bree raced up the stairs, flying into the master suite. Only the thought of waking Mel—and having to explain to her why she was slamming doors—kept her from flinging the door shut behind her. She forced herself to close it gently—though she took vicious satisfaction in snicking the deadbolt into place.

She couldn't believe the asshole had only kissed her because he wanted to kiss Maggie Tate.

Talking about her *eyes*. Her stupid freaking turquoise eyes. Her damn *Maggie* eyes.

She stalked over to the open bottle of champagne she'd left chilling in the bucket earlier. The bubbles had likely all gone flat and the ice had all melted, leaving the bottle sitting in a bucket of cold water that dripped all over the carpet as she poured a glass all the way up to the brim—easier to do now that there were no bubbles taking up space.

How dare he?

Though, yes, okay, fine, *she* was the one who had kissed *him* and he'd merely responded to the all-you-can-kiss buffet she'd laid out for him, but really, did he have to be thinking of another woman? Even if it was another woman she was paid to impersonate.

She downed a hefty swallow of champagne, choking

a bit when the bubbles—more of which remained than she'd anticipated—hit the back of her throat. She coughed, shaking her head—then took another swig, just as large in defiance of the damn bubbles. In defiance of everything.

The man had ruined a perfectly good kiss.

A perfectly *amazing* kiss, if she was honest. Quite possibly the best kiss she could ever recall having. Though, if she was honest, it had been a while since she'd had anything to compare it to.

She didn't really date. Which had something to do with the fact that most of the men she met in the art world were either gay or married or both, but it wasn't *entirely* due to that.

She'd dated in high school, and even had a few pretty darn good kisses, even if she was considered something of an oddity in rural Minnesota. Her angsty teenage *artiste* phase had been indulgently acknowledged by the people of her town, but never really accepted. If she hadn't also been "pretty" in the classical sense, she probably never would have gotten a date to prom. And she had wanted a date to prom—even if she wanted to buck the system and take down the patriarchy, she still wanted to be accepted. To be wanted. To be loved.

Three things she seemed to have spent her life singularly failing at.

She'd never really felt that way in Clement. Accepted. Understood. Her parents, her friends—they loved her, but no one got her. When she'd gone to college, she'd thought that would be it, the moment when people saw the value in her, but that hadn't quite gone the way she'd thought it would and she'd found herself a college dropout driving her beat-up car across country toward the promise of Venice. The promise of acceptance. The promise of Zander and all his stupid lies.

She couldn't believe she'd told Cross about that. But he'd been so open after his own confession, and the words had just popped out.

Kind of like that impulse kiss. Another in a long line of impulses that hadn't turned out as planned.

Her arrival in California hadn't ended quite how she'd envisioned either, but she had ultimately found what she was looking for in Venice. A sense of community. Of shared purpose. And the promise that if she could just make a name for herself in the art world there, she would finally be accepted for exactly who she was.

She'd dated occasionally, from time to time over the years, but nothing serious. It was easy to avoid any sort of serious emotional attachment. All she had to say was that she was focusing on her work—which was true, but it wasn't the whole story.

If she was entirely honest, she wanted to make something of herself. To prove to all those people who thought she was a little too different, a little too odd to really fit in, that she really *did* have a place. That she did have worth. And that she was worthy of love.

Part of her had always thought that when she finally hit it big her love life would simply fall into place. Like the universe would acknowledge that she was enough of a catch to deserve love. She'd be good enough. If she could just make it.

It had never really surprised her, when her dates didn't want to turn into boyfriends. The subtext beneath all those perfectly painless breakups had been clear. She was fun, but she wasn't worth the commitment. Not yet.

And there was Cross, telling her the same thing all over again. Accepting her kiss—because why not? But seeing Maggie when he looked at her. Maggie and her freaking turquoise eyes.

Bree downed the rest of the champagne and stormed to the bathroom, yanking open the drawer where the contact lens case was hidden.

She popped out the lenses, dropping them into the saline-filled cups, blinking rapidly. Her eyes hurt more now than they had when she'd put the lenses in for the first time, raw and scratchy. Tears gathered at the sting, clinging to her lashes, and she glared defiantly into a reflection that still looked entirely too much like Maggie Tate, even with the wrong colored eyes.

She wanted the hot pink streaks in her hair, the funky pixie haircut, the clothes that felt like hers and not the silky designer bathrobe that probably cost as much as her freaking car.

This was undoubtedly the world's stupidest tantrum—the girl who was angry to be trapped in a movie star's life—but she hadn't expected the experience to make her feel like the person she was when she wasn't Maggie Tate was so…worthless.

She stared into her reflection, the moisture in her eyes—from the contacts, damn it—sliding down her cheeks. This was who she was. The girl looking out of someone else's eyes, begging to be seen.

She itched for her camera, itched to be able to show people what she saw, but even if she had it, would she be able to? Or was she, as Olivia Hwang had so casually condemned her, just another beautiful and boring thing?

* * * * *

He'd screwed up.

Cross knew it as he tossed and turned that night—tormented by a hurricane of questions and doubts about his mother...his sister...and Bree. He arrived in the fitness studio at the crack of dawn the next morning, needing to talk to her, needing to explain, but Bree wasn't there.

He shouldn't have let that kiss happen. Shouldn't have kissed her back. And he sure as hell shouldn't have said all that about his family and the freaking field house. His only excuse was the cumulative effect of the day, the freaking emotional hangover.

It was dark. It was intimate. They were together, trapped inside this crazy bubble where the regular rules didn't apply and he'd forgotten for a second that he had one job—keep her safe and keep his hands to himself. Where had his freaking professionalism gone?

In the light of day, he couldn't imagine why he'd wondered, even for a second, if she was really Maggie. Mel hadn't been trying to give him a message. The two women were so different it was obvious—and Candy was with the real Maggie.

He should let it go and be grateful that Bree had pulled away when she did, before things could go too far, but it bothered him that she thought he only wanted Maggie Tate when Bree was so much more.

He knew he should be professional. He *wanted* to be professional.

But he also wanted her to know that he hadn't been kissing Maggie Tate last night. He'd been kissing her.

Which was probably the last thing he should tell her because it couldn't happen again. Cross didn't operate on the happily-ever-after spectrum. Even if the job hadn't been in the way, he wasn't looking for another relationship. He wasn't built that way. His marriage had proven that.

But Bree was strong. She was smart. If he explained that he couldn't get emotionally involved, she would understand. They could keep things light. Casual. As long as they were careful and none of it spilled over onto Maggie, what could the harm be?

The door to the fitness studio opened and Cross came to attention—but it was Mel, not Bree, who poked her head inside.

"She isn't here?" the taller woman asked, though the answer was obvious.

"No." The single word sounded inexplicably guilty to his ears.

Or maybe *explicably* guilty. Since just last night Mel had told him to keep his distance and not half an hour later he'd been making out with the woman in question.

"Huh." Mel departed as abruptly as she'd arrived—leaving Cross alone with his tangled thoughts.

He started to follow—Bree had to be in the villa because the sensors hadn't gone off, he could help Mel find her—but his cell phone rang and he fished it out of his pocket instead.

Mayor Mike.

He hadn't realized he'd been expecting to see his mother's number until he saw the mayor's. It was early in Iowa. Before dawn. But Mayor Mike was putting in long hours leading up to the dedication.

The dedication.

Suddenly Cross felt sick at the idea of a two day ceremony honoring his father. Was this why his mother hadn't wanted to go? Because of his half-sister? But that didn't make any sense because she'd never had any trouble honoring his father in the past. Why start now?

Did anyone else know the truth? Did the rest of the

town? His mother had said they kept things quiet—what did that mean? That no one knew? Or that they all kept the secret?

He'd wondered, last night in the middle of the night when nothing seemed clear, if he was overreacting to the news that his father had cheated. He knew a lot of his teammates had cheated on their wives—the culture of professional sports didn't exactly discourage it. He'd never felt the same sense of betrayal from learning about a teammate's infidelity. So why should he react so strongly to learning the truth about a father he'd never really known—

But that was it right there. He'd never really known his father. He'd only had the stories. Growing up there had been two role models in his house—his mother and the legend of his father. To find out the legend was a lie...he couldn't help wonder what else about his life was a lie.

His mother hadn't told him about the other woman. The less-than-perfect aspects of his father's legacy. Without that letter, he might never have known. He'd Googled in the middle of the night—his father's name, his half-sister's name—and found nothing. The story, if there ever had been one, had been buried. All the world knew was his father, the god.

Big Aaron. Pride of Harris. Perfect husband. Perfect father. Best ball player ever to live in the history of ball players.

Why had his mother continued to perpetuate the myth, why had she been a part of what now seemed like a giant conspiracy to reshape his father into a decent human being, and why should they honor the man if everything about his life was a lie?

What else didn't he know about the man?

The ringing stopped, the call going to voicemail, and Cross made no move to listen to it. He couldn't handle Mayor Mike right now. Couldn't handle the enthusiasm. Couldn't handle the idea of everything he'd done in the name of his father since he left the NFL, pouring money into Harris in his name.

The name of a man he didn't even know.

He pocketed his phone and returned to the front of the house to focus on the job. That was what he was good at. The best at, damn it.

The main floor was still quiet. No sign of Bree. Though he found Mel on the patio with her breakfast, tapping away on her tablet, when he went out to check the perimeter security one more time.

She looked up when he opened the patio door—and he tried not to let the memory of what had happened the last time he'd been out here show on his face. "The eagle has landed," she said dryly.

Cross frowned as he took a seat opposite her. "What does that mean?"

"It means there's been a sudden surge of new arrivals on the other side of the resort. Dominique called. Apparently the resort policy is not to refuse a room to anyone as long as they don't bother other guests or try to infiltrate the VIP side, but she wanted to make sure Maggie didn't have any restraining orders against members of the press that they should be aware of." She glanced back down at her tablet. "I've been checking various travel sites as well and it's suddenly gotten very hard to find space at the closest resorts on the main island—the ones which would have the easiest boat access to the villa. Looks like we're about to be under siege."

She smiled smugly—and Cross reminded himself

that this was exactly what they wanted. They wanted the parasites to swarm around them, because if they were here, they weren't in Fiji.

But he'd have to step up his game and be even more diligent about Bree's safety with so many of the bastards nearby looking to get a shot of her. And any further kisses—on the patio or otherwise—were absolutely out of the question. Not that he'd been planning more kissing.

It was game time. And he knew better than to let himself get distracted on game day.

* * * * *

If Bree had felt trapped in the gorgeous villa before, that was nothing compared to the intense feeling of claustrophobia she had now.

She could tell herself it was only because they were under siege and her already controlled movements had been restricted even more, but she was afraid it had more to do with him. Cross. Now that she'd kissed him, her edgy awareness of him seemed to have heightened to ridiculous levels.

And it didn't help that her stupid heart felt like it *knew* him after the way he'd shared himself last night. She wanted to know more. She wanted to know everything. To lose herself inside his perspective. To wallow in getting to know him—

But that wasn't a good idea. Even if she didn't have that niggling voice in the back of her mind telling her he'd only kissed her because he saw Maggie when he looked at her.

At least they hadn't been caught.

If some early bird paparazzo had managed to get a shot of them in the shadows of the patio last night, the story doubtless would have broken by the time she woke up—late and mildly hungover after she polished off the rest of the bottle of champagne. So they were safe on that front. Thank God. Though they'd have to be much more careful now that the buzzards were circling.

Not that they would have anything to be careful *of*. Not that it would ever happen again. Obviously it wouldn't happen again. This was not the time to be screwing up her shot at sixty K with a stupid infatuation.

In the glaring light of morning, her mistake was all too clear. She'd let the stress of the situation and the false sense of intimacy get to her. She'd never been particularly good at managing pressure—though this was the first time she'd reacted with a full frontal kiss assault.

She just needed to relax—maybe she could talk Mel into smuggling her in a camera. That would calm her down faster than anything else. Give her something to focus on. Maybe Maggie was taking up an interest in photography. Or doing research for a role. There were dozens of reasons why Maggie Tate might need a camera.

When she found Mel and asked her, the manager seemed puzzled by the request—as if she couldn't imagine what Bree would want to take pictures of while she was under glorified house arrest—but she agreed to look into it for her, after reminding her for the fifth time to stay inside and keep her head down. Apparently they didn't want to tease the paparazzi with her presence yet, instead frustrating the bastards and making them frantic to get the shot—which was fine with Bree, since she didn't exactly want her hangover face splashed over every tabloid in America and neither did Maggie.

Several "tourists" with telephoto lenses had already been caught trying to sneak onto the property, but hunkering down inside the house just made her feel restless. She read one of the books the resort had stocked the bookshelves with—but her focus only lasted for a few minutes at a time and she couldn't get absorbed in the story. She worked out—twice—but even the endorphins from running couldn't counter the tension that seeped into her blood whenever she entered the fitness center, as if some part of her was constantly waiting for Cross to appear.

Dominique came by that afternoon to discuss more wedding stuff, but Bree's focus was fragmented and the wildly accommodating wedding planner promised to come back another day.

And the siege continued.

The siege of freaking boredom.

Bree had never been officially diagnosed with any kind of attention disorder. Her very logical, very driven parents didn't believe in them, didn't want anyone putting the idea in Bree's head that she wasn't capable of focusing perfectly well on her own. Which she appreciated on one level—but there were days she would kill for some freaking Adderall. Days when her brain skipped like a stone on a lake and she couldn't get it to stop.

Then Cross walked into the kitchen where she'd been rattling around, shuffling through cupboards in search of inspiration, and all of her focus tightened suddenly on the awkwardness in the air between them.

Mel had gone off to touch base with the other team on Skype. Kaydee had taken Cecil Two for a walk—since apparently photos of her assistant and her dog were the perfect thing to confirm to the press that

Maggie was there without giving them the money shot they wanted.

But that meant neither of them were there to act as a buffer—and Bree needed a buffer.

He looked good. Better than good. Better than a man had a right to look. His skin was a bit more golden than it had been when they first arrived on the island, which complimented the dark array of browns in his eyes. His hair was two shades lighter, with more streaks of true platinum blonde in the mix. It had grown a little longer—still short, but starting to reveal a natural waviness. With his long golden lashes, there was something of the sexy surfer about him, giving him the illusion of being relaxed—and she knew that was an illusion. His jaw was as tight as ever, his shoulders bunched and his walk the strong, purposeful stride of a man who moved through the world with strength and focus.

Totally unlike her.

She'd dated jocks in high school and things had always ended predictably enough—with her feeling like she wasn't quite right. Wasn't quite good enough. She didn't need any more of that feeling, so it was just as well she and Cross would be staying away from one another.

Except he seemed to have missed the keep-your-distance memo when he leaned against the island and said, "Look…about last night…"

"We don't have to discuss it," she said quickly, flicking a glance toward the stairway Mel had disappeared up.

"I know the difference," he said, the words seeming heavy with meaning and it took her a moment to figure out what he meant.

She'd accused him of not knowing who he was kissing. Not knowing the difference between her and Maggie. "I know you do," she assured him, though she knew nothing of the kind. "But we still can't...there are other reasons."

"I know. I completely agree," he said with demoralizing alacrity. "I just didn't want you to think—"

"I don't. We're good."

She had a job to do. He had a job to do. End of story.

Whatever she'd thought she felt last night was only the product of stress and too much moonlight. Not to mention the champagne. Though admittedly she hadn't had much *before* the kiss. Still. It couldn't happen again. She couldn't be jeopardizing her future for a silly flirtation with no future anyway. And guys like Cross didn't want girls like Bree. Not for keeps.

He nodded, hands thrust deep into his pockets. "I should probably..." He didn't say what he should probably do, vaguely indicating the rest of the house, as if there was pressing work for him there.

"Good idea." Her gaze went to the blinds that blocked every window. As far as they knew, there were no paparazzi physically within telephoto distance of the villa, but Mel and Cross had decided better safe than sorry, closing up the indoor-outdoor villa like they were battening down for a hurricane.

It was pretty insane, the degree to which Maggie's privacy was invaded when she wasn't even the source of a particular scandal. No wonder she'd wanted to hire Bree to distract the paparazzi from her wedding.

Five days down, sixteen to go. Then Bree could go back to being invisible behind the lens of her camera, sixty thousand dollars richer. She could handle two weeks of sexual frustration and boredom mania. Easy.

Cross began to move silently out of the room and she watched him go, irrationally hypnotized by the sight of him. A door slammed upstairs, making her jump and jerk her gaze guiltily away, toward the stairs as Mel appeared. She lifted her tablet above her head, fury sharpening the lines of her face.

"What the *fuck* did you do?"

CHAPTER FIFTEEN

Apparently it took longer for a photo of an illicit kiss to hit the tabloids than Bree had thought.

She sat in the theatre room—the villa's other windowless space, which had become their war room—sinking down into the plush couch and doing her best to look invisible as Mel glowered at everything and Cross paced.

"It had to be Kaydee," Cross announced as he stalked from one end of the room to the other. Bree grabbed the ottoman, pulling it out of his way so he could pace unimpeded. "From the angle, the shot had to have been taken from inside the house. Cecil even barked at the door. He must have been barking at her. All of the resort staff had left for the night. So if you didn't take it—"

Mel looked at him as if the suggestion was insultingly stupid. Kaydee hadn't been invited to the damage control meeting, still on her walk with Cecil Two, oblivious to the drama inside.

"I hope she was well compensated for that shot, because she's about to be fired." Mel glared at both of them, as if implying that Kaydee might not be the only one. "Though she shouldn't have had anything to shoot."

Bree sank down, trying to think invisible thoughts. They were waiting for a Skype call from Maggie—

apparently Cross's colleague Candy was doing something on their end to ensure the call would be one hundred percent secure—and the waiting was horrible.

She'd almost definitely lost her job. She'd be lucky if she didn't get sued for breach of contract, damaging Maggie's reputation like this, but the ax hadn't fallen yet. It wasn't official. Not until Maggie said the words—and waiting for her to say them was making Bree feel physically ill.

"The odds of her getting the shot without us seeing her were extreme," Cross argued, still pacing.

"And yet she got it."

Yes, she had. Several shots, actually. One of a couple locked in a kiss that could not be mistaken for anything but raw and sexual—but neither of them was clearly identifiable in that photo so another had accompanied it. Taken through the living room window. His hands on her face, her expression dazed as she gazed up at him in the moments after the kiss—her face clearly visible. Maggie's face.

Cross's identity was less certain—though it was alleged in the accompanying article. But regardless of who the man kissing Maggie Tate was, it certainly wasn't Demarco Whitten. Not tall enough. Without Demarco's close-shaved head. And even in night vision green, the fact that his skin was the wrong hue was blindingly clear.

Demarco Whitten. The groom of the freaking wedding she was supposed to be planning.

How could she have screwed up so epically? How hard was it to pretend to be Maggie Tate for three weeks and keep her freaking lips to herself? What had she been *thinking*? Because she couldn't blame Cross. She was the one who had instigated the kiss. Even after he'd warned her that she could never let her guard down here. Even after Mel had warned her to keep her distance.

She'd said as much as soon as Mel showed them the pictures. *It was my fault. Don't blame Cross.* But Mel seemed determined to blame both of them, and Cross—when he wasn't obsessing over how Kaydee could have gotten the shot—was equally willing to claim his share of the blame. *I knew better*, he'd growled—and Bree had felt even worse.

He'd known better. And she'd ruined *both* of their chances.

She knew how important his job was to him. It was his entire freaking identity and she'd savaged his reputation as effectively as if she'd set out to do it.

Mel's laptop, which she'd set up on the theatre room's low faux-stone drink table, trilled suddenly, announcing the incoming video call, and Bree cringed, sinking deeper into the couch. Mel took her place in front of the webcam and Cross rerouted his pacing to bring him around so he could see the screen as Mel connected the call.

Maggie appeared on the screen, flanked by Demarco Whitten and a petite woman with spiky blonde hair whom Bree mentally placed as Candy. The movie star looked good—tanned and beautiful. And pissed. Very, very pissed.

Maggie's angry turquoise eyes instantly locked on her. "What the hell, Bree?"

Bree cringed, obviously not doing nearly as good a job as she might have hoped at being invisible. "I'm so sorry."

"Well, of course you are," Maggie said, "but what am I supposed to do with that? The entire world thinks I'm making out with my bodyguard."

Bree stiffened on a surge of irrational defensiveness on Cross's behalf. As if he was just a bodyguard...

"It had to have been Kaydee," Mel interjected, surprising Bree with her defense. "No one else could have gotten the shot, so obviously she'll be fired—"

"No," Maggie interrupted quickly. "Kaydee stays. We might still be able to use her. This isn't about blame. It's about damage control. What do we do?"

A beat of silence followed the question, and Bree knew she ought to keep her mouth shut and just be relieved that she hadn't already been fired, but if the last twenty-four hours had proven anything it was that she was terrible at doing what she should do. "We could lean into it," she blurted.

There was a flicker of lag in the video feed and then Maggie's voice came through, staticky and broken. "What does that mean?"

Bree thought fast, making it up as she went. "We were supposed to distract people from your wedding, right? So we *really* distract people from your wedding," she said. "We post a press release that you and Demarco have broken up and I mope around here looking heartbroken. Meanwhile, you two are getting hitched five thousand miles away." And it had the added bonus that she stopped lying to the people of the Luxe resort about holding a wedding there. No more stringing poor Dominique along. "We'd have to reveal that you had a double at the end of it, and you probably wouldn't be able to use me again, but for now..."

Maggie's frown had morphed into something speculative on the first sentence, but she still looked skeptical, until Demarco announced, "I like it."

Maggie glanced at her sweetie, her expression softening. "It could work," she admitted. She looked back to the screen. "You and Cross can play all lovey-dovey. Give them plenty to look at."

Bree flushed at the idea of faking a relationship with Cross. "I don't know about that..."

Maggie's expression darkened instantly. "You didn't have a problem kissing him before."

Bree flushed, glancing over her shoulder toward the bodyguard, who hadn't said a word—even though it would be his lips she'd be using to sell this story. She appealed to him with her eyes, begging him to come up with some excuse why they couldn't fake a relationship, but her pleading eyes must not have been nearly as eloquent as she thought because he said, "I'm in."

"Bree?" Maggie demanded, and she felt her face heat even more.

It was her only shot at leaving here with the sixty thousand—and she owed it to Maggie after so royally screwing up—but what was Cross's excuse? Why would he put himself in the middle of a media shitstorm like that? Because it would be *him* in the middle, not some character he was playing like Bree was.

Her stomach roiled, but it was his call to make. Her choice had already been made. Kissing Cross had almost cost her sixty grand. She could sure as hell kiss him to get it back. "Of course I'll do it."

"Excellent." Maggie rocked back in her chair, her expression triumphant. She looked to her fiancé. "I guess our next step is drafting a press release announcing our break-up." She cocked her head. "Maybe you can be overheard fighting on the phone and the press can get a picture of you tearfully begging Demarco to forgive you."

Bree's stomach revolted at the idea of putting her acting to the test in that way, but Mel stepped into save her. "It will look too staged," the manager argued. "You would never go out somewhere anyone could hear you to have a screaming, crying fight—and for the next two weeks, Bree is you."

Maggie wrinkled her nose. "Right. So I guess a press release."

"I'll have something drawn up immediately," Mel assured her. "They'll be expecting a reaction to the photos."

"Excellent. Coordinate with Demarco's team. I'll leave it in your capable hands," Maggie said, waggling her fingers at the video. "Good luck!"

The call ended, but no one moved.

Bree couldn't speak for anyone else, but she was frozen by a mix of dread and relief that she'd never experienced before. She hadn't ruined everything—that was good—but from here on out…

She had no idea what she was doing.

"Is Kaydee really staying?"

"I don't love it, but Maggie's right. She can still be useful. You'll have to talk to her," Mel said. "Convince her you broke up with Demarco. Here, give me the ring." Mel thrust out her hand and Bree tugged at the replica on her finger. The humidity made it tight and she twisted, scratching her knuckle when she finally managed to yank it loose. "Be upset that the news leaked," Mel coached, accepting the fake. "But not too upset. Demarco wasn't right for you. You're crazy about Cross."

Bree blushed, avoiding looking at Cross. "Are you sure that's a good idea?"

"It was your idea." Mel frowned. "And at this point it's the only logical thing to do. We make you two into a show, and then when Demarco and Maggie are ready, we reveal the truth. That she was with him all along, desperately in love, and you were hired to give her five seconds of privacy."

"You don't think her fans will mind being lied to?"

"We'll spin it as a necessary evil. Which it is. But you don't need to worry about any of that. I'll handle all the press releases. You just keep Kaydee on the line for a couple more weeks."

"Right," Bree agreed, still unable to look directly at Cross. She could do this. She had to.

All because of one little kiss.

* * * * *

She was waiting for Kaydee when the girl came back from the world's longest walk with Cecil. Mel had speculated that Kaydee was probably meeting with her media contact and getting instructions or giving another "exclusive" interview, but Bree was supposed to pretend that none of them suspected anything—though how Kaydee could actually believe she hadn't been found out was baffling to Bree. She'd done a terrible job of covering her tracks, but the younger woman was smiling and confident when she walked through the patio doors with Cecil.

"There's my baby," Bree cooed at the dog, who bounded over to greet her, his little tail sweeping the floor enthusiastically. Cecil had grown on her over the last few days and she'd actually started to enjoy having him around, when he wasn't yelping like a dying seal. She scooped him up into her lap, cuddling him close and taking comfort in his soft weight in her lap. "Was he a good boy?" she asked Kaydee.

She hadn't had much direct contact with the girl over the last few days—at least not without Mel or

Dominique around. Bree had made a practice of avoiding being alone with her, never entirely certain what to say, but Mel had insisted that she had to do this part herself.

"He was an angel," Kaydee promised. "He fell asleep on the beach and he looked so sweet I didn't want to wake him, so I just stayed there until he woke up."

So that was her excuse for being gone so long. Bree pretended not to suspect the flimsy story, lifting Cecil up to her face. "Did somebody have a nice nap? Did you? Yes, you did."

Kaydee's gaze locked on her left ring finger—and the distinct lack of a nine karat piece of bling. "Where's your ring?"

"We've called off the wedding." Bree gave a mildly irritated sniff—as if the change in her relationship status was a minor inconvenience—and settled Cecil into her lap, stroking his silky head. "Demarco and I rushed into things so fast and we really wanted it to work—but I think we both knew it wasn't right. I'm sure you could tell I was having second thoughts and he was too." She sighed. "Then when those pictures came out this morning..."

"Pictures?" Kaydee asked with forced innocence.

Bree flapped a hand as if they were nothing. "Just some sleazy photographer hiding in the bushes who got a shot of Cross kissing me. Can you imagine a grown person skulking around prying on private moments for money?"

"You were kissing the bodyguard?" Kaydee asked, in an impressive imitation of surprise.

"We've been talking some since we arrived on the island," Bree admitted, not having to force her blush, "and he's a really great listener, you know? I just feel like he understands me—like the deeper me—and when Demarco saw the pictures, he wasn't even upset. I think he knew that we were never meant to be."

All of which was true, for Bree. And somehow lying to Kaydee didn't feel quite so wrong. Maybe because the younger woman had been sneaking around taking pictures behind her back, but Bree felt absolutely no guilt about selling this particular story. Though she did try to stick to the script Mel had given her.

"I think we were more in love with the idea of one another than actually in love with each other, you know?"

"Absolutely," Kaydee agreed, nodding eagerly. "I was wondering if something was wrong when you suddenly stopped talking about Demarco. You haven't been talking to me at all."

Because I don't trust you any farther than I can throw you. "I know. I've just been so conflicted. And now...I don't know. Maybe Cross is the one I'm really meant to be with. Maybe he's my soulmate and Demarco was just the man I needed to help me see past the bodyguard to the man, you know?" She gazed out over the crystal blue waters. "Maybe this is my love story."

"Maybe it is," Kaydee agreed, the perpetual yes-woman.

It was all part of the script Mel had given her, but Bree was afraid of how real the words felt. They didn't feel like a lie—and that was terrifying, because Cross hadn't spoken to her since he slipped out of the theatre room that afternoon. She didn't know how he felt. She only knew that she felt entirely too much.

And that scared her like nothing else.

CHAPTER SIXTEEN

The ocean glittered like aquamarine gems in the morning sunlight, so exquisitely beautiful it didn't need to say anything, it just reached into your soul and spoke—but Bree couldn't enjoy the view. She was too busy scanning the landscaping for the telltale twitch of a palm frond or reflection off a lens.

The press release had gone out last night. Mel had informed her that morning that it was having the "desired effect." Whatever that was. The manager had also met with Dominique, discreetly informing the woman that due to their current circumstances there would no longer be a wedding, but they had decided to stay for the rest of their planned vacation regardless.

So now it was on to phase two. No more fake wedding prep—which was good. But now she had a fake relationship to worry about—which was not so good.

Mel had decided on the balcony off the master bedroom for their first "appearance" as a couple. Apparently several members of the press had been stopped trying to get close to the villa and Mel was confident at least a couple had slipped through the cracks and were now lurking in the bushes, waiting for their chance.

It was a decidedly unsettling thought.

Bree wanted to make things up to Maggie—and God knew she didn't have a choice if she wanted to walk out of here paid and unsued—but she couldn't get comfortable with the idea of faking it with Cross. It wasn't that she wasn't attracted to him. Obviously. It was...she didn't know what it was, but she was excruciatingly uncomfortable as she donned her padded bikini for the staged Sunbathing with New Beau on the Balcony scene that Mel and Maggie had agreed should be their first photo op.

She added a sheer white cover up and was fussing with her hair, trying to make it look like the stylists always managed to, when a soft knock sounded on the door. "Come in," she called without turning from the vanity, hyperaware of the sound of the door opening and closing behind her.

"You almost ready?" he asked, his voice deep, and Bree swallowed, forcing herself to turn away from the mirror.

"I feel like I ought to feel guilty for lying to Kaydee," she said as she turned and caught sight of the man in her room—and her mouth went dry.

Bree had overheard him arguing with Mel about whether or not he needed to "show off the goods" during the photo op. Apparently Mel had won.

Cross was wearing the same board shorts he'd worn on the jet-ski two days ago, but this time there was no t-shirt covering the impressive muscles of his chest and abs. He looked like something out of a men's health magazine. Or Playgirl.

Bree blushed, unable to meet his eyes—and trying desperately not to stare at the cut of muscle that angled down into his shorts. The David had nothing on Aaron Cross, Jr.

His body was art in motion, sensuality in every shadow, and she shivered at the beauty in his strength—though he might not appreciate being told how beautiful he was. Guys could be so touchy about things like that, especially big strong macho men.

"Don't feel guilty," he said—and it took her a moment to realize he wasn't forgiving her for gawking at his abs. "She hasn't exactly proven herself trustworthy."

"True." Bree swallowed thickly. "You ready for your close up?" she tried to quip.

"As ready as I'll ever be." There was a note in his voice, a note of resignation, a *let's just get through this* tone, and suddenly Bree realized why she was so uncomfortable playing lovey-dovey with Cross.

He didn't want to.

The idea that a man she had a huge crush on was being forced to pretend to like her was demoralizing in the extreme. Yes, he'd kissed her before—or rather he hadn't shoved her away from him when she'd kissed him—but she still couldn't escape the niggling doubt that he'd only done it because he saw Maggie when he looked at her. The movie star, the goddess, the fantasy.

Now he had to pretend to want her, the pale imitation of Maggie—and it was her fault they had to do it.

He crossed to the balcony doors, but she stopped him before he opened them.

"Why are you doing this?"

He froze at the soft question, turning back to face her, frowning gently. "We shouldn't talk about this here."

Right. He'd warned her about microphones that could be aimed at windows to hear inside. Telephoto video cameras with lip readers. Not to mention Kaydee simply eavesdropping. There was nowhere in the villa that was one hundred percent private, but she needed this answer before they started this.

She came closer, until they were separated only by inches, and then repeated beneath her breath, barely moving her lips, so low no microphone could possibly catch it. "Why are you doing this?"

She wanted him to say he didn't mind. That it was okay. That pretending to fall in love with her wasn't such a hardship.

He met her eyes, something in his gaze softening, gentling, compassion in the look. Compassion and a kind of connection, acknowledging this *thing* that lived between them, the live-wire of want.

Say it, she willed, not certain what she wanted him to say. But then he spoke, the words barely audible. "This account is important to EP."

She rocked back on her heels, feeling the words like a slap. "Right." The job. He was all about the job. She nodded. "Time to get to work."

He opened his mouth, as if he would say more, but she was already moving around him, past him, out onto the balcony to do her freaking job—which now involved playing the freaking lovers on the balcony like Romeo and freaking Juliet.

Joy.

* * * * *

He shouldn't have lied.

When she'd asked him, point-blank, why he was doing this, he could have told her the real reason, but some self-preservation instinct had kicked in instead and he'd gone for a simpler truth.

He *was* doing it for the job, for Maggie and EP, but

that wasn't why he'd said yes so damn fast when Maggie had proposed the idea. Bree had looked so crestfallen when she realized they'd been caught on camera, so broken by the idea that she'd let Maggie down. She'd hunched down on that couch in the theatre room like a prisoner waiting for her turn at the gallows, her expression so perfectly miserable he would have done anything to wipe that look off her face.

Which was a dangerous line of thinking. He needed to be focused on doing the best job he could for Maggie and EP, not on the way Bree's heartbroken eyes had made his chest ache.

His inability to ignore the way Bree made him feel was what had gotten them into this situation in the first place—lounging on a balcony, pretending to trade sweet nothings as they basked in the sun and waited for the paparazzi.

It would be easier if he could keep this about the job. Cleaner.

They would play the couple for two weeks, and then they would reveal the truth. Bree was the decoy and Cross had been hired to feed into the distraction. Admittedly, he hadn't originally been hired to kiss her, but a good security specialist knew how to adapt to evolving situations. He was still doing the job he'd been hired to do.

He was just doing it shirtless on a balcony now.

While Kaydee was walking Cecil this morning, they'd been coached by Mel in the theatre room—the room with the best soundproofing in the house and therefore their chosen strategy chamber. They would lounge—lazy, comfortable, two new lovers with nothing better to do than bask in the sun—which would apparently drive the gossip websites crazy because how could Maggie *possibly* be lazing around with her new lover when she'd just jilted poor Demarco.

More exposure. More focus on them. More cover for the real Maggie.

He strode over to the long, low lounge chair with its thick white cushions and stretched out on it. It wasn't really big enough for two people, but he slid to one side and jutted his chin at her. "Come here," he rumbled.

They'd planned this, choreographed the shot they would give the paparazzi—provided any of them had managed to find a perch high enough to see onto the balcony. He knew what was coming, but he still found himself not entirely prepared for the sight of her crossing the distance between them. He couldn't see her eyes behind the sunglasses, but he could feel them on him as he stretched out a hand to her. She took it and he tugged her down against him, half on top of him, folding his arms around her as she smiled against his lips.

The kiss wasn't heated. It wasn't a repeat of the other night, with tongue and hands everywhere and that crazy rush of desperate need. This one was sweet. Temptingly so. Drawing him in. Alluring in its slow, lazy exploration, until he forgot about cameras and plans and just kissed her.

When she lifted her head, he wished the sunglasses hiding her eyes would vanish. He wanted to see if she had that same dazed soft-focus look she'd had the other night. If she would look at him in that way only Bree had. But the sunglasses blocked her eyes from view— and that was probably for the best. This was a job.

She settled against him, cuddling against his side, gazing out over the water, and he reached for one of their props—a crossword puzzle they were supposed to pretend to do together. Which, according to Mel, would demonstrate that their connection was mental as well as physical.

Bree lay against his side as he idly studied the clues. "Did you talk to your mom?"

* * * * *

Cross stiffened beneath her and Bree knew instantly that she'd said the wrong thing. Always blurting out the wrong thing. Her thoughts had been spinning after the kiss and she'd needed to say something, but she regretted it as soon as she felt him somehow pulling away from her even though there was no room for escape on the lounge.

"I'm sorry," she tried to backpedal.

"It's fine," he said, his voice hard, everything about him suddenly hard and stiff.

Awkwardness swamped her. The same awkwardness she'd felt when he'd pulled her down for a kiss. Not that he wasn't a good kisser. Not that the moment hadn't been perfectly choreographed. It was that fishbowl feeling. Like nothing about the moment was theirs. Like they were only kissing for the cameras. For the screaming fans eagerly downloading the shot.

As his lips had brushed hers, she'd had a sudden surge of empathy for Will and Kate and all the other royals with their staged balcony kisses and forced romantic moments. How perfectly miserable.

Though perhaps more miserable for her because she wanted him to want to kiss her for real. Not for the cameras. Not for the job. For *her*. If only wishing it could make it so.

And then she'd gone and said the stupidest thing possible.

She really needed to stop feeling sorry for herself. A gorgeous man had kissed her on the balcony of one of the most gorgeous villas in the world, looking out over what had to be one of the most gorgeous beaches in the world. Life didn't get much better than that—even if it was only her life temporarily. She ought to be enjoying this, but she couldn't seem to get her head in the right place. In any kind of place. Her thoughts kept skipping around, stones on a pond, the ripples bumping into one another, never still.

Ripples of his kisses. Of his dark eyes. Of the strong, direct way he spoke to her.

Far too many of her ripples were about Cross.

She needed to get her head on straight. She'd already screwed everything up once because she let her agitation drive her to the point of impulsiveness—which never ended well for her.

She needed to be calm. Zen. But there was nothing Zen about the way she felt when he shifted beneath her, settling her more firmly in his arms.

She wanted to talk to him, wanted to ask him the thousand questions that were on her mind, but she'd already overstepped and she needed to focus on sounding like Maggie. What would Maggie say to a new lover? What would Maggie want to know?

"Where's Cecil?" The dog. She had been reduced to talking about the dog.

"Inside asleep on his bed," Cross answered. "I think the sun might be too hot for him out here."

"It's almost too hot for me out here."

She hadn't meant to attach any innuendo to the words, but Cross looked down, the left side of his mouth tipping up in a wicked smile. "Maybe we should go inside and cool off," he said, his voice low and sexy, and all at once she was drowning in innuendo.

She'd never thought the words *cool off* could sound quite so dirty.

"Good idea," she whispered, suddenly breathless.

For a long moment, neither of them moved, then Cross slowly shifted, setting her off him just enough to unfold his long body and rise to his feet. She let him pull her up beside him—and tight against his chest.

It's all an act, she reminded herself as her heart rate went into double time. This man, this serious, sexy, hunk of a man, was playing his part perfectly—and she needed to do the same. So she pushed back in his arms, slanting him a flirty look from beneath her shades, and wrapped her hands around the sun-warmed skin of his biceps, pulling him with her even as she walked backwards toward the balcony doors.

"You look overheated, Mr. Cross," she purred.

"Do I?" he asked, the words dark as her back came up against the balcony doors and his front pressed against her, pinning her to the glass. Then his mouth was on hers and—shit, they hadn't scripted this kiss.

It was hot and open-mouthed and left no question where this was going as he wrapped one arm around her waist, lifting her off her feet, against his body, until they were the same height and she could twine her arms around his neck and kiss him on his level. His other hand scrabbled beside her hip and it wasn't until the door at her back suddenly gave way that she realized he'd been groping for the handle.

They staggered inside, locked together, the kiss going on and on, not stopping, not even for air. He shifted her weight to one arm again and she felt him reach blindly behind for the door, flinging it shut hard enough to rattle the glass—and Bree turned her head at the sound, breaking the kiss.

Cross lowered her to the ground slowly. Bree's bare feet touched the floor, and she braced herself against him as her knees wobbled. The blinds were closed. They were inside. Out of sight. No more show to put on. But it took her a moment to step away from him. To find the strength in her knees.

"I'm sorry," he murmured, so soft she could barely hear the words. "I shouldn't have ad libbed."

"No, it was good," she whispered back, trying to hide her breathlessness. It had been more than good. It had *melted* her, but he seemed so calm, like he could just flip a switch and turn off the performance. "The photographers may not have been able to see us in the lounge chair anyway."

"I just don't want you to think I'm taking advantage—that you have to go along with something you don't want in order to stay in character."

"You think Maggie Tate isn't perfectly capable of asserting herself and shutting you down if she feels like it? The press would probably love that even more than a kiss."

"I didn't want you to feel like you have to."

"Of course not. I wanted to." And then, realizing what she'd blurted, she blushed, lowering her eyes.

"Right," he murmured. "Good."

Awkwardness filled the air between them. She'd never been so confused about where she stood with a man who'd kissed her multiple times before, kissed her like she was *everything*, but then she'd never pretended to be a famous movie star in a relationship before. That did have a way of complicating things.

She cleared her throat softly, trying to return to professionalism. "I think that went well," she whispered.

Cross nodded silently, glancing at the closed blinds as if looking for the microphones or sonic lasers or whatever crazy technology the paparazzi would use to listen in on them. "I should go," he mouthed, and her heart sank.

She hadn't realized how badly she'd wanted him to stay until that moment, when he squeezed her hand—as if to say good job, a nice little pat on the back—and then he was walking away from her. Stealthily out the door of her bedroom, leaving her there in a puddle of want.

Was he just being a gentleman? Was that why he was walking away from her? Trying not to pressure her? Trying not to cross a line? Because that was sexy and all—but it also left her in a welter of doubt about *what he wanted*.

On the balcony when he'd pulled her into his arms, so fast and perfect, there hadn't been any doubt. But as soon as the door shut between them and the outside world, he'd come to his senses.

Did he not really want her? Was he only playing a part? When she'd said she'd wanted to kiss him, he hadn't said it back. He'd just said *good*—whatever that was supposed to mean.

Was *she* the one taking advantage of *him*? She'd kissed him the first time. The only times he'd initiated anything were when they had to for the cameras. Was he really not interested?

She wished she knew him well enough to know. She only had a few pieces of the puzzle that made up Cross. Had she offended him by mentioning his mom again?

Did he even like her?

Bree flung herself on her back on her bed, staring up at the tray ceiling and trying not to groan in frustration.

Trying to figure out the puzzle of Cross.

An image flashed in her mind—like one of her collages with the small photos creating the larger whole, but this time it wasn't a street scene or a wave, it was Cross's face. And each puzzle piece that created the whole was another confusing moment. The kiss. The jet-ski. Those moments in the dark when he'd been moving, all fluid grace. She could see it—the pieces of him composing the larger whole—but sadly it didn't tell her anything else about what he wanted.

The man. The myth. The mystery.

Who she really needed to stop falling for.

She needed to keep her distance. That was the only solution. Now if only she could do that while pretending to fall in love with him.

CHAPTER SEVENTEEN

You look overheated, Mr. Cross.

Those words. That sexy little purr.

Overheated didn't even begin to cover it. His body temperature had been in the red zone ever since she'd given him that little come-hither grin—but she'd turned her face away the second the door had closed behind them, when they didn't have to keep up the act anymore, the signal clear.

I wanted to.

Her voice echoed in his thoughts—so maybe the signal hadn't been so clear, but he'd walked away. For his own self-preservation if nothing else. They were working together—albeit in an unusual way—and they needed to keep things as professional as possible. He already had Candy smirking at him every time they Skyped. He'd already snapped at his colleague about putting him in for the job—the last thing he needed was her pushing more of her meddle-in-his-love-life agenda.

He was perfectly capable of making his own choices, damn it. And he didn't need to do anything else to muddy the waters of his professional relationship with Bree.

Her kisses may be hot enough to get him hard in two-point-two seconds, but he needed to keep his distance. And a cold shower—something to stop the highlight reel of that kiss from playing over and over again in his mind.

His room was dark when he entered, the drapes drawn against prying eyes, and Cross didn't bother to turn on a light, moving straight to the bathroom and only flicking on the light over the shower after he kicked the door shut behind him. He cranked on the water, shucking his board shorts and stepping beneath the spray before it had time to warm up—and swearing profusely at the chilly blast.

Which did nothing to dispel his thoughts of Bree.

He should have stayed in the master suite. That had been the plan. Kaydee was in the house somewhere. She might see that he wasn't with Maggie right now and suspect that their "relationship" wasn't all Bree had been telling her it was—but he'd known if he stayed in the master with Bree, with the enormous bed so close, something would have happened that was far from professional.

He shuddered under the water as it slowly warmed, doing his damnedest *not* to think of how she'd looked and felt stretched out in the sun. She'd looked relaxed, but he'd felt the tension in her body. Bree may know how to throw herself into fun, but she didn't know how to do nothing any better than he did. The lazy, lounging photo op hadn't suited her any more than it had suited him. Though she'd certainly looked the part.

The bikini covered more than most—but he knew that was because it was also designed to amplify what she had up top. He knew from seeing her in the gym that her natural lines were more streamlined. Not willowy, that wasn't the right word. It implied a flimsiness that didn't fit. No. Bree was more aerodynamic. Like a high end sports car. All sleek lines and lethal sex appeal.

Cross cursed, closing a fist around the erection that refused to go away. It wasn't natural, this reaction to her. He needed to get it under control. Take the edge off. His hand worked roughly up and down his shaft, eyes closing and head falling back as the muscles in his neck went loose. All he was seeing was Bree anyway. Challenging him with her eyes. Teasing him with her smiles. Pushing the limits, always pushing. She'd be like that in bed—enthusiastic. Demanding. Her hands on him. Her mouth…

He groaned roughly, working himself to a fast, rough release, leaning into the forearm he'd braced against the tiles. He breathed hard, the water pouring over his shoulders, warm now, almost too hot, and felt the heat seep into his bones.

But the relaxation didn't penetrate all the way. That edge was still there. Beneath the surface.

He would run it off. He pushed away from the wall, briskly washing himself off and turning off the water. Five minutes later he was in workout clothes, jogging down the stairs to the fitness studio.

He didn't see Kaydee—or Bree—as he avoided the windows—since as far as the paparazzi knew he was getting a different kind of exercise—and strode quickly into the cool, air-conditioned quiet of the studio.

He only realized he'd been straining his ears for the whirr of the treadmill as he approached when he found the room silent and empty. He moved to the treadmill, stepping on and cranking it up until he could stretch out his stride without bothering with a warm up—his muscles were plenty warm, thank you very much.

His feet pounded and he cranked up the speed again.

He'd never liked running on machines. For lifting

weights they were fine, but when it came to running he'd take a track or a beach or pretty much *any* place where he could see the ground disappearing beneath his feet rather than a machine. He never felt like he got anywhere. Never felt like he accomplished anything. And if he wanted to put on an extra burst, to challenge himself up a hill or try to lap another jogger on the track, he had to ask the freaking machine to give him that program.

Did Bree prefer running on the treadmill? Or was she only doing it because she couldn't run outside as Maggie?

I wanted to, her voice whispered in his mind and he shuddered. How much of what she did here was her and how much was because she was trapped in Maggie's life? He didn't really know her—just as Candy had taunted him—and the more he learned, the more he felt there were more layers to uncover.

He hadn't realized how restless being caged in the house was going to make him. How restless it must have made her. They were alike in that, he knew. The agitation.

She got it. Because she felt it too.

His ex had never understood. Not that she'd tried very hard.

He shook away the thought. Why the hell was he thinking about Lauren? His ex was ancient history. And comparing her to Bree? He barely knew Bree. All he knew was how she kissed. And that was the kind of thinking-with-his-dick shit that had gotten him married to Lauren in the first place.

The fitness studio door swung inward and Bree froze on the threshold in her own snug little workout outfit, her wide eyes locking with his in the mirror. He saw the moment she made the decision to leave, her gaze shuttering before it flicked to the side and she murmured, "Sorry," starting to turn away.

"Wait. Bree." Cross broke stride, nearly braining himself on the nearby stationary bike as he leapt off the whirring treadmill to intercept her.

He slapped a hand on the door to the fitness studio to keep it from closing between them, ready to sprint after her, but she'd stopped at the sound of her name, though her expression remained wary as she faced him. Uncertain.

I wanted to. That voice again. Bree's voice. Cross frowned, realizing for the first time that his father's voice had been quiet the last few days. He didn't hear it around her. That thing inside him, constantly pushing him to be more, to never stop, to always try harder—it was quieter in her presence. He could breathe with her. And he didn't want her to walk away. He didn't want to lose that.

"Can we talk?"

* * * * *

He wanted to talk. She'd just finished giving herself a pep talk about staying away from him and now the man who had done such a good job of keeping himself distant from her wanted to talk.

Of course he did.

She stood in the small hallway outside the fitness studio, hyperaware of every gorgeous inch of him, and knew she should say no even as she heard herself murmur, "Sure."

He caught her hand—and Bree was so distracted by the feel of his warm, calloused fingers curled around hers that they were several feet down the hall before she realized she was following along obediently.

"Come here." He ducked into the theatre room—one of the few rooms in the house without windows or exterior walls and therefore one of the few places they could talk privately. He released her hand and turned to shut the door behind them—and Bree tried not to deflate at the loss of contact as he sealed them inside.

She'd been in this room a half a dozen times in the last two days, but suddenly she had a new awareness of the intimacy of the dark wood paneling—and of the giant couch that looked more like a bed that could sleep six.

Bree carefully avoided looking at that couch, moving toward one of the overstuffed ottomans.

"What did you want to talk about?" she asked, her voice low even though this was one of the few places in the house they could speak freely.

"I thought maybe we could get to know each other a little. It might make things easier, don't you think? For the roles we're playing?"

For the roles. Of course. She blushed, embarrassed that she'd thought he might actually be pulling her in here to have his way with her. "How is knowing me going to help you seduce Maggie?"

She needed to squash this stupid crush she had on him. He was a jock, an achiever, the kind of person who glided through life from success to success, king of all he surveyed, and she was the weird art chick who didn't have the talent to succeed in the non-conformist art world. Their lives were too different. *They* were too different.

Cross shrugged, moving to the couch/bed and lowering himself on the edge as if it was nothing. "It could make us more comfortable around each other."

Half of his mouth tipped up in a crooked grin. "Honestly, I like being around you. I have these...I don't know, not voices in my head, I'm not crazy, but sometimes I hear echoes of things people said to me once, haunting me, you know? Like they're half my thoughts and half memories I can't escape, but when I'm with you, they're quieter. It's like they don't matter so much."

She felt her face heating, always blushing with him, her heart humming with warmth at his words, though she tried to keep her voice professional. "I have those too," she admitted softly. Those awful echoes. *Not everyone has what it takes. You can't just* decide *to be an artist.* "Why are we never haunted by people telling us how awesome we are?"

"I don't know. That'd definitely be better." He studied her for a moment. "We have a lot in common, you and I."

She arched a brow. "And here I was just thinking how different we are."

He didn't see her when he looked at her. He saw perfect, polished Maggie or he wouldn't be saying that. He wouldn't be so interested.

"You're from the Midwest, right?" he asked.

"Minnesota," she acknowledged. "A small town where I never really fit in." *Because I was never good at being what people wanted me to be. Because I'm not "normal" enough to date the hot jocks.* She needed him to know she wasn't anything like Maggie.

"Me too."

Bree arched a wry brow. "You didn't fit in?" she asked, not bothering to hide her skepticism.

"Small town."

"Yeah, I have a feeling our experiences were pretty

different. I wasn't the football star."

He met her gaze directly, mirroring her droll eyebrow lift. "You think my life was perfect just because I played ball?"

She flushed, ashamed by the assumption. She had thought that. She'd put him in the hot-jock-with-a-perfect-life box the second she met him and had ignored any information about him that didn't feed into that stereotype—because it was easier to think of him that way than to acknowledge he might be real. He was already sexy enough. If he was sexy *and* real, how was she supposed to resist that?

When he'd told her that stuff about his father, she'd ambush-kissed him. What would she do if he started talking about his childhood?

"I shouldn't have assumed. I always seem to say the wrong thing. That stuff about your mom—"

"That wasn't you. That was me. You didn't say anything wrong. I just—" He scrubbed a hand down his face. "I don't like not knowing things. It's been driving me crazy not knowing whether it was you or Maggie I've been guarding all these years and that was nothing. This…"

"Isn't it better to know the truth now?" she murmured. "To know who your father really was? He had feet of clay, sure, but that also means he was *real*, not some fantasy that someone dreamed up. Isn't that better?"

"But how do I know which parts were real and which were bullshit?"

She grimaced. That was the tricky part about lies. They made you question everything you'd ever believed to be true. "Do you remember him at all?"

Cross grimaced. "Only the memories that people tell

you about—half my memories are stories. *Remember how Big Aaron used to carry you around on his shoulders after the games? Remember how Big Aaron taught you how to throw your first football?* Things like that. Things I'm not sure if I remember or if I've just been told so many times I built the memory from the stories. None of it feels real. I was *five*. I remember my mom shaking, crying in the bathroom after the funeral when she thought I couldn't see her. That felt real. Because it scared the shit out of me. I'd never seen her shake like that. Like she was breaking apart."

"It was just the two of you after that?"

"My grandparents helped some. We moved back to Iowa—he'd been playing for the Broncos and I have vague memories of a big house with all the rooms done in white and a pool, but after he died, yeah, it was just us. Well, us and the ghost. The legend of Big Aaron. She never dated again, because no man could compete with the myth of my father—and now I find out she's been lying to me for twenty-five years about who he was."

"Are you sure that's what happened?"

"She admitted it. After my half-sister sent me a letter asking to meet me, my mother admitted it was true. That she'd known."

Bitterness was tight in his voice and Bree didn't know what to do to ease it. "Have you reached out to your sister?" she asked instead.

"Not yet. She left her phone number, but I haven't...What would I even say to her after all this time?"

"Hello? Nice to meet you?"

He grimaced and shook his head, clearly not ready to go there yet. "I just need to focus on this. On getting through this job. And on not murdering Mayor Mike when he won't stop nagging me about the damn field house."

Bree tried not to take offense that the job with her was something he needed to *get through*. "That's the dedication your mother didn't want to go to? The field house you're giving the town?"

"My *father's* field house. Hell, I'm not sure *I* want to go to the dedication anymore."

"Yes, you do. *You* built it. You're giving it to the town. Not your father. The way you feel about him may be changing but you're still doing something good. *You* accomplished that. Wouldn't you regret it if you didn't see it through?"

Cross studied her, frowning, and she was certain she'd said the wrong thing again, crossed some line. Then he said, "How do you do that?"

She swallowed at the intensity in his gaze. "Do what?"

"See right through the bullshit to the heart of things?"

"It's easier to see from the outside—when you're not in it emotionally."

"I don't think that's it. You're a remarkably intuitive person—has anyone ever told you that? I bet you'd be amazing at two truths and a lie."

"What's that?"

"It's a game—and a great way of getting to know one another and testing how well you're able to read someone. Each person takes a turn telling the other three things about themselves—two of which are true, and one of which is a lie. Then the other person has to figure out which is which."

She shook her head, already feeling like Cross saw too much of her. "I don't really like tests."

"It's not a test. It's a game. And you'd be great at it."

"Somehow I doubt that."

"You need to have more confidence in yourself."

"Truth. You're good at this game."

He chuckled. "That isn't how it works."

"Two truths and a lie?" She pretended to think it over before holding up a single finger, "I'm being paid a ridiculous sum of money to sit around and do nothing on a tropical island and I can't even do that without getting caught kissing the wrong guy."

Cross grinned, shaking his head. "That doesn't count. Besides, maybe I'm just irresistible."

He was that, but she grabbed a pillow and chucked it at his cocky face. He caught it, laughing, his dark eyes freaking *twinkling* in a way that was wholly unfair as he flicked it aside. "Want me to go first?" he asked.

She wasn't sure she wanted to play at all, wasn't sure it was a good idea to keep getting to know Cross because the more she did, the more he started to feel *right* to her in a way she knew he shouldn't. But part of her also *really* wanted to play—the part that threw caution to the wind and ran headfirst into anything that made her heart race—and that part always won.

"Yes." She waved a hand at him. "Go."

CHAPTER EIGHTEEN

Two truths and a lie. He didn't know why he'd thought of it. He hadn't played in years, but Cross was oddly excited about playing with Bree. He'd already told her more about himself than he ever confided to most people in his life, he realized as he ran through the options of which truths he could use.

Maybe he'd start with an easy one. Something she already knew. He met her eyes and held up a single finger. "I grew up in a small town in Iowa where my father was worshiped as the local deity because he was the first person in Harris to ever make it big, so I spent the first twenty-six years of my life being compared to him and failing to live up to the legacy of Big Aaron Cross."

She frowned—as if trying to see if there was some shred of a lie mixed in with the truth as he raised a second finger and continued. "Everyone hunted where I grew up. I killed my first deer when I was seven and went on to compete in sharpshooter competitions starting when I was twelve—and I won all but two."

Her brow furrowed further as she concentrated and he lifted a third finger. "I retired from football when I was twenty-six after I tore my ACL in the last game before the playoffs." She sucked in a breath—as if the idea of him in pain pained her. And something about the look in her eyes made him add one extra truth. The one he'd never told *anyone.* "But I could have come back. The doctors told me I could make a full recovery, but I didn't want to. I used that injury as my get out of jail free card." He spread his hands wide. "So? Which lie did I tell?"

She shook her head. "That's easy. You couldn't have come back. If you could have, you would have. You don't know how to give up."

She was wrong, but not about him. Somehow she was right about him and wrong about the lie. "Actually, I never fired a gun until I was recruited to work at Elite Protection."

The certainty fell off her face. "Seriously?"

He shrugged, as if it was nothing. As if giving up his entire football career had been a breeze. "Everyone thought I would do whatever it took to come back—and I did the rehab. But when it came time to play again, to run the combine and show my coaches that I was back up speed, I threw my tryout. I pretended my knee was hurting and I'd lost a step. And everyone was so sympathetic, so understanding. They'd all seen athletes try to come back and not have it—and the fact was I might not have had it even if I had given it my all, sometimes people just don't come back, but I didn't try. I didn't want to."

She blinked, studying him. "How is that possible? You seem so…driven."

"I know." He grinned. "That was why no one suspected I was faking. They couldn't imagine I wouldn't kill myself to win."

"So why didn't you?"

He shrugged, but he wasn't dismissing the question, just rolling his shoulders, trying to unknot the tension that had taken up residence there. "A lot of reasons. I'd spent my entire career—from the time I first started showing my speed in high school, all the way through college and into the pros—knowing that one bad hit could end it all. I'd had injuries—more injuries than I could count—but none of those moments where you're carted off the field on a stretcher and all your teammates are down on their knees with their helmets off praying you'll be able to walk again, let alone play—and thanking God that it isn't them. It's this ghost that hangs over you—the knowledge that it can all be gone in a blink, everything you've worked for your entire life vanishing like that." He snapped his fingers. "And when it finally happened, after the pain and the shock, I realized there was something else underneath it—relief. The other shoe had finally dropped. I didn't have to wait for it anymore. Everyone rallied around me during the months in recovery and rehab—so determined to keep my spirits up, telling me that I could do it, I could get my life back—and I realized I wasn't sure I wanted it back."

"Why not?" she asked, hanging on his words.

"I'd been told my entire life that I owed it to myself to use my talent. That I owed it to my father's memory, to my town, to my mother, to my coaches. I'd bought into the idea that my life had one path—football. I dropped out of college for the draft—because of course I would. Nothing mattered more than playing in the NFL. But when my ACL was shredded, I started seriously thinking about what I would do if I *couldn't* play ball anymore. And I had no fucking idea, but it sounded *amazing*." He grimaced. "Sorry. Language."

"I don't care if you swear. I've heard the words before."

"My mom hates it when I swear." At the thought of his mother—of the Lie—his smile dimmed. "I'd always been told who I was—Little Aaron. Big Aaron's kid. Big Aaron's legacy. But when I got injured, for the first time I had to think about who I would be if that wasn't who I was anymore. It was...*freeing*."

"Do you ever regret it? Not going back?"

"Sometimes." He couldn't believe he'd admitted that to her, but Bree somehow knew exactly which questions to ask to make him want to tell her everything. "I wish I could say no, that I never looked back, but that's bullshit." He grimaced, propping his forearms on his knees. "I don't really watch football anymore. Every time I do, I see a play and I think *I can do it better*. Which might be bullshit. I think I could have come back. That I could have been just as fast, just as lethal on the field, but I'll never know for sure and sometimes that competitive instinct rises up and I want to prove that I can. Still, that injury, it was like a giant flashing neon exit sign had popped up in my life and if I didn't take it I might never get another chance." He shook his head, looking up and meeting her eyes. "I've never admitted that to anyone."

Her eyes went wide. "Really?"

"Not even Tank—Julian Tancreado. My friend who got me the job at EP." He snorted. "Hell, not even my mother. She would not have understood."

"Wow." A flush rose to her cheeks and her eyes shuttered.

She was such a contradiction—impulsive and shy by turns, bold and hesitant, and just so real. There was something about her, something about this place. He wanted to know *everything* about her.

"Your turn."

THE DECOY BRIDE

* * * * *

Oh shit.

He'd told her something real. And now she felt like she owed him the same, but the idea of revealing herself to this man was suddenly terrifying. "I..."

"Two truths and a lie," he reminded her. "Anything you want."

She opened her mouth, probably looking like a gaping fish, but the pressure to open up to him was making her choke. Why did they have to get to know one another anyway? But he'd been so honest, she felt like he deserved nothing less from her—even if the idea of exposing her truth to this man scared her shitless. She wasn't usually afraid to be herself—she was who she was and the rest of the world could take it or leave it—but something about the fact that it was *him*—his approval mattered. Even if she didn't want it to. Even if she told herself he was just some dumb jock.

He was so much more than that. Somewhere in the last few days he'd started to matter in a way that made her incredibly nervous.

Two truths and a lie.

She swallowed and held up a single finger. "I dropped out of college and moved to Venice to try to make it as an artist when I was nineteen—and I've been struggling ever since." That was true enough. She held up a second finger, reaching for something he wouldn't believe. "I was a cheerleader in high school." His eyebrows flew up, but he didn't interrupt. "Full on pom-poms and ponytails. And I was *good*. High kicks, splits, you name it." Cross grinned, clearly trying to restrain his reaction as Bree flicked up a third finger and tried to come up with a lie—somehow that was much harder than the truths had been. What was she supposed to lie about? "I'm an amazing painter. I win competitions—"

"You already told me you don't paint."

She grimaced. Okay, yeah, she had said that. So she needed a better lie. "Okay...my best friend thinks I date too much and I should swear off men for the foreseeable future." At his look, she narrowed her eyes. "You told me one you'd already told me too."

"But you didn't know if all the details were true. You realize you kind of already gave away which one of those was a lie?"

"Fine." She glared at him, bracing for his follow-up questions. She shouldn't have asked so many; she'd opened the door for him to do the same. Now she wished she could retract all her curiosity and pretend it had never happened.

"You were really a cheerleader?"

"Just freshman year," she admitted. "My mom really wanted me to fit in—and I did. It took me a while to realize that playing the part of the popular girl made me feel like I was putting on a show." She grimaced. "And here I am again. Putting on a show as the popular girl."

"Or helping her, depending on how you look at it. What kind of artist are you?" he asked and she tried not to squirm.

"Photography and mixed media."

"But no painting."

"No." She scrunched her nose. "I'm not a painter."

He considered her across the distance between them. "There's a story there."

How did he know that? How did he see through her so easily? She almost said *let's talk about how bangable I told my BFF you are instead*—but that felt like cowardice. He'd told her about this huge turning point moment in his life—but he'd come out the other side stronger.

Proud of who he was. She...well. She hadn't.

Bree swallowed. "Yeah. There's a story."

How did she get here? Sitting in the theatre room telling him the defining stories of her life? How did this man, this typical jock fratboy man, slip so easily past years of defenses?

But then she met his eyes—burnt umber and amber and so damn accepting, as if there was nothing she could say that would make him turn away from her, and suddenly she was talking.

"My parents are not artistic." She grimaced—talk about an understatement. "They insisted that if they were going to pay for school, I was going to get a practical, bankable degree. My mom was pushing for accounting, while my father was convinced I would make an excellent teacher—and both of them thought it was adorable when I talked about my art, as long as I knew that couldn't be my career. Elementary school art teacher was about as close as we ever got to agreeing on my future."

Cross nodded, but didn't speak, his gaze on her steady and dark.

"I was undeclared, but there were a few art classes for non-majors and I took all of them my freshman year, telling my parents I needed the elective requirements anyway. There was this one...a beginning painting for non-majors class. It was everything." She sighed, the memory of how she'd felt all those years ago incredibly vivid. "The professor was this energetic, charismatic man who wore paint-splattered Sketchers and jeans and told us to call him Billy and talked about how everyone had art in their soul. I *worshipped* him." She swallowed thickly. "His class was the first time I really thought about trying to be an artist for real. He was so encouraging. I remember this group project at the end of freshman year where he told me he could tell I really loved to paint, that he could *see* my passion—and I thought that meant I was talented. I actually thought he was telling me to become an artist. Then sophomore year came."

She cringed at the memory. "I loved my art classes. I didn't want to have to fill my schedule with things I didn't care about. I was ready to defy my parents and declare as an art major. I planned to figure out some way to pay my tuition myself, because I knew I was meant to be an artist. On some fundamental level, I knew that was who I was. But there were all kinds of forms to fill out and I didn't have the chance to declare before fall semester, so I wasn't technically eligible for some of the major-only art classes. I couldn't fit the Painting for Non-Majors class that I'd taken freshman year into my schedule again, so I registered for one of Billy's just-for-majors advanced painting courses." She was looking at Cross, but no longer seeing him, seeing only that studio, the easels in rows. "It was the first week of classes and I hadn't realized how tight my schedule was. I had to run from one side of campus to the other to get to my painting class on time and by the time I got there it was already starting so I grabbed a space and set up. I had all my materials. I was so ready. So excited to be there with the real artists. Not just the dabblers from the non-major class. These were my people. I felt like it was happening, I was finally becoming the person I was meant to be." Stupid, *stupid* girl.

"But then when class was breaking up, Billy asked me to come see him in his office." She shook her head at the memory. At her incredible naiveté. "I thought he was going to advise me to declare as an art major.

Maybe offer to be my advisor."

She'd been so incredibly wrong.

Not everyone has what it takes. You can't just decide to be an artist.

"Did he do something?" Cross asked, his expression dark—and she was so deep in the story it took her a moment to realize what he meant. The professor inviting the young student to his office. She hadn't even thought of that.

Bree shook her head. "He told me I was presumptuous," she said, the words low.

"What?" Cross frowned, visibly confused.

"He said I'd disrespected him by assuming I could join the class without his prior permission." She shook her head ruefully. "Billy always said everyone was an artist—that we all had it inside us—but that was in the non-major class. He didn't really mean it. He was *angry* at me for presuming to think I could be a painter. I would hold the *real* artists back, he told me. I didn't have the training. I didn't have the technique. I didn't belong." She grimaced, quoting, "'*You can't just decide to be an artist. That isn't how this works, Bree. Not everyone has it.*'"

"Ouch."

She laughed without humor. "Yeah. I was destroyed." God, it had killed her. She'd been so sure and then the rug had been yanked out from under her. "It was embarrassing—sitting there in his office and I couldn't stop crying. I told him I couldn't fit the non-major class into my schedule and he suggested photography." She would never forget it. The patronizing tone. The consolation prize. "*Anyone can take a picture.* That's what he said. And I'd never felt so worthless in my life. But I did take the photography class. And I was good at it. But nothing felt the same."

School. Her dreams. She'd been broken. Feeling like she would never be good enough.

"It wasn't just that I didn't want to paint anymore. I didn't want to be there. It felt like the soul had gone right out of me—so when an art dealer I met online said I should come out to LA for a show because my photos showed real talent, I jumped at it. And when he turned out to be a scam artist who just wanted to sleep with me and steal my rights and claim my work as his own, it kind of felt like a fitting end to the whole saga. Except I loved LA. I loved Venice. I met some artists selling their work on the beach and they were everything I wanted to be. They were *doing* it. It felt right. So I stayed. And my friends told me I was good, that I shouldn't give up, that I should keep learning—but from life not from classes, because art professors were sanctimonious assholes who were just bitter because they hadn't been able to make it as artists themselves. At least that's what they said. And that's what I did. I stayed and I learned and I worked. But now..."

"Now?" he prompted.

She looked at him and for the first time since she'd started her story she saw him again—and the reality of this moment in her life sank in. "What if I never make it? What if I really don't have what it takes to have a career as an artist? Did I just waste the last ten years of my life?"

"No." His denial came without hesitation. "You were chasing a dream. That's never wasted."

"Even if you fail?"

"Especially if you fail." He sounded so certain.

She eyed him skeptically. "Especially? How's that work?"

"You had to keep going without the validation of success. That takes a ton of bravery."

"Or stupidity."

"Bravery," he insisted. "I'm serious. I couldn't do it."

"Fail? I believe that."

"*Try*," he said. "Let myself do something I'm not one hundred percent positive I can master. I don't do anything unless I know I can be the best—which means sometimes I watch opportunities pass me by." He grimaced. "There's a job opening at my company. A junior partner position. More administrative, less time in the field—Candy put my name in for it. The bodyguard who's with Maggie? She thinks I can do it."

"And you don't?"

"No. I do. I think I'd be great at it, but I don't...I don't try for things I'm not sure of and there are too many reasons my boss would pick someone else. I don't know how to fail."

She snorted. "You should take a page out of my book. I'm *amazing* at it. Years of practice."

"You can't be an artist without putting yourself out there, though."

"I thought athletes had to overcome all sorts of adversity and try-outs and stuff."

"Yeah, but I felt like I could control all that. If I trained the hardest, if I made sure I was the best, there was never any risk. The only failure I felt like I couldn't control was my divorce."

Divorce. She didn't know why she was so shocked—maybe because she'd been making out with him and that felt like a pretty big thing not to know about someone who'd had his hands on your ass. He'd said he was married to his work—and never mentioned that he used to be married to someone else.

"You were married?"

CHAPTER NINETEEN

He hadn't realized he hadn't told her. It felt like Bree knew everything there was to know about him now, but from the shocked expression on her face, he'd failed to mention his ex.

"It was over a long time ago," he explained. "Pretty much as soon as it became apparent I wasn't going to make a triumphant comeback to the NFL. We got engaged right before I got drafted and divorced as soon as I could no longer provide her with the football wife life she wanted."

"Ouch."

He shrugged. "We're both better off. I'm better at being single. Though my coworkers and their wives seem to find that hard to believe. There's been a marriage epidemic at Elite Protection in the last few years and now they've all become matchmakers."

She made a face. "As if we have to be paired off to be complete. My best friend is exactly the same way. She just got married and the happy hormones have clouded her brain and she can't seem to stop insisting that I need to date more."

"Exactly," he agreed. "I'm perfectly happy on my own. And I'm sure as hell happier than I was when I was married."

"You don't think you'll ever do it again?"

"Honestly?" He shook his head. "I doubt it. I don't think I'm wired that way. I mean, I love women, don't get me wrong, and I'm not a player. I'm not just looking to get laid, but that forever love bullshit—I haven't seen a lot of examples of that working out." He cocked his head. "What about you? Why don't you like to date?"

At any other time it might have been a strange thing to ask, but the last few minutes seemed to have broken down all the rules around what was and wasn't safe to say.

"I don't know." Bree shrugged. "I guess I always felt like I was waiting to be successful first." She bit her lip, twisting a loose thread on the ottoman. "Every time I go on a date and the guy asks what I do and I say I'm an artist and then they ask what I *really* do for a living since I couldn't possibly be making a living that way...I guess I just wanted to be able to say this is who I really am, that it was my only job—and once I could say that then the right person would magically appear. Like once I'd made it as an artist I would be worthy or something. Which I know is silly, but that's why I don't date."

"You *are* an artist, you know. Even if you aren't making a living yet."

She rolled her eyes. "Says the man who's never seen my work."

"I see you. I see the way you see the world."

* * * * *

Bree blinked, startled.

It was a strangely erotic statement. That he saw her. And he saw the artist in her. She shivered in spite of herself and looked away from the man seated across from her, forcing her gaze away from the arm porn he was displaying with his forearms braced on his knees.

He was too dangerous. Too sexy by half and there he was telling her the one thing she'd always wanted to hear. She couldn't let herself get swept away by the words.

"We'll see," she said to the wall. "When this is over, if I haven't screwed up again and I actually come away with the money, I'll have bought myself a couple years to try to make it. After that..."

"You had no way of knowing Kaydee would take that picture," he argued, defending her, and she looked back at him. "I didn't know and it's my job to be aware of my surroundings."

"We still shouldn't have done it." Even if she couldn't quite bring herself to regret it.

"True," he agreed. "But we're still doing what we were sent here to do. Creating a distraction. We definitely have the attention of the press now."

She snorted. "That we do."

They'd been getting reports all day from the hotel's security desk. About photographers being caught on the property and did Maggie want the hotel to press trespassing charges on her behalf? It was surreal.

"I kind of thought she was overreacting," Bree admitted. "When Maggie first talked to me about using me as a wedding decoy. I thought the entire plan sounded like something out of a movie with a particularly thin plot, but now I can see why she wanted me here. I can't imagine the kind of scrutiny she lives with every day—millions of people obsessing over who she's kissing and why."

"It's a crazy world," Cross agreed.

"Do you think they'll make it?" Bree asked. "Maggie and Demarco? I mean, they barely know each other and they can't hide out forever. Once they come back, their lives are going to be under constant examination. It would be one thing if she were marrying someone who wasn't famous in his own right, but Demarco Whitten?"

Cross shrugged. "I can see the appeal."

"Athletes stick together?"

He shook his head. "He's probably the first person she's met in a decade whom she was sure wasn't using her."

Bree blinked. She hadn't thought of it that way. All she'd seen was the emotion. The impetuous, emotional, I-always-get-what-I-want-when-I-want-it actress marrying a man she'd only known for a few weeks. She'd dismissed Maggie's perspective.

"When you're as famous as Maggie Tate—and as rich," Cross added, "it can feel like everyone in your life wants something from you. That they're only there because they want to use you to get what they need. My wife was like that. She was good at hiding it, but she tied herself to me because she liked me well enough and thought I had a chance to make it to the pros. I liked her because she wasn't from Iowa and she didn't know who my father was, but she knew my stats better than I did. We met in college, but she majored in being supportive of my career. She conditioned me to think of her as the one who had stuck by me in college when my schedule was ridiculous, so I would be the asshole if I didn't stick by her when things started going well. Of course I didn't see any of that until the door was hitting her ass on the way out of our marriage."

"She used you."

"Oh yeah. And I knew it on some level the entire time, even if it wasn't obvious until the end. Like this hum, you know? Always in the background? And Maggie has that too. Probably louder than mine since she's a much bigger star. Even when she's dating other famous actors, that's no guarantee they don't want to use her to raise their capital. But with Demarco—he's already a multi-millionaire in his own right, so he's not after her money. His contracts aren't based on popularity—at least not solely on popularity. His stats matter the most. Being with Maggie might get him an extra endorsement deal or two, but the bulk of his life is something she can't help with—other than to cheer him from the sidelines. She knows he isn't using her. Not the way most people do. So yeah, I'm not surprised she fell for him so fast. That's intoxicating shit."

"You really think they'll make it?" Bree asked softly. She'd never been the type to believe in fairy tales, but she wanted that for Maggie, wanted the starlet to find someone who made her feel like she was valuable, just for herself.

Cross shrugged. "Who can say? I'm not really the love-conquers-all type," he said, echoing her thoughts, "but after all we're doing to give them a clean start, I hope they work."

She met his eyes and a moment of understanding passed between them, seeming to stretch and tighten in the air around them. His brown eyes were so soft beneath their fringe of blond lashes.

The door opened and Bree jumped in guilty reflex as Mel's head popped through the opening, followed by her entire body when she saw them. "There you are."

She looked back and forth between them, as if puzzled to find them in the same place—though maybe she was more puzzled that they weren't sitting closer to one another after the make-out session that had been caught on candid camera the other night.

"What's going on? Anything I need to know about?"

Bree blushed as Cross shook his head. "Just talking. What's up?"

Mel's face brightened. "I have an idea."

CHAPTER TWENTY

Mel's idea, it turned out, was a romantic evening for Maggie and Cross. Candlelit dinner on the patio. A moonlight walk along the private beach, hand-in-hand, gazing sappily at one another.

Apparently the early reaction to the Cross kiss and the break-up statement was...less than favorable toward Maggie.

Which Mel volubly cursed herself for not predicting when they'd agreed on the damage control plan yesterday. The "DeMaggie" fans had been vicious in the wake of the press release, labeling her a cheater and a whore, and Mel wanted to shift the narrative. Maggie was in love. This was emotional, not sexual—or at least not entirely sexual. And Demarco had broken up with her before anything happened with Cross.

Mel was still working out how to make that last part public in a subtle way—and working up a script for Bree's next conversation with Kaydee—but holding hands on a moonlit beach was supposed to help with the rest of it.

Mel had insisted on full Maggie hair and make-up—which involved nearly two hours and four different applications before it met with Mel's approval. It was, apparently, vitally important that she *glow*. Mel repeatedly encouraged her to be glowing with happiness. Bliss, if she could manage it.

So as Bree slipped her hand into Cross's for the moonlit walk portion of the performance, she tried to do her best to project bliss...and to hide her discomfort.

They weren't just playing at being lovers anymore. They were playing at love. And her stomach churned nervously at the thought. She'd never actually been in love before, but after their afternoon in the media room everything already felt different. More intimate somehow. As if knowing him better made all of this more real. And that was dangerous thinking.

Especially when he squeezed her hand and she looked up, getting lost in his eyes, and needed to remind herself this was an act.

"You know those reality dating shows?" she blurted. "*The Bachelor* and *Marrying Mister Perfect* and *Shot at Love* and all those?"

Cross's brows arched. "I haven't seen them, if that's what you're asking, but I know they exist. My boss's sister went on *Marrying Mister Perfect* and we did security for one of their dream wedding special things."

"One of my old roommates used to be obsessed with those shows—" She froze. Shit. She was supposed to be careful about what she said. Had Maggie had roommates? Before she hit it big in Hollywood? Oh well. She'd already put her foot in it now and it would only make it look suspicious if she backpedaled, so she pressed on. "Anyway, all of these shows have these dream dates. Elaborate set ups with candlelight and champagne and string quartets. Formulaic just-add-water-for-romance dates—and every time someone faced the camera and talked about how romantic it was, I wanted to scoff because it felt so forced. So fake."

And here they were, walking barefoot on a beach in

the moonlight, holding hands and trying to convince the cameras they couldn't see that this was romantic. Just add water.

"They've been doing those shows for years," Cross murmured. "You'd think they would have figured out that romance isn't about where you are or what you're doing." He glanced down at her. "It's about the person you're with."

Her heart thudded hard at the words. They came to the edge of the water and he stopped, turning to face her at the edge of the waves. Then he slid his hands into her hair, cupping her head and she gazed up at him, helpless to look away even if she had wanted to as his eyes grew heavy-lidded and his lips lowered slowly to hers.

The kiss was sweet. Delicate. Lazy and delicious, with none of the balcony's heat and frantic rush. His mouth moved slowly over hers, as if they had nothing but time—and she grew more and more uneasy the longer the slow, sensual kiss lasted. Fast and frantic was easy. It was safe. It was getting swept away and losing your head. This...this was something else and she wasn't braced for it.

She went up on her toes, gripping his shoulders for balance and his hands moved from cradling her head to steadying her, strong and solid on the back of her ribcage—but they didn't roam. He didn't touch her anywhere else and she had to fight the urge to squirm in his hold. They were selling romance. Not sex, damn it.

A wave hit her ankles, flowing over her feet, the water shockingly cold, and Bree gasped in surprise, breaking the kiss to look down at their feet where the water foamed over them. When she looked up, Cross was smiling down at her, his expression warm and gentle—as if he was perfectly satisfied by the tepid, romantic kiss. As if his thoughts hadn't been pinging around like a ball in a pin-ball machine the entire time they were locking lips. Or maybe that was just her. Maybe she was the only one who couldn't do intimate and romantic without feeling like there were a thousand ants crawling beneath her skin.

"The water's colder than I thought it would be," she said, in the lamest possible conversational gambit.

Cross moved without missing a beat, bending and scooping her up. She yelped in surprise, clutching at his shoulders, but she needn't have worried he might drop her. His hold was steady, one strong arm supporting her back, the other curled beneath her knees. Cold water dripped from her feet to the sand below, but suddenly she wasn't so worried about the chill. Even with the cool breeze off the water, it was warm in Cross's arms.

His face was closer to hers in this position and she could see his eyes, even in the low light, the darkness of them. "You have the prettiest eyes," she murmured, the words out before she realized she was going to say them.

"Not half as gorgeous as yours," he replied in a husky tone that did things to her insides, lowering his head to take her lips again.

It should have been the world's most romantic moment—but once again her brain refused to shut up, whispering that they weren't her eyes. They were Maggie's eyes. And he wasn't cradling her in his arms because he wanted to. He was doing it because he needed to sell the romance with Maggie.

Bree lifted one hand to his cheek, feeling his stubble against her palm, and leaned into the kiss, trying to lose herself in it, trying to quiet the whispers in her head, but

Cross broke the kiss at the first brush of tongue, giving her a wry smile. "Maybe we should take this inside..."

She knew that was the plan, but she still gave him a look of playful disappointment. "What? You don't want to try the *From Here to Eternity* thing in the waves?"

"As much fun as sand in unmentionable places sounds...No. I'd rather have your undivided attention without having to worry about the tide coming in and drowning us both."

She smiled. "Fair enough."

She shifted in his arms, expecting him to set her back on her feet, but Cross apparently wasn't done with his knight-in-shining-armor routine. He turned and started back up the beach toward the villa with her still cradled in his arms.

"I can walk, you know," she reminded him wryly.

"I know," he agreed. "But I'll take any excuse to have you in my arms. Humor me."

She knew the words were for show and not for her, but Bree shivered at the impact of them nonetheless. The man knew how to turn on the romance when he wanted to. "How did your ex-wife let you slip away?"

The words popped out without conscious direction—she really needed to stop doing that—and she realized what a mistake they were when Cross's shoulders tensed beneath her hands. They were at the edge of the patio now and he lowered her to her feet on the pavers.

He might have set her down anyway, but it sure felt like he was setting her away from him after what she'd said. Bree cringed, reaching for him, trying to apologize with her touch. "Cross...I didn't think—"

She never thought, it seemed.

"It's okay," he assured her, gently sliding his hands into her hair again. "We're okay."

He lowered his head to hers for another too-gentle kiss. So respectful. So freaking *chaste*.

And the doubts whispering in her head only got louder. She went on her toes, trying to pull him closer, trying to turn up the heat, but he smiled against her mouth and lifted his head, his hands stroking through her hair. Soothing. When the last thing she wanted was to be soothed.

"Do you want me?" she blurted and his eyebrows flew up, his eyes glittering with amusement.

"That's a question?" He stole a quick kiss off her lips—so fast she didn't even have time to hunger for more—and then he turned her toward the door, tucking her under his arm. "Come on. Let's go in."

She looped her arm around his firm waist, walking at his side and trying to look adoring and lovey-dovey—and not like her favorite toy was being taken away from her. Because as soon as they got inside, out of the view of the windows, they would separate. No more kissing, no more cuddling, no more pretty words unless Kaydee was within earshot.

And that was for the best. She just needed to keep reminding herself of that—though it was getting harder and harder to think of why. Why not let herself fall for Cross? Why not enjoy this moment with him for as long as it lasted? What was the harm really?

But then they were inside, the drapes were drawn behind them, and Cross released her, giving her a smile that was friendly, but lacked the extra heat, the *intent* of his earlier smiles, reminding her that this was a show and she needed to stick to her part.

They moved together up the stairs and he paused for a moment outside her door.

"Good night," he mouthed, not even whispering

since they'd become so paranoid about bugs—and she didn't have the guts to stop him from walking away. To tell him that it didn't have to be good night. To invite him into her room and see where things went.

He was already down the hall, slipping silently into his own room and Bree swore softly to herself before opening the door and retreating into the master suite.

She'd left her cell phone in here, set to silent mode, and it flashed from the bedside table, beckoning her back to reality. Seeing a missed call from Andi, she retreated into the master bath and turned on the shower, letting the water disguise the sound as she sank down on the plush vanity stool and dialed Andi's number.

"Bree?"

"Hey. I just saw I missed a call from you."

Andi practically spoke over her. "Yes or no. Does your top secret Maggie assignment involve making out with Hot Cross on a tropical island? Because I just saw some photos..."

"You can't tell anyone!" She clenched the edge of the vanity. "We're running interference for Maggie and Demarco. *No one* can know I'm here."

"I knew it!" Andi crowed triumphantly. "Ty told me I was going down a crazy conspiracy theory rabbit hole—"

"Andi, he can't tell anyone!" Heartthrob Ty Walker's Twitter account was legend. One stray tweet and it would all be over.

"He won't breathe a word," Andi assured her—and Bree melted with relief. "You think we've never wanted to get away from the limelight? Why do you think we're getting married in Clement?"

"Because you love it and that's where you fell in love?"

"Well, yeah," Andi admitted. "But also because we want to get hitched *without* the media circus. Trust me. We get it. We won't do anything to spoil it for you or for Maggie. But why didn't you tell me Hot Cross was a famous football player?"

Something hard settled in the pit of her stomach. "Is he famous?"

"Apparently he went to UCLA around the same time Ty did—they didn't know each other or anything, but Ty knew who he was. Total hotshot. I mean, he's no Demarco Whitten, but he's not far off."

Deep down, she'd suspected as much. She may not know much about football, but the way Cross talked, part of her had known that he was out of her league. "I never heard him talk about playing football before this week. He was always just the bodyguard."

Andi snorted. "*Just* the bodyguard. You should hear the way they talk about him. Like he's one step down from Jesus. And if he hadn't torn his ACL he would have totally gotten that walking-on-water thing down too. No one is even remotely surprised that a guy like Aaron Cross Junior would be dating Maggie Tate." The short pause was loaded with questions, but Andi only asked, "So what's going on with you two?"

Bree felt herself blushing, grateful Andi couldn't see her. "Nothing. It's just for the cameras."

"Really?" Andi's tone was somehow both disappointed and relieved. "Because when I saw that kiss…"

"It was just a stupid impulse thing," Bree said, knowing Andi knew her well enough to accept the *I-wasn't-thinking* excuse. "I was going stir crazy and we were trying to get media attention here so it stayed off Maggie and Demarco…" Though not like that. She'd almost ruined everything. "But it's not...we're not actually *together*."

"Oh. Well. That's probably for the best," Andi said.

Bree wilted. *Was it?*

"I was all for him when he was Hot Cross the Sexy Bodyguard," Andi chattered, "but Aaron Cross Junior former NFL hero...I don't know. You hear all those stories about football guys taking one too many hits to the head and snapping and taking it out on their girlfriends."

"Cross isn't like that. He couldn't be less like that."

"I'm sure he doesn't seem that way, but how well do you really know him?"

After this afternoon? Pretty damn well.

But Bree kept her mouth shut. She didn't want to talk about Cross or the feelings she should or should not be having for him.

Though a few minutes later, when she ended the call with Andi, she couldn't help typing his name into Google on her phone. The most recent stories were all about him and Maggie—the pictures seemingly everywhere.

And of all the comments—good, bad and *very* ugly—about the idea of Maggie and Cross together, not one of them said he wasn't famous enough for her. No one thought Cross was out of his league with Maggie Tate...which just went to show how far out of her league Bree was with him.

Good thing she didn't have feelings for the man.

CHAPTER TWENTY-ONE

"Remember, act naturally."

Bree resisted the urge to roll her eyes at Mel's oh-so-helpful advice. She felt like a secret agent with her phone's earbud in one ear and Maggie's manager spying from the next room. Kaydee would be down any minute to take Cecil for his morning walk and Mel had set the scene so instead the perky assistant would find "Maggie" crying into her mimosa over all the untrue rumors about her and Demarco.

Mel had prepped Bree on what she was supposed to say, but hadn't trusted her to improvise if Kaydee questioned her, so Bree now had to pretend to be listening to music on her phone when Mel was really feeding her lines through her earbud.

They'd officially graduated to espionage, but she still had to sell it, so instead of focusing on how ridiculous she felt, she concentrated instead on what Maggie must feel when she saw how people were bashing her in the media. She managed to dredge up a few tears and blinked to encourage them as she heard footsteps on the stairs.

Moments later, Kaydee strolled into the living room and found her curled up on the couch, sniffling and blinking back tears as she cuddled Cecil.

"Maggie?" Kaydee asked. "Are you all right?"

THE DECOY BRIDE

Bree jerked as if startled and pretended to hit pause on her phone. "I'm sorry. I was just listening to our song. Have you heard the things people are saying? As if I'm a horrible person for cheating on Demarco when *he's* the one who broke up with *me* before I even *thought* about kissing Cross."

Kaydee's dark eyes were unnervingly shrewd as she frowned. "You have to understand why they would think that. You were still wearing the engagement ring in the pictures."

"Because I was hoping he would come to his senses!" Bree exclaimed. "I kept hoping that if I just kept planning the wedding as if nothing was wrong, then nothing would be wrong, but *he* broke *my* heart and now everyone is acting like he's the wounded party."

"Well, you do have a history."

"What's that supposed to mean?" Mel said in her ear a fraction of a second before Bree snapped, "What's that supposed to mean?"

"Oh come on, Maggie. You know you aren't entirely innocent here."

Lost, Bree waited for some hint from Mel what the hell Kaydee was getting at, but the manager was silent. "Demarco was the one who wanted to call off the wedding," she insisted, reverting to the script Mel had given her—but then the manager herself stalked into the room.

"Kaydee. You're fired."

"What?" The girl laughed. "No, I'm not."

"I assure you, you are. Cross will supervise you as you pack your things and then escort you to the other side of the island where you can make your own arrangements to get back to LA."

"Are you going to let her talk to me like that?"

Kaydee asked Bree, her manner worryingly confident.

Before Bree could speak, Mel cut in, her voice harsh. "I have confirmation that you are the one who leaked that photo of Maggie and Cross," she said, as if they hadn't had that confirmation for days.

"You can't just fire me," Kaydee sputtered.

"I definitely can," Mel assured her. "I can also sue you for violating your NDA, so if I were you I'd contact a lawyer as soon as you get back."

"And how am I supposed to get back? It's like insanely expensive to fly here."

"I suggest you take it up with your friends at the *Fame Game*, since they are the reason you are no longer employed."

Kaydee turned to Bree, her eyes flashing with barely contained anger. "Are you sure you want to let her do this?"

The threat behind the words was vague—and all the more unsettling for it. But again, before she could speak, Mel stepped between them.

"Cross is waiting in your room to help you pack."

"Fine," Kaydee snapped. "You can clean up your own dog shit."

She stalked out of the room and Bree held her breath until she was gone, her muscles still tense. "Were you planning to fire her all along?" she asked Mel.

The taller woman sank down onto the sofa opposite her, her expression more troubled than Bree had ever seen it. "Not necessarily. But I was ready for the possibility. I should have fired her weeks ago. As soon as I started to suspect she had some knowledge she was dangling over Maggie. A little tattling to the tabloids is one thing, but blackmail is something else entirely."

"Aren't you worried she'll tell whatever she knows?"

"She'll be too busy defending herself. We already have the papers drawn up to sue her for violating the NDA as soon as she steps foot back in LA. If she has half a brain—or decent legal counsel—she'll know to keep her mouth shut."

"And if she doesn't?"

"Then we come after her for blackmail, and everything else I can throw at her. No one threatens Maggie."

That was a nice thought, but Maggie hadn't wanted Kaydee fired—and Bree wasn't sure how she'd react to Mel's initiative.

"So now what?" she asked.

"Now we keep playing the game. Do you have your bikini?"

* * * * *

When Cross stepped onto the pool deck and saw Bree already stretched out in a bikini, her bare skin glistening in the sun as she waited for him to begin another day of Mission: Romance, he had to wonder if Mel was deliberately trying to give him the worst case of blue balls in the history of mankind or if that was just a natural side effect of spending so much time with Bree and not being able to touch her for real. He'd taken matters into his own hands in the shower more than once over the last couple days, but his body still reacted to the sight of her, waking up and sending blood rushing south.

"Good morning," he said, bending to brush a light kiss across her lips—because that's what he would do if they were a couple. And because he wanted to.

He'd gotten addicted to the taste of her over the last few days, and it was getting harder and harder to draw that line between what he was doing for the cameras and what he was doing because he wanted to.

He'd escorted Kaydee off the premises—which didn't mean there weren't still cameras aimed their way, but it *felt* more private now, and his palms itched to touch her as he stretched out on the lounger beside her—face down so she wouldn't see the way his body was getting ready for business at the sight of her.

He'd done his morning sweep of the property, finding no listening devices, and checked in with the resort's security, getting their logs of people they'd stopped from approaching the villa—which brought him to the second portion of his working day: laying around doing nothing and pretending to be in love.

If the last week had taught him anything, it was that neither he nor Bree were particularly suited for a life of idle luxury. They both chafed under the restraints of inactivity—as she'd proven with that first kiss. The memory of it, the taste of her wildness through her lips, made even more blood rush south in his body and Cross cursed under his breath.

The pool wasn't heated. Maybe it was cold enough this morning to douse his lust.

He stood, keeping his back to Bree so she wouldn't see his affliction, and dove into the water. *Fuck, that's cold.* It closed around him, an icy shock to the system and he shuddered at the impact—but at least he had something to think about other than Bree.

He surfaced, sucking in air through his teeth and swimming over to the shallow end where the sun would have had more of a chance to warm the water this morning. A man-made waterfall poured into the pool and he swam beneath it, letting the falling water drown out his thoughts.

He didn't know how long he sat like that, eyes closed beneath the fall of water, before a pair of hands slid over his chest—startling him so much he jerked, taking in a mouthful of water and choking as he opened his eyes to find Bree sleek and slick in front of him.

"Sorry," she said, yanking back her hands as he coughed and choked, moving away from the fall of water. "I didn't mean to startle you."

"It's fine," he assured her, taking a seat on an underwater ledge. "I didn't hear you get in." Because he'd been trying to drown out the thought of her. Trying *not* to picture her diving into the water and rising out of it like something from one of his teenage fantasies.

She treaded water in front of him, her strokes smooth and easy—someone who had swum all her life. Cross was a decent enough swimmer, but she looked natural in the water. Like a freaking nymph.

She glided over to him, perching sideways on his lap, though the buoyancy of the water made her seem like she was barely there, like she could float away at any moment. Her hands came to his chest and he wasn't sure whether she was using him for balance or teasing him when her palms smoothed slowly over his pecs. She leaned in, until her mouth was a whisper away from his ear, until he could feel the movement of her lips against his lobe when she whispered, "Is this okay?"

Okay? Try fucking incendiary.

Instead of answering her, he turned his head, catching her lips and kissing her hard enough to make her fingers flex on his chest. They were supposed to be sweet. They were supposed to be romantic.

But he was only human.

The slight taste of salt clung to her lips from the saltwater pool and he wrapped his arms around her, kissing the taste from her lips, slipping his tongue between them where hers was there to meet it. She pressed closer to him, the water facilitating her movements as she slid higher up his lap until her thigh pressed against his erection. She whimpered eagerly into his mouth—and the sound about killed him.

Only the primitive, instinctual knowledge that she wasn't safe here—exposed to the prying eyes of those fucking telephoto lenses—kept him from stripping her bare and doing every wicked thing he could think of to her. Instead he shifted, trying to get his feet under him, trying to get his arms around her—and that part was easy, but he stumbled when he tried to stand, lurching against the side of the pool with her cradled high in his arms, never breaking the kiss, because to stop kissing her would be to stop breathing—but fuck, he was going to kill them both if he didn't watch where the hell he was going. He finally, reluctantly, broke the kiss, but he didn't loosen his hold.

He waded through the shallow end toward the steps, cradling her sleek, slippery body against his chest. But she wasn't sitting passively in his arms. She nibbled his earlobe and he lurched to the side, barely keeping his balance in the water as he carried her out of the pool. Her hands were everywhere, stroking his neck, his shoulders, nails lightly grazing his nipples until he growled, "Behave."

She chuckled darkly in response.

The house wasn't far—but the shelter of the cabana was closer. There was a daybed in the cabana. And heavy burlap flaps that closed out prying eyes. That was all he needed.

He laid her down on the daybed, releasing her only long enough to go back to the door and untie the ribbons holding the flaps open. One of them knotted when he tried to undo it and he swore, all thumbs as he wrestled with the ties until it finally fell closed and he turned back to the bed, his mouth watering at what he saw.

She was exquisite.

Lying on the bed. Propped on her elbows. The long, lean line of her legs. The curve of her hip. The dip of her clavicle. *Fuck*, she was gorgeous.

He froze, staring at her, and reminded himself that it had been a performance to this point. But now they were alone and he needed to know that she was still with him. "Do you want me to stop?" he asked, his voice gravel rough.

She bit her lower lip, the even white teeth pressing into the plump, kiss-reddened pad—and then she shook her head. "No."

Thank you, Jesus.

He didn't remember getting to the bed. He just knew he was suddenly against her, over her, and the press of her skin against his made him lose his mind a little. What was left of it.

Then he was kissing her again, heavy and deep, his tongue thrusting into her mouth, fucking her mouth, losing his fucking mind in her. He stroked a hand down her side and her skin was cool from the water. He warmed it with his touch. His body felt like a furnace right now and he needed to share his heat with her. She shivered as he caressed her stomach, gliding up over her ribcage to cup her breast. He growled at the layers of fabric and padding between his hand and her skin, breaking the kiss to press his mouth beneath her jaw, breathing in the scent of her. Saltwater and jasmine and need.

"Cross," she gasped, her hand gripping his wrist

where he cradled her breast. "Wait."

He groaned, that single word *killing* him, but he forced himself to go still above her. *Shit shit shit shit shit.* "Wait?" His voice barely sounded human, guttural and dark.

She took a deep breath, the movement lifting her chest into his hand, but he managed not to twitch a single muscle. He lifted his head, gazing down into eyes that were suddenly disconcertingly uncertain. She wet her lips. "I just..."

God could not be this cruel. She could not be stopping him. *Why* was she stopping him? Seconds ago she'd been breathless. Her legs had been moving restlessly against his. She'd told him not to stop and then...what had happened? What had he done?

He removed his hand from her breast, rocking to his side next to her, and she released his wrist. Had he gone too fast? Pushed too much? He was always pushing...

"What kind of car do you drive?"

"*What?*" He'd been prepared for a lot of questions. That wasn't one of them. She wanted to know what kind of car he drove before she slept with him? That didn't sound like Bree.

"I just...I realized I didn't know and I thought..."

Okay. So it was some kind of weird getting-to-know-you thing. Like *don't sleep with someone if you don't know their last name.* Fine. He could handle that. "A Lexus. I drive a Lexus LC."

Her expression fell, her body shifting subtly away from his. "I was afraid you were going to say that."

He frowned. "Why were you afraid? What does that have to do with anything?"

But she was already moving away. Slipping off the bed, reaching for a towel and wrapping it around herself, hiding her body from him.

"Br—" He barely stopped himself from saying her name out loud. They were still outside. They could still be overheard. "Maggie. Come on."

She shook her head, padding toward the door. "I'm sorry."

She was gone before he could argue. Not that he could have argued. He had no idea what the fuck he would have argued with because he didn't know *what had happened*. One second everything had been good and then—*bam*. Blue balls.

"*Fuck*," Cross swore, long and loud, not caring who heard him. He could not catch a fucking break.

CHAPTER TWENTY-TWO

It had been his car. The one in the driveway that day Maggie had summoned her. He'd dropped by to talk about security. She didn't know why she hadn't put the pieces together before, but when he'd been kissed her just now she'd heard Andi's voice in her head, talking about how he was the kind of guy who would date women like Maggie Tate and all of a sudden it had clicked.

He drove that sex-on-a-stick Lexus. And she'd thought it might be Maggie's car. He *belonged* with Maggie. Not with some art chick who couldn't even pay her rent without pretending to be someone else.

He'd grabbed her breast—Maggie's breast, with all that ridiculous padding—and reality had hit her like a lightning bolt.

She might not know anything about sports, but she knew how the world worked and the perfect people like Cross didn't end up with the also-rans like her. She hadn't really realized what a big deal he was before—he'd just been Cross. Hot Cross, her harmless crush. But now he was the hot-shot Lexus-driving NFL-star who could get someone like Maggie Tate if he wanted.

A guy like that would never want anything real with her.

Not that she wanted something real. She'd just

wanted him.

This morning, when he'd appeared, shirtless and mouthwatering, on the pool deck, her heart had stuttered in her chest and she'd lost track of the world for a moment. The kiss he'd given her had been perfectly nice—a light good morning hello between lovers—but she'd wanted so much more. She hadn't wanted respectable and sweet. She'd wanted heat and insanity. And she'd already proven she had the world's worst impulse control.

When he'd splashed into the pool and swum over to tip his head back beneath the waterfall, she'd given in to her urge to join him—and to see if she could push him past respectability and back into heat.

And it had worked. God, had it ever worked. Until she remembered that he was lightyears out of her league.

She'd run. Into the blinding sun that bathed the pool deck and then up the steps and across the patio into the air-conditioned chill of the house, shivering as she raced up the stairs and into her room. She crossed the master suite to the balcony and the view, waiting for the beauty to soothe her, but nothing did.

She still felt that restless whisper beneath her skin, the need that never entirely went away when he was near. If only he'd been a bad kisser. If only every time he touched her didn't set a new bar for how good she could feel. If he was going to be out of reach, he could at least do her the courtesy of being undesirable. But no. He had to be fantasy-perfect in every way.

A guy like that would never want a girl like her. When they seemed to, it was a lie. Every time.

Except he did. Right now, she was sure he did. Even if it was only temporary.

She didn't trust easily, even if she was impulsive, but she *trusted* him.

Hell, maybe the fact that he was out of her league was for the best. She'd be able to keep her heart out of the equation if she remembered how different their worlds were. Just a fling. A pure fling. Her one chance to be with a man like him.

No. Not a man like him. Her one chance to be with *him*. With Cross. Strong and gorgeous and protective and so freaking *hot* she nearly singed her fingertips touching him.

What the hell was she doing, walking away? This was the fantasy. Where was her freaking impulsiveness *now*?

She spun away from the view, the towel falling forgotten to the balcony floor as she moved quickly through the master suite, picking up confidence and speed as she went until she was nearly running when she hit the stairs down to the pool deck.

He wasn't in the cabana any more. He stood beside the lounge chair where she'd left her sunglasses and her book earlier when she dove into the pool. He turned at the sound of her bare feet slapping against the tile and his eyes widened when he saw her. She didn't know what he saw on her face, but he braced his feet and barely swayed when she collided with him, her arms around his neck, momentum carrying her body against his chest and her feet lifting off the ground as his arms closed around her.

Her mouth crashed against his and Cross didn't miss a beat, kissing her back hungrily—but before she could do more than moan her relief, he lifted his head, breaking the kiss, his eyes searching her, dark and questioning.

"What happened?" he asked, still holding her against him, off the ground.

She shook her head. "I was stupid."

His eyebrows arched. "And you're smart now."

"Very smart," she promised, putting a hand to the back of his neck and pulling him toward her for a kiss that seared her nerve endings. He didn't resist—thank God—his mouth moving persuasively over hers.

As if she needed persuading.

He lifted her higher and she wrapped her legs around his waist, locking her ankles at his back and grinding her core against the hard ridge of his erection. Fuck, that felt good. Especially when he closed one of his large hands on her ass and pressed her tight against him, making them both groan.

"You're driving me crazy," he murmured against her lips, and she felt the fizzy urge to laugh, the idea that she could make him wild going straight to her head like champagne bubbles.

They were moving—and she realized belatedly he was taking her back to the cabana and shook her head. "The bedroom," she whispered in his ear, feeling him shudder at her breath against his neck. He changed course without a word, every step sending shivering friction through her body where it was pressed against his. The chill of the air-conditioning hit them as they entered the house, but it only made the heat of his skin against her that much more of an erotic contrast. Hot against cold. Softness against strength.

And God, he was strong.

Up another flight of stairs, not even breathing hard. She thought he would put her down as soon as he kicked the door shut behind them in the master suite, but he showed no signs of tiring, one arm beneath her ass and the other banded behind her back, both holding her as if he could do it all day. She'd always been on the scrawny side, but she wasn't a feather and the idea that he could manhandle her however he wanted was really fucking hot.

He kissed her, his tongue thrusting against hers in a sensual echo of the act she wanted, the need building in her blood until she was squirming against him, anything to get him to stop screwing around and strip her bare and *do this already*.

She might have said that out loud because he stopped nuzzling her neck and chuckled darkly, crossing to the bed in three long strides.

She unhooked her ankles and let her legs drop down so she was kneeling on the bed, facing him as he stood beside it, and his hands, no longer occupied with holding her against him, skimmed up the sides of her body.

Her uncertainties tried to creep in when his palms brushed the outer curves of the wonder-bikini. Maggie had generous Cs and Bree's barely-Bs were bound to disappoint if he was expecting Maggie Tate's legendary curves. But Cross caught her lips, distracting her, and his hands moved quickly over the complicated network of strings at her back, releasing the bikini top so quickly she could only gasp against his lips as he flung it away. She barely had a second to worry that he would be disappointed by her flatness before he was leaning back, his hands sliding up her ribcage until the curves of her breasts rested on the webbing of each hand and he groaned, his eyes locked on what he held, dark pupils glazed with a look that couldn't have been further from disappointment.

He looked dazed. Wild. She arched into his hands,

encouraged by the gleam in his eyes as he bent and set his mouth to one nipple. A high cry burst from her lips, startled by the sharp jolt of sensation as his mouth tugged hard on the sensitive peak. She'd always been sensitive, but this. "*Fuck.*"

He growled against her skin, turning his head, his stubble a delicious coarseness against her skin as he turned his attention to the other nipple, the fingers of one hand pinching the one he'd just left until she squirmed, gripping his shoulders to stay upright. Heat pooled between her legs—and he hadn't even touched her there yet. His teeth gently tweaked one taut nipple and she gasped, "*Aaron,*" making him smile against her.

He could smile all he wanted, as long as he didn't stop.

His mouth still on her breast, he pressed her back until her shoulder blades hit the comforter and she threw her head back—which exposed her neck and he wasted no time taking advantage, nibbling there while she twisted beneath him, her aching nipples pressed to his chest, trying to figure out how the hell she could get back in control of the situation.

She'd never been like this. Mindless. Consumed.

Sex was fun, sure, and it felt good, but this...this was tension and heat and *need* and if something didn't give soon she was going to *die*. His weight left her suddenly and she released a helpless keen of disappointment—too far gone to even be embarrassed by the sound—but then his hands were gripping her bikini bottoms and she was lifting her hips to help him slide them down faster.

She thought he'd be back—his weight over her, pressing into her—and she widened her thighs to make room for him between them, but it wasn't his hips she felt there. His palms pressed her thighs apart and then his mouth was on her center and she was arching, keening, digging her heels into the coverlet, trying to find purchase, trying to find anything to hold on to as he hooked her knee over his shoulder, sliding a finger into her, curving it high and—

Bree screamed, losing her mind. His tongue. His fucking tongue. He kept licking. Didn't let her come down, pushed her so high she was shuddering, jerking, crying, making sounds she'd never heard, let alone made, and Cross—one hand in her, one on her waist, holding her steady—he shattered the world.

She covered her face with both arms, when he finally let her come down, breathing rough, ragged breaths as she felt the bed move and knew what he was doing. She heard the bedside drawer open. The tear of foil. The sound of wet fabric hitting the floor as his board shorts came off.

She lowered her arms, not wanting to miss the view.

He stood at the edge of the bed, sliding the condom on, his eyes on her. They looked almost black and her breathing, which had begun to calm, went ragged again. God, he was gorgeous. Art in motion. An erotic masterpiece. He crawled over her, bracing himself on straight arms above her, and her aesthetic appreciation was abruptly lost in something more carnal.

"Are you ready?" he growled—and she almost laughed.

Are you kidding? she wanted to say. *I'm a puddle of orgasms and need.* But she didn't have words. She didn't have anything but touch and taste and smell and God, the sight of him. Her legs were splayed bonelessly wide and he lowered himself slowly between them—but with his eyes at a level with hers, her core lined up with his stomach, not his lean, sexy hips and the delicious hard-on there.

He kissed her, and it was one of those kisses—slow and deliberate and drugging. Where was the frantic thrust of tongues? The fierce rush of heat? How was he not losing his mind? He hadn't just come his brains out all over the bed more times than he could count. That was her. Why wasn't he *hurrying*?

But this man, with his exquisite control, the kiss seemed to say, knew exactly what he wanted, and he wasn't going to rush.

Muscles loose with release began to tighten again with anticipation. He reached between them, one finger unerringly finding her clit and tapping her there, sending shivers of aftershocks through her body, as if she hadn't already literally come until she couldn't come anymore.

Cross rumbled something close to her ear, but she couldn't process words anymore because he was hooking his elbow under one of her knees, opening her to him, his cock pressing into her, slow and thick and God, she was losing her mind, losing her sense, losing everything but the feel of him filling her, stretching her—*fuck*, he was big and then his other arm was beneath her other knee and he was lifting her pelvis off the bed, angling her up, on his knees, sliding deep and *damn*, the man was strong, and she couldn't move, couldn't do anything but reach over her head and brace herself against the headboard as he lifted her just a little higher and *fuck* what did he hit in there because her toes were curling again and she was gasping, couldn't breathe, coming so hard she couldn't breathe, and he was thrusting, harder now, the slap of flesh loud in the room and every time he hilted he hit *that spot* and her vision went black again. Every. Fucking. Time. Then he was swearing, the stream of blue words feral and raw as he yanked out, wrenching a cry from her and flipped her so fast she was bracing her hands on the bed before she saw him move, her knees still held off the mattress by his strong hands, lifting her as he drove back into her and—Christ, it was better. How could it be better? She pushed back against him, deaf to the sounds she was making and he slammed into her one last time, stiffening, holding her tight against him as he came and she screamed along with him, losing her mind all over again.

CHAPTER TWENTY-THREE

No one had ever told her sex could be like that.

She'd seen porn, seen the writhing and the screaming and the moaning, but she'd always sort of thought that was the male fantasy, not the female reality. The sex she'd had had always been nice, but sort of...tame before. And now...

Damn.

She lay on the bed afterward, staring at the ceiling and trying to come to terms with the fact that she'd just had porn star sex. Cross was breathing hard at her side, flat on his back, staring up at the tray ceiling as well.

It was a nice ceiling. The resort had spared no expense. And at least if she kept staring at it she didn't have to look at the man who could turn her into a shameless porn star with one touch.

She felt like every muscle in her body had been wrung out. No wonder people said sex burned calories. She wasn't sure it had, the way she'd done it before, but this...yeah. That had been aerobic.

"Wow," she said, when she was able to form words.

Cross chuckled, low and smug—and she decided she would allow him smug. The man deserved smug. He was *good* at that. Fucking *fantastic* at that.

Which was amazing. As long as she didn't think about how he'd gotten to be so fantastic. He'd obviously had a lot of practice. A lot more than she had, anyway. Not that it was a competition. But still, her insecurities flickered to life at the reminder that this man had probably spent his entire football career from high school to the NFL tripping over women who wanted nothing more than to help him hone his sexual skills.

The large body at her side moved before she could fall completely down that particular mental rabbit hole. He rolled away from her, disposing of the condom, and then he was back, reaching for her, curling his body around hers, and it felt so good she forgot to be insecure.

"You called me Aaron," he rumbled.

"What?" She couldn't see his face, tucked with her back to his front, but his voice was teasing in her ear.

"There was a lot of Oh God, Aaron. Harder, Aaron."

"Oh." She blushed and ducked her head, unsure whether she should be embarrassed by the things she'd said—though he seemed to like it—or apologizing because she knew he preferred to be called Cross. "Sorry about that."

"No. I kind of like it when you say it," he murmured against her neck, and she relaxed against him, nestling closer. "Can I ask you something?"

"Are you shy now?" she asked incredulously.

He chuckled, a low dark sound. "Not hardly." He shifted her in his arms until she was on her back and he was on his side beside her, looking into her eyes as he asked her, "Why did it matter what I drove?"

"What?" she asked vaguely, hoping to play dumb, though she could feel herself blushing and his direct gaze offered no escape. She squirmed, looking away.

"Hey. Look at me."

She sighed gustily and admitted, "I thought it was her car. When I first saw it at the house." She made a face, mouthing *Maggie's* in a belated attempt to keep from being overheard saying something she shouldn't. She lowered her voice to a whisper. "You drive the same kind of car that a movie star would drive. It's credible that a guy like you would be with someone like Maggie Tate." She shrugged then, hoping the negligent gesture would make the words she was about to say seem worldly and indifferent. "It doesn't make sense for you to be with me."

His eyes darkened. "That's bullshit."

"Is it?"

"I *am* with you," he said.

But for how long? She didn't say it. They hadn't talked about the future. They hadn't talked about more. And he'd already been very clear that he wasn't looking for marriage and kids and happily ever afters.

Not that she was looking for that, necessarily, but it made her nervous, not knowing what the future held. Not knowing how long this would last.

So when he bent his head to kiss her, she twined her arms around his neck and pressed up into the kiss, enjoying the moment, because at any second the moment could be gone.

* * * * *

In the short time he'd known her, Cross had learned that he and Bree were *very* different. She was artistic and impulsive where he was disciplined and driven, but in one crucial way, it turned out they were perfectly matched: neither of them had an off switch.

If he had two modes—push and push harder—Bree only had one—go. His exes had often bitched that he was relentless, not knowing when to stop, but Bree gave him a run for his money.

He should have known an affair with her would burn hot and fast. After that first time in the suite, things between them didn't so much progress as erupt. She became his instant obsession—and the feeling appeared to be mutual.

It was surprisingly *nice* being with someone who matched him in that way. Who even outpaced him. When they physically exhausted one another the voice inside him that always pushed him quieted for a moment and they could just *be*. Or at least he could. Even after he'd made her come screaming, she often still had energy, her body restless against his. Over the next couple days, he started taking it as personal victory when he could not only make her lose her senses, but also make her come until she was boneless and immobile.

She was a challenge—and he loved to win.

Neither of them had any balance, any perspective, but that was perfect for a fling. This thing between them wasn't built to last, but it felt fucking incredible in the moment. He couldn't remember ever being with someone he'd sexually clicked with so completely.

They still played the lovey dovey couple in public for Mel's agenda, but in private it was raw heat and sexual marathons.

Not that it was all sex. On the second morning after their affair started, he pulled her into the theatre room—yes, because he wanted to have sex without worrying that he would say her real name when he came—but also because he just wanted to talk to her when they didn't have to worry about anyone hearing her being her non-Maggie self.

Bree was restless, already pacing in the space when he closed the door behind them, the shower sex they'd had earlier apparently doing nothing to calm her down.

"Aren't they married by now?" she demanded. "I know the days are all sort of blurring together, but it's been over a week and they wanted a two week honeymoon, didn't they? Shouldn't the deed be done by now?"

"Apparently there have been a couple delays." He relayed what he'd learned from Candy's latest report. "It's been raining and Maggie wants the photos to be perfect so they're waiting for a clear day."

Bree snorted. "They should have come here and we could have gone to Fiji."

He couldn't argue with that. The weather had been perfection. The tropical storm that had threatened a few days ago had swung north of them, far enough away that they hadn't gotten even a drop of rain. Cross had almost been disappointed when he'd seen the forecast, because a hurricane might have scared away some of the photographers. Or at least given him an excuse to keep "Maggie" holed up in bed all week. Not that he needed an excuse.

"I just wish they would get to it already," Bree declared. "Not that it matters since we'll still be here distracting from their honeymoon, but at least I'd feel like we'd accomplished something when they're actually married, you know?"

He stepped into the path of her pacing, wrapping his arms around her. "You're terrible at patience, you know that?" She made a face and he dropped a quick kiss on her mouth to distract her. "You should take it as a compliment that they aren't in any hurry. They're enjoying being hidden away and confident that we can keep the heat off them."

She grimaced, leaning back in his hold even as she

gripped his biceps. "I didn't think I would be so bad at keeping this up, being her for three weeks."

"Are you kidding? You're amazing at it." He pulled her closer, bending to bite her lower lip. "You're just wilder than she is. Not as domesticated."

Her smile glinted, wicked and inviting. "You going to tame me?"

He grinned, lowering his head. "Why would I want to do that? The wildness is the best part."

Half an hour later, he lay on the oversized couch with Bree sprawled across him, his thoughts tracking back to their earlier conversation as she began to fidget. He stroked a hand through her hair—silken, blonde, and so exactly like Maggie's. But now when he looked at her he couldn't help but see the differences.

He brushed his thumb over the line of her upper lip, the shape of it ever so slightly different than Maggie's, though he'd never noticed it before they came to the island. "You look so different to me now."

"That's because you've seen me without the Wonderbra," she said, grinning. "Once someone points out the differences it's easy."

"Yeah?"

She held up a finger. "I'm shorter than she is." Another finger joined the first. "Flatter than she is. Blonder—though don't tell her I told you that. Younger—though *definitely* don't tell her I told you that. And our eyes are different colors."

Cross frowned, staring into the turquoise eyes that had been staring back at him all week. "What color are your eyes?"

"Sort of grey-ish hazel. Nothing special."

"Will you show me?"

She opened her mouth, but no words came out. At

length, she frowned. "Why?"

Because I want to see the real you.

He frowned, unsure where that thought had come from—and careful not to say it aloud. He didn't want to give her the wrong impression about what this was. They'd been careful so far to keep things easy. Undefined.

He liked what they had now, liked being with her, but he wasn't looking for forever. Better if they kept things casual. Better if he didn't have to worry about disappointing her.

"No reason," he said finally. "Just curious."

Mollified, she rolled off him, reaching for the clothes that littered the floor. "Has Mel said anything to you about how Campaign True Love is going?"

"Not yet," he admitted, catching the boxer-briefs she tossed at him and standing to put them on. "Though honestly I don't see the point of trying to convince the world Maggie is in love with me when she's going to reveal she was with Demarco the whole time."

"Mel is protective of Maggie," Bree commented. "I don't think she likes anyone saying anything bad about her, even if it is just temporary."

A high pitched whine sounded outside the theatre room door and Bree padded across the room in her panties and padded sports bra, opening the door a crack to let Cecil slip inside. "Were you lonely, furball?" she asked the dog, crouching down to scratch his ears before he darted over to Cross to receive the same tribute.

Cross's cell phone rang from his pants pocket as he was bending to pet the dog and Cecil yipped, scampering over to growl at his jeans until Cross fished out the phone. His mother's name showed on the screen and he frowned, sending the call to voicemail and tossing the phone on the couch.

"Still dodging calls?"

He grimaced, shoving his feet into his jeans and yanking them up around his hips. "I don't know what to say to her."

"Have you heard her side of the story?"

"I don't need to hear her side." He yanked his shirt over his head more forcefully than necessary, nearly tearing the fabric.

"You sure about that?"

"Positive."

"What about your sister? Have you contacted her?"

"I will," he promised—promising himself as much as her. "I just need a little more time to process it. I'm not ready for it to be real."

"I think I'd be impatient to know the truth."

"I am, but I also…I don't know. I don't want to call her when I'm still mad at him. My father…" He shook his head—simultaneously having no words and too many words to describe the man. "He was a great football player. I've seen the tapes. He was fast—faster than me, as no one would ever let me forget because sportscasters love nothing more than to compare our 40 times. He played wide receiver and I played defense—cornerback, the position that defends against the wide receiver and I can't count the number of times commentators speculated that my father would have been able to get separation if I'd been covering him. I have been compared to him my entire life, in every way we can be compared to each other. When we made varsity in high school. When we became starters. How high we were drafted. But that shit? That's fine. That didn't bother me. I may have spent my entire career chasing a ghost, but I could handle it. He *was* better than me. That's fine. But the fucking lying? The rewriting history? Why do that? Why lie?" He shook his head, frustrated.

"You could ask her that," Bree commented, the words light, without judgment.

"I'm not ready to talk to her. Because I know if I do right now all I'll do is yell about the lies. About the freaking illusion that is my father."

He expected her to argue, but she merely nodded. "I hate illusions too."

"Yeah?"

"Zander? The guy who lured me out to LA under false pretenses? I think the worst part wasn't that he'd lied or wanted to use me—it was that I'd built my entire self-worth around the idea that what he'd said was true and suddenly everything I wanted to believe about myself had no foundation. I felt so stupid for believing him. Stupid for wanting to. I couldn't stop feeling like I should have known, like it was my own fault I'd been taken in. So I spent the next decade trying to peel back all the illusion in Hollywood. I hate the fake shit we all project to try to look like we're successful or happy or like we don't have regrets, because who do those lies help? They don't help the people who are struggling and feeling like they're faking it and any second someone is going to discover the truth. We aren't perfect, but we all try to sell the lie. Facebook perfect. It didn't help me when I came out here on the promise of a stranger. And it didn't help you—giving you this unrealistic ideal that you spent your entire life trying to live up to. As if you have to be perfect to be worthy. So, I get why you would be mad at the illusions—I get why you would be pissed at your mom. But she's still your mom. And this is still your sister. And if I found out I had a sibling, I wouldn't wait around before calling her. Because you never know when someone needs you."

Cross stared at her, this woman who somehow sliced straight to the heart of everything. Straight to the heart of him.

"I'll call her," he promised.

Bree smiled. "Good."

She turned away, finishing dressing, and he watched her, his thoughts swirling.

He couldn't help but admire her, and envy her that knowledge she had, down to her core, beneath all the restless energy that rustled over the surface. She *knew*. Who she was. What she wanted. She had a calling. A purpose. A certainty that she was doing something she was meant to do with her life.

The way she felt about her art came through every time she spoke about it. It was who she was. But more than that, it gave her meaning. Something Cross wasn't sure he'd ever had, even when he was doing what he thought he was best at—playing ball. It had never meant anything. He'd never been happy. Not the way she was, completely separate from the idea of success. He didn't know how to be happy like that. He only knew how to win.

How did she do that? How did she cut right down to the heart of everything and see?

He crossed the distance between them in two strides, taking her face in his hands. "You're amazing. You know that?"

"Do I?" she whispered, looking up at him, and he didn't have the words to explain. He didn't have words at all. So he explained the only way he could.

He kissed her. Admiring her. Worshiping her.

...and eventually shooing Cecil out of the room and

taking her against the wall because he had no restraint where she was concerned. No limits.

But also no illusions.

With Bree, there were no illusions. Only them.

CHAPTER TWENTY-FOUR

Bree's life sometimes felt like a history of mistakes. A catalogue of them. But none had ever made her feel quite as nervous as this.

She rushed in. She always rushed in. She let the energy beneath her skin drive her to recklessness. She always had.

It had made her parents crazy when she was a toddler—running straight toward danger, giggling all the way—and then it had made them even crazier as a teen—breaking curfew and then sneaking out when she was grounded for breaking curfew. It wasn't that she didn't like rules. It wasn't that she didn't understand what they were there for. And it wasn't that she didn't try to be good. She knew when she was disappointing people and she *hated* disappointing them, but all of her efforts to be the good daughter, the good *anything*, always ended the same way. With restlessness. Impulse. And a mistake.

This thing with Cross. This wild, reckless, wonderful thing with Cross. It was a mistake. She could feel it. But she couldn't regret it. Yet.

Though she was freaking out a little.

Okay, a lot.

The sex was great. No complaints there. They had the kind of physical connection she'd always thought was exaggerated for effect in books and movies—but that was no guarantee this was never going to hurt.

She was falling for him. And scared shitless that it was a one way street.

She still hadn't shown him her real eyes. She knew he wanted to see her without the contacts. He'd seen her without the make-up designed to make her look like Maggie—but that was in the shower, when he'd had other things distracting him.

If she took away that last layer of illusion between them. If he really *saw* her, and then walked away...She was afraid she wouldn't be able to handle the rejection. That was the thing when you stripped away the illusions. You couldn't pretend they weren't rejecting *you*.

They knew one another now. She knew he wanted to be seen as more than a jock. He'd confessed to her, during their quiet talks in between bouts of sexual Olympics, that he'd decided to continue the interview process for the new job at EP, though he still worried that all anyone saw when they looked at him was the dumb jock.

She'd been forced to realize how important his job was to him—which she'd known before, but now she knew why and that knowledge drove home with more force why he felt he needed to succeed. This was his identity. His self. And if it came down to a choice between her and his work, she was pretty sure she knew which one of them would lose—and it wouldn't be the respect he'd been striving for his entire life.

A couple days after that moment in the theatre room when everything started to feel too real, Cross was called away in the middle of the afternoon to deal with some security issue.

It had started to rain that morning—apparently mirroring the weather in Fiji where Maggie and Demarco were still unmarried at last report—and the weather made Bree restless and edgy. At least she chose to believe it was the weather. She refused to consider it might be anything else. Like Cross's absence. Or her own nerves that she was falling for a man who would never love her back.

She descended the stairs, looking for distraction, and found Mel in the living room with Cecil Two—and, surprisingly, three of the maids who took care of the house, who had been incredibly stealthy up to now.

"Maggie!" Mel smiled, standing up as Cecil scampered over to yip at her ankles until she scratched him. "Just the woman I was hoping to see. I have some scripts for you to look over—"

She knew that code. The "scripts" were really scene ideas Mel had drawn up for Bree and Cross to act out. Hyper-romantic set-ups designed to make it look like they were deeply in love. Forcing them to gaze soulfully into one another's eyes over moonlight, candlelight, any kind of romantic lighting Mel could find—

"No."

"Excuse me?" Mel asked, drawing herself up at the hard tone in Bree's voice. One of the maids went still in the doorway, but Bree didn't soften. She couldn't play anymore. She couldn't pretend. Not when the feelings were starting to feel entirely too real.

"I don't want to see any more of those scripts. I'm done. I need a break."

Mel blinked, visibly surprised to see her in diva mode—but she shouldn't have been. Bree should have been doing this all along. Maggie wasn't easy. She wasn't biddable. Bree had been too obedient. But she couldn't be obedient now.

She bent, scooping up Cecil, and plucked Mel's tablet off the end table next to the couch. "I'm taking a break," she announced, head high, and marched out of the room—straight to the fitness studio where the door sealed behind her with a satisfying click.

She could have gone to the theatre center, but her recent memories of that giant couch were too tied up in Cross right now. She wanted someplace she could be alone. Someplace she could be Bree.

Nudging an inflated exercise ball out of the corner, she sank down onto the mats in its place, tucking herself against the wall. Cecil wriggled in her arms to get comfortable, licking her chin with fast, frantic licks before tucking his little head against her neck, his weight warm against her chest.

She propped the tablet on her knees, flicking through the screens, knowing exactly what she was looking for.

Every day, Maggie's LA-based publicist had an assistant compile every media mention of the star into a single file—talk shows, internet articles, all of it—and emailed them to Maggie for her to look at or ignore at her discretion.

Bree huddled in the corner, and brought up the file, tapping the link to run the video feed. The screen lit, a familiar entertainment news anchor's face appearing.

"Tonight! Is it true love for Maggie Tate and her new squeeze, former-NFL heartthrob Aaron Cross? Or is this just a rebound from sexy baller Demarco Whitten? Our panel weighs in!" The clip cut instantly to the panel discussion and Bree found herself watching with bated breath as they began to argue about her relationship. Of the five panelists, it quickly became evident that there were two on the side of true love, two on the rebound sex train,

and one who thought it was pure down and dirty boot-knocking.

"*Look at the way he looks at her!*" Panelist Number Five exclaimed. "*That is lust, boys and girls. A textbook case. Whatever she might be feeling, he's just in it for the sex.*"

"*Are you kidding?*" Another panelist argued. "*Look at that intensity! Look at that focus! He's not just trying to figure out when he can get her naked again. He's listening to her.*"

"*A man can listen if he thinks he's about to get laid.*"

"*It's not about how he looks at her,*" another insisted. "*It's about how she looks at him. And she doesn't look at him like she looked at Demarco.*"

A photo popped up on the screen—one of the few pictures of Maggie and Demarco together, laughing together, Maggie ducking her head and flicking a gaze at him beneath her lashes. "*She's twitterpated,*" the panelist declared. "*But with this new guy...*"

Another picture replaced the first. Bree and Cross. On the beach. Holding hands. But she wasn't looking at him directly. Scared to look in his eyes—like gazing straight into the sun—

"*She's holding back!*" the panelist insisted. "*Total rebound. Mark my words, Maggie Tate is still in love with Demarco.*"

When that segment finished, the screen flickered and the argument continued on another network—different panel, same arguments, but different pictures. Bree's stomach clenched when this particular show flashed both pictures up as a split-screen. For a moment she panicked, sure someone would see the differences between her and Maggie, but they were too busy analyzing her sex life to notice the shape of her upper lip.

The third clip didn't focus so much on the love triangle aspect, taking more of a *Who is this Aaron Cross anyway?* angle—and asking whether the former football star was using her to try to reclaim his own fifteen minutes of fame. Her stomach—already clenched nervously—began to ache as she listened to the debate.

Especially when a photo of his first wife popped up on screen.

Gorgeous. Poised. Tall. With cleavage that made Maggie's look paltry. Her long blonde hair flowed over her shoulders. She looked like someone who belonged with a star athlete.

The commentators discussed his illustrious career. How he had been on his way to becoming a household name when an injury ended his career. How he could have written his own ticket as a broadcaster if he'd wanted to when he retired. How the world was Aaron Cross's oyster...

And every time they said his full name, *Aaron Cross*, as if they didn't know he liked to be called Cross. As if they didn't know *she* was the only one who got to call him Aaron and then only in bed...

The door opened and she looked up, tapping pause on the clip reel as Cross stepped into the fitness studio. "There you are. Mel said you seemed upset."

"Did she?" The words came out harsher than she expected and Cross's eyebrows slid upward.

"You okay?"

Cecil, belatedly realizing his best friend had arrived, began to wriggle in her arms, his tiny nails scratching the skin of her arms until she guided him to the floor so he could run to greet his hero. Cross bent to pet the dog, but his gaze stayed on Bree.

"I'm fine," she assured him, though she felt like ants

were crawling beneath her skin. "Just seeing what they're saying about us." She turned the tablet screen to show him—only realizing it was frozen on a picture of him with his wife when his expression went stony.

"I guess I should have expected them to dig up Lauren." He straightened, crossing the distance between them to sink down on a weight bench across from her, Cecil wriggling for attention at his feet. He absently reached down to stroke the dog. "What's she saying?"

"They're just talking about her at this point."

He nodded. "Probably only a matter of time before they get her in there for an interview. She's probably negotiating for the best deal. She always knew how to work things to her advantage."

Bree studied his face, the tension in his jaw as he continued to frown at the tablet screen. She turned it away, pressing a button to make it go black and setting it in her lap. "Are you worried about what she's going to say?"

"I haven't talked to her in years, but I'm sure whatever she says will make her look good. That was always one of her skills."

"I'm sorry your personal life is getting sucked into this."

He grimaced, shrugging. "Maybe she'll keep pushing for more money until the truth comes out and everyone realizes I'm not really with Maggie. There would be a sort of poetic justice in that, if she stalled to extort them and it bit her on the ass."

"Does she have a story worth extortion?"

"Maybe. I don't pretend to understand what's newsworthy these days. Though if she's honest she can't say that much against me. Just that I never loved her, probably. And that she doesn't think I'm capable of loving another human being."

"Cross...You know that isn't true." Bree rose awkwardly to her knees and crawled across the distance separating them, stopping when she was kneeling in front of him, with Cecil excitedly trying to climb her to get closer to Cross. She placed her hands on his knees, staring up into his eyes.

"It's not false. I didn't really love her. I was just good at going through the motions." He continued to look in her eyes, but the look in his made her stomach clench. "I like you, Bree. I really like you, and I don't want to hurt you. But you should know, I'm not that guy. I don't do love. I don't know if I can." He grimaced. "I'm sure some psychotherapist would have all kinds of theories about my mom and my dad and all my baggage about love and marriage, but the truth was I married Lauren because I thought I was supposed to. I wanted to be the good guy who was faithful and stuck by the girl who stuck by him. We'd been dating all through college and I always liked her, but the hearts and flowers, *this is the one* bullshit that everyone writes songs and sappy love poems about? That wasn't us. That isn't me. I don't have that in me."

"But you took care of her. You take care of people. That's how you show you love them."

"I took care of her because she was my responsibility, because I thought I should. That isn't love."

She shook her head. "Maybe love isn't the same for everyone. Maybe you shouldn't judge how you feel based on how other people tell you it's supposed to feel."

His eyes darkened. "I don't want you to get your hopes up—"

Hot, ugly embarrassment seared through her at his

words and she couldn't let him finish, pushing off his legs and standing, suddenly restless. "I'm not saying I want you to love me. This isn't about me. This is about you. You can love someone if you want to. You can do anything you want."

She stalked to the other side of the fitness center and back, pacing around the heavy equipment, her arms tight around her middle. He *could* do anything he wanted. That was Cross's whole schtick. Super achiever. The perfect human specimen. The kind of man who belonged with the Maggie Tates of the world.

Whereas she…

She was happiest with her life when she didn't have to hold it up against anyone else's standards of success. She had goals that gave her purpose. But when she looked at her life alongside his, she was embarrassed by the scale of it.

Her beat up old car—because she couldn't afford a new one. The apartment she couldn't really afford on her own. Her total lack of savings. Lack of a retirement plan. Lack of a job with a future or a 401(k).

She'd been working for a decade and all she had to show for it was a non-starter of an art career. Was it time to face reality? Was it time to think about what she could do with her life to be a contributing member of society and support herself like a grown up? Her life, her choices, they looked irresponsible alongside his. What would she bring to a relationship with a guy like him?

Don't get your hopes up.

"What are we doing?" she asked, her voice coming out sharper than she'd intended, almost shrill.

Cross frowned in confusion, still sitting on the weight bench, petting the damn dog. "What do you mean?"

Her nerves were tight. She didn't trust easily, but she

had trusted him from the beginning—and that scared the shit out of her. Suddenly everything felt too real and she was out there with her feelings exposed, all by herself in the cold and he was telling her not to get her hopes up. "The whole world thinks you're with Maggie Tate. And they believe it. You're that kind of guy."

He rolled his eyes. "I'm not any kind of guy."

"You aren't a millionaire?"

His cheekbones flushed, as if the talk of money embarrassed him. "I had a few good years."

"So you are. You're rich."

"What does it matter?" he argued, his eyes darkening. "It's not a competition."

"This from the man for whom everything is a competition?"

"What you do, without needing to win at it, knowing that it's meaningful—that matters. I admire that. I admire *your* success," he said.

But she wasn't successful. And the only reason he thought she was, the only reason he saw her as an equal was because he still saw Maggie when he looked at her. He saw this luxurious villa. He'd never seen her apartment. He saw the helicopter rides. He'd never seen her car. He didn't *see*. Not the starving artist. Only the movie star.

"That isn't me, that success. That's her. You still see her." All he had ever seen when he looked at her was Maggie.

"Don't be ridiculous," he snapped. "You're nothing like Maggie."

She flinched at the words, freezing in place at the rough tone. "You're right. I'm not."

But she'd gone and fallen in love with a man from Maggie's world. Who couldn't be farther from hers. A man who *didn't want her to get her hopes up.*

She was moving toward the door, fleeing before her brain even caught up with the impulse. "I think this was a mistake."

"Bree!" he called behind her, but she didn't stop. She didn't turn. She was already through the door, leaving him swearing behind her as it closed.

CHAPTER TWENTY-FIVE

Cross swore under his breath, collecting the tablet and trying to figure out what the hell had just happened. They were good this morning when he left her in bed. He'd been called away to do his job, but that had happened before and he'd never come back to this. What had changed?

He pulled up the video she'd been watching, resetting it to the beginning and studying it for some clue as to what could have upset her—but all he saw was that the plan was working. People were discussing the relationship, the possibility of love. People weren't calling Maggie names anymore. Mission accomplished.

So what the fuck was Bree's problem? What the hell had made her pick a fight with him? Because he'd felt that shift in the room. She'd been spoiling for a fight. Did she really think he couldn't see how different she was from Maggie? Did she honestly think she was just a place-filler for the movie star?

When he exited the fitness studio onto the main floor, the maids were gone—as was Mel who had directed him toward the fitness studio when he asked where Maggie was, warning him that she might not want company. Maybe he should have listened—and maybe he should give her time to cool off now—but instead he took the stairs up to the master suite two at a time.

He raised his fist to knock—with no idea what he was going to say when she answered, but he was good at figuring things out on the fly. He'd cross that bridge when he came to it. But before his knuckles could land on the wood, he heard her cell phone ring inside the bedroom and a breathless, "Andy? Hang on."

His hearing sharpened at the man's name—but all he heard was the interior bathroom door shutting and the sound of running water. Bree wanted privacy to talk to Andy. Whoever the hell that was.

Not that he was jealous. The strange man's name simply drove home the truth of how little he really knew about Bree's day to day life. Andy could be a coworker—an agent, a fellow artist, an art dealer.

Somehow in the last week and a half they'd gotten to know one another on a startlingly deep level, but the basic, everyday stuff had been skipped. It was disorienting. Making him feel like everything was more intense than it was. They were stuck on an island together, sharing the most intimate details of their lives with one another, but he didn't even know where she lived.

That was the illusion of this place. That he knew her. That what they were doing here would matter when they got home. But the truth was, for all this concentrated time together, it was like one of those reality shows Bree had talked about. A reality distortion filter where everything seemed more important than it was.

When they got back to the real world, his perspective would be back and the need to chase her down and make sure she knew he saw *her* and not Maggie wouldn't seem quite so urgent. Making sure everything was okay between them wouldn't feel like the most important thing in his life.

He just needed space and the reality of their day to day lives. Then he wouldn't need her like this.

* * * * *

"Andi? Are you still there?"

"I'm here. Are you okay?"

Bree sank down onto the vanity stool, staring blindly into the shower stall where steam was starting to rise from the water she'd cranked up to drown out the call. "I'm fine," she insisted, though she still felt raw from the conversation with Cross downstairs. "Why? What's happened?"

"Nothing, I just...Ty was telling me I was being ridiculous, but I saw this picture today on the cover of a tabloid of you and Cross and I just...I don't know. I wanted to call. You looked really...involved."

"I slept with him," she blurted out, the admission coming out of its own volition, but it felt so damn good to have someone she could talk to she couldn't regret the words, even when Andi groaned.

"Oh honey."

"I know. I know it was stupid. We come from totally different worlds and he's completely out of my league, but there's this thing between us, this connection, and I couldn't not do it."

Andi huffed. "Okay first off, that thing about him being out of your league is bullshit—"

"You were the one who was all worried because he was a hot shot NLF star!"

"Because they're conditioned to be violent and have brain injuries! Not because he was too good for you. If anyone is too good for anyone—"

"It's the failed artist who's never done anything with

her life?"

"Stop it. You're amazing," Andi snapped. "I would have fallen apart without you after my divorce. You put me back on my feet and let me heal and never stopped looking out for me. He should be so lucky as to have someone like you."

"He doesn't want someone like me." She grimaced, admitting, "He doesn't think he wants anyone."

She could hear Andi's frown. "What does that mean?"

Bree closed her eyes, trying to find the words to fit the fears that had been whispering in the back of her head all morning. "He doesn't think he's capable of love. He's...competitive. He doesn't like being vulnerable or feeling out of control..."

Andi groaned. "And there's no less controlled feeling than loving someone."

"He won't let himself," Bree said, the words settling, hard and true, against her sternum. "He always has to be the best—and if it comes down to a choice between me and his job, he will always take the job. He will always want success more than he wants me." *And I've fallen in love with him.*

She couldn't say the last words, but she knew Andi heard them when her next words were, "Is there anything I can do?"

"You're already doing it," Bree murmured. It felt good to talk to someone, even if there was no solution. "I guess I don't know whether I should retreat now or ride it out until it dies on its own."

"I know what I would do," Andi said, sympathy rich in her voice. "But then, I was always the one who ran away. You were the brave one."

"Was I?" she asked weakly.

"Honey. You moved to LA when you were nineteen with pennies in your pocket because you knew you were meant to be an artist. That's *brave*."

"Or foolish."

"It takes a lot of bravery to be foolish. You should tell that to your Cross."

"He isn't my Cross."

But he was her Aaron.

Andi didn't push it, that wasn't her style, and they got off the phone a few minutes later with Bree feeling lighter, but no closer to knowing what she wanted to do.

She turned off the water, her eyes itching from the steam, and she reached in the drawer for the contact case. She plucked out the contacts, dropping them into the saline and rubbing her eyelids at the relief.

Cross wanted to see her eyes. She still hadn't shown him their natural color, often forgetting to take the contacts out and sleeping in the uncomfortable things until she woke up with her eyes burning. Not that she'd been intentionally avoiding showing him her natural eye color, just that they had a tendency to get carried away and removing her contacts became a low priority.

Well. That. And she'd been avoiding showing him her natural eye color.

Her eyes weren't special, and part of her worried that as soon as he saw them he'd realize she wasn't special either.

But she could be brave.

Bree strode quickly out of the steam-filled bathroom before she could change her mind, through the master bedroom and onto the landing beyond. "Cross?"

She didn't know what she was going to say to him when she found him. She couldn't even remember what she'd said to him when they'd argued in the fitness studio, only those awful words: *Don't get your hopes up*.

Was that what she was doing? Getting her hopes up? Setting herself up for failure?

She ought to be used to it by now.

He wasn't in the outdoor living room or the pool deck. The fitness studio and the theatre room were both empty—and she was almost relieved because she would have had to be completely herself in either of those rooms and she wasn't sure she was ready for that. He wasn't on the beach or in any of the villa's public areas. Starting to wonder if he'd gone off on some security mission as he'd gotten in the habit of doing since the paparazzi arrived on the island, she headed upstairs to try one last place.

The door to his room was cracked open. She tapped on it and it swung soundlessly inward, revealing Cross sitting at the desk, his large body hunched forward over his laptop. He rocked back in his chair when the door opened, watching her, not smiling in greeting, waiting for her to set the tone—and she didn't know what to do. She didn't know what to say—so she went on instinct.

Crossing the room quickly, before she could lose her nerve, she climbed onto his lap, facing him, wedging her knees beside his hips in the rolling desk chair. "I'm sorry," she said—not even sure what she was apologizing for, just knowing that she needed to make it right. Whatever it was, this thing between them that was out of balance, she needed to balance it. She needed to fix it. She needed *him*. No matter how dangerous that was to her heart.

She followed the words with a kiss, framing his face with her hands, feeling his stubble against her palms as his arms closed around her—but the action was more automatic than impassioned and he was barely kissing her back.

When she broke the kiss, he was frowning, his eyes on his hands on her waist. "I'm not sure this is a good—"

No. She cut him off before he could get the words out, blocking them with another kiss, more aggressive this time, with tongue and arching her body against his and grinding closer, trying to make him lose his mind so he would forget the brush-off words she knew instinctively he'd been about to say. If she could just kiss him long enough, he would forget the distance he was trying to put between them. Their natural chemistry would kick in and he would devour her. If she could just kiss him long enough...

But he set her away, murmuring, "Sweetheart..." and gazing into her eyes, his own so sympathetic it made her chest ache—

He blinked, his gaze sharpening, hands coming up suddenly to frame her face as his spine straightened. He whispered, "Your eyes," and the vise in her chest squeezed even tighter as he studied them without the contacts, his expression slowly softening. "They're beautiful," he breathed. "*You're* beautiful."

The vise didn't loosen, if possible it tightened even more until she couldn't breathe at all as she held his gaze.

She felt like she was balancing on a high wire and any direction she stepped she could go plummeting back to earth—and she wanted to stay up in the heavens a little while longer. Even if at some point she would have to fall back to reality. She wanted to live in this moment when he was looking at her like she mattered. Like she was everything. Like she, *Bree*, was beautiful.

He kissed her, his lips gentle and sweet against hers,

and she closed her eyes against the flood of feeling pressing up in her chest. She held his shoulders for balance as the world seem to tilt slowly off its axis. His mouth moved over hers, more intent now, drawing her into the depths of him and she went willingly, boneless and helpless to resist him. She'd never be able to resist him. How could she want to?

He lifted her, carrying her to the bed without breaking the kiss. He laid her on her back on the coverlet and she sank into the softness of the comforter as his weight pressed her down. On and on he kissed her and she never wanted this moment to end, scared of the reality that would intrude when it did. But when he lifted his head, it wasn't to pull away. He brushed stray tendrils of hair away from her face, meeting her eyes, and shaking his head once—that movement as if in answer to some internal question she couldn't interpret—and then he was kissing her again.

Their sexual marathons weren't always fast and frantic, but there was always a momentum to them, a force of building need that drove them inexorably forward—but this. This was different. They weren't pushed by lust, thrown into the bonfire of need and consumed by it. This was a lure. A draw. A tether to something deep in her soul, pulling her down, pulling her toward him until she couldn't feel where he ended and she began.

Their clothing wasn't torn away in a frantic rush; it was drawn off slowly, almost reluctantly, as if each of them knew that each inch of skin revealed was another barrier between them removed and those barriers were the only things keeping them from melting into one another entirely.

She was breathless and terrified and holding him as

close as she could, kissing him as hard as she could, hoping he wouldn't see the truth in her eyes and pull away. That this was different. This was more. This was *everything*.

Then he was there, condom in place, sliding into her, and she was trying not to cry, biting her lip, because nothing had ever felt so good...or so raw. So open and vulnerable. Like he could reach right out and snatch the heart out of her chest if he wanted to and there was nothing she could do to stop him because it was his. Everything she was was his.

He whispered her name, her real name, against her temple, and then he was moving. Slow and hard.

Everything felt different. The tension in her body, the vulnerability in her chest—it all tied together into one knot of emotion and she was scared of its release, pushing back against it, scared of what she would say and what he would do if he heard her say it. So she bit her lip. She closed her eyes. She turned her head to the side and tried not to feel, tried to concentrate on the physical sensations, on his body moving, slow and delicious, above her and his mouth teasing the sensitive spot at the side of her neck.

But the feelings in her chest kept getting tangled up with the need, especially when he whispered her name, his voice thick and dark as he praised her. *God, you feel good. Come on, baby. Look at me. Let me see those eyes. Come for me.* She opened her eyes and he was there, his own nearly black with need, his face straining, so focused, so *Cross*, and her release came in an unexpected rush, flowing through her body, melting her down to nothing as he came the same way—slow and hard and groaning low.

His weight pressed her down into the mattress, his

breath heavy in her ear, and she held on tight—not wanting him to move. Not wanting reality to set in. When he slipped free of her body and rolled away to dispose of the condom, Bree curled on her side away from him, tugging the edge of the comforter over her, and when he came back he curved his body around hers, adjusting the blanket over both of them against the air-conditioned chill and spooning her as he often did after sex. Nothing was different, she told herself.

But everything felt different.

She was in love with him.

Completely, stupidly in love with him.

And she wasn't stupid enough to think he felt the same way. She knew he didn't want this. Knew how all those sentences she hadn't let him finish ended. He didn't want her getting hurt. He didn't want her getting her hopes up. Maybe this wasn't such a good idea.

She knew that. And her stupid heart loved him anyway.

So what was she supposed to do with that?

Heavy footsteps thundering up the stairs interrupted her train of thought. Cross lifted his head, his body still curled protectively around hers, as they heard a heavy pounding on the door to the master suite next door and Mel's voice calling out. "Maggie? Cross?"

He rolled away from her, collecting his clothes. She was sitting up in her nest of covers, but Cross was fully dressed again and halfway to the door when Mel banged on it. He opened it, using his body to block her view of Bree on the bed—as if Mel didn't know they'd been sleeping together for days.

"What's wrong?" he demanded.

Mel's gaze flicked past him, taking in Bree's comforter-wrapped presence without a flicker of an eyelash. "Pack your things," she told them both. "We're going back to LA."

"What?" Bree said, brilliantly, as Cross asked, "When?"

Mel's gaze turned back to him, the next word hard. "Now."

CHAPTER TWENTY-SIX

What the fuck just happened?

He'd been working, focusing on the job and trying not to think about Bree and the fact that he needed to nip this thing with her in the bud before it got any more complicated—and then she'd waltzed into his room, straddled his lap, and the nip-it-in-the-bud plan had been losing traction even before he'd seen her eyes.

He'd never realized before how eye color could completely change a person's face. Or maybe it was just Bree.

Maggie's eyes were her signature—bright, shocking aqua blue. Bree's eyes were so different. A pale grey with a hint of blue and spokes of yellow, right around the iris when he looked closely—and he had looked closely. He'd fallen into her eyes. And then the rest of it had sort of happened. Whatever that was.

He didn't have time to dwell on it now. He had a job to do.

Mel hadn't said what the emergency was, only that they were needed back in LA *yesterday* and she would explain on the plane. The manager had hustled Bree back to her room so she could become Maggie again, and was now on the phone arranging their flight plans. A battalion of staff from the resort were due any second to pack Maggie's things for her, but no one was packing

Candy's precious equipment but him, so he needed to get his ass in gear so nothing got left behind.

Candy would kill him if a single gadget was lost or damaged. He jogged through the house, collecting the extra security devices he'd put in place with Cecil yipping excitedly at his heels, delighted by the game. He packed his own things quickly and added his bags to the pile the swarms of staff were building by the front door when Maggie emerged from the bedroom.

And it was Maggie.

Massive sunglasses covered her eyes, but he didn't need to see them to know they would be turquoise. Her hair was tucked beneath the giant floppy hat—the same damn hat she'd worn when they first arrived. Her posture was Maggie's posture—arched to show off her assets to best advantage—and she crouched, cooing at Cecil and picking him up to cuddle him into her arms as a maid trotted at her side with his carrier.

Pure Maggie. No trace of the woman he'd made come all over the bed upstairs.

Mel rushed into the room then, hurrying them all out the door as the bellboys loaded their bags onto the parade of golf-carts that would take them and their belongings to the helipad. Cross hopped into the golf cart with Maggie/Bree and Mel and they were rolling, the villa disappearing as the cart zipped down the path.

* * * * *

It all happened so fast, Bree was grabbing for Cross's hand on the helicopter before it hit her that it was really over.

She had no idea what had happened to send them fleeing back to LA, no idea if she was even supposed to still be pretending to be in love with Cross, but either way, right now she needed his hand in hers as the helicopter swooped into the air and the contents of her stomach swooped up toward her tonsils.

She tried closing her eyes, but that only made it worse, so she stared at their hands instead, his strong fingers wrapped solidly around hers. Cross would never let anything happen to her. She believed that. Unfortunately, even Cross couldn't change the laws of physics and if something went wrong while they were in the air he couldn't exactly save the day like a freaking X-Man.

She knew she was squeezing his hand too hard—she could see the white impressions her fingers were leaving on his skin—but she couldn't help it. She hated this feeling. Like she could plummet to her death at any moment and there was *nothing she could do about it*.

Just like falling in love. A hysterical laugh tried to bubble up her throat and she swallowed it down.

God, she was such an idiot. What was she doing with him? She knew it wasn't going to end well. What kind of girl threw her heart at a man who told her right off the bat that he wasn't looking for a relationship? Who did that?

The helicopter touched down near the airstrip and Bree's death-panic eased enough for her to focus on the present. She climbed out of the helicopter, clinging to her hat with one hand and Cecil's carrier with the other. He'd gone nuts the second he heard the helicopter blades and had tried to climb into Bree's hair, scratching all the way until they could get him shoved inside his carrier. She hadn't been able to hear him on the flight, but he was still yipping hysterically as Bree followed Mel away from the damn machine as quickly as her sky-high heels would allow.

"Don't worry, baby," she promised him, "you don't ever have to go on the fucking deathtrap ever again."

His yipping subsided with a little whimper—and Bree knew exactly how he felt. Yanked around from place to place with no control over his own life, forced to ride freaking helicopters against his will. Poor baby.

Mel spoke with the pilots while Cross oversaw the porters loading the luggage onto the plane and Bree climbed onboard with her dog—useless and ornamental as ever.

It might help if she had the first clue what the hell was going on.

Had there been some kind of threat against Maggie? And if so, why was Mel running the show and not security-badass Cross? Was something wrong with the real Maggie?

Bree had taken a minute to Google Maggie's name for clues while she was putting on her make-up, but she hadn't seen anything out of the ordinary. Certainly nothing that would have caused Mel to go into full-on SWAT tactical exit mode.

She sank down onto one of the seats on the plane—and the reality sank in that they were really leaving.

She'd gone stir-crazy in the villa, but now that they were leaving, now that it was over her chest ached. She didn't know where she stood with Cross after that last...whatever the hell that was in his bedroom. It felt like there were a thousand things unsaid between them, things that would never get said now that they were leaving the island.

Everything was going to change.

They took off within minutes and Bree wasted no time releasing Cecil from his carrier. The dog whimpered as he scrambled into her lap, shivering his displeasure at being airborne again. She stroked his silky ears, murmuring unintelligible words to comfort him—and herself—until Mel returned from speaking to the pilots and plopped down facing Bree and Cross.

Cross had been looking out the window, but at Mel's appearance he leaned forward in his chair, propping his elbows on his knees and demanding, "All right. What's going on?"

Mel's face remained expressionless, the careful blankness of years of practice. "There's another story."

Bree frowned. "What kind of story? I Googled and I didn't see anything new."

"It hasn't broken yet," Mel explained. "The reporter contacted Maggie's publicist for comment. It'll be going live in the morning—just in time for all the morning shows. We're going back to LA so we can get in front of it."

Something wasn't adding up. "What kind of story needs us to go back to LA? Is it about me? Did they find out I'm—"

Mel held up a hand. "We don't know all the details yet, but we might need to reveal you as the decoy early. We'll know more when we land in LA. Until then the best thing we can do is try to get some rest so we're fresh to deal with this."

"To deal with what?" Cross asked. "You haven't told us anything."

"All we know right now is that there are some questions about the timeline and who Maggie was with when."

"That's it?"

"We'll know more in LA." Mel shot her a stern look. "Don't borrow trouble."

Cross frowned. "Can I have a word with you?" he

asked Mel and the manager nodded, the two of them moving to another part of the plane to conspire with one another.

Bree glared after them, curled up with Cecil.

None of this made any sense. And she couldn't even concentrate on all the what-the-hell-is-going-on-with-Maggie panic because she was too busy drowning in what-the-hell-is-going-on-with-Cross panic.

He hadn't looked straight at her since Mel had interrupted them—and yes, she knew he was in work mode, but she couldn't help feeling that everything was over. Not just their time on the island, but *them*. Whatever story was about to break, it was hard for her to imagine a scenario in which Maggie would need her to continue to play lovers with Cross once they got to LA. Maggie might not need her at all—and if he wasn't guarding her anymore, if she wasn't Maggie...she didn't know what that meant for them.

She hated illusions, but she'd been living inside one for the last week and a half...and now it was gone. And she missed it.

CHAPTER TWENTY-SEVEN

Cross and Mel were on their phones the entire flight—and their electronic focus only became more complete when they landed. It was late. Close to midnight in LA—which meant her body thought it was three in the morning—but Bree only managed to doze a little in the car ride from the airport, too nervous to really sleep.

She knew they were heading to Maggie's mansion and expected to find it dark and empty, but when they pulled into the driveway every light in the house was on and the outdoor floodlights showed an array of cars already parked in the driveway—including her Honda and Cross's Lexus, as if she needed another reminder that their lives didn't match.

The gate closed behind them, sealing out the rest of the world—though Bree hadn't noticed any paparazzi on their drive in. Maybe they hadn't caught on to the fact that "Maggie" was no longer in the Caribbean.

She climbed out of the car, Cecil Two snoring softly in the carrier in her arms, and trudged toward the house, trying to quell the feeling that she was walking toward the guillotine. Until she knew more, there was no sense borrowing trouble, like Mel had said, but she had an uneasy feeling the others knew more than they were telling her.

Especially when she stepped in the front door and

the first voice she heard was Maggie's.

"Maggie's back too?" Bree turned to frown at Mel, but the manager was ushering her deeper into the house. "What's going on?" she demanded, digging in her heels.

"Damage control," Mel said flatly, putting a hand on her back and gently shoving her back into motion.

But that didn't make any sense. Maggie had been in Fiji. The flight was longer. She shouldn't have been able to get back before Bree unless they'd left their island hours before Bree'd left hers.

Mel ushered her into the library—but Maggie's raised voice carried easily through the open doors.

"I love you! You know I love you!"

"Do I?" Demarco's answer was clear as day and Bree cringed at hearing the evidently intimate conversation, even if they were shouting. She stood perfectly still—as if that would make the eavesdropping less egregious—and held Cecil Two's carrier to her chest.

"I would have married you in the rain," Demarco declared. "You were the one who needed more than you and me and a ring. Now I see why."

"But it wasn't me! Baby, it wasn't me. It was the decoy!"

"I know it was you, Maggie!"

"Demarco!" Maggie's last wounded shout was accompanied by the slamming of a door—and another shrieking, "Demarco!"

Cecil Two startled awake at the sound, releasing a shrill yelp. Bree sucked in a breath, trying to be invisible, but the divine Miss Tate had heard the dog and appeared in the doorway a moment later, with her own Cecil at her heels.

She looked magnificent. And tragic. Like the heroine

of a Shakespearean drama in the last act when everyone started dying.

Tears glistened on her cheeks, but her head was held high, her eyes blazing as they locked on Mel. "I told you not to fire her."

Kaydee. Shit.

Now was clearly the time to keep her mouth shut, but Bree had spent the last six hours wondering and she *had to know*. "What happened?"

With a sharp, humorless laugh, Maggie flung a hand at the table. "Don't you read?"

Bree hadn't noticed the print-out lying on the table, but now she set down Cecil's carrier and sank down on an ottoman, gathering up the papers that looked like they'd been thrown there. They were out of order, but it didn't take her long to get the gist. The article's title was *The Many Men of Maggie Tate*. And there were photos. Not just of her and Cross. Of Maggie with several other men who were most certainly *not* her fiancé, including several of her exes—but that was nothing alarming. There was no reason to think the pictures were recent.

Until she read the article.

Apparently there were "witnesses" claiming at least two of the photos had been taken since Maggie started dating Demarco—one of them only two weeks ago at a club in LA, only days before they'd flown to Fiji. Which certainly explained why Demarco wasn't feeling the love tonight.

A pair of crystal-studded Louboutin sandals stopped in front of her and Bree looked up into Maggie's tragic, noble face—a face that somehow managed to be even more radiant with tear tracks streaking down her cheeks.

"I need you to say it was you," she said.

Bree blinked as she suddenly realized what Mel meant by *damage control*. "What?"

* * * * *

Cross had thought the plan was doomed to failure the second Mel had told him about it on the plane. He'd wanted to tell Bree, to warn her of what was coming, but Mel had insisted it was vitally important to Maggie that she be the one to ask Bree for this "personal favor" in person. When he'd pushed back, she'd reminded him that the client was always right.

Which was bullshit. In security, the client was only right when their opinion didn't compromise their safety—but in this case there was no safety concern at risk so he was forced to keep his mouth shut and focus on his phone for the entire damn flight because if he looked at Bree he knew he would say something he was going to regret.

Telling Bree that Maggie wanted her to take credit for all of her affairs wasn't his job and he needed to focus on doing his job—even if keeping it from her felt like a shitty thing to do.

He'd gotten too caught up in Bree at the villa. It was time refocus his priorities.

So he kept his face carefully blank and tried not to notice the horrified shock in Bree's eyes as Maggie went on.

"You'll come out as my decoy, confess you were the one who made out with Cross, and then also admit that it was you in these photos with Alec and Franklin."

"But it wasn't," Bree said, sounding a little dazed, and Cross resisted the urge to go to her.

"But it could have been." Maggie knelt in front of her, taking her hands as Bree shook her head. "Bree. I need you to do this for me. Demarco doesn't believe me. He thinks it was me. He's refusing to marry me." Her eyes glistened, pleading—and Cross realized that it wasn't her looks or her talent alone that made her so successful, but some combination of the two that enabled her to be breathtakingly gorgeous and utterly vulnerable at the same time. When most humans were ravaged by emotion, Maggie was somehow elevated by it.

"It *was* you though," Bree reminded her. "You cheated on him and now you want me to lie to him so he'll marry you?"

"It was Alec!" Maggie pleaded, tears trembling on her lashes. "I can never say no to Alec."

"Then maybe you shouldn't be marrying Demarco!"

Maggie stood abruptly, stalking across the room in her four-inch heels. "You think this is funny? You think my life is a joke?" she snapped. "That I just exist to provide tabloid stories for your entertainment? You think I don't know that you're all laughing at me?"

"No one is laughing, but if you were making out with Alec two weeks ago, what makes you think you're ready to marry Demarco today?"

"I love him! I'm not a doll in a show. I have feelings!"

"I know you do," Bree raised her voice, the two Maggies facing off across the room. "But so does Demarco. So do I." When Maggie didn't react, she threw out her arms. "So does Alec! And he can tell everyone that I'm lying."

Both Cecils yapped excitedly.

"We'll say he didn't know. You were pretending to be me—and I didn't know either."

"So now I'm the sociopath who runs around pretending to be you?"

"You always pretend to be me. How is this different?"

"That's a job! This is..." She released a frustrated breath, shaking her head. "I don't want to be famous, Maggie. Especially not as the girl who impersonated Maggie Tate so she could hook up with her exes. That's crazy. And that story will follow me around forever. It will be attached to *my* name."

"So it's fine as long as you're attaching scandal to my name, but not the other way around?"

Neither of them looked at him, but Cross could feel their sudden awareness of him in the room with them. He and Bree had attached a scandal to her name. They'd been caught together when they both had a job to do. He'd almost screwed things up—not just for Maggie's reputation or his own, but for EP as well.

He could have lost his job. His reputation. His potential to be a partner at Elite Protection. It wasn't the same thing to Bree. It was just money. She was an artist doing this as a side gig, but for him, this was *who he was* and he'd let the romance of the island mess with his freaking mind until he nearly lost sight of that.

He didn't make mistakes like that. He was the best. He worked the hardest. He never lost focus. *Never*.

She was a play-it-by-ear, live-by-impulse kind of woman and he'd almost let the temptation of her ruin his career.

"I won't pay you." Maggie's words were stark in the silence that had fallen in the den. "Not a penny. Not unless you say it was you."

Bree's mouth fell open, her eyes wide and hurt. "I did everything you asked. I gave up my life to be you—"

"To suntan on a beach, boo hoo. And you couldn't even do that right." Maggie's expression hardened.

"You were in breach of contract the second those pictures of you kissing Cross hit the internet. I don't owe you a dime and I don't see why I should have to give you anything if you don't say it was all you. All of it."

"Maggie..." Mel said softly—but the movie star shot her a glare and she fell silent.

Bree looked at Cross for the first time since Maggie had entered the room. Her eyes searched his, as if seeking out an ally, some hint of support, but he couldn't move. She looked away from him, shaking her head bitterly. Her eyes glittered as her head turned back to Maggie. "I can't do it. I can't be you anymore, Maggie. I'm sorry."

"I'll sue," Maggie threatened.

Bree lifted her chin. "Do it," she said defiantly. "I don't care."

She turned on her heel and fled the room. Cross took an instinctive step after her before he stopped himself.

It wasn't his job to comfort her. He forced himself to turn back to Maggie and Mel—and found both women watching him.

"Mr. Cross," Maggie said, her voice cool and calm. "Mel tells me I can count on you. That you're a team player."

He nodded, nervous at the look in her eyes.

"I'm sure you can see which course of action would be better for Elite Protection," Maggie went on with a distinct lack of the subtlety she was known for. "I need you to persuade Miss Davies to see reason."

Cross swallowed around the dread in his throat. Apparently it wasn't his job to comfort Bree. It was his job to convince her.

CHAPTER TWENTY-EIGHT

Bree made it as far as the driveway before she realized she didn't have her car keys. All of her things were tucked away in the closet of an upstairs guest room, waiting for her to shed her Maggie persona and return to her real life.

She would have to go inside to get them before she could escape, but right now the idea of going back into that house for any reason made her shudder. She wasn't a person to them. She was a tool. A get-out-of-jail-free card for Maggie's relationship. And if she did this now, who was to say Maggie wouldn't ask her to do it again, who was to say she wouldn't be the decoy, shopping on Rodeo Drive so Demarco didn't know that Maggie was cheating on him with one of her exes. Who was to say she hadn't *already* been used that way.

It had seemed so harmless before. Helpful even. But now the wrongness of the lie suffocated her.

And Cross hadn't said a word.

How could he stand there and go along with it, by his silence if not by any word or action? Mel was the one who had tried to speak on her behalf, but even she had fallen in line with Maggie's demands. All of them asking her to do this.

Not that she should be surprised. She should have known. Mel had always been Team Maggie first and foremost. She knew that. But she'd thought that Cross was different. That they were a team.

The front door opened. Cross stepped out onto the landing, with Cecil Two cradled in his arms, and Bree nearly cried with the relief at seeing him. She did have an ally.

Nothing had ever looked better than the tall, strong man in the simple, dark suit he'd changed into on the plane, with the tiny furball in his arms. It was bright as day beneath the floodlights that lit the driveway and she could clearly see the concern in his eyes as he strode down the steps toward her.

"Are you all right?"

"Can you believe this?" she asked, still having trouble wrapping her head about the last fifteen minutes. She reached for Cecil and Cross relinquished the silky soft comfort of the dog into her arms.

"Is it really so different?"

She took a step back so fast she nearly stumbled, holding Cecil up like a shield. "You're on her side?"

"It isn't about sides." His voice was so calm and soothing it made her want to scream. "Think about this. You'd get the money to support yourself while you're doing your art and all you have to do is what you've always done. Be Maggie."

"When I was Maggie before it never involved hurting anyone! At least not that I knew about. But now she wants me to lie to her fiancé. That's *wrong*, Cross. How can you not see that?"

"Maggie's powerful. She could sue you for damages."

And suddenly she realized why he was here. "She could sue Elite Protection, you mean. She could mess with your perfect career. With your shot at that promotion."

"This isn't about me."

"Isn't it? You're the one out here trying to talk me into lying to save Maggie's ass." She shook her head, backing away until her butt hit her car. "Why are you here, Cross? For Maggie? For Elite Protection? So you can *win*? What's more important than the truth to you, because I thought the lying bothered you as much as it bothered me."

"It isn't the same thing. We're protecting our client—"

"By lying to her fiancé? By lying to *everyone*?"

"That's what you do! You pretend to be Maggie. You *lie*."

"Well, I don't want to do it anymore!" she shouted at him. "I am done, all right? Done with the illusions. I can't anymore. This has gone far enough. I'm not going to let her use me to hurt Demarco."

"She's sorry—"

"Because she got caught! And now instead of being honest, she's trying to foist it off on me. Aren't you the one who can't even talk to your mother because she lied about your father's affair?"

"Don't bring my family into this," he growled.

"I'm sorry." She knew his father was a sensitive spot for him, a low blow, but it was hard to think rationally with her thoughts scrambled by everything that was happening. "You have to see this is wrong—"

"I did at first," he admitted. "But if you think about it—yes, it's wrong, but it's a small wrong that could solve a lot of problems—"

She frowned, her brain catching on the way he said it. "What do you mean 'at first'? When did you find out about Maggie's plan?"

He grimaced and she knew she was going to hate his answer. "On the plane. Mel made me promise not to say anything. Maggie wanted to tell you—"

"Maggie wanted to blindside me! Maggie wanted to pressure me into saying yes before I could think it through! Maggie wanted to use me and you knew it and you *helped* her!"

She'd known. She'd known if it ever came down to a question between Elite Protection and her, she would lose. She just hadn't expected being proven right to sting quite so much.

She knew he needed success like he needed oxygen and she didn't represent success, but this feeling, this betrayal, choked her. She'd *loved* him. How stupid was she?

"How much?"

The words seemed to fall between them, incomprehensible even in their simplicity. She frowned, confused. "What?"

"You know I have the money. And I know you need it. How much for your cooperation?"

She stared at him. He wanted to pay her to lie. Just to make the client happy. Just to make the problem disappear. "Fuck you."

She tucked Cecil against her chest and stalked past him back toward the house, the little dog growling as if he sensed her anger. She no longer cared about avoiding Maggie. She just wanted to get her things and get the fuck out of here.

Cross chased after her. "Bree. Be practical."

"*No.*" She whirled to face him at the top step, glowering down at him. "*Fuck* practical. That isn't me. None of this is me. I know you want some perfect, *practical* Stepford girlfriend who will do anything to help you succeed, but this is *wrong*, Cross. And if you can't see that, what blinded you? The money? The power? The celebrity? Do those things really matter to you so much? Do they really make you happy? Is anyone in this entire fucking mess *happy* if I lie? Is *Maggie*, married to Demarco and knowing he only took her back because she lied to him? Are you? Knowing you gave up your integrity for a freaking *job*?"

His expression darkened. "We can't all be as righteous as you."

"It isn't righteous. I've just been on the other side. And so have you." But he wasn't listening to her now. He was stuck in trying to save his own ass, not hearing a word she said, and she couldn't do this anymore. "Use my name," she said. "Tell the press I said whatever the hell you want me to say. Put words into my mouth. I won't contest whatever story you put out, but I'm done. I'm out. I'm not doing this anymore. Tell her she can sue me if she wants to. It's not like I have any savings for her to take anyway."

Bree turned to stalk back through the door and straight up the stairs to collect her things. There were no footsteps behind her and she refused to turn back, refused to look to see if he was happy to have won. Because she definitely felt like she'd lost.

* * * * *

"Max. We may have a problem."

"One second." Cross heard a muffled sound, like his boss murmuring to someone with the phone covered and a door closing. "I assume this is the Maggie Tate situation?"

Cross glanced at his watch, belated realizing it was nearly one in the morning. "I'm sorry. I didn't realize it was so late." His body was still on island time and the combination of the floodlights and everyone being so awake at Maggie's place had screwed with his time sense even more.

"You're fine," Max assured him, as sharp and businesslike as if he was always pulled out of bed in the middle of the night. "What's going on?"

"We may be in breach." He braced himself for his boss's reaction, ready to hear any number of words. *Fired. Suspended. Demoted.*

"Is this still about the photos of you kissing that girl? Because Candy brought me up to speed when she and Pretty Boy got back tonight and it sounds like Maggie Tate may not have a very good case for claiming you negatively impacted her reputation since she apparently did plenty of that on her own. Unless it was the decoy who kissed those men."

"No, it was Maggie. But she wanted Bree to say she did it. She's threatening everything she can think of to make that happen."

"And the decoy's refusing?"

Cross opened his mouth to tell Max the truth, but the same thing happened to his voice that had happened when he was talking to Maggie and Mel after Bree drove off in her Honda. Instead of telling them all that Bree had essentially told them to use her name but keep her out of it, he said, "Yeah, she said no. No way."

"Good for her."

Cross blinked at Max's blasé tone. "Maggie's pissed. She's threatening to sue everyone."

Max snorted. "She isn't going to sue. It would only drag the whole situation into the light and make her look even worse. All she's likely to do is talk shit about us to her famous friends."

"Which could kill our business."

"Well, it won't be good for it," Max said dryly. "But it also won't be the first time we've had someone who thinks they're a god gunning for us. Did you ever meet Hank the Hammer?"

"The wrestling guy?"

"He hired us to upgrade the security on his house and thought Candy should be one of the perks. It's a minor miracle she never handed him his testicles on a silver platter, but in the end we handed him off to another company and he talked shit about us all over town. And we're still going strong."

"That's Hank the Hammer. This is Maggie Tate. Are you seriously saying you're not worried at all?"

"About Maggie? Nah. She'll calm down. You okay?"

I asked a woman I care about to lie about sleeping with other men and when she said no I offered her money to do it. I'm just peachy. "I'm good."

"This thing with the decoy—"

"It's over. You don't need to worry about me being distracted."

"I wasn't—"

"I'm back and ready to focus on work one hundred percent." He would make up for the last couple weeks. He would be flawless.

A long pause met those words, and, finally, "Okay."

CHAPTER TWENTY-NINE

"I can't believe you made it!"

It was definitely a sign of what a horrible human being she was becoming that Bree had completely forgotten it was Andi's birthday when she drove straight from Maggie's house to Ty and Andi's place in the middle of the night.

"And you brought a dog..." Andi went on, eyeing the Cavalier King Charles spaniel clutched in her arms.

"This is Cecil. Cecil Two. My decoy dog," she blurted. "I'm sorry to come so late."

"You're here. You can be as late as you want." Andi reached through the open doorway, pulling her into the house, which was still brightly lit, music softly playing from the living room. "You know Ty—he hates to let a party end, but Jade's asleep upstairs so we're pretending we're all responsible adults down here. God, it's good to see you."

Standing in the foyer, Andi hauled her into her arms and Bree squeezed back—maybe hanging on a little too long and a little too tight because Cecil whimpered in protest at being squished and Andi leaned back in her arms, searching her face. "Are you okay?"

"I..." She tried to answer, tried to play it cool, but tears welled in her eyes.

"Come here." Andi grabbed her hand, leading her

away from the party and up the stairs. Bree leaned back against her grip.

"Your guests…"

"They've seen plenty of me. I haven't seen you in weeks."

Bree stopped resisting and let her best friend pull her upstairs, needing her too much to let her guilt over taking Andi away from her birthday party make more than a token appearance.

Andi led her to the sitting room attached to the bedroom she shared with Ty and softly closed the door behind them. None of the voices from downstairs carried this far, leaving them perfectly alone. Andi put her back to the door and crossed her arms over her chest. "Okay, what happened?"

"Nothing," Bree protested, knowing her tone sounded more defensive than believable. Andi arched her brow skeptically and Bree tried again. "It's your birthday."

"Technically it's after midnight and yesterday was my birthday, but even if it was, who cares? You were there for me three hundred and sixty-five days a year when I needed you. Now I'm here for you. So tell me what's wrong."

It wasn't the words so much as Andi's calm, steady presence, her certainty that they could deal with this, whatever it was, that made Bree choke up again, tears welling in her eyes. "I love you, you know that?"

"Okay, now I'm really worried," Andi teased gently, putting a hand on her arm and guiding her toward the nearest chair. When they were both seated—Bree deflated into her chair with Cecil cuddled close and Andi perched on the edge of hers, leaning forward, ready to help—she gently prompted, "Bree?"

She'd come here to tell Andi everything, but now she opened her mouth and couldn't find the words.

"Did you kidnap the dog?"

Bree laughed, tears leaking out with the sound, the dam holding back her feelings cracking. "I'm pretty sure he's actually my dog. Maggie gave him to me."

And then the entire story came pouring out. All of it. The decoy job and Maggie's plans to marry Demarco. The stupid, impulsive kiss with Cross that had tilted everything on its axis. Maggie calling them back and demanding Bree take credit for hooking up with half of Maggie's exes. Cross taking Maggie's side and Bree walking out...without the money. She stroked Cecil's silky ears as she spoke, trying to absorb comfort from his soft, warm weight.

"And now I'm right back where I started," she concluded, sniffling pathetically. "With nothing—only now a movie star might want to sue me or paint me in the tabloids as some kind of psycho stalker who ran around pretending to be her and hooking up with all her exes."

Cecil put his paws on her chest, his tiny rough tongue licking the salty wetness from her cheeks. Andi had come out of her chair, toeing off her heels and kneeling at Bree's feet, both of her hands wrapped around one of Bree's.

"Honey..." She may have glossed over that whole falling in love with Cross thing a little, but from the look in her friend's eyes she wasn't fooling Andi. "I know it feels horrible right now, but you don't have nothing. You have your friends. Your family. Your *art*. Olivia Hwang gave *you* a show at her gallery—"

"No, she didn't."

"What?" Andi frowned, confused.

"I lied about the show. I just didn't want to tell you that Olivia Hwang thought I was a talentless hack."

"Don't say that—"

"I thought if I could do this one job for Maggie I wouldn't have to worry about money for a while and I could buy myself a little more time to get my big break."

Guilt flickered in Andi's eyes. "Why didn't you tell me you had money problems? I never wanted to leave you in the lurch by moving out—"

"Don't you dare apologize to me for being happy and having a good life you want to live with people you love."

"But if I hadn't moved out…"

"We could both be miserable?"

Andi's eyes glittered worriedly. "Are you miserable?"

"Of course not," Bree insisted, though she couldn't have said at that moment whether the words were true or false. "Though I may have to move back to Clement and live in my parents' basement, like all self-respecting thirty-somethings."

She groaned, dropping her forehead on top of Cecil's silky head. He wriggled in her arms, trying to lick any patch of skin he could reach. "Maybe I should have done it. Just said whatever they wanted me to say. I told Cross to go ahead and do whatever they wanted anyway. At least if I'd stayed I would have the money—and I'd know what they were planning." She lifted her head, meeting Andi's eyes. "Do you think I'm an idiot? Should I have played along?"

"You have to listen to your gut—and stories like these have a way of following you around."

Andi should know—she'd been part of Ty's social media & PR team when they first met. She'd seen the business of fame from every angle. "It wasn't my reputation I was worried about," Bree admitted. "It was the lying. Not just to the press, but to Demarco. And the people who thought they were going to get to host a Maggie Tate wedding. And everyone who got so excited to meet me because they love Maggie Tate. I started to feel sick with all the lies."

"It makes sense," Andi said softly. "After what happened with Zander."

Bree pulled a face. "This isn't about him. He doesn't affect me."

Andi's eyebrows arched skeptically, but she didn't say anything. She didn't need to.

Okay, yes, maybe she had a little bit of baggage about liars. Who didn't? Lies *hurt* people and she couldn't be part of that anymore. It wasn't a harmless little impersonation anymore. It was *wrong*.

"I just can't believe Cross asked me to do it," she whispered.

That had been the betrayal. She'd expected it of Maggie, who had so many people telling her whatever she wanted was right that she couldn't possibly have any idea of right or wrong anymore. She'd even expected it of Mel, who always did whatever was best for Maggie. Always.

But Cross...

"When did you fall in love with him?"

She looked at Andi—who evidently hadn't been fooled for a second—and grimaced, resting her chin on Cecil's head, who gave a comforting little whimper. "Does it matter?"

Andi shrugged, reaching out to scratch Cecil Two under the chin. "I didn't think you liked dogs."

"He grew on me," she murmured—and she wasn't

only talking about Cecil Two. Cross had snuck in under her defenses when she wasn't looking and then there she'd been. Hopelessly, stupidly in love with someone who would never love her back. "I knew better," she murmured. "He's so freaking obsessed with winning. He has to be perfect all the time—he'd never be with someone who makes mistakes. Who's impulsive and reckless and tempts *him* to make mistakes. Even if he wanted someone—which he doesn't. He's totally focused on his career. On being the best at it." She shook her head at her own stupidity. "He even *told* me that he doesn't think he knows how to love someone."

"Men are bastards," Andi declared. "Don't they know a woman can't be expected to resist a man who needs her to teach him how to love?"

Bree snorted, not quite managing a laugh. She felt hollowed out, her insides scraped empty of everything that made her feel. "I knew it wouldn't work, but I really, *really* wanted to be wrong, you know?"

"You want me to have Ty beat him up? He's a lover, not a fighter, but he really likes you. I bet he'd be down."

Bree sniffled through a laugh. "No offense, but I think Cross can probably take him. He's trained in all sorts of scary shit."

Andi squeezed her hands. "You know you're staying here, right? As long as you want."

"You barely have space for the four of you."

Ty might be a television star, but he was a superstitious one and he still lived in the house he'd had when he got his big break—only now he lived there with Andi, his daughter Jade, and his daughter's aunt on her mother's side. The public areas may have been renovated to a modern shine, but the house wasn't large and Bree refused to impose.

"We'll make the space," Andi insisted, but Bree was already shaking her head.

"I think…I think it may be time to…" Emotion welled up in a rush at the words she couldn't quite get out. "I'm not making it, Andi," she whispered. "I think it might be time to give up." The last two words were choked out.

"You don't mean that. You can't even say it without crying," Andi said.

But she did mean it. She just hated it. And she couldn't seem to stop crying long enough to explain. She didn't want to give up on her dream, simply saying the words out loud felt like it had broken something inside her. Her art was her identity. But how long could she fail before she accepted that she would never succeed?

She'd told herself a thousand times that she just had to keep trying a little longer, that her big break was coming, any day now—but how many times could she be expected to pick herself up after yet another rejection, yet another failure, yet another sign that she was wrong and she didn't have what it took?

Maybe Billy hadn't been cruel when he'd kicked her out of that class. Maybe he'd simply been trying to spare her the pain of working for a decade only to discover she didn't have what it took.

She'd wanted this for so long she didn't know how to want anything else, but was it time to be practical? Was it time to find another dream? One that wouldn't leave her taking any job she could find to support herself so she could keep on failing?

Was it time to stop dreaming and start living? Start putting together a life she could be proud of and stop pinning her hopes on a someday that might never come?

Andi rose up on her knees, wrapping her arms around Bree and hugging her with Cecil squirming between them. "Everything's going to be okay," Andi murmured. "It's going to get better. I know it is."

Bree held on tight, trying to believe her, trying to hope.

But the words felt like a lie.

CHAPTER THIRTY

"Bree! Bree, wake up! It's Maggie!"

Bree came blearily awake, batting away the hand shaking her shoulder and feeling like she'd had about two hours of sleep. "Here?" she mumbled.

"On The Morning Show," Andi clarified, standing over her, fully dressed and so alert it was almost insulting as Cecil Two yipped excitedly, dancing around Andi's ankles.

After the sob-fest in the sitting room last night, Andi had worried about Bree driving and since the party had broken up by then, Bree had let her friend persuade her to crash on the couch in the living room—though only after apologizing profusely for ruining the end of Andi's birthday celebration.

Andi refused to hear a word of it, insisting that the scales were still tipped far in Bree's favor in terms of who had supported whom more and that she was glad to finally be able to be there for Bree.

Bree had stayed—and tossed and turned restlessly on the couch, her thoughts refusing to let her sleep, continuously cycling through a highlight reel of everything that had happened in the previous twenty-four hours. Cross...Maggie...her ultimate failure as an artist...

The merry-go-round of regret had circled in her brain

all night, keeping sleep at bay until she must have finally fallen into a fitful sleep around dawn.

"Where is everyone?" she asked as she sat up, rubbing the sleep from her eyes.

"Ty took Jade to the bookstore—as soon as we could pry her away from Cecil Two. I thought you might want some quiet this morning."

Bree cringed, hating the idea of disrupting their lives. "I'm sorry—"

"Stop," Andi insisted. "I know our mothers hammered that Minnesota nice shit into us, but if you apologize to me one more time I'm...I don't know. I don't have a good threat. But I promise I'll be very irritated with you. I get to take care of you for a change, so suck it up and say, 'Thank you, Andi. I love you, Andi.'"

"Thank you, Andi. I love you, Andi," Bree parroted, though tears gathered in her eyes with the sincerity of the emotion behind the words.

"No crying," Andi insisted, swiping at her own eyes. "We're on a mission."

"Maggie's really on The Morning Show?"

"I had it on in the kitchen, but I paused it as soon as they announced who their next guest was. Do you want to see?"

"Absolutely." Bree stood, smoothing the wrinkles from her slept-in clothes. "Better to know what they're saying than wonder."

Cecil Two scampered at her heels as she trailed Andi into the kitchen, where Maggie's face was indeed frozen on the screen. Her stomach pitched and she wondered where her cell phone was, if Mel or Cross or any of them had sent her a message. But before she could chicken out and go looking for her phone, Andi lifted the remote.

"Ready?"

Bree nodded, and the interview began.

She barely heard the intro and the first question over the ringing in her ears. Something about the article that had broken that morning and an offer for Maggie to give her side of the story...then came the words Bree had been dreading.

"*I have a decoy,*" Maggie said on screen. "*Someone who, for security reasons, takes my place during certain public appearances. That is who was caught on camera kissing my bodyguard. I have never been involved in any way with Aaron Cross.*"

"*And the other photos?*" the interviewer, known for her puff-pieces and delicate handling of celebrity egos, prompted gently.

Bree held her breath.

"*Those were me.*" Maggie admitted, gazing straight at the interviewer, and Bree's breath whooshed out. "*One was taken before Demarco Whitten and I became serious about one another and the other was as part of a chemistry test for a future project, so really the whole thing was quite innocent, but when you're a celebrity, people are always ready to assume the worst.*"

"*And Demarco? Did he assume the worst?*"

"*I will always care about Demarco, but even someone who is used to being in the public eye isn't always prepared for what my life is like and ultimately we came to the decision that our lives weren't compatible, no matter how much we care about one another. I have to respect his choice.*"

"She just made him look bad for dumping her after an article came out claiming she'd cheated on him," Andi marveled. "She didn't even give the cheating story time to gain traction before she defused it. Smart. She is good."

"She told the truth," Bree murmured, confused. "Sort of."

Andi muted the television as the interview concluded and the host threw to the next segment. "What does that mean for you?"

"I have no idea."

"Do you think Cross…?"

Bree shook her head, feeling like she'd missed a crucial piece of the puzzle. "I don't know." She became aware of her surroundings. The kitchen. Andi's happily-ever-after in progress. "I should go home. Start packing."

"Bree…"

"I can't stay, Andi." She bent, gathering Cecil's warm mass in her arms. "It's time to leave LA."

* * * * *

Her apartment looked exactly as she left it—which was somewhat disorienting since she felt so completely different. It seemed wrong that the apartment, as a reflection of her, hadn't undergone some fundamental transformation, but it just sat there, as sparsely furnished and littered with prints stacked in random places as ever.

She stepped through the door ready to pack, on a mission, determined to do this—but she was distracted by the sight of the pieces she'd pulled out for the Olivia Hwang showing, neatly stacked next to the futon.

Setting Cecil down so he could explore the apartment, she stared at the first print—a bridge scene—and tried to see it with impartial eyes. Tried to see what the Olivia Hwangs of the world saw when they looked at it.

She flipped to the next print, and the next, barely

aware of the passage of time. She felt like there was some truth right on the edge of her brain that she couldn't quite see yet, teasing her, out of reach.

It could have been five minutes later or three hours when a knock at the door pulled her out of her distraction. She looked up from her spot sitting on the floor, with her prints spread out around her, propped against every available surface in the apartment. Cecil raced from the tiny eat-in kitchen toward the door, barking hysterically at their visitor.

The knock came again—firm and direct—and her heart began to pound as fast as that fist on her door as she realized who must be on the other side.

He could have gotten her address from Maggie. He could have come to... what? Apologize? Beg forgiveness? Swear his undying love for her?

Bree scrambled to her feet, smoothing the loose tendrils of hair that had slipped from her ponytail behind her ears. She ran her hands down her skirt—and realized she hadn't changed since the plane last night. Maggie's clothes. Now dirty and slept in. She felt grimy and probably looked worse, but she didn't have time for vanity as the pounding came again.

"Coming!" she called out, so he wouldn't give up and leave.

Please don't let him leave.

She navigated her way through the minefield of photos littering her floor and smoothed her hair one last time before reaching for the doorknob. She held her breath as the door swung open and revealed...

"Mel."

"Hello, Bree."

Her face flushed and she realized she was more embarrassed to be caught looking like roadkill by

Maggie's perfectly put together manager than she would have been by Cross. "What are you doing here?"

"I come bearing your check," Mel said with a wry smile. Cecil whined excitedly and circled Mel's ankles until the manager bent and scratched him beneath the chin. "We could have direct deposited the money like we usually do, but Maggie thought this would be more appropriate. More of a cinematic moment."

"That sounds like Maggie," she murmured, still trying to catch up. "I thought she wasn't going to…"

"To pay you? Don't listen to her temper. She's really much kinder than her tantrums indicate. And sixty thousand is nothing to her. You could have held out for more. We were paying more for the villa than we were for you."

Bree watched as Mel removed a check from her bag. "It's a lot to me," she whispered, hating the admission.

"It is to most of us," Mel agreed. "And Maggie caved as soon as I pointed that out to her. She just wasn't willing to hear it last night. It had been a long day."

Realizing she was being rude, Bree stepped back. "Would you like to come in?"

Mel smiled, crossing the threshold and looking at all the art debris that cluttered every surface. Cecil darted around the room, delighted to have more of his people together.

"I've never been to your place before," Mel mused. "We always have you come to us." There wasn't much room to stand—and nowhere to sit that wasn't covered by artwork, but Mel seemed perfectly at home standing in the center of the chaos as she turned to face Bree. "Maggie wanted me to tell you that she's sorry."

"Is she okay?" Bree found herself asking. "I saw the interview this morning…"

"Maggie's always okay," Mel said with a wry smile. "Even when she isn't. Foisting the problem off on you wouldn't have solved anything. She was mad when Cross told us that you'd refused to cooperate—"

"What?"

"She might have thrown her People's Choice Award across the room, but Cross stood up for you. Said it wasn't right of her to ask you to lie for her, and she saw that. Once she calmed down." Mel smiled. "She's always hated the word no. But give her a week and she'll be begging for you to come back and decoy for her again."

"I don't know..." Bree shook her head. "I've been thinking about moving back to Minnesota."

Mel's eyebrows flew up. "Really? Wow. I did not call that one."

She shrugged. "I just think it might be time, you know. Get a real job."

"I thought you were an artist," Mel said, and Bree swallowed thickly at the easy simplicity of the words. As if you could just decide to be an artist.

"I'll never stop taking pictures, but maybe this isn't the way, you know?"

"And that means you have to leave LA?"

Bree nodded. "Clean break. It's for the best."

Mel nodded slowly. "Does this have anything to do with a certain former football playing bodyguard?" When Bree blushed, she smiled indulgently. "I did live in a house with you guys for almost two weeks and while I may be very good at pretending not to notice things, I'm not blind."

Bree swallowed. "It's over now."

"Is it." The words were a statement more than a question, but Bree defended herself.

"It never would have worked anyway. We're much

too different."

"Really?" Mel's eyebrows couldn't get any higher. "You surprise me, Bree. I didn't take you for a quitter. I thought you were braver than that."

"Yeah, well, sometimes bravery is just stupidity in another package. I've decided it's time to smarten up. In all areas of my life."

"Well." Mel smiled sadly. "For what it's worth, I thought you were good together." She nodded to the photos decorating the couch. "And those are beautiful."

Bree grimaced. "But what do they *say*?"

Mel shrugged. "What does any beautiful thing say? *Look at me. Love me*." She laughed low. "Or maybe my perspective is skewed by six years of Maggie." She handed Bree the check, reaching out to hug her with her free arm. "Keep in touch, all right?"

And then, with one last cuddle for Cecil Two, who sat at her ankles with his little tail sweeping briskly back and forth across the floor, Mel left her there. Alone with her beautiful things, her decoy dog, and a check in her hands.

Bree stared at the check. Sixty thousand dollars. Money she no longer felt like she'd earned. This money had been her goal for the last not-quite-two weeks, and now she couldn't imagine depositing the check.

It felt strange, the future in her hands, her new lease on life.

If she kept it, she could do anything she wanted. Stay in LA. Pursue her art.

But was that still what she wanted? Or did she want to go home with a clean slate like she'd told Mel?

"What do you think I should do?" she asked Cecil, but he merely gazed at her with his dark, liquid eyes—reminding her that it was probably time for his dinner.

After filling the little bowls she'd bought for him that afternoon with food and water, she found her phone among the things she'd dropped when she came home, but there were still no messages from Cross. No news alerts with her name attached. Maggie had kept her personal details out of it. Was that Cross's doing? And if he had been her champion, why hadn't he come to see her? Except…he had no reason to. They were over. She'd sensed it on the plane, before they even got back to LA. This thing between them…it had been a Caribbean fling, destined to die in the Angelino air.

It was probably a good thing he hadn't come to see her. She hadn't showered since the last time she'd done it with him in that giant frosted glass master shower at the villa, and she was probably starting to smell.

She picked her way through the art explosion in her living room, setting the check on the counter as she passed on her way to the bathroom and the shower which would hopefully clear her head and make her feel more human—but her gaze caught on a stack of magazines tucked under the coffeepot she hadn't used since Andi moved out.

Maggie had given them to her so she could study her expressions and practice in the mirror. Image was everything.

Look at me. Love me.

Cecil whined at her ankles as she picked up the coffee pot, setting it aside and flipping open the top magazine, studying the lines of Maggie's face, the layers of her smile. Always so careful to be perfect.

Bree flipped through the pages—more faces, more smiles, everyone wanting to be seen, everyone hoping to be loved, and also so scared to let anyone see beneath the surface. So scared to fully invest in love and risk their hearts. Hope and fear in every smile. Desire and control in every pouty, sultry look. A kaleidoscope of contradictions.

So beautiful. But what were they saying?

Bree grabbed the stack of magazines, sinking to the floor, her surroundings forgotten as she fell into that place where only images spoke.

CHAPTER THIRTY-ONE

"Focus!"

Something hard hit his ankles, sweeping his legs out from under him, and Cross hit the mat hard, trying to roll with the fall, but a weight slammed into his shoulders, driving him to his stomach on the mat and wrenching one of his arms behind him until he tapped out.

Candy bounded off him as soon as he patted the mat in surrender. "Dude. You really suck today. I was hoping you would be one of those guys who deal with heartbreak by channeling their emo crap into intense badassery—like Liam Neeson in *Taken*—but you're just distracted. It's very disappointing. And kind of pathetic."

He rolled to his feet, only slightly favoring the left side she'd kicked the shit out of earlier. "I hate you, you know that?"

"Now, Crossy baby, you don't mean that."

"Crossy baby?" Another voice joined the conversation as Pretty Boy stepped into Elite Protection's sparring ring. "Should I be jealous?"

"Your fiancé is a pain in the ass," Cross informed him, and Pretty Boy grinned broadly.

"I know. Isn't she great?" He hooked his arm around Candy's shoulders and she leaned into him, grinning evilly. "You about done here? Max wants to talk to you."

"Please, take her," Cross urged, reaching for his towel.

"Almost done," Candy said. "We were just about to talk about the girl."

"No, we weren't," Cross corrected—before he realized that by even acknowledging the existence of the girl he'd lost ground. It'd been six days since they'd gotten back and he'd managed to avoid thinking about Bree by putting his head down and focusing on work.

At least he'd been able to avoiding thinking about her *constantly*.

"I feel like we were," Candy insisted.

"Yeah, man, what's going on there?" Pretty Boy asked and Cross shot him a glare that made Candy snicker.

"Hadn't you figured out he's the touchy-feely one in our relationship? He talks about feelings and shit *all the time*. It's kind of horrifying." She reached for her bag. "So this girl..."

"There's nothing to discuss."

"I feel like there is," Candy insisted and Cross rolled his eyes, moving away from the sparring mats. "You're obviously upset about something," Candy said, her footsteps following him even though Max's office was in the other direction.

"I'm not upset."

"I feel like you are."

He spun to face her. "Candy. Let it go. It's none of your business."

Candy was unimpressed by his glower. "Cross. We're family—"

"Are we?"

"—and as family it is our right, dare I say, even our

duty to tell one another when we are being giant idiots. And I will admit I don't know all the details of what happened between you and Decoy Girl, but I have a strong feeling that you're being a giant idiot. So as your friend and coworker and honorary obnoxious older sister, allow me to offer you some free advice."

"Will you stop chasing me if I listen to this?"

"For now, yes."

He folded his arms. "Okay. Go ahead."

"Apologize."

"For what?"

She shrugged. "All of it. Whatever you did wrong."

"What makes you so sure I'm in the wrong?"

"You're male, so statistically, it's likely that you are, but whether you're wrong or not is irrelevant. Apologize anyway."

"Whether I'm wrong or not?"

"This is good advice," Pretty Boy piped up from where he was waiting at the sparring mats.

Cross shot him a glare, but Candy wasn't done. "You can be proud and alone or you can apologize and get your girl back."

"She isn't my girl."

"But you want her to be, don't you?"

"Candy. I'm not that guy, okay? I don't need love to complete me. And you need to back off. I'm not looking for a girlfriend and if I were—" He shook his head. "I'm just not, okay? I have other shit on my mind."

Which was a total lie. Even with his mother calling him every day and the dedication looming and that damn letter from his sister begging him to make that call, and with the way he'd been throwing himself into work ever since he got back in an attempt to redeem himself after the fucking Caribbean debacle, he didn't have anything else on his mind. No matter how badly he wanted to. Bree kept invading his thoughts. It turned out what happened in the Caribbean didn't necessarily stay in the Caribbean.

He turned and continued stalking toward the changing rooms and this time Candy didn't chase him, though she did call after him, "Remember, if you want to talk about your feelings, Pretty Boy is here for you!"

Cross snorted, but didn't stop walking. He didn't want to talk about his feelings. He didn't *have* feelings, damn it. At least not about Bree.

He wasn't a good bet, romantically, and the sooner everyone realized that, the better. His ex-wife had certainly told him what a disappointment he was in the love department enough times. And it wasn't like his family was full of healthy examples.

But Candy was right about one thing. He had been off, and he did need to focus. She was just wrong about what he needed to do to get his head back in the game.

It wasn't Bree. It was the rest of it. Everything he'd been avoiding.

So when he got out to his car, he pulled the letter from the glove box...and made the call.

* * * * *

Through no fault of his own, his flight was late arriving in Des Moines, but Cross still felt inexplicably guilty as he rolled into town in his rental car only minutes before the first of the dedication events was supposed to occur—as if his reluctance to be there had somehow caused the headwinds.

He'd texted his mother that he would meet her at the town square, where the mayor would be making a "small speech" about the effort to build the field house.

It was his first communication with her in almost two weeks. Even after he spoke with Rachel the first time, he hadn't been ready to talk to his mother yet.

His sister would be arriving tomorrow.

That first conversation, when he'd called her from his car, had been predictably awkward. He'd apologized for not calling sooner and explained that her letter had been a shock—that he had not, in fact, known about her until the day he read it.

She'd been cautious too—as if she was feeling him out as much as he was her—and he'd liked her the better for it, but after their second conversation, she'd agreed to come to the dedication of their father's field house. It seemed only fitting that she be there.

The official ribbon cutting wasn't until tomorrow, but Mayor Mike had two days of "festivities" planned and Cross—though his feelings were still mixed on the subject—had agreed to attend all of them. The speech. The cocktail reception. And then tomorrow the official ribbon cutting.

The parking around the town square was full, and even the side streets nearby were lined with cars, forcing Cross to circle farther and farther away from the square before he finally found a space. Music floated through the air from the square as he jogged back toward the steps of city hall where a microphone had been set up for the mayor.

He hadn't expected a crowd for the bureaucratic showboating of the mayor's speech leading up to the dedication. In spite of Mayor Mike's references to *gala events* implying layers upon layers of pomp and circumstance, Cross had failed to recall exactly how much his small town excelled at making a big deal out of absolutely anything. He should have known. The tree lighting ceremony every December was an all day event.

There was actually a crowd as the high school band finished playing and the mayor stepped up to the microphone. It looked like half of Harris had turned out for the event. Cross fell in at the back, nodding absently when a few of the townspeople standing closest to him did double takes and waved when they saw him, their faces lighting.

He'd been back dozens of times in recent years, not only for planning the field house, but also for Christmas and his mother's birthday. She'd moved back to Harris after his father's death because this was where her parents were. His grandparents had died a few years back, but Linnea Cross had stayed, even when Cross offered to fly her out to live with him. She'd never been a city person. Hadn't particularly liked being an NFL wife. But she'd loved her husband—and few places on earth was Big Aaron worshiped more than he was in Harris.

At least that was why he'd thought she'd stayed at the time. Now, nothing was certain

His parents had gotten married right out of high school and Cross had been born while his father was still playing college ball. His mother had never finished college, but she'd worked as a secretary for twenty years at the city hall and now stood beside Mayor Mike, evidently having gotten over her reservations about attending the dedication enough to be lured on stage. She seemed to radiate modest pride as Mayor Mike, who looked like he'd just graduated from college, waxed poetic about the honored donors who had contributed to the Field House Fund, with special thanks to the Cross family.

Mayor Mike had wanted Cross on stage with him,

and he silently thanked the headwinds that had given him an excuse to text the mayor and back out of that part of the spectacle. He was here to support the field house, but his feelings about the entire experience were decidedly mixed.

He probably wouldn't have gone at all, but he kept remembering what Bree had said about it being his accomplishment as well as his father's and he hadn't wanted to miss seeing it complete.

Mayor Mike had a tendency to get carried away, but thankfully his speech was relatively brief. Once he'd finished his remarks and the high school band had started playing again, Cross wove his way through the crowd that had started to drift en masse toward the gazebo at the center of the town square where the high school football team and cheerleaders were setting up for some kind of fundraiser—now that the mayor had primed the pump by talking about the generous donors who had given them the Field House.

Cross made his way instead toward the stage, forcing himself to smile at the frequent shouts of "Little Aaron!"

He was thirty years old and six feet three inches tall—and the entire freaking town still called him *Little Aaron*.

Except his mother.

"Aaron! You're here." The mayor had already left his perch on the steps when his mother spotted him. Smiling and reaching for him like nothing was wrong— but that was Linnea Cross's way, apparently. Never acknowledge when something wasn't perfect.

He pushed down that bitter thought, hating the way it had infiltrated his feelings toward his mother, and bent to hug her.

"Hi, Mom." He folded his mother into his arms,

marveling as he always did at how small she was. She'd put on a fair amount of padding over the years, but the top of her head didn't even come up to his clavicle.

She turned her face to the side, pressing her cheek to his chest and whispering, "I'm so glad you're here."

He felt something unknot in him at the familiar feel of her—even if part of him was still angry at her deception. She was still his mother. Still the one person he'd always wanted to protect above all others.

"Did you make it in time for the speech?" she asked when he pulled away. Not *I'm sorry for lying to you your entire life about the existence of your sibling.* Just *did you catch the speech*? Cross's jaw worked.

"Yeah." He stepped back. "I made it." He jerked his chin toward the football team, suddenly eager to get this over with. "Should we head down there?"

"Oh, no, that's for the team—you'll meet them tomorrow at the ribbon cutting. We have the VIP reception next. At the VFW. Didn't Mayor MIke send you the itinerary?"

"He did," Cross admitted, but he'd been avoiding thinking about this event as much as possible over the last couple weeks, so he hadn't really looked at it. "I didn't take a close look at the times."

"Well then it's a good thing I did," she said with a forced smile. "Come on. Everyone is dying to ask you what Maggie Tate is really like. Gossip about you and that movie star is the only thing people in this town are more excited about than the dedication."

The words were nervous chatter, her posture stiff, and it was instinctive for him to want to put her at ease, but instead his own words were awkward and stiff. "That was just a stunt. Maggie and I were never together."

"Well, you can't blame me for wishful thinking."

Is that why you never told me about my sister? The words were on the tip of his tongue, but they weren't alone. More and more faces he recognized were nodding to them and calling out greetings as they neared the VFW.

He'd come here not only for the dedication and because he wanted his sister to feel like she was a part of something that had been built in their father's honor, but also to talk to his mother. To finally clear the air, once and for all.

But now wasn't the time.

A fact which became glaringly evident when Mayor Mike bore down on him as soon as he entered the VFW hall.

The VFW building wasn't far from the town square, and there were already over a dozen people inside, where plastic flutes overflowed with Costco quantities of champagne and teenagers in football uniforms carried trays of hors d'oeuvres.

"There he is! The man himself!" Mayor Mike exclaimed, loud enough for the entire room to hear him as he descended on Cross. "We were afraid you weren't going to make it."

"Just some headwinds," Cross said, keeping his own voice at a normal speaking level since he had no interest in performing this conversation for the whole town.

"You should have been up there with me," Mayor Mike continued at full volume. "After all, this is your baby more than anyone else's. I'm just the bureaucrat— you're the heart and soul behind the Aaron Cross Senior Field House."

Cross gritted his teeth around a smile. "I don't need to be up on the stage."

"Humble. Just like your father."

Cross ground his molars harder to avoid pointing out that Mayor Mike hadn't even been born when his father died and couldn't possibly know whether the man was humble or not. In Harris, every virtue was always ascribed to Big Aaron first and anyone else second.

"I wanted to ask you about that victory flag again," Mike began, and Cross broke in.

"Actually, I was thinking about that. I think it would mean more to the students if they raised the money to get the flag themselves. It would really be *their* victory flag that way."

Mike visibly deflated, but he acknowledged, "Yeah. Yeah, that's a good idea. But the bleachers—"

"Are good. Everything is good. You did a good job, Mike. But now we're done. Both of us. Enjoy it." He clapped the mayor on the shoulder and moved away before the man could come up with another way to ask him for money. He'd done enough for the town for now.

And yes, *he'd* done it. In his father's name, sure, but he was the one who'd funded the project and kept Mayor Mike in check when he wanted a facility that would have made a Big Ten football coach proud. He wouldn't be giving any more money to the monument to his father. It was a public building—the town could support the maintenance on their own field house.

These last few months he'd grown bitter about Mayor Mike's demands—long before he'd been disillusioned about his father. He'd started to resent the time suck and money drain that the field house had become, but now as he strolled through the VFW, chatting with the townspeople and receiving their thanks for everything he'd done, he was reminded that it hadn't all been for his father.

It had been for the town. For his old football coach. For the students and athletes who would come after him—and maybe make it even bigger than either Aaron Cross ever had.

He had actually done a good thing.

He chatted with the townspeople and sipped champagne, avoiding his mother when she tried to catch his eye and Mayor Mike when he tried to catch his arm. He'd been braced for the usual questions—about his father, how his knee was doing, if he missed the NFL, if he still talked to his buddies in the NFL, what he'd thought of this game or that one, when he was coming back to Harris to stay, there was always a coaching job open for him if he wanted it...

And he got those, but this time, peppered in with the usual refrain was a new theme.

How long have you been dating Maggie Tate? Did you bring Maggie Tate with you? Did you really steal Maggie Tate from Demarco Whitten? Guess he should have known better than to go up against a Cross, eh?

It was immediately apparent that none of them knew the whole story. None of them had even heard of the existence of a decoy—and no matter how many times he explained that he hadn't ever dated Maggie Tate, that it had just been a stunt designed to draw attention away from the real Maggie for security reasons, none of them believed him. They all thought they knew the truth and they didn't care to hear anything that didn't confirm what they already believed. Even when he denied it, they patted him on the back and commended him on his discretion, winking and grinning.

It was his father all over again. If it didn't fit into their idea of the legend, it didn't exist. And he was so tired of legends and lies.

"I'll be damned. Aaron Cross, in the flesh."

He turned, hoping his forced smile was some semblance of pleasant and trying to keep from cracking the plastic champagne flute in his grip—but his stiff smile fell into a natural one as soon as he saw who had come up behind him. "Reg?"

Reggie Purcell grinned at him, toasting him with his plastic champagne flute. "In the flesh."

One year behind Cross at Harris High and the starting quarterback Cross's junior and senior years, Reg had been good—good enough to get a scholarship to play college ball, if Cross remembered correctly—but if Cross had lived in his father's shadow, Reg had lived in his. Though he'd never seemed to mind. Reg never seemed to mind much of anything, always with that loose, easy smile—and stoned off his ass half the time when he wasn't playing ball.

Though that had been high school. He wore a tie and button down shirt now as he rubbed elbows with Harris' most respectable citizens—though his smile was still loose and lazy as he clasped Cross's hand.

"When did you move back?" Cross asked.

"Couple years back. I'm an architect now, if you can believe it."

"No shit." School had never seemed to interest Reg much—of course, in Harris none of the star players had ever been encouraged to study much beyond their playbooks.

Reg grinned, entertained by his shock. "No shit. Turns out being good at calculating angles is good for more than just throwing a football. Who knew, right? No one ever told me that before I left Harris."

"There is a slight football obsession here."

Reg snorted at the understatement. "Heard you were

hooking up with Maggie Tate. That true?"

Cross grimaced. "No. Not true."

"Yeah? So you mean you hot shot NFL guys aren't swimming in hot actress ass? You're ruining all my fantasies of what I could have had if I went pro." The words were as light as everything Reg said—as if nothing he said could be taken seriously, but Cross hesitated long enough for a small, curvaceous woman with a massive pregnant belly to appear at Reg's elbow, shooting him a glare.

"Hot actress ass? Really, Reggie?"

Reg's grin grew even wider as he slung his arm over the woman's shoulders, tucking her against his side. "You know your ass is the only hot ass I care about, but I gotta give Cross shit about his pathetic inability to score with Maggie Tate." He flashed his shit-eating grin at Cross and tilted his head toward the woman under his arm. "This is my Millie. She teaches English at the high school now and she won't even let me smoke the pot she confiscates. Can you believe it?" Millie elbowed him in the ribs hard enough to make his body sway, but he just laughed. "You got a girl who keeps you on your toes, even if you couldn't lock down Maggie Tate?"

"Reggie. Rude."

"What? I'm just asking."

And for some reason, unlike all the times when his happily coupled-off coworkers had asked him about his love life, Cross didn't mind the question. He wasn't tempted to bitch about everyone who was married trying to inflict that state on every innocent bystander they met.

He just thought of Bree.

He'd been doing a good job of not thinking about her for the last few days—at least insofar as he wasn't obsessively thinking of nothing but her—but now he couldn't help thinking how different this would be if she were here.

She'd be watching everyone, fascinated by things he didn't even notice. What would she see here? Would she be annoyed by the hypocrisy of his father's legend? Or would she see something else entirely in the town's celebration and their rabid fixation on a football hero who'd died over twenty years ago?

What would the people of Harris think of her? Half of them would probably think she was Maggie, even if they told everyone she wasn't—until she did something on impulse. Something purely Bree. He couldn't predict what it would be. He could never predict her—but he knew it would be an adventure if she came here. She made everything feel that way—

A clinking sound echoed through the room and all eyes turned to where the boy mayor was tapping a fork against an empty champagne bottle, in the absence of glass champagne flutes. "If I could have your attention for a moment—"

"Oh joy. Another speech," Reg muttered under his breath, and his wife shushed him.

Mayor Mike began waxing poetic about the heroic accomplishment of the field house and the words washed over Cross. *Honored to be part of...incredible spirit of collaboration...the culmination of the efforts of so many...but one member of our community...*

Cross tuned in as he realized the mayor wasn't just blathering. He was making a toast to *Cross*.

"I think we all know that the Field House would not exist today without the incredible generosity of a certain someone and I would like to take this opportunity to give special recognition to the guardian angel without whom the Field House would have remained a pipe dream. Ladies and gentlemen, please raise your glasses to Aaron Cross Junior."

A cheer went up and he jerked his chin in a nod to acknowledge the praise, feeling inexplicably awkward. As if his patronage were a lie.

Would he have done it if he'd known the truth about his father? Would he still have built the field house? He'd been wondering that a lot over the last few days.

When he'd quit football, he'd felt guilty for not trying harder to go back. He'd felt guilty for finally going his own way and not trying to be his father version 2.0. So he'd built the field house—using the money left over from his NFL contracts after Lauren took her cut. He'd set aside some for his mother's retirement and then sunk the rest into the field house.

Because he felt like he'd failed a ghost. And now, knowing the ghost wasn't the man everyone had said he was—or if he was that he was something else too, someone else's father—he had to wonder if he would have done it, if he'd known.

But he wasn't ready yet to consider whether it was a good thing he hadn't known. Just like he wasn't ready to talk to his mother.

He slipped out of the cocktail party as it was winding down, cutting through the familiar side streets to get back to his car and then driving out to the high school to see what he'd built.

It really was beautiful.

Bigger than any high school needed, and state of the art, but still functional. A ribbon that would be ceremonially cut tomorrow had been strung across the doors, but Cross circled the exterior, studying the words that had been etched into the stone.

The Aaron Cross Senior Field House and Athletic Center.

He'd done this. Not bad for a dumb jock from a hick town.

"Aaron?"

He should have known she would follow him. And perhaps on some level he'd expected her to. There was something sort of fitting about having this discussion here. At the monument he'd built to the man he'd thought his father was.

He turned to face his mother. She stood, nervously twisting the strap of her purse between her hands.

"You left without saying goodbye," she murmured.

He looked back to the building, shaking his head. "I don't know what to say to you anymore. I don't want to be angry at you, but I'm afraid if I talk to you, I'll start yelling." And he'd never yelled at her in his life.

But there was one thing he needed to say. One thing he needed to know. Even if it led to the yelling.

"Why didn't you tell me?"

CHAPTER THIRTY-TWO

"You were so young," she murmured.

"I'm not young anymore," he snapped, then forced himself to stop, closing his eyes, concentrating on the June heat pressing against his skin. "Sorry."

"Don't apologize. I'm the one who should be apologizing. I didn't intend to keep it from you. I just never knew when to tell you. I didn't know how. How do you tell your son his father—whom he idolized—had a child with someone else?"

"And who taught me to idolize him?" he asked, looking up into her face, softened by the years.

"Parenting is harder than it looks, you know," she said softly. "You want to protect your kids, even from the truth. I always felt like I was walking a tightrope with you. Trying to avoid tainting your memories of your father. Always trying to focus on the positive. Maybe I went too far."

"It felt like he wasn't even human. This god I had to live up to."

"Oh, Aaron, no. I never meant for you to feel like you had to live up to anything."

"Are you kidding? I've been compared to him my entire life. Compared to him and found lacking, like he's some kind of unattainable superhuman god. The myth of Big Aaron. And you fed into it. You hid my half-sister from me."

"What was I supposed to do? Talk to my child about the other women? Discuss the paternity suit we paid to keep quiet?"

"Why pay to hide the truth at all?"

"Because it was your name too!" The words were loud enough to startle him. "What was I supposed to do? Tarnish the name he gave you? I only wanted to protect you and maybe I went about it the wrong way, but I couldn't talk to you about my husband. He was your father. And he was a good father. A good athlete. And on the whole, not a bad man, even if he wasn't the most faithful."

"Why didn't you leave him?"

She smiled, huffing out a soft breath. "That question always sounds so simple but it's not. I thought about it. Maybe things would have been different in the long run if he'd lived, but at the time all I could think was how much he loved you and you loved him—even if you don't remember it now—and I couldn't take you away from that. As long as it didn't touch you, I could tell myself it didn't touch our family. So I kept his secrets. Far longer than I should have. And yes, I convinced myself that you didn't need to know. They never reached out to us until now—"

"I still deserved to know."

"I know." The words were weary, exhausted. "But I couldn't tell you. I'm sorry."

He swallowed thickly, shaking his head. "You let me build a monument to him. I've been chasing a ghost who was never real."

"He *was* real, Aaron. And he did love you. No one is all good or all bad. We're all somewhere in between. You have to take the bad with the good."

"But I only ever heard the good."

"And that was my mistake. I see that now. I worried that my bitterness would taint your feelings for him, so I overcompensated, but you never need to feel like you have to live up to him. I am *so* proud of you. You are a thousand times the man he was. You always were. You never needed to compete with him." She shook her head, her chin wobbling. "I only wanted you to be happy." She searched his eyes. "Are you happy, Aaron?"

He gazed into his mother's eyes—and realized he had no idea how to answer her question. He wasn't sure he'd ever known how to be happy. How to release the constant need to do more. To be more. He didn't know how to just *be*.

Until Bree.

He missed her, like an ache in his chest. She'd made him feel…everything.

Before her, his life hadn't really been a life so much as an endless series of tasks to complete, but with her…she made every second feel alive—and as if it was enough, as if he was enough, like he didn't have to keep striving. He'd never felt that before. Not Cross, the chronic overachiever.

He still wanted to push himself to be the best, but it felt different now, like a goal more than an imperative. He may not be good at being happy yet, but with Bree…

"I'm getting there."

* * * * *

After the conversation outside the field house, they went back to his mother's house—the same one he'd grown up in and which she refused to move out of. They sat in the kitchen, at the familiar cracked wooden table, and talked until midnight.

Cross had always thought they were close, he'd always thought he could tell her anything, but now...they just talked. About everything and anything. He wasn't trying to be perfect for her and she wasn't trying to sugarcoat the truth for him. She told him stories about his father he'd never heard—some that didn't show him in a glowing light, but also some that did, and some where she was groaning and smiling at the same time, and for the first time his father didn't seem like some ideal he had to live up to. He just felt like a man.

He'd been angry at his father as much as his mother these last few weeks—very ready to hate him for betraying his mother, the feeling all the more extreme because of the perfect picture of his father he'd built in his head, but he found himself letting go of that as well.

Yes, he'd been an asshole sometimes—but he *had* been a prince among men sometimes too. Aaron Cross Senior was just a man—and Cross realized he'd come to terms with that not a moment too soon when he arrived back at the field house the following morning.

It was early, over two hours before the ceremony was supposed to start, but there were already members of the Dedication Committee rushing around getting things ready. He stood over to one side, beneath the giant engraving of his father's name, and waited. He hadn't thought about the fact that other people would be here when he'd suggested this for their first meeting, thinking only of the fact that it was someplace honoring his father.

Their father.

He was early—but Rachel was too.

He'd had a vague vision of his half-sister in his

head—and that vague image had looked a lot like Jennifer Aniston, he realized now, when a woman who looked more like a young Sophia Vergara approached him warily. She was tall, with long, dark brown hair pulled into a ponytail, dark eyes—and his father's mouth. That was the moment it went from feeling surreal to stunningly real. She smiled, nervously, hesitantly, and it looked familiar.

"Hi," she said cautiously, stepping out from behind her car—and he realized she was also about thirteen months pregnant.

"Rachel?" he asked awkwardly.

"Yeah," she said, looking as uncomfortable as he felt, and he suddenly wished Bree was there. She wouldn't be able to stand the awkwardness. Her energy would blast through it and she would put everyone at ease by asking the wrong question which somehow turned out to be exactly the right question.

"It's nice to meet you," Cross said, stiffly, extending his hand for her to shake—and hearing Bree's exasperated voice in his head. *Would you just hug her already? She's family.*

Rachel took his hand and they shook awkwardly. He released her hand and shoved his deep into his pants pockets. He'd dressed up a little, wanting to look nice for the dedication…and to make a good impression. She tucked a strand of hair behind her ear, chewing on her lip, and studied the building. "So this is it, huh? The field house you were talking about?"

"Yeah." He half-turned to face it.

"Big."

"Yeah." *Say something, you idiot!* "You said in your letter some things had changed for you recently?" he blurted.

"Yeah." Rachel put both hands on her belly. "You could say that."

"Is your...husband...?"

"The father isn't in the picture," she said, the words fast and hard, and Cross's eyebrows went up.

"Do I need to kick the shit out of someone?"

"Is that part of the older brother service? Offering to beat up jerks for me?"

"Always," he promised, before sobering. "I'm sorry he was a jerk."

She laughed softly without humor. "Yeah. Me too. But he taught me some stuff. Got me to reach out to you."

"I'm glad you did."

"Are you?" she asked, her voice shaking a little. "I wasn't sure...I didn't know you didn't know. About me and my mom."

"My mother told me some of it last night. Not everything. Apparently you weren't the only paternity claim, but you were the only one that turned out to actually be his."

She cringed. "I feel like I owe your mother an apology."

"You don't. You didn't do anything."

She shook her head ruefully. "My mom...she doesn't always think things through. I'm the planner. The organized one." She grimaced. "Perfectionist."

"Me too. You think we get that from him?" The idea that his drive to be perfect might still be Big Aaron's legacy—just not in the way he'd thought—was oddly comforting.

"I don't know. Do you remember him at all?" she asked. "I have a picture that was taken when I was two. He's holding me on his shoulders, but I don't remember any of it."

"I only remember bits and pieces—and most of it is stuff people told me about so I'm not sure how much I actually remember myself. He seemed like the tallest man in the world and he had a loud laugh—that's mostly what I remember. But growing up here—Big Aaron is pretty much the town mascot."

Rachel nodded at the building. "I can see that."

"I'm glad you could make it for the dedication. Seemed like you should be here too, when we're honoring Big Aaron's legacy."

Rachel frowned. "You're being surprisingly cool about all this."

"I had a few weeks to think about it." And he had Bree's voice in the back of his mind, whispering about how Rachel must be feeling. Seeing things differently.

"Can I ask you something?"

"Anything," he promised, ready to answer any of her questions about their father.

"Are you really dating Maggie Tate?"

He released a groaning laugh. "No. I'm not."

"Dang. That would have been really cool."

"I do know her though," he offered, suddenly wanting to impress his sister. "I work her security detail sometimes."

"It looked like *working her security detail* involved making out from the picture I saw."

"Actually Maggie has a decoy—a woman she pays to impersonate her in public sometimes so she can have some privacy. I was…involved with her for a little while."

"And you aren't anymore?"

"Honestly I'm not sure what we are anymore. She's kind of mad at me. I might have been an idiot."

He'd definitely screwed things up with her.

He remembered with vicious clarity the look in her eyes when she'd thrown that final volley at him that night at Maggie's. He'd told himself it was for the best that it ended when it did, that he couldn't give her what she deserved anyway and it was better to cut ties now before either of them got in too deep...but it didn't feel like it was over. And the longer he tried to stay away, the more he missed her every day.

"And what?" Rachel asked, startling him out of his thoughts. "You're just going to let her walk away? What if she's The One?"

"I don't believe in The One," he said, the words automatic. But with Bree...

Was she The One? Was she *his* One?

He'd never really bought into the romantic crap before. His mother's love for his father had always felt more like a fable than something between real people—like the exaggerated perfection in a celebrity magazine, not the real moments. Like the way she laughed when she left him in her salt spray on the jet skis. Or the restless way she moved—constantly in motion.

Or the look in her eyes when he'd offered her money to lie.

She had no reason to forgive him, no reason to want to talk to him again.

"You scared to show her your softer side?" Rachel asked.

"I don't have a softer side. And I don't get scared."

She snorted. "All right, tough guy," she said, as if she knew he was lying.

Because he had been scared. Scared shitless. He'd thought love was something you did. Something you perfected. Motions to go through. That was what it had been with his first wife. A role to perform. And he'd tried to be good at it. He'd thought he was good at it—and she'd left him anyway. And when she had, when she'd packed her things and walked away, he hadn't felt anything.

He'd known then that he was broken. That he didn't know how to love—and that he didn't need the kind of pressure trying to play at love caused him. He didn't want to lead someone on by going through the motions—so he'd always kept things casual. And he'd thought he was happy that way.

He'd been wrong about a lot of things lately. Maybe love wasn't something you performed. Maybe it was something you felt. Maybe it was that moment when it felt like something in your chest reached out to the other person and all you wanted was to see them smile one more time.

"She might not take me back."

"True," Rachel acknowledged. "But you never know until you try."

Maybe she wouldn't forgive him. He could admit, the idea of throwing himself at her mercy and begging forgiveness scared the shit out of him...but Cross didn't hide.

When something scared him, he ran right at it, screaming all the way.

CHAPTER THIRTY-THREE

For nearly two weeks, Bree had waited for Cross to come knocking at her door. Not all the time. Not even more than two or three times a day, but every time her phone buzzed with a text message she wondered if it was him—before she picked up her phone and saw the message came from Andi or her mom.

Her mother was euphoric that she was moving back to Clement—which Bree tried not to find annoying, but it was an ongoing battle. To her mother this wasn't her admitting defeat and retreating home in disgrace, it was her waking up and making responsible, forward-thinking decisions with her life. Her mother dreamt of her in a stable, nine-to-five job with benefits, oblivious to the fact that that stability made Bree feel like she was walking through life in a straitjacket.

She hadn't picked a date yet, for moving back. Once she did, it would feel final, it would feel real, and she wasn't ready for that yet.

If these were going to be her last days living as an artist in LA, she didn't want to waste them. She'd fallen into her art—spending every waking moment working and coming up for air only when she realized she hadn't eaten all day or she couldn't remember the last time she'd showered.

It was a minor miracle she was clean and fed when

the knock came at her door that afternoon, setting Cecil into a barking frenzy. The knock was too tentative to be Cross, though her heart still surged as if it might be him.

But when she opened the door, her shock was more complete than if it had been Cross.

Maggie *never* came to her.

The actress stood on the landing, with her celebrity disguise of a baseball cap and giant sunglasses obscuring her face—though it was the oversized hoodie that really sold the look. She reached up, plucking off the sunglasses and revealing nervous turquoise eyes. "Can I come in?"

"Of course." Bree opened the door wider and Cecil darted out, bouncing ecstatically at the sight of his goddess.

The actress bent to pat him and murmur, "Hello, baby," before crossing the threshold—and stopping dead, staring around her. "Oh."

Bree's apartment was rarely clean under the best of circumstances, but after a week where every available space had been commandeered for her new project she had to admit the living room did look a little terrifying. Like a paper cyclone had hit it.

"Are you packing?" Maggie asked tentatively as Bree closed the door and Cecil began to wiggle frantically at her feet in a bid for attention. "Mel said you were leaving."

"It seems like it's time." Bree gathered up Cecil so he would stop harassing Maggie, tucking him against her chest. "Look, I'm sorry—"

"No." Maggie faced her, shoving her hands in the pockets of the hoodie. "I need to apologize. You were my friend. Pretty much my only friend if friends are the people who tell you what you need to hear rather than what you want to hear. I shouldn't have asked you to take the fall for me. I'm sorry about that and I came here to thank you for saying no."

"Really?" her voice cracked on the word.

"I was pissed," Maggie admitted. "Like, *really* pissed—at you, at Mel, at Kaydee—at everyone but myself because I didn't want to face the fact that *I* was the one who screwed things up with Demarco. Not any of you. Kaydee saw me kiss Alec." She grimaced. "That's how she got the job—and she's saying she wasn't violating the NDA because the things she's talking about publicly all happened before she was an employee."

"So she's getting away with it?"

"Oh no, we're suing her into the next century. She violated that NDA a dozen different ways—even if that wasn't one of them. The pictures alone..."

"I'm sorry. I feel like I started all of this."

"You didn't. I did. And I need to be the one to stop it. It was the right thing to do, come clean about everything. I don't know when people stopped asking me to do the right thing. I get so used to everyone doing what I want that sometimes I forget that just because I want it doesn't mean it should happen." She laughed softly. "Like marrying Demarco. I think I probably would have driven him crazy."

"Did you love him?" Bree asked gently.

"Yes?" Maggie answered, but it sounded like a question. "At least I loved the way it felt to be with him. He won't even talk to me now. Not that I blame him." She swallowed, smiling weakly, and reaching out to ruffle Cecil's ears where he lay in Bree's arms. "I kinda suck at being alone. And I know no one wants to hear the movie star whining about her perfect life—"

"Hey," Bree grabbed her hand, realizing for the first time that Maggie's hands were surprisingly small. "I've been you, remember? I know how lonely it can be."

Tears filled Maggie's eyes as she smiled. "I just wanted someone to be mine, you know? My family isn't...they aren't there. And everyone you meet in this business wants something from you and you feel like you can't let anyone in, but then you feel lonely *all the time* and everyone thinks they have the right to judge you, especially when you do stupid shit like make out with an ex who dumped you and suddenly wants you again and you know it's stupid, but you can't stop looking for love in all the wrong places until everyone in the entire world thinks you're ridiculous except your dog."

She was blubbering by the end and Bree wrapped an arm around her, squishing Cecil Two between them—who whined softly and licked Maggie's chin. Bree went up on her bare toes so they were the same height. "Hey. Who cares if people think your life is ridiculous? What does it matter as long as you're happy?"

"But I'm not happy," Maggie whimpered, then sniffled. "God, I'm sorry. I'm the worst. Crying all over you after I was *horrible* to you."

"You weren't horrible. You were human." Bree guided her over to an arm chair she'd picked up at a yard sale, brushing photos off the seat to make a space for both of them to perch on the edge, holding onto the movie star as she cried and Cecil crawled all over her, a silky, wriggling puppy comfort machine.

Maggie lived in the lap of luxury, isolated in her perfect world. She didn't have a family. She didn't have support that wasn't on her payroll, but she was just looking for love in all the wrong places—like *everywhere*.

THE DECOY BRIDE

"Maggie Tate isn't my real name, did you know that?" she asked when she collected herself, softly stroking Cecil Two. "Dolores Margaret Terchovsky. Sexy, right? I picked Tate because of that band. The Fifth Horseman? Lorenzo Tate? I thought Maggie Tate sounded like an actress. Like someone powerful and important. But I never feel powerful and important. I just feel trapped and alone."

"Maybe you should get away for a while—not to get married, just to get away from the pressure."

"It follows you," Maggie murmured.

"I could decoy for you," Bree offered. "On the house."

"No," Maggie squeezed her hand. "It's time for me to live my own life." A photo ripped from a magazine crinkled beneath her as she shifted and Maggie glanced at the debris around them. "What is all this?" she asked.

"I'm not sure yet," Bree admitted. "Something I'm working on." At Maggie's frown, Bree stood, making a decision on impulse—like all of her best decisions. "Come on. I'll show you."

Cecil leapt off Maggie's lap and danced around their feet as Bree led the way into Andi's old bedroom, which she had taken over as a studio when her roommate moved in with Ty. Her new project was propped on her largest easel, lit by the natural light that filled the back half of the apartment.

"Oh my God," Maggie whispered, staring, and Bree's stomach churned as nervously as it had when Olivia Hwang was looking at her stuff. Cecil darted into the corner, burrowing into the little nest he'd made for himself there in a splash of sunlight.

"It isn't done—"

"You're an artist?" Maggie asked, yanking her eyes

off the piece to stare at Bree.

"Sort of."

Some of her other pieces lined the walls, including the ocean scene that Olivia Hwang had called pedestrian, which curled in the corner like the wave it was. "Why did you never show me any of these?" Maggie demanded.

She shrugged. "Everyone wants something from you. I've been you. I know that. And I didn't want to be another one of those people." Honesty forced her to add, "And I think I wanted to know that I could make it on my talent, not because I randomly happen to look like somebody famous."

Maggie moved closer to the new piece on the easel, studying the details. It was the same kind of piece as the wave—photos in a collage to create a larger picture—but it was *different*. The end effect wasn't of another photo; the larger piece looked like a painting, with brush strokes composed of photographs with ragged edges carefully frayed. It was vague, impressionistic, vaguely Van Gogh in feeling.

"It's you..." Maggie murmured.

And Bree blinked, surprised she'd seen the difference. That she hadn't seen herself. "Maybe..." she admitted. It was an eye, the side of a face, vague and unformed.

"I don't know how you did this," Maggie murmured, her gaze caught on the half-finished piece. "How you took all these pictures that all seem to only see the surface and turned them into something where all I can see when I look at it is loneliness and hope." She leaned forward, peering at the small photos. "They're all you, aren't they?"

"How can you tell?" She'd gone through hundreds of

magazines and fan sites, pulling pictures of herself-as-Maggie, with another pile of the ones where she wasn't one hundred percent sure which one of them it was, but Maggie had known at a glance.

Maggie reached out to touch one of the pictures—one with Cross. "Are you in love with him?"

"Who?" Maggie gave her a *really?* look and she grimaced. "Does it matter? We're so different. And he doesn't want me anyway. He doesn't *do* love."

"And if he did? Would you take him back?"

Bree shook her head, but it was more confusion than denial. "I don't know. It's a moot point anyway. I haven't heard a word from him since we got back. That sends a pretty clear message. And honestly, it's for the best. I'm getting ready to leave LA and he would only confuse things."

"So you wouldn't want to see him? If he came knocking at your door?"

He isn't going to do that. He'd proven that by the last two weeks. And she refused to be the girl who hung onto a man who had made it clear he didn't want her. She was stronger than that. "No. No, we had our chance."

"Men are idiots," Maggie agreed, then her eyes were back on the collage. "But this is incredible. Promise me you'll show it?"

"I'd have to get a showing first," Bree said dryly. "And no, I don't want you to ask someone to show it for me. I actually..." She hesitated, but blurted out the rest. "There's a gallery owner—an important one—who offered to look at my stuff again at some point and I've been debating showing her some of my new work. I'd probably be setting myself up for failure again—"

"Do it."

Bree swallowed thickly, her own eyes on the piece. "I didn't make it to show anyone," she admitted. "I'm not even sure I legally could since all the photos are probably copyrighted. I just…I had something to say."

Maggie didn't look away from the easel. "Why are you leaving LA?"

"Because it's time. Because I failed. Because I failed consistently for ten years and at some point you have to see the writing on the wall."

"Bullshit."

Bree blinked. "Excuse me?"

"Do you know what the difference is between those who succeed and those who fail?"

"Talent?"

Maggie gave her a hard look, unamused. "The successful people keep going after they fail. They learn from their failure, but they never stop trying. Stupid, dogged determination. That's what success is. Don't give up, Bree."

Bree swallowed, looking into Maggie Tate's incredible turquoise eyes. "That's a good speech. Is that from a movie?"

"I do occasionally have moments of genius of my own," Maggie said with a wry grin.

Bree met her eyes, her heart warming at the sight of this woman who could have been her sister. "Thank you."

"Hey. What are friends for?"

"I'd like us to be friends," Bree said.

"Really?" The movie star at her side looked at her, her eyes vulnerable.

"Yeah. You've gotta have someone in your life who will tell you when you're being an ass."

Maggie laughed. "Thank you. I appreciate that. And

it goes both ways." She nodded to the portrait. "You have to show this. Bree, it's perfect."

"It's not finished yet," she murmured.

Maggie's mouth twisted in a wry smile. "Honey, none of us are."

CHAPTER THIRTY-FOUR

One month.

One month had passed since she'd first shown Olivia Hwang her work and she felt like a completely different person. Was that Maggie? Cross? Her? What had happened? How did a woman go through thirty years of life evolving at a snail's pace and then suddenly change overnight?

She popped open the hatch on the Honda and her chest filled with feeling at the carefully packaged pieces inside. Something like pride.

Olivia had been skeptical when Bree called to schedule a second viewing, asking pointedly if she was sure she was ready—though the subtext in her voice had clearly been, "Am I going to regret giving you a second chance?"

Bree had insisted she was ready, but she knew this would be her last chance with this gallery. Olivia Hwang wasn't going to keep taking the time to see her work if she wasn't blown away by today's pieces. But this time instead of paralytic nerves making her want to puke all over the sidewalk, all she felt was a low buzz of excitement.

She knew—*knew* who she was and what she had to say and if Olivia Hwang hated her work she would meet Andi and Maggie later for a consolation martini and then start approaching other galleries. Other dealers. Hell, she would take her work to farmer's markets, but she wouldn't ever give up because she had a voice, she had something to say, and *this* was who she was meant to be. And it was worth all the work she had to do in between so she could afford these moments.

Though Maggie had talked her into cashing the check, so she wouldn't need to do any side gigs for a while even if her work didn't start paying for itself.

She wasn't betting her future on this moment, but she *wanted* it. She wanted Olivia Hwang to love her work. She wanted the affirmation that she was good, but she didn't need anyone else to tell her she had what it took. She did. Because it wasn't just talent. It was perseverance. And she wasn't giving up. It was only a matter of time before she caught. And maybe it wouldn't be big, maybe it would just be small steady work. And if it didn't happen until she was eighty, she'd still have a pretty good life, filled with pretty good art.

She'd turned over a new leaf—even buying some paints and adding a few swipes of color to a few of the pieces. She wasn't going to live her life by anyone else's opinion anymore. She knew what beauty said now.

And maybe she was making a mistake. Most of the pieces she was showing today weren't finished—but it was Maggie who had given her the idea that maybe they didn't need to be. They were *people,* her pieces, and weren't all people works-in-progress?

She certainly was. Though she felt a little more complete now. She'd called her mother last night—and the conversation hadn't gone nearly as badly as it might have considering she'd opened with "I'm not coming home."

"What do you mean? Not until next month?" her

mother had asked.

"Not at all. I'm staying in LA. And I'm going to keep trying to make art my life. I know you hate the instability of it—and sometimes I hate that too, but I feel like I can never say that to you without giving you ammunition that you can use to try to make me give up my dreams. Because I don't want a stable normal life with a picket fence and three kids, Mom. I dream of art showings and people being moved by my work, but mostly about that moment when I'm creating and it feels like I disappear and the work takes over and I *know* I'm doing what I was meant to do with my life. I *love* that, Mom. And I know you don't get it, but can you try to love it too? For me? Because I'm not ready to stop being me."

"I don't want you to," her mother had whispered—and then they'd cried, but they were good tears. It had been a good handful of days. So good she almost didn't miss him.

"Do you need a hand?"

She turned, expecting to see Olivia's assistant—what was his name again?—but instead her smile of greeting froze on her face when she saw Cross standing on the curb. As if conjured by the stray thought. As if it was the most natural thing in the world.

As if she hadn't been starving for the sight of him for the last two and a half weeks.

"What are you doing here?" she demanded, the words coming out harsh.

"Maggie told me you'd be here."

She looked up at the gallery and back into the trunk of her car. "This isn't a good time."

"I wanted to come see you before, but Maggie refused to give me your address because she said you were working on something important and I deserved to suffer. It was Candy who talked her into telling me you'd be here today—"

"That still doesn't explain why you're here." It had been weeks. Any hope she'd had that he'd realize she was more than a fling had hardened into a tough, defensive shell.

"I'm an idiot."

"Okay."

His mouth twitched in a not-quite smile as he stepped off the curb, and she fell back a step. "I came to tell you that I'm an idiot and to apologize."

Perfect Cross. Always trying to be perfect for everyone. That must be what this was. She glanced into the trunk, seeing nothing. "Mel told me you wouldn't let them use my name. I know you didn't have to do that."

"Yes, I did."

She looked back at him then, shaking her head slightly. "I only meant you don't have to apologize for that. I know you stood up to your client for me and I appreciate it. You don't have to feel bad about asking me to lie."

"That's not what I'm apologizing for," he said, then added hurriedly, "though I am sorry for that too."

"Why are you here, Cross?"

He flushed and she realized he no longer looked like master of the universe, commander of all he surveyed. He looked nervous.

"I met my sister," he blurted. "In Iowa."

She blinked, startled by the sudden change of topic, but curious in spite of herself. "How was that?"

"It was good. Great, actually. Awkward at first and I kept thinking if you were there you'd know what to say—"

"I probably wouldn't have."

"It was at the dedication of my father's field house. My field house. People kept asking me if I was dating Maggie..." He met her eyes and something flickered in his gaze. "I spoke to my mother. About my father's myth. She told me some stories about him—stuff I'd never heard. Stuff that made him real. Turns out she wasn't the head of the Cult of Big Aaron like I'd thought. She just didn't want to tarnish my memories of him—or have me grow up with everyone knowing he'd cheated. So she deified him to protect me."

"Wow," Bree murmured, unsure what to say.

"And I realized some things. About us."

"Cross..."

"Bree." He took another step toward her and she stumbled, falling back until they were standing on opposite sides of her raised hatchback. "I want you back."

She shook her head, looking anywhere but him—the pavement, the gallery behind him, the art in the back of the Honda. "I rushed in with you. I'm always rushing into things, but it was a mistake. I overinvested and everything happened too fast—"

"I like fast. You're impulsive. I love that about you."

Something deep inside her went still at his words—not quite the ones she wanted to hear, but so damn close...

"My mom said something, about wanting me to be happy, and I thought maybe I should give that a try, but I don't know how to do it without you."

She raised her gaze to his, but wasn't able to form words as he stepped forward and took her hands.

"You are the first person who saw me and made me feel like I didn't have to do any more or be any more than I already was. I could just *be* with you—and yeah, that scared the shit out of me and so I put up walls, but you got inside them anyway. You make me feel alive, but this isn't just about me. I want to be what you need too. I want to make you happy. Do you think you could give me another chance to try?"

The still part deep inside of her wanted to say yes, wanted to believe he meant it, but the hard outer shell had her shaking her head. If she opened herself up to him and he ghosted on her again…

"I can't—"

"I love you," he blurted.

She yanked her hands free. "You said you didn't know what love was."

"I didn't. I thought it was my mother's Greek tragedy or some kind of part you had to play. You were the first person who made me see that it's *this*."

"What 'this'?" she demanded, needing the words and almost angry at him for daring to say them.

"Caring about someone like this, where I want you to be happy above all else, and I want to be with you, even when you make me crazy, because any second with you is better than it could ever be without you because all I do is miss you like a piece of my heart has been carved out of my chest when you aren't around. Like a piece of me is missing right here." He tapped his chest.

She shook her head, scared to let the words in, scared to believe them.

"I got married last time because I felt like I should. It was just another way to do what I was supposed to, but with you…I know you don't care what anyone says you should do and you probably shouldn't marry me, but I want to marry you, Bree—"

"*Cross.*" When the hell did they get to marriage? Five

seconds ago she was trying to decide whether she was ready to *date* him again.

"Not because I should, but because I want everyone to know that I love you. I want *you* to know it."

"Are you *proposing*?"

"Yes? No. I don't know." He shook his head. "I'm going to. I'm going to do it right. I don't have a ring—"

She laughed. "You think I need a ring?"

"I feel like I'm screwing this up. I don't know why I'm talking about marriage—I mean, I want to marry you, but this probably isn't the best time—"

"And you always have to be the best," she teased.

At the quirk of her lips, something hopeful lit in his eyes. "You deserve the best," he murmured.

She felt her smile start to spread, something warm unlocking inside her, something she hadn't been able to evict from her heart, no matter how she might have wanted to. Something she'd pressed down and ignored, throwing herself into her work, until it bloomed again, as bright and vibrant as ever. "Maybe I don't want the best," she said softly. "Maybe I just want you. Maybe I like it when you get it wrong."

"Yeah?"

"Maybe I'm stupidly in love with you too."

He closed the distance between them, threading his hands into her hair. "Yeah?"

"Yeah."

And that quiet, still place inside her became a heartbeat, strong and sure, as he bent his head to whisper, "Thank God," against her lips. She clutched his shirt, kissing him until that beat spread light all the way to her fingertips and toes, until she felt like she was made of joy and any second she would float right off the ground.

A throat cleared behind Cross, a dry feminine voice interrupting. "Ms. Davies? Are you ready to show me those pieces?"

EPILOGUE

One year later...

The Hwang Gallery was overflowing on the night the Bree Davies Collection was to be unveiled to the public for the first time. The paparazzi swarmed the street outside—thanks, in large part to the presence of Maggie Tate, close personal friend of the artist.

Elite Protection had provided security for the event, ensuring that Maggie and the other Hollywood power players who had chosen to attend the event would all be unmolested by the press. Cross had handled all the details personally.

He was rarely in the field anymore, since he'd become Max's second-in-command and begun taking on more and more of Elite Protection's administrative tasks in the year since Max and Parvati's daughter had been born. Fewer personal protection jobs meant more reliable hours that got him home to Bree at a reasonable hour—though half the time she didn't notice what time he arrived because she was so engrossed in her work.

Olivia Hwang had taken one look at her new pieces last year and declared that Bree needed more for a full show—and so she'd thrown herself into her work with single-minded focus for the last year, creating a collection she could be proud of.

And God, he was proud of her.

Of all the successes of his life, he'd never felt such triumph as he did now, watching her smiling as she accepted compliments on her work.

She'd moved into his house when her lease expired last July, commandeering the rooms with the best light and spreading her chaos into every inch of the once pristine, expressionless space—and he loved every bit of it.

He still had a tendency to work too hard—but so did Bree and he knew how to play hard now too. Luckily neither of them had any desire to have children, because their offspring would undoubtedly starve before their first birthday with both parents off obsessing about something—though Cecil Two always managed to get fed. He was even getting a little fat—often conning both of them into giving him dinner.

Bree's solution to his tubbiness was to arrange extra playdates with the original Cecil and Candy's dog Wicket. Which meant more time with her friends, Andi often joining them.

Bree had marveled to him the other night how full of people her life had become.

She had no filters, telling him everything as it crossed through her brain—about how she'd never felt like she had many people who accepted her as she was, but now she was surrounded by friends who knew her and loved her just the same. Even her relationship with her parents had improved.

They'd flown in from Minnesota for the opening and were currently telling everyone who would listen that they were the parents of *the artist*. Simply proud, with no qualifications. No urging her to move back to Minnesota, no talk of a fall back plan. Just pride.

Thankfully they didn't seem to mind that she'd been living in sin with Cross for the last year.

His half-sister was here somewhere, with his adorable baby niece, whom his mother couldn't seem to stop cooing over—though thankfully she seemed to have accepted he and Bree didn't have any plans in that direction. Though she still dropped frequent hints about the wedding.

They'd been engaged for nearly a year now, but at this rate he was going to have to whisk her away to a private island to get her to stop working long enough to marry him. He'd heard worse ideas. A little honeymoon at the villa...

Bree bounded over to him, with Cecil Two in her arms. "Why didn't you tell me Candy's husband was the son of Lorenzo Tate?"

"Why didn't Candy tell you? You talk to her as much as I do."

"He wants to buy the Candy portrait and I told him he couldn't afford it—which apparently was extremely wrong. Are all of your friends stupid rich? Because really that's just elitist."

"Says the woman who is best friends with a movie star."

"Maggie is *dying*, by the way—she named herself Tate after his father. She couldn't believe she'd been guarded by Lorenzo Tate's son and she had no idea because everyone calls him Pretty Boy. You really shouldn't have kept that from me."

He snorted. "I promise the next time I learn one of my coworkers has a famous parent I will be sure to call you immediately to tell you."

"Thank you. Speaking of Maggie, she wants to know if you're going to feel emasculated if I'm suddenly richer than you are."

"If you're richer than I am, does that mean you're finally going to trade in the Honda?"

"Bite your tongue. That car is my baby. Oh! There's Andi and Ty!"

She rushed away to greet her friends and Cross grinned after her. The show was a success. She was a success. And *this*, this was what success felt like. Finally.

Yes, sometimes she forgot he existed and fell into her work for days at a time, but when she came out, she always came straight to him. Falling against him on the couch, pressing her ear to his chest. Covered in paint and paste and exhaustion. He would put his arms around her as she listened to his heart and they would sit together and just be.

Happy.

THE END